# The Story

The Arlin Trilogy: Book 1

# The Story

ONDREA KEIGH

The story, all names, characters, and incidents portrayed in this production are fictitious. No identification with actual persons (living or deceased), places, buildings, and products is intended or should be inferred.

ISBN: 979-8-9872442-1-0 (paperback)

ISBN: 979-8-9872442-0-3 (eBook)

Book Cover by Emily's World of Design

Map by Emily's World of Design

Editing by Laura Ebersole

Published by Lyonsword Publishing

ondreakeigh.com/lyonsword-publishing

To my family,
who have supported me in all my writing adventures.

THE NORTHERN CONTINENT
THE NORTHERN COUNTRY
THE NORTHERN MOUNTAINS
THE NORTH TOWN
THE WESTERN ISLAND
THE WESTERN ISLAND COUNTRY
THE WESTERN SEA
THE EASTERN ISLAND
THE EASTERN ISLAND COUNTRY
THE EASTERN SEA
THE GREAT VOLCANO
THE VILLAGE
THE VALLEY
THE FIELD
THE FOREST
THE WOODS
THE TOWN
THE HILLS
THE SOUTH TOWN
THE SOUTHERN MOUNTAINS
THE SOUTHERN COUNTRY
THE SOUTHERN CONTINENT

# Chapter 1

BLOOD POOLED ON THE wooden floorboards as I walked across the room and glanced out the window. No people, no noise. The muddy streets were devoid of movement, save for a few windows that danced with the light of a candle, casting lively shadows on the streets below. So far, no one seemed to have heard the struggle. I took a deep breath and shoved the dark feeling in my gut down again as I ran my fingers through my short, sun-bleached brown hair. I turned from the window to examine the body on the floor. The man looked no older than me, probably around thirty, and his casual clothes and boots were those of an off-duty soldier. His once white shirt was now stained with his blood, a sleeve and hand scorched by fire, and his eyes glazed over and void. His death was not without reason. This soldier I had just killed had turned against the man in charge, General Delaney. After his betrayal—and many instances of defiance—General Delaney had ordered him gone.

The general was well liked by the people, but in a town ravaged by murderous beasts every two to six years, he had no tolerance for rogue soldiers. And as the next war was nearing, he had even less tolerance for defiance and more need for money to fund the upcoming fight with the Great Beasts of the Southern Mountains.

The general's men who had accompanied me went to work cleaning up the bloody mess we had made as I turned and began searching through the man's house. The man now lying dead on the floor had been tasked with finding something valuable, and now that task fell to me. I had only learned about it a few days earlier when General Delaney called me to his mansion on the Crescent Hill.

"We have a problem," the general had begun as he placed a hand on my shoulder and guided me into his office. "One of my soldiers has failed to bring me something I tasked him with finding," he stated with a disappointed frown. "I tried to help him stay focused, but it seems he lost his wits and has turned on me. He is now a danger to everything I have built here since the last war ended. If he defies me, then everyone else will lose faith in my abilities to protect them as this next war grows near."

It had been General Delaney's ancestors who helped vanquish the Great Beasts of the Southern Mountains during each war since the very first one occurred centuries ago, and it was General Delaney who had helped the whole town get back on its feet after the last few wars.

"What was he looking for, sir?" I asked.

"He was looking for a book," the general stated as he took a seat at his desk, gesturing for me to sit opposite him. I chose to stand.

General Delaney crossed his arms over his desk, and the long fingers of his right hand formed an "L" that he rested the side of his face in. His eyebrows raised and his forehead wrinkled in a concerned expression as he continued. "Sadly, I think we have lost him. You know what happened the last time someone defied me," he said solemnly. "A beast of the Southern Mountains was allowed across our blockade, and we all very nearly died." He leaned back in his elaborately carved chair and regarded me with a thoughtful frown. "We can't risk letting this man live. This is not the first time he has failed to follow through on direct orders, and if he can't follow such a simple order as delivering a book, then he is a threat to our very existence in the face of these beasts. If I can't get treasures like this book, then I will not have the wealth I need to build the Town back to what it once was, and I won't be able to fight off the beasts each time they come," he explained.

The general told me how he had given the soldier as much time as he needed, money, a comfortable place to live, everything he wanted, and all he had to do was find and deliver the book. But when the time came to give it up, the soldier had refused and taken it for himself.

General Delaney had even gone to the soldier and given him a chance to explain. The man's explanation had been that it wasn't worth giving up, and something about General Delaney not knowing how much it was truly worth. I assumed the general knew its exact worth. Although he acted as though the book were no more impressive than all the other treasures that he collected to use for funding, I had learned over the course of the last two wars and the fourteen years since I joined the general's army that he didn't often bother with items that were not impressive. It was more likely that the soldier just wanted the wealth for himself and had decided to risk trying to keep it instead of handing it over.

But whatever the book's value, it was none of my business. General Delaney could do as he wanted with the book. Plus, what he did with the treasures he gathered usually helped the Town. All I cared about was that he paid me when I found what he was looking for.

Now I was here, watching this man's blood stain his own floor. I took another deep breath. Everyone who joined General Delaney lived a great life. When I first joined the general's army as one of his soldiers, I thought that was the life I wanted. I was sixteen years old and eager to fight the beasts I had grown up fearing. My father had fought in previous wars, and I remembered admiring him as a man with a purpose in a world with no hope. Once I joined the fight, it was General Delaney who taught me everything I needed to know. He taught me politics, how to follow orders, and how to fight the beasts. In return for my services and loyalty, he protected my family and me and provided for us throughout the wars.

And so, I fought alongside my father in battle with the beasts. But after eight years and two wars, I grew tired. I had watched the world burn twice, saw the people's pain, and felt loss deeper than I could imagine was possible. So, about five and half years ago, after the last war ended, I left the army. But I had no other skills than those of being a soldier, so I became somewhat of a soldier for hire. Though I worked mostly for General Delaney, I spent my time retrieving objects, protecting people, and even killing for whoever paid the right price. Working for more people paid better, but things were different now. Some of General Delaney's soldiers had no problem with endless wars, playing the part, and doing dirty deeds in the name of survival, such as the men with me now. And I had been that way too, even as I worked for other employers, but not anymore. Not since that night. Not since I saw those glittering green eyes.

I blinked hard to erase the image in my mind. *Not now. I need to get this done.* Feelings resembling regret or guilt had been plaguing me recently. But it was just because I was tired. *That is it,* I thought. *I'm just tired. I just need a break. After this job, I will take some time off.*

With that thought in mind, I continued my search for the book. The soldier's modest living quarters didn't offer much in terms of hiding places. There was a set of drawers, a bed, a fireplace, one chair, and one table. All his belongings were stored neatly in their places. After rummaging through everything the soldier had owned, I came up empty. My life had been so easy lately; why did this have to be so hard? And right when I was low on energy and motivation.

"What did you find?" asked Valdra, General Delaney's right-hand man, as he approached through the back door. Tall and broad shouldered, Valdra was an imposing figure, especially in the ankle-length, black leather duster that all of the general's high-ranking soldiers wore.

"Nothing. If he had it, he hid it, and there is no sign of it anywhere. I told you we shouldn't have killed him immediately," I said as I glared at Valdra, moving my own black leather duster aside and placing my hands on my hips. This had been an execution, but one I had been trying to avoid. When Valdra's irritating fascination with fire scared the man into pulling a gun on him, I did what I had to. I had killed many beasts but only a few men in my life. The latter had gotten easier over time. Somehow that made my gut twist.

Valdra crossed his arms, the leather of his long coat creasing near his elbows. "You know, a week ago you would have barged in here ready for a fight," he said with a grin. "What's gotten into you?"

I shook my head. "Nothing." I pinched the bridge of my nose. "I'm just tired," I explained as I turned and walked toward the door, stepping over the dead man's leg as the general's men continued cleaning up the mess we made. *I am just tired,* I repeated to myself. But last week was before I had stared into those green eyes. Something about them had changed me. I wasn't about to tell Valdra that, though.

Exiting the house, I glanced over my shoulder and saw Valdra watching me as I walked to my horse. I put my foot in the stirrup of Jeb's saddle and swung into the worn leather seat. I had been a great leader in battle, but between wars, that was not my job. I just did as I was told. Finding leads was Valdra's job, and once he found one and discussed it with General Delaney, he would pass it on to me with instructions.

I nodded to Valdra and cued Jeb to head toward the Kuzmich Inn, my path dimly lit by lanterns left burning above homes and the few businesses open late into the night.

I pulled the collar of my black leather duster up higher and wrapped the coat tighter around my body to shield me from the light, cold wind. The Town was moderately empty tonight, but my mind was a constant barrage of thoughts, and I needed some company as a distraction.

I rode through the Town listening to the sounds of a group of soldiers doing their rounds, their horses plodding through the muddy streets as they ensured the area was safe from beasts. Though the creatures had not shown their ugly faces for nearly six years, they were bound to show up any time. That sound of horses on muddy ground brought back painfilled memories I wished I could forget. Memories of leading men and woman into battle against hideous beasts whose full strength I did not understand. But that war was over; now, it was just me. Just me waiting for the next horde of beasts to call us all back into war once again.

Rain started to fall as I neared the noisy inn. I left Jeb at the inn's stables and headed toward the front door. A smile fought its way onto my face as I heard hearty singing pierce through the old, worn, green door. Above the door hung a sign bearing the name "The Kuzmich Inn." As I opened the door, the sound of singing became distinctly louder, no longer cut off by the door. I approached the bar and I waved at Missy, the sweet-spirited bartender whose long, strawberry-blonde hair hung in curls over a faded green dress. She waved back and smiled, her freckled nose scrunching slightly as she did, then went to work filling a mug with ale.

"Benjamin!" a big, burly man yelled with glee from the other side of the bar.

"Where have you been?" said the red-headed woman with him as she rounded the bar to greet me.

"I've been working, Nadia. That's what people like me do. We work all day and all night until we can't handle it anymore. Then we come and see you and Ivan and have a good time," I responded with a tired smile.

Nadia laughed as she wrapped her strong, lean arms around me in a hug. "You should take more breaks. We miss seeing you."

"I have been doing a lot of work for General Delaney. You know that," I said in a halfhearted tone.

"Yeah, remind me again what it is that you do for General Delaney during these beastless days?" said Ivan as his well-tanned face lit up in a playful expression.

"The general hired him privately, Ivan, remember?" said Nadia playfully as she jabbed him in the shoulder. "He finds rare valuables now!" she stated as she turned her grin toward me. Her wide blue-green eyes were bright against her fair skin and seemed to always match whatever she was wearing.

"Oh, yeah! He's a treasure hunter!" Ivan snapped his fingers as if he had suddenly remembered, and a cocky grin appeared below his bushy, auburn handlebar mustache.

I rolled my eyes. "I am not a treasure hunter. I just happen to find things for him occasionally, so please keep your outlandish adventure ideas to yourself tonight, Ivan," I said with a groan. "I need a break."

I sat down at the bar on one of the red leather topped barstools and caught the ale that Missy slid across the counter. I lifted a hand in thanks and then let it fall to my forehead, meeting with my other hand before I ran them over my face. I slouched in my seat and retreated behind my upturned collar. Ivan settled in beside me, and I could tell by the look on his face that tonight was not the night I would get a break from his grand visions of adventure.

I worked for General Delaney as one of his soldiers, doing whatever he needed of me, available to fight the beasts whenever they should arise. But Ivan had been trying to convince me to go after the Beast of the Woods again. General Delaney's ancestors had offered a great treasure as a reward to anyone who could kill it—an offer that still stood to this day. They had claimed it attracted the

Great Beasts from the Southern Mountains. The rumor was that the Great Beasts were trying to use its soul to enhance their ranks.

Whether it was true, partially true, or completely false, I had no idea. I didn't much care anymore, nor did anyone else in town. I had been sent a couple times by previous employers, and once by General Delaney, to figure out how to kill the Beast of the Woods, but failed. No one could even enter the Woods without dying, and the Beast remained inside, protected by the invisible boundary around its dense, tree-lined edge.

"You know, word around town is that the Beast of the Woods was seen moving through the trees on the Woods' edge a few nights ago. Maybe the general will send you after it again and give you that big reward for killing it." Ivan's grin was wide, but his eyes were distant with wonder. "Imagine the things you could do with such wealth!"

*And there it is,* I thought with a sigh. *He's never going to stop trying to convince me to go after that thing.*

"It's just a story, Ivan. You know the Beast isn't real," said Nadia as she rolled her eyes. "And even if it was, there is no way you would be able to catch it. You're too slow and easily distracted," she teased.

Ivan frowned. "Keep thinking that, sister, but one day I'll catch the Beast and build a grand house on the Crescent Hill right next to General Delaney's, and all who see it will marvel at the one who caught the Beast!"

Nadia laughed out loud. "Oh, that's hilarious! And let me guess, you will have horses and dogs and birds for hunting; all you could want, General Delaney would grant you when you drag that beast's lifeless body to his feet!" she said in a theater-worthy monologue of Ivan's delusions of grandeur.

I tuned them out as they laughed and argued back and forth over each other's outlandish ideas of who was more capable of catching the Beast of the Woods and what they would do with the reward. What they didn't know was that the Beast was real. I knew because I had seen it myself, only a week ago. Eyes like emeralds glowing in the dark, its fur so black it vanished into shadow when the creature went still. Those eyes had been burned into my memory. I wanted them, but not in a covetous way. There was something about them. It was like they were calling my name. It was like I was missing part of myself and only the Beast of the Woods could grant it. All I knew was that when I saw it there, at the edge of the Woods that night, I had felt an odd sense of hope, but that hope was just outside my reach. My soul within me was drawn to it like nothing I had ever known. The Beast had vanished at the sound of an oncoming traveler, but those eyes were a sight I would never forget. Like a light in a dark cave, they had drawn me in and stirred something within me.

I shook my head. *That animal I saw was not the Beast people say lures people to their death, or lures the Great Beasts to attack,* I thought, trying to convince myself. *It's just a myth.* A myth curated by a story that had been told and written about for centuries. A story that had faded in popularity with every war that was raged by the Great Beasts that came from the Southern Mountains and beyond. In the story, the Beast of the Woods resembled a large melanistic cat, just like the creature I had seen. Though that dark coloring was rare, large cat-like creatures existed all over the world. *But none with those sparkling emerald green eyes,* I thought to myself. I let out a hard breath, and the room around me came back into focus. It was just a myth...just a story.

Ivan smacked me on the arm with his large, strong hand, and I was suddenly aware that he was talking to me.

"Something grand, I bet," he was saying.

"What?" I asked.

"The job General Delaney has tasked you with this time, what is it exactly?" Ivan inquired, leaning forward with anticipation.

"He wants me to find some rare, old book," I said, waving my hand dismissively. "I guess it was once a common book but might be worth something now that it is no longer in print. I got the impression it is part of his project to fund the coming war. He seems excited about it, but based on descriptions of the book, it's not all that impressive. Brown leather cover, with a faint imprint of a simple design in the upper right corner." I took a swig of my ale and thought back to my conversation with the general when he gave me the assignment. He had mentioned a threat to everything he had built, but maybe he was just exaggerating. I had been less cooperative than usual in the past week, and he could have just been trying to motivate me.

"Maybe it's a map!" announced Ivan.

"Nice try, Ivan," I said. "It's no map. Just an old book that contains an old story. That's all."

Ivan wiggled his eyebrows up and down and said in a low voice, "It's a map, and you know it." His grin widened.

I rolled my eyes, and he laughed his roaring, contagious laugh. I couldn't help it. I smiled. It felt good. *This is why I come visit this place,* I thought as I looked around at the smiling faces. *Not for the drinks, but for the people.* This place was like its own world. When

I walked through that green door, the hopelessness of life vanished as I entered the world of Nadia and Ivan, the Kuzmich twins.

"I'm not a treasure hunter, Ivan," I said, trying to suppress my smile. "I just do what the general tells me, and sometimes that involves finding valuable things." *And other times, it means doing some dirty work,* I thought, my mood darkening again. *"It's just a job."* I heard General Delaney's voice ringing in my ear. Toward the end of our meeting, I had found myself asking if a less permanent solution would suffice. *"We can bring him down to your holding cells and keep him there. He may come in handy later if we still can't find the book,"* I'd suggested. Though I had killed plenty of people for General Delaney over the years, the prospect suddenly made my stomach churn. *"It's just a simple job, Ben,"* he had said. *"Once you complete it, you will feel much better. That's all. It's not complicated."* But for some reason, lately, it felt like things were getting more and more complicated. Wishing it all could go back to being simply, I pushed past the gut feeling that killing him was the wrong answer. "All I care about is getting paid," I told the twins.

Finally letting it go, Ivan and Nadia invited me to a game of darts. After I won, I spent the rest of the evening engaged in conversation and a few card games, but eventually I needed sleep. Around midnight I got up to leave, thanking the twins and Missy for a good night and laughing with the inn's guests as I bid them farewell. Once outside, I headed to the barn to tack up Jeb for the ride home.

As I led Jeb out of the stables, I got the distinct feeling that I was being watched. I glanced up and down the quiet streets around me. No one was there. People were all inside, either sleeping or having a good time. I shivered. This feeling had started only two days after I saw the Beast. *If someone is watching me, they are experienced,* I thought as I swung into the saddle. Since I had joined the wars with The Great Beasts, I had developed a good sense of my surroundings, but every time I thought I knew where the feeling of being followed was coming from, I would spin to find nothing but empty air. As Jeb began to walk, the feeling returned briefly, and I checked over my shoulder. Nothing.

As I rounded the corner to exit the Town and head up the eastern side of the Crescent Hill toward home, I found myself stopping at the signpost that marked the main entrance to the Town. Many people over the years had gathered in this town and the nearby land to find safety and hide from the Great Beasts. The signs had been placed here long ago to guide travelers. They were so old, in fact, that the roads they had once pointed down had long since disappeared, lost to time. Now, they simply pointed in the general direction of each location. The signs had been repaired many times, but apparently no one had ever thought to change them.

This signpost at the edge of the Town was one of three, the other two located between here and the two distant mountain ranges to the north and south. Places that had high beast populations had a beast's head carved into the wood before the place name, and some of the signs were laden with mementos of those lost to beasts on their travels. Seeing the sign always reminded me of how dull life was. The generic names on the signs reflected the detached feeling of hopelessness that seemed to grip the land and all who lived in it. At the signpost's top was a small pointed wooden plank that read "The Town," angled directly toward the Town's center. The Town had expanded over the years to accommodate more people, so the signpost was now nearly within the Town itself. Just below the top sign was another pointing directly across the road. It read "The Woods" and had a beast's skull and bones etched into it, indicating imminent death if one entered, rather than just danger. Below those two signs was a collection of wooden indicators that pointed out the directions of other notable locations such as "The Forest," "The Hills," "The Crescent Hill," "The Northern Mountains," "The Southern Mountains," and more such generically named ports and seas. *No point in giving the land a beautiful name if it is just going to get destroyed by war with the beasts,* I thought.

As I contemplated the depressing names, my attention was gradually drawn toward the Woods, which lay directly in front of me on the other side of the main road. Half of the Woods protruded from the Forest, which separated the Town from the far-off volcano and the Northern Mountains beyond. The Woods were only a mile or so wide, the trees standing in a perfect circle, with foliage so dark and thick you couldn't see past the outer layer. I had never really paid much attention to them before. Until the night I saw those eyes. The green eyes came to me again in my mind's eye. I stared at the tree line, hoping to get a glimpse again, but nothing appeared. *Maybe I am losing my mind,* I thought. *Maybe I just imagined it.*

I left that thought at the Woods' edge and turned right, following the road along the length of town before continuing up a dirty stone path on the low-set eastern edge of the Crescent Hill toward the place I called home. It was a grand stone house that General Delaney had given as a gift to my father for his service in a previous war. But since the most recent war ended, I had wanted nothing to do with it. Too many memories of what I had lost roamed its halls. I passed the house's vine covered stone archway that framed the front door and rode toward the brown barn in the back, where I dismounted Jeb before leading him into the barn and closing the door behind me.

After tending to Jeb and feeding him, I climbed up to the loft. I had turned it into my home about five years ago. The loft's wooden floor and crossbeam ceiling were not as fancy as the house I had once lived in, which sat only a few yards away, but somehow it wasn't as full of painful memories. Or at least sometimes it wasn't. And I still had many good memories that I had made in the barn before I was old enough to see the effects of the wars.

I sat on the edge of my bed and let my tired muscles relax. Most nights, sleeping out here was peaceful. Other nights, I wondered what I was doing out here when I had a grand house to live in. I didn't know what I was doing anymore. *I just want a break,* I thought to myself yet again. *But from what?*

I lay down on my bed and looked through a nearby window up at the stars in the sky. *There are no beasts to fight right now,* I thought. *This is my break.* But somehow, that made me feel worse.

# Chapter 2

GREEN EYES STARED BACK at me, steady and intense. Longing filled my soul. Through those eyes was a grand, wondrous place, but one I couldn't really see or understand. It was more like a feeling. Something within me longed to be in that world. The emerald eyes called to me, sparkling and drawing me in. I stood so close, but they looked so far away, far beyond my reach. Something kept us apart. Something I could not see.

I snapped awake, at what, I wasn't quite sure until I saw him. Standing in the shadows on the other side of the room was one of General Delaney's personal messengers, identifiable by his knee-length black duster. Sighing, I released my grip on the knife hidden under my pillow.

"What do you want? I am trying to sleep," I groaned as I rubbed my face and swung my still-booted feet to the floor.

"The general wants you to follow up on another lead. Someone on the other side of town says they know the book's whereabouts."

I glared at him. "It's the middle of the night. Can't this wait until morning?"

He smiled. "Actually, it's only about two hours before sunrise." His expression turned serious. "You know how it is. If you do this for him, he will give you what you want."

"And what is it that he thinks I want?" I glared at him, not quite sure why I was so irritated. This was a totally normal situation for me.

"A break." The messenger looked at me with dead eyes.

It was a true statement, but one that left a lot of wiggle room as to what General Delaney might think a break consisted of.

The messenger sighed and pushed off the wall he was leaning against. "You know he is just trying to keep you from falling deeper into whatever it is that you are falling into."

I sighed, ignoring the man's attempt at making me feel better. "Fine. I'm coming," I said as I got up.

"Valdra will meet you at the bottom of the hill in ten minutes. Don't be late," he said as he disappeared down the loft's ladder.

I got up, rinsed my face in a nearby washing bowl, and grabbed a bite of bread and cheese and an extra coat. Strapping my twin triple-barreled flintlock pistols around my hips, I headed down to the main barn area, where I saddled Jeb.

The general's soldiers sneered at the way I treated Jeb and often used to explain that I should use one of their horses that had, supposedly, superior training. But they had long since learned that I would always refuse and finally stopped offering to have one brought to the house for me to use on missions. Though Jeb's training might be unorthodox, I preferred him, especially on these early morning missions. I never knew what to expect on an early mission, and Jeb was more reliable.

After I met Valdra, we set off toward the other end of town. Although it was still dark, the Town was just beginning to come to life as we rode through the streets. I pulled up my hood, less to shield me from the cold and more to keep people from seeing my face. If whoever had been following me was still doing so, I didn't want to give them any help. I had no idea who they were or what they wanted, but the last thing I needed was them interfering with this mission when I was already distracted and tired.

Valdra led the way down a street until we arrived at a modest house. We dismounted the horses and left them standing in front of the single-level building as we approached on foot. The house was small but well kept. It wasn't fancy, but it was styled with clean, dark wood and delicate carvings in the framing around the windows and doors. The home had a peaceful air about it. Mary would have described it as quaint. I smiled as I imagined her standing next to me in her favorite faded red dress with small yellow flowers, white lace around the neckline. She would have loved the flowering vine that arched over the front door. It had been nine years since her death. The pain of sorrow had barely dulled over time. If I let my memories take me, I could almost feel her hand on my arm. Her bright smile overtook my imagination as I momentarily forgot what I was doing, her brown eyes flashing through my mind with almost childlike joy. Her laugh rang soothingly in my ears.

"This place gives me the creeps," said Valdra with a sour expression.

His words yanked me from memories of my past, and I looked at him. Behind whisps of his long jet-black hair, his gray eyes darted uneasily over our surroundings. He slipped his hand into his jacket to rest on the hilt of a knife I knew was concealed at the small of his back. Despite my positive impression of this place, I put my hand on one of my revolving triple-barreled flintlock pistols just in case. Valdra and I had worked together for years and gotten to know each other well. I had learned to pay attention when he felt uneasy.

"He knows we are coming. But we are better off making a statement from the get-go," he explained. "He has a reputation as a swindler, and I don't want him thinking he can play tricks with us. I want to be out of here as fast as we can," he said crossly.

As we approached the door, I leaned toward Valdra. "Let's not kill this one, okay? If he doesn't know where the book is, we should just put a watch on him and hope he leads us to it."

Valdra looked at me for a moment as if trying to gauge my intentions. It seemed he had started to pick up on the recent change in me, and it was beginning to concern him. But instead of interrogating me, he nodded and fell in behind me.

Out of the habit of dealing with people who were less than interested in having me in their homes, I turned the handle and kicked the bottom of the door. It swung open quickly, slamming against the counter behind it as I pulled one of my twin pistols from its place in my belt and stepped into the main room.

The home was as modest inside as it was outside. A table sat in the center, with sleeping areas and a ladder to the loft on the left and a fireplace framed with two chairs to the right. No hidden corners, save for the back of the loft.

A woman sat in front of the fireplace in the far chair, which was angled a little toward the front door. She flinched and looked at us as the door rammed into the counter, her mouth hanging open in shock and her hands clutching the chair's armrests. Her dark brown eyes looked to Valdra, and there was a flicker of something across her face. Fear? Though I was surprised to see a woman, since Valdra had mentioned a man, I checked the room and glanced over her to see if she had any weapons. She wore a brown and gray dress, and her curly dark brown hair was woven into a thick braid that hung over one shoulder. Having grown up with Nadia, I had learned that thick braids and dresses offered surprisingly opportunistic locations for hiding weapons.

The woman's mouth closed, and an irritated frown creased her tawny forehead as she raised an eyebrow. "Can I help you?" she asked as she stood, placing the book she had been reading on a small table next to the chair. Her hands remained at her sides, not reaching for any potentially concealed weapons. But her stance was balanced, as if she had some form of combat training. I couldn't help but wonder if she chose to put the book down to free up her hands for access to something more deadly. However, finding no immediate threat, I holstered my gun.

I looked at Valdra and whispered, "I thought you said it was a man."

He shrugged. "I didn't really know for sure. I just assumed..."

I shot a stern look at Valdra for his unfounded assumption as the woman cleared her throat. "Just because my first reaction was not to scream doesn't mean I want you standing in my house without permission. So, you'd better explain yourselves, or I may just scream to make a point," she said as she crossed her arms and glared at us.

"We are here for information," I said, choosing to ignore the awkward situation. "Information on a certain book."

She raised an eyebrow and gestured to the book she had put down when we had so rudely barged into her home. "This is the only book I have. You can take a look if you want."

I glanced at Valdra, who was scowling darkly. "Tell us where the book is," he demanded.

I stepped toward him and put a hand on his arm. "Just give us a minute," I said. He frowned but complied.

I looked at the woman and asked, "May I sit?" She briefly regarded me with a suspicious glare, then nodded and sat in her chair.

I approached the fire and took a moment to warm my hands before sitting in the chair closest to the door. As I sat down, I looked at the book this woman had been reading. It was small, brown, and unimpressive. I looked for the title but couldn't see it.

I placed my elbows on my knees and turned away from the fire toward the woman so I could keep an eye on both her and Valdra, who still stood by the door. "What book are you reading?" I asked the woman.

"It is my favorite book. My father gave it to me when I was young," she said calmly, watching me carefully.

"What's it about?"

She studied me with her brown, inquisitive eyes, and for a moment, I thought she was going to tell me to get to the point or leave. But instead, she leaned back in her chair and simply explained, "It is about love."

I heard Valdra groan in the background. I ignored him and continued. "How so?" I asked.

This gentle approach was relatively new to me, but for some reason, I didn't have the energy for my usual brash forcefulness. Plus, there was something about this woman. I couldn't put my finger on it, but she was...different. Something about her attitude stood out to me. Most people these days were either pretending everything was okay or blatantly lost in the hopelessness of perpetual war. But this woman was not like the others. Something about her was different. I couldn't quite put my finger on it.

She leaned forward with a smile and said, "A woman falls in love with a man from another town. She is different from other woman, and the townsfolk dislike that about her. But the man she falls in love with loves that about her. He doesn't care what the people think, but rather that he found the one with whom to share his life."

"Hmm." I leaned back in my chair and examined her. She was beautiful, in a subtle kind of way, as if what made her truly beautiful was worn in a place deep within. She sat straight, but not stiff, her slightly broad shoulders rounded under her sleeves with a subtle muscular tone, the sinews of defined muscles in her forearms making it clear she did her own work. She was strong and had knowledge in her eyes. I looked around the room. Her bed was made, and the place was clean. No sign of anyone else having been there recently.

"Where is your family?" I asked.

"Should I share such information with a stranger who let himself into my house?" she said with a cocky smile.

"No, I think not," I said as I regarded her with a soft smile of amusement.

Her response to this situation seemed a bit odd. She was calm, and though she had been irritated initially, she seemed to be enjoying herself now.

"This book we are looking for—my companion over here heard that you know where it is. It's quite valuable, and we must return it to its rightful owner," I lied.

"Was it stolen?" she asked, tilting her head slightly to one side.

"It was lost. And we need to find it," I responded simply. Lying again.

She looked at me with penetrating eyes, then nodded. "I suppose something that is lost should be found," she said slowly. "But I am afraid I cannot help you," she said at a more normal speed, seeming to dismiss whatever she had been skeptical about. "As I said before, the only book I have is the one I have here." She picked up the book and held it out to me. "Would you like to take a look?"

I wasn't a fan of these overly romantic novels people were reading these days. Plus, this one didn't look like the one I was looking for. Too thick. No symbol in the top corner.

I shook my head. "No thanks. But if you do find the book, be sure to let me know," I said as I stood, a little frustrated that we had come down here for nothing.

"How will I know if I have found it? I don't know what book it is," she responded.

"It is rare. It tells the story of an ancient prince. Do you know it?" I asked conversationally.

"I must say I have heard of it. But I believe all printed copies were burned for warmth, along with most other books and belongings during the wars with the Great Beasts," she pointed out, sounding as if she was sorry to disappoint me.

I nodded. We had obviously gotten bad information. This woman knew nothing of the book, and it dawned on me that Valdra had said she would know we were coming, which was clearly not the case.

"Well, if you see a copy, please let me know," I said as I turned to leave.

"I will. How should I contact you?" she replied.

"You can leave a note with the owners of the Kuzmich Inn. Nadia or Ivan," I explained, briefly turning back toward her as I spoke.

She nodded. "And if you should ever come this way again, I would appreciate a knock on the door before entering," she said with a smile.

I paused, then returned her smile. "Of course. I apologize for that. We didn't expect..."

"A woman?" she said with a raised eyebrow.

I found myself feeling quite embarrassed suddenly. "We heard you were a man who deals in valuable items," I tried to explain, hoping I didn't sound like I was making excuses.

Her eyebrows shot up in understanding, and she said, "Oh, you are probably looking for my neighbor. See, we share a wall," she said as she gestured to the wall the fireplace was set in. "Many people think this place and his are one. I would go next door and speak to him about your book."

"Oh." *That explains it,* I thought. I glared at Valdra. "I apologize for the mix-up, ma'am," I said as I turned back to face the woman, offering a small, respectful bow while simultaneously wondering why I was being so polite.

"Apology accepted. Like I said, just make sure you knock next time," she said with a smile.

Her smile shone in her bright eyes, and I found myself trying to keep my mind focused on the task rather than her. She was a unique woman compared to others in town. She was not seductive, but there was something attractive about her. Polite, but without allowing others to take advantage of her. Calm and unbothered by what had happened. And there was wisdom in her eyes. She was no fool. I had never met anyone like her before. Except Mary. Well, actually the two were complete opposites in appearance, and where Mary had a more childlike joy, this woman's joy was more firm, confident, and weathered, yet unbroken. But this woman's eyes contained a quality I had once seen in Mary. *Contentment!* That was the word I had been looking for. Contentment, a rare quality in this world. I found myself filled with hesitation, not wanting to leave. I felt as though I could talk to her all day. A feeling I had not felt about anyone in a long time.

I blinked and abruptly bid her a good day. I had no time for women. I had a job to do. If I didn't do it, I would fail General Delaney and, in turn, would put the people of this town in danger.

Valdra and I exited the woman's house and approached the neighboring door. This time, I knocked. A short, thin, pale man with wire-rimmed glasses perched on the end of his nose opened the door. As soon as he saw us, he snapped, "You're late."

When I hesitated, Valdra pushed past us into the house without waiting for an invitation, and I followed.

"Sorry, there was a bit of a mix-up with your neighbor," I said.

Valdra glared at me. He clearly thought I was being too soft. In our line of work, we never apologized.

"That odd lady?" replied the man. "Ha! She is harmless and sweet and knows of the book. But I doubt she knows where it is located. I, on the other hand, can point you in the right direction!" he announced. "For a price, that is," he said, grinning as he rubbed his hands together eagerly.

Valdra smiled tensely. "General Delaney is willing to set you up nicely." He looked at the wall the man shared with his neighbor. "And in a place with its own walls," he said in a disgusted tone.

The man clasped his hands together. "I look forward to joining him on the Crescent Hill. But how do I know he will come through? I will need...assurances," he said, raising an eyebrow.

Valdra reached into his pocket and took out a money pouch. He dumped the contents onto the nearby table and tossed the bag on top. The man stepped forward and stared greedily at the money as he ran his fingers over the shiny gold coins.

The man grinned. "This last week, I had a conversation with a friend who saw the very book you are looking for. It is owned by a woman who lives in the mountains. You can find her where the two rivers join to form the river that runs under the Town into the Woods," he stated as he grabbed the money off the table and placed it back in its bag.

Valdra and I glanced at each other and then back at our host. "The mountains?" I asked. "You called us out here just to send us to the mountains? We were under the impression that you had the book on you," I said in irritation.

"It is there, I promise!" The man's eyes snapped up to meet mine before flicking back and forth between us, trying to gauge our intentions.

"And how do you know this?" I asked, placing a hand on one of my pistols.

"My source saw her with it!" he responded, clutching his money bag. "My source was in the Southern Mountains on a hunting trip just last week, and the old lady was there reading it."

"Hunting in the Southern Mountains is illegal. Who is your source?" demanded Valdra, taking a step forward and snatching the money bag from the man's hand.

The man stared at Valdra, his eyes growing wide. He swallowed. "Okay, fine," he announced with a nervous shrug, "I didn't overhear anything. I was in the mountains and saw her myself. Now, I did my good deed for the day. Give me my money and leave," he said with a slight tremor in his voice.

Suddenly, Valdra stepped behind our host. Before I could react, Valdra slid a knife across the man's throat, catching him as he began to crumble, before covering the open wound with a kitchen towel. The man grabbed at his bloodied neck in a desperate attempt to hold on to the life now gushing from his body. But it was no use.

I stepped backward to avoid the spray of blood as Valdra lowered the man to the ground and wiped his blade on the towel. Then he stood and began rummaging through the man's things to make it look like he had been killed in a robbery gone wrong. Once satisfied, Valdra headed for the door.

"Where are you going?" I snapped. I followed, exiting the house just in time to see him headed for the woman's house next door. "Do not lay a hand on her," I growled and drew my pistol for the second time today.

Valdra froze. "General Delaney will not be happy that you dared cross me," he said with smooth intensity as he slowly turned his head to gaze at me. I could see my actions had surprised him. We were not exactly friends, but we had worked together many times, which had garnered a certain level of trust between us. And I had just pointed a gun at him.

"It is just a book, Valdra, and she has nothing to do with this!" I snapped as I relaxed my hand, pointing the pistol at the ground.

"She knows we went to see him," he replied in a low voice as he continued toward the woman's door.

"Well, you should have thought of that before you made another mess!" I hissed through gritted teeth. "She knows nothing, you made it look like a theft gone wrong, and no one will even think to look until tomorrow anyways."

"It is tomorrow," stated Valdra as he reached the door.

As it dawned on me that the sun was just breaking the horizon, Valdra barged into the woman's house. I ran in behind him but froze. She was gone. Everything looked the same, but the fire was out, and she was gone. She must have left while we were talking next door. *A fool she most definitely is not,* I thought.

"We will post a watch and have her disposed of when she returns," Valdra grumbled as he slipped out behind me. I stared at the empty chair by the fireplace, caught off guard by how relieved I was that no one else had to die today. Especially her.

I frowned in thought as I turned toward the door, placing my pistol in my belt opposite its twin. I could not let them kill her, but I knew I had already crossed a line General Delaney would not be happy about. Valdra had his favor. Not me. No matter how much General Delaney told me he liked me and would care for me, something of late told me I was running out of rope. My opinions were only valuable as long as they were helpful. And lately, they had been more challenging than helpful. *The last thing I need right now is to be jobless and homeless.* For now, the woman was safe. I would have to think of a way to keep her out of Valdra's trap later.

I exited the house to find Valdra on horseback waiting for me. He said nothing about my outburst or pointing my gun at him, but his horse shifted nervously, sensing his irritation. I swung up into my saddle and listened as Valdra tasked me with retrieving the book and the old lady from the mountains.

"You aren't coming?" I asked. In the past, we went on these retrievals together for safety reasons. We were often not the only people out looking for these treasures, and others had learned that if they followed us, all they had to do was fight us for them before we made it back to the general's mansion.

"Don't mess this up, Benjamin," he said over his shoulder, ignoring my comment as he turned and headed off, likely to update General Delaney.

I watched him leave, then gazed at the distant mountains for a moment before turning toward the center of town. *All I have to do is get the book and the old lady. It is just a job.* I sighed and repeated that thought over and over as Jeb began walking in the direction I pointed him. *It is just a job. And I will keep doing these jobs until the next beast attacks and the whole process starts all over again,* I thought hopelessly.

# Chapter 3

THE TRIP THROUGH THE mountains to where the two rivers met would take about two days if I went at an easy pace. I tried to find out if the old lady ever left and came to town so I could just grab her here. But after asking around, I learned that she only came to town for three days each month on a cart to sell her tapestries before returning home with food and supplies. I was also told that occasionally people would go visit her to listen to her read the story in the book I was looking for, but she didn't carry the book with her into town. And, just my luck, she had already returned home for the month.

So, I bought some rations for the trip and stowed them in my saddlebags before heading out of town, toward the Southern Mountains. I clucked to Jeb, and he shifted into a comfortable walk as we started our journey to retrieve the book and its owner.

It was the end of winter, and spring had begun. But the cold weather still lingered, and spring showers looked to be on their way. We rode for hours, following the dirt path that wound its way through the land, which transformed from bare and unpopulated to rolling lightly forested hills stretching toward the rocky mountains in the distance. With nothing to do but sit and think, my mind wandered to the woman I had met that morning. I hadn't realized just how tired I was of the blood spilled on these missions until I met her.

I had been a beast fighter in the war and seen many people die. But these missions were different. In the war, the Great Beasts had been the ones killing people. But on these missions for General Delaney, I was the one killing men and women. My mind's eye played back images of the people I had killed. A man I had stabbed in the back, literally, because he had stollen from the general. A home burned to the ground because someone wanted revenge. A father's life taken by a bullet from my pistol—a weapon my own father had given me. A sudden feeling of guilt left a bad taste in my mouth. My guilt only deepened as I recalled seeing Valdra rush into the woman's house with the intent to kill her. I didn't know why I was the one who felt guilty. But I did, and that feeling was becoming far too common. Guilt and regret. I wasn't sure why these feelings were arising now. I had encountered them before on similar missions, especially my first. Over time it had gotten easier to take a life. For a long time, I was able to brush it off and move on. But recently it had been affecting me more. I couldn't sleep without being haunted by memories of the people I killed. Their faces. Their last words.

Suddenly, the feeling of being watched returned. I turned to glance over the trees and trail behind me, but once again, there was nothing. Confused, I tried to think back to when this feeling had started. I initially thought it was about two days after I saw the Beast, but the more I thought about it, the more I vaguely remembered times before that when I felt like I was being followed. *No, it must have been when I saw the Beast of the Woods,* I told myself. Or maybe I was losing my mind to the lull of the mysterious creature. It had been said that the Beast lured people to itself, to their death. Or maybe I needed a break, and that was all just a story. Or worse, maybe someone had found out that I saw the Beast and was stalking me to find out if I knew how to kill it. The reward offered by the Delaney family was attractive to many people.

Whatever was happening, I did know one thing. I was tired. So, after checking once more to ensure no one was following me, I let the thought slip from my mind as I was rocked to sleep by Jeb's gentle, swaying walk.

Those eyes. Green as emeralds, they blazed back at me. They called to me. I tried to get to them but the deadly boundary at the edge of the Woods made me stop. Each time I reached toward those eyes, I was crushed by guilt, regret, anger, and frustration. All the memories of my past missions and the people I had killed. All the decisions I had made that got me to where I was. They seemed to pile onto my shoulders, weighing me down.

My outstretched hand reached for the Beast of the Woods. I wanted to go to it, as if it were water in a parched land. But the weight on my shoulders grew until I was pulled away from the Woods and the Beast within them. I searched for the eyes. Those green eyes. They were there. I found them. But I could not reach them. They were intense and bold. I yearned for them. No, for something within them. But I was too weak to get to them. I blinked, and darkness consumed me.

I snapped awake so violently that Jeb pranced with worry. "Easy," I told him as I stroked his neck. His brown, black-edged ears flicked back to listen to my calming word.

Long ago, I had taught him to listen to my words, to know what they meant. "Easy" was his cue to calm down, and he did so. I scratched his favorite spot at the base of his mane to reward his response as I glanced around at where we were. Still on the trail headed toward the mountains.

Jeb stretched his nose out in pleasure, and I smiled. I gently rested my hand flat on his neck, signaling that the petting was over as my mind wandered back to my dream. It still sat deep in my bones, and I shuddered. The memory of those eyes at the edge of the Woods would not leave me alone.

Jeb and I rode on, past a signpost marked with a beast that indicated I was still traveling toward the Southern Mountains, until we came to a stream. This unique stream ran north, starting in the Southern Mountains and flowing through the Hills to the back edge of the Town, where it disappeared underground before supposedly coming out somewhere in the Woods, though no one had confirmed that in centuries. If I followed this stream toward the Southern Mountains, it would eventually join with two small rivers just within the base of the Southern Mountains. No one really knew how these rivers and streams worked because the water flowed in an unusual way. The small rivers that joined at the base of the Southern Mountains created a single river that somehow grew even smaller the closer one got to the Woods, rather than joining into a larger river. On the other side of the Woods, three rivers flowed uphill from the Eastern and Western Seas and the Great Volcano, each getting smaller as they traveled through the Forest and ending, supposedly, in the Woods as well. No one seemed to know where the water was going once it reached the Woods, as there were no lakes or other bodies of water near the Woods. Many believed there was a deep pool within the Woods, but that had never been confirmed. A few believed the rivers were created at the beginning of time and helped keep the Beast of the Woods alive. I didn't much care how they were made, just that they pointed me in the right direction.

Jeb and I would travel upstream, camping for the night by the caves where the Hills began. The next day, we would follow the stream, as it got bigger, all the way through the Hills to the other side, where the terrain would give way to the first few rocky outcroppings of the Southern Mountains. It was within those beginnings of the bigger mountains that the two rivers met and, hopefully, I would find the old lady with the book.

As I rode up the length of the stream and watched it grow into the wider river, I couldn't pass up the opportunity to wade in before it got too big and the currents grew too strong. I signaled Jeb to stop, and he did so. I removed his tack and let him roam and take a drink in the river as I took off my boots and rolled up my pants to wade into the gently flowing waters. It was cold, but the noon sun warmed my back.

I ran my hands through the water and over my head, rinsing my face and hair. I had to make camp before dark, but the sky had cleared and there was no sign of rain, so I decided to sit on the bank and let Jeb enjoy a bite to eat.

Ten minutes later, we were back on the trail. The dirt path led through fields of green grass and patches of green trees of all shapes and sizes. I spotted occasional rabbits and squirrels snacking and playing, pausing briefly to watch us pass by as birds trilled from the treetops, alerting the world around us to our presence in their land. The wildlife grew more and more sparse the closer one got to the mountains, probably due to the Great Beasts' looming presence in the mountains. So, I likely wouldn't see as many animals as we approached our destination. It seemed even the wildlife knew the beasts were to be avoided at all costs, something this old woman didn't seem to understand. The section of the Southern Mountains where the old lady lived was tall enough that it would likely have some snow this time of year, but not nearly as much as the massive peaks just to the south. So, I anticipated that tomorrow's travels wouldn't be too bad.

"Remember the first time you saw these mountains, Jeb?" I asked.

Jeb's ears flicked back to catch my words.

"The sun was shining, and Mary and I were picking flowers in the Hills, taking her pregnant mare on a gentle walk around her father's property. Suddenly, your mother went into labor a week early." I laughed at the memory. We had decided to stay in the Hills that night, watching the stars and keeping an eye on Mary's horse as it tended to little Jeb. Then we returned to her father's farm the next day.

My mood shifted. "I miss her," I said to Jeb. "You're the only one I can say that to these days."

Jeb's ears flicked forward suddenly at the sound of rustling in the bushes. A rabbit jumped out, and, after tensing momentarily, Jeb licked his lips and released a sigh, and I relaxed along with him. I chuckled. "Life can be stressful, can't it, Jeb," I said as I scratched his favorite spot on his neck. "But the problem always seems to be simpler than we make it," I mused.

We picked up the pace and continued on, arriving at the caves near the beginning of the Hills and setting up camp just as the sun went down. Because there was no war now, there were very few beasts out and about. But still I habitually checked the scattered bushes for tracks and kept a close eye on the shadows among nearby trees. Despite needing to keep an eye on my surroundings, I always slept better out here. The quiet, cool night air was soothing, and I slept soundly that night for the first time in weeks. No dreams of green eyes or feelings of guilt or hopelessness. Just a good night's sleep and the breeze blowing through tall grass and trees as the sound of the river lulled me and Jeb to sleep under the stars.

The next day we trekked on, steadily drawing closer to the mountains and closer to where the two rivers met. The sky had yet to let loose any water, but signs that it had done so in recent nights began to appear. As we reached the other side of the Hills, patches of snow became more and more frequent as the landscape shifted from rolling green hills and caves to rocky paths and frozen dirt.

As we climbed to higher altitudes, the view of the Hills rolling between us and the Town was spectacular. Below us, to the north, beyond the Hills and the Town, the Woods lay in a neat circle. The Town and the Crescent Hill bent around the southern half of the Woods in a crescent moon shape, the Forest extending from the opposite side like a blanket. From here, I could see both the Eastern and Western Seas spreading out farther than the eye could see. With the Forest stretching between the seas, it looked as though the land might connect all the way to the Northern Continent, too far to see from here. But I knew a man-made channel cut through the land, creating the two continents. What I could see was the Great Volcano. It loomed far off in the distance, on the other side of the Forest but just before the Channel, a thin trail of smoke rising from its scorched top. Though we were too far away to see what dark land lay around its base, I knew it well. For at the Great Volcano, the most recent war had ended. *And so did what little of a life I'd had left.*

I turned from the stunning view, leaving the memories of war behind me, and continued south. As Jeb picked his way through a snowy patch, we suddenly heard a sound in the distance. A scream. Jeb's ears shot forward and we both froze, waiting to see if it was just a hawk or something worse. The sound came again. It was definitely a human scream.

"Run!" At the sound of the word, Jeb leapt from a standstill to a gallop as I steered him toward the scream. I doubted that it was a wise decision, but we ran anyway. We banked around a large rock and came to a small clearing surrounded by rocks and clusters of shrubs and trees to find a man. Horseless and unkempt, he looked to be in his mid to late twenties. He was little shorter than me, his jet-black hair a mess and his dark olive skin smeared with dirt and dust. His once nice clothes were askew, his shirt one button off. He was desperately scrambling away from a pack of wild dogs who were gathering around him. They were likely strays that had formed a pack, and they were now going after the man's bag, which I assumed contained food that they desperately needed after a long winter.

"Charge," I said quietly to Jeb. At the word he had learned during the war, Jeb lunged toward the dogs. Baring his teeth at them as he ran, Jeb used his natural herding behavior to chase them off. Once the dogs were on the run, I gently rested the right rein on Jeb's neck and let the other hang loose on the left side, signaling him to turn to the left and go back the way we had come. As Jeb came to face the man, I whispered the word, "Stop." Jeb responded immediately, and I studied the man on the ground before us.

The man scrambled to his feet, gathering his bag and travel bedding from what appeared to be his choice of a camping spot. "Thank goodness you showed up when you did! Those dogs would have eaten me alive!" the man wailed.

He frantically ran his hands over his disheveled hair and began brushing dust and dirt from his rumpled and frayed clothes. As I watched in amusement, he continued to brush dirt off his belongings and stow his things in his bag or in straps under its base. Once he finally got himself under control, he approached me with his hand outstretched, though he avoided Jeb as if he were a leper.

I leaned down and shook his outstretched hand as he said, "My name is Otto Bilden. Thank you for your assistance."

"You're welcome," I said slowly, studying him.

With that, Otto bowed, turned on his heel, and walked in a straight line for three steps before stopping and spinning around to face me again.

"Do you know, I have no idea where I am. You don't happen to have a map on you?" Otto asked, leaning forward a fraction to examine my saddlebags.

I narrowed my eyes, unsure what to think of this Otto fellow. "Not one on paper. I keep my maps in my head," I explained as I crossed my wrists and rested them on Jeb's saddle.

Otto lifted his chin and raised an eyebrow. "I see. Well then, maybe you could scoot forward and offer me a ride to the nearest town," he said, shooing me with one hand.

I let out a breath and sat up straight. "I'm afraid I'm going in the opposite direction." I lifted the reins slightly and Jeb walked forward, passing Otto and heading south once again.

"Well, you will need to come back some time. I'm in no rush. Plus, you look like you could use the company," said Otto as he began to follow me.

I sucked in a deep breath. Company was the last thing I needed. "I don't need anything but to get where I am going. Town is that way." I pointed behind me. "Have a nice walk." Otto was walking next to Jeb now, once again eyeing him as if he had the plague. "Plus, you don't look like the horse-riding type," I added.

"I have never understood why someone would sit on a horse when they could ride in a carriage, but my options are limited," he stated with conviction.

I ignored him.

"Fine! I will walk on my own!" said Otto, sounding offended.

"Have fun," I said sarcastically.

Jeb and I continued up the path, but when I glanced over my shoulder, I caught a glimpse of Otto gingerly picking his way over rocks and jumping out of the way of something I couldn't see. He was definitely not from around here. He seemed just the type to go out into nature to try to find himself and end up in a ditch within an hour. But I couldn't have him following me around, so I left him and went on my way.

Jeb and I arrived at the old lady's house around sundown. The rivers met literally in her front yard, though the house was well concealed and easy to miss. I would have ridden right by it if it weren't for the smoke from her chimney. The house was built into the exposed roots of a huge tree. It was carved out of the tree itself, blending in so it looked like a tree and nothing else. Only the small puff of smoke that had found its way through a hollowed-out branch made it recognizable as a living space.

I dismounted Jeb and approached the nearest root, and, unsure what exactly to do, I knocked. There was no response. I knocked again, and to my surprise, a response came from behind me.

"That is not the front door," I heard a voice say.

I spun around, my hand on my pistol, only to find an old lady standing near Jeb. Though her voice had sounded young, she looked to be in her late seventies, with tan, aged skin that indicated years of hard work in the sun. Silky gray and white hair hung loose down to her waist over a brown dress and a brown shawl, and she carried a staff in one hand and a basket of fruit in the other. She offered Jeb an apple, which he accepted, his head bobbing in pleasure.

"It's not a typical house," I replied, slightly embarrassed.

I eyed her staff, wondering if she had ever used it for anything other than walking. She fit right in with the surrounding colors and terrain and had gotten much closer than I would have expected, making me wonder about her past and what kind of life she had lived that taught her to walk so quietly. Despite her silent approach, she didn't look to be a threat, so I relaxed. Besides, Jeb seemed to like her.

"No, I suppose not, but it's a good one," she said with a smile as she approached me.

I nodded. For some reason, I was unsure how to handle the situation. I was used to getting things done swiftly, with a gruff forcefulness that had become a habit, but I seemed to have less and less energy for that type of approach lately. Despite the good night's sleep, I still couldn't muster up enough energy to badger an old lady.

"You came for the book, didn't you?" she said as she walked by me.

I straightened. "How did you know?"

She smiled. "An old lady in the mountains doesn't have much—only a couple of possessions in my grasp. You are not the first." She approached the tree and entered under a branch about four feet to my right. "Won't you come in for tea?" she asked kindly.

I frowned after her. I wasn't normally met with such a peaceful reaction, and, for the second time in three days, I did not know how to handle it. With nothing else to do, I removed Jeb's bridle and loosened his saddle before joining the old lady in her home.

The inside of the house was surprisingly comfortable. A rocking chair sat in front of a fireplace that used one of the branches as a chimney, and a chair and table sat in the main area, with a bed in the corner to the left. It was simple and rustic, yet cozy. Despite the apparent age of the tree, the wood walls seemed to fill the room with the smell of fresh-cut wood. Woven baskets filled with edible plants and fruit hung above the table, and curly designs were etched into the rim of the single window, which was concealed on the outside by branches.

"Sit; I'll put some tea in the kettle," said the old lady as she shuffled toward the fireplace.

I sat down and regarded her with what I hoped looked like a stern expression. "You must know that I am not here as a guest. I was sent by General Delaney to retrieve you and the book." I paused. *Why am I telling her that instead of just taking her?*

The old lady smiled. "I know. Would you like some bread?" she asked as she pulled out a loaf to have with the tea.

I stared at her, confused, then shook my head. "No, we need to be on our way," I said.

She turned and set a teacup and a plate with bread on the table in front of me. "The sun is down. Stay the night. We can leave in the morning."

*Oh, right,* I thought as I pinched the bridge of my nose. I had been so distracted by this unusual situation that I had completely forgotten what time it was. Then something about what she had said dawned on me. "You mean you'll go with me?" I asked. "Willingly?"

The old lady smiled again and walked over to her bed. She reached under the pillow and pulled out a small, thin, brown book. She walked over and sat down at the table with her tea, then placed the book in front of me. I picked up the book and read a few pages at random before I examined its cover. The unusual symbol, though worn and nearly invisible, was right where it should be. This was the book I was looking for.

"Many seek this book," she said. "Some want to learn. But many want it for other reasons. Some say that the story tells of a powerful ancient king. Others believe it tells of the origins of the Beast of the Woods." She smiled. "Some even believe that it says the Beast can grant any wish one desires, save that pertaining to life. Still others say that if one kills the Beast, one can take that creature's soul and use it to gain eternal life," she said with raised eyebrows and a sparkle in her eye.

"It's just a story," I responded irritably.

She looked at me, her face calm and eyes inquisitive. "Who told you that?"

I frowned. "Everyone knows it's just a story that people tell each other. I've just been told to retrieve it, and I do what I am told."

She smiled. "Oh, well, if everyone knows it, then it must be true." She chuckled to herself and took a sip of her tea.

I ran my hands over my stubble-covered jaws and momentarily massaged my temples. "I don't have time for this," I mumbled.

"On the contrary, you have all night," she said with a grin.

I sucked in a deep breath. "I am not talking to you about this," I said as I stood. "We will wait until morning and leave at first light. You have a cart, right?"

"Yes."

"Do you have a horse then?"

"No."

"You don't have a horse, but you travel to town once a month." I stared at her, confused. "What happened to your horse?"

"It recently passed," she said simply, but her eyes remained fixed on me as a subtle smile tugged at her lips.

I huffed. "Fine, we will have to hitch the cart to Jeb," I said, more to myself than to her.

The old lady stood. "There is a blanket near the fire; you can sleep there. Keep the fire going, or it will get deathly cold in here at night."

I nodded, then paused. "Last I checked, it's not very polite to have the guest tend to the house," I said, annoyed.

The old lady giggled. "You said it yourself; you are not a guest."

I rolled my eyes. *I can't take this right now.* Glaring at the back of the old lady's head, I downed my warm tea, grabbed the bread, and headed outside to tend to Jeb.

Once I returned, I added wood to the fire and got comfortable on the floor with the blanket. I laid my head on my arm and watched the orange flames jump around in the fireplace. I glanced over my shoulder at the old woman lying on her bed and then back to the fire. She couldn't go anywhere without a horse, and Jeb wouldn't go for anyone but me. With that in mind, I rolled over and watched the flames until I fell into a restless sleep.

The next morning, the old lady rose early and made breakfast. Once our stomachs were full, I took the book from the table, and we went outside to prep for the journey. When I had finished saddling Jeb and had placed the book in his saddlebags, I turned to see the old lady come around the corner of her tree house with a donkey in tow.

"I thought you said you didn't have anything to pull the cart with," I said, my anger flaring slightly.

"You, my boy, need to learn how to ask the right questions," she responded, chuckling as she began hooking her donkey up to the cart.

I stared at her in disbelief. *Don't bother with this crazy lady,* I told myself. Irritated, I turned my back on her and finished gathering food for the journey, placing it in Jeb's saddlebags with the book. Once we were both ready, we headed out down the mountains toward the Hills and the caves.

We traveled in silence until we reached a fork in the road, and a realization stopped me from going down the path I had followed on my way up. Even though I hadn't felt anything since I left town or seen any evidence that I was being watched, someone could be following me, so I decided to take a different route back down to the Town to avoid running into them on the trail.

As we traveled, I observed my new companion. The old lady was intriguing. She irritated me to high heavens, but I didn't always know exactly why. She was gentle, but her eyes were filled with knowledge and understanding. She had marks on her skin that told of a life filled with many hardships, both from daily life and the treatment of others. Her knuckles and hands were scarred from work, and a long, jagged scar stretched down her right forearm. Both wrists showed old, subtle scars, possibly from chains, and a thin scar, made more visible by her dark tan, ran along the left side of her jaw. Yet despite her appearance, she commanded no hostility. Like the river we were following, she had a beautiful confidence about her, touched by the sharp rocks of this world but filled with the grace of someone who knows where she came from and where she is going. The unfamiliar sensation of jealousy rose within me for a moment, but I pushed it aside.

We reached the caves about an hour before sunset and stopped to set up camp. I picked a cave that had a good view of the trail passing by its large opening and checked the bushes surrounding the mouth of the cave and the trees and tall grasses beyond for anything that might pose a threat as we slept. When I was satisfied that we would be safe, I removed Jeb's tack and let him roam free while the old woman removed the donkey's tack and set him up in a makeshift enclosure that would keep him from straying too far from camp. Thankfully, I didn't have to stray too far myself before I found and caught us a couple rabbits for dinner, returning within the hour.

As we finally settled down to eat, I heard rustling in the bushes near the edge of the cave entrance. I jumped to my feet and drew one of my pistols in the smooth, well-practiced motion of someone with a lifetime of experience. But rather than a beast of the mountains or a thief looking to steal our belongings, out stumbled Otto. He froze in shock at the sight of my gun, and his hands stiffly flew up.

"What are you doing here?" I moaned as I holstered my weapon and sat down again.

"Oh, hello!" he said while nervously smoothing out his ragged, once white shirt. "I, um, didn't mean to startle you. I just saw the fire from over there and thought I would come see who was here," he explained. His hair was sticking out in every which direction, and he looked even dirtier than before. His travels had apparently not gone well, especially considering that we were only a half hour's walk east of the campsite I had made on the way up. He was most definitely still lost. "Would you mind?" he asked as he moved to sit near the fire.

I opened my mouth to reply, but the old woman interrupted me. "Of course, you can join us," she said. "We would love your company."

"No, we wouldn't," I snapped. "Otto, go make your own camp!"

"Oh, come now," said the old lady. "He just needs a place to sleep. Here, eat something," she said as she handed him some meat.

"Thank you!" said Otto as he sat and grabbed some more food. "To whom do I owe the pleasure?"

"I am Ruth," responded the old lady.

"It is nice to meet you, Ruth. I am Otto Bilden. I am at your service!" he said proudly.

"It is so nice to meet you, Otto. Where are you traveling to?" asked Ruth.

"I...I am traveling to the Forest. My father was a great natural philosopher, and he loved to study the Forest. I thought it was an odd thing to study," he said with a thoughtful expression, "but now that he is gone, I feel it is my duty to continue what he started," he said nobly.

*Oh, great!* I thought. *A rich philosopher with no sense of direction. That's exactly what I need on this trip.*

Ruth and Otto continued their conversation while they ate. Ruth said she had lived alone in the mountains most of her life, and she was the only person in the country with a copy of the book I had been tasked to retrieve.

"What is the book about?" asked Otto.

"It is about the beginning of life as we know it," she said with a smile.

"You mean when the kings fought over the land and dug the Channel?" he asked.

"No, no," she said with a smile. "Before that. These days many fight over the land, taking what they can when they can get it. But in the beginning, there was only one king, a prince, and their wonderful kingdom."

I groaned. "There was no such thing," I said impatiently.

Ruth ignored me and continued, "This king created the Forest and a wonderous kingdom that encompassed the whole forest and more. The Forest was a grand place back then," she said with a far-off look in her eyes, "filled with creatures of all kinds."

"Well, what happened?" asked Otto. "The Forest is fraught with danger, and the Woods are untouchable, and that beast within them is causing all this war, attracting those beasts from beyond the Southern Mountains!" he exclaimed.

"Ah, so it seems. But all is not as it appears, my dear friend," she said with a smile. "That forest is a wonderful place. We have just forgotten."

I frowned. *Yeah, right,* I thought. *I have been in the Forest. There is nothing wonderous about it.*

A subtle sadness seemed to fill her voice. "The people were deceived by greed." She paused for a moment before continuing. "The King was a good king and always gave them the choice to stay or leave. But when the people left, no one stopped to think about what impact it would have on them or the land in which they lived."

"If it was so grand there, why did people leave?" asked Otto incredulously.

Ruth smiled, studying him. "Greed can be quite convincing, Otto," she said simply.

Something like guilt flickered briefly across Otto's expression. "Well, it's a horrible place now," he said dismissively. "I have studied it! They were right to leave since it was going to turn so sour," he claimed.

Ruth continued studying him, but after a moment she took his cue and changed the subject. "You said you are a natural philosopher, did you not?" she asked him.

"Yes!" he said proudly. "Well, my mother was, and I followed in her footsteps. It is quite a fascinating field," he said.

"I thought you said it was your father," I said suspiciously as I took a bite of meat.

Otto looked at me with that same flicker of surprise in his eyes. "Oh, I…I guess I must have misspoken. I meant to say my father was a natural philosopher."

"What does he do now?" I asked as I watched him fidget. Clearly, he was lying. Earlier, he had said his father was gone. Which sounded like he was dead.

"He is in shipping," he said flatly. "We are from a seaport town on the Eastern Island."

"Hmm." The Eastern Island Country, as people usually called the main seaport town on the Eastern Island, was home to one of the biggest shipping ports among the islands in the Eastern Sea. *If Otto's father is in shipping, they are probably one of the richest families in town,* I thought.

Deciding that whatever Otto seemed to be hiding probably didn't have anything to do with me, so I left them to converse about natural philosophy and stories. I was not thrilled with Ruth now inviting guests on our trip, and I had no energy left after a restless night in her tree house. *Once we arrive back in town, Otto will go on his way, and I will deliver Ruth and her book to the general.* With that thought in mind, I stoked the fire, lay down, and let myself drift off to sleep.

At some point in the night, I was startled awake. Unsure what had woken me, I scanned the area. Ruth and Otto were both asleep, so I looked out the cave entrance at the moonlit terrain beyond. The first thing I noticed was Jeb's outline. He was standing near the entrance to the cave, looking toward something I could not see. I watched him for any signs that whatever was out there posed a threat. Jeb suddenly flicked his tail up and down hard and broke from a standstill into a prancing trot toward our cave, nickering softly to draw my attention as his search for safety brought him near.

I was up in an instant, waking the others.

"What's the matter?" Otto asked groggily, rubbing his eyes.

"There's something out there. I don't know what, but I don't want to stick around and find out," I said.

Without protest, Ruth grabbed her donkey and set up the cart faster than I would have thought possible for someone her age. I tacked up Jeb while Otto complained about having to ride in such an unsightly cart.

"Would you rather ride double with me?" I snapped.

Otto eyed Jeb with a look of disgust. "I will take the cart over the animal any day."

He climbed into the cart, and we set off down the path. I let Ruth and Otto go ahead as I checked our flank. What I saw sent chills down my spine. Two men and a woman seemed to materialize out of thin air, facing the caves with swords drawn. Their shadowy cloaks moved like fog as, on silent feet, they approached the cave we had just left. *Who are they?* I thought, transfixed for a moment by their mysterious cloaks. *Am I seeing things?* I blinked hard. *Maybe my exhaustion is taking a toll and my mind is just playing tricks on me.* Either way, I decided I had no desire to stick around and find out who they were and why they were here.

At the gentle touch of my reins on his neck, Jeb turned and followed the cart. I suddenly had an urge to avoid taking Ruth to General Delaney's. Assuming they were real, perhaps those three people at the cave were the reason for the feeling that someone had been following me. I didn't want them putting General Delaney's plans in jeopardy. I frowned at that thought. They wouldn't dare follow us to his mansion. Even if they did, it wouldn't put his plans in danger. *It might put me in danger.* I glanced at Ruth. *It might put Ruth in danger.* Maybe that was what I was more worried about.

Over the years, many thieves had targeted the wealth the general gathered to fund repairs after each war. On multiple occasions, Valdra and I had found ourselves under siege from treasure hunters out for the same items. Many believed that repairing the Town was pointless since another war would come, and they wanted that wealth for themselves. I rubbed my right thigh, recalling the time I had almost died from an infected knife wound I had sustained on one of my first missions after leaving the army. It was because of that mission that Valdra and I usually worked together. If he had been there, I never would have been wounded. This time, probably because I had pointed a gun at him, he was not here to watch my back. I heard General Delaney's voice echo in my ear. *"It is my job to protect this town and those who live in it, Ben. And it is your job too."* As I watched Ruth handle her cart, the book in Jeb's saddlebag suddenly felt very present. *I could take the book and let Ruth go home,* I thought. *If those people only want the book, I could find a way to make it obvious that I have it now. Then Ruth would be safe, and I could take the book to Valdra and the general without her.* But Valdra had told me to bring her back with the book. I shook my head in frustration. It wasn't my job to be concerned about Ruth's safety. It was my job to get the book, and her, back to the general.

Pushing my worries from my mind, I herded everyone forward. We kept a much faster pace than the day before, but not so fast as to put us in danger of crashing the old cart. Thankfully, the sun came up only an hour after we left the caves, which made travel easier. Once I felt we were out of harm's way, we relaxed our pace, and my mind wandered back to what I should do with the book and Ruth.

As we traveled, I kept feeling Ruth's eyes on me. Every time I looked up, she would smile, then go back to steering the cart. *That smile.* It was as if she knew something that I did not. It made me shiver.

As we got closer and closer to the Town, I began to feel a pull toward the Woods. Ever since that day I saw the Beast on its boundary, I felt drawn to it. Those green eyes stared back at me in my mind's eye. *Why?*

I must have said the question out loud because Ruth's cart pulled up next to me and she smiled. "Now, that is a good question," she said with a childlike gleam in her eye before she chuckled and drove her cart past me.

I did not know what to think of this woman. But for some reason, the more I traveled with her, the less I wanted to put her in danger from whoever was following us. In just two days, this woman had changed my mind about...something, though I couldn't quite put my finger on what.

As we drew nearer to our destination, I could not shake the feeling of the book heavy in Jeb's saddlebags and the image of the armed thieves showing up at the cave. Ruth seemed happy to go where I was taking her, but the closer to town we got, the worse I felt about bringing her along.

As the Town came into view, I involuntarily brought Jeb to a stop. As he stood, stamping his hooves with desire to follow the others, I looked from the Town to Ruth and back. "I have a job to do, and I will do it," I told myself out loud. Suddenly, those green eyes jumped to my mind again, and my gaze drifted to the Woods. As I stared at their thick foliage, I wondered again if the Beast had just been a figment of my imagination. But I knew deep within me that it wasn't. *It's there,* I thought to myself. *I know it's real and is in there watching me.* I knew it. I could feel it. *Why?* I thought again. Then Ruth's words came to mind. *"Now that is a good question."*

# Chapter 4

As we entered town, Otto parted ways with us. Well, to be more accurate, I forced him to part ways with us.

"You can't just leave me here! Where will I stay?" he complained.

"Stay wherever you want. You're rich, right? The world is yours!" I said sarcastically as I steered Jeb in the opposite direction, leaving Otto standing at the edge of the Woods with a look of disbelief on his face.

"But—!" he protested.

I ignored him and kept walking. Ruth seemed content to do the same, though she wore that slight grin on her face as our gazes met. Guilt washed over me as I once again wondered if I was putting her in unnecessary danger by bringing her back with me. But I pushed the thought down. *Not now,* I told myself. *I have a job to do, and the job is almost over. Ruth will be fine, and I will get a break soon.*

As we traveled up a wide, hedge-lined stone path to General Delaney's grand house on the Crescent Hill, I felt the tug of the Woods again. I must have glanced at them because Ruth appeared next to me again and spoke.

"They are an enchanting place, are they not?" She looked me in the eye with a joyful, almost childlike expression. "It is said that many are drawn to the Woods—to the Beast within them. Yet entering that place results in death," she said, almost as a question.

"Yes." I straightened in my saddle and frowned. "Death is what would come of it. That makes the decision easy," I said in frustration, though I was not exactly sure why her words irritated me so.

"True. Though the pull is there, it is easy to resist. It is easy to choose this world over that one. But this world still ends in death. So, what does this world have that the Woods do not?" She was silent for a moment. "Or maybe it is the other way around." Again, she smiled as if she knew something I did not. "Maybe it is what the Woods have that this world lacks."

Clucking to her donkey, she continued on toward the looming mansion ahead of us. My gaze shifted to the Woods again. Ruth's words were like a slap in the face. *"This world still ends in death...Maybe it is what the Woods have that this world lacks."* Those words stuck in my mind, echoing within my skull. I shook my head to clear them from my mind and turned my attention back to the mansion before us and the job at hand.

General Delaney's mansion at the top of the Crescent Hill had a round drive with a fountain in the center. The building was three stories of expertly hewn stone, marble, and wood, and its property sprawled over something like six acres. Leaving Jeb and Ruth's cart outside, we approached the tall oak front door. Its solid gold handles seemed to slither out of the wood. Though they did not bear any specific resemblance to a creature, they had always reminded me of snakes.

We were ushered into the high-ceilinged entryway by one of General Delaney's beast-fighting soldiers. He had many of them, and they were led by Valdra. I had worked with them in the past quite regularly, now only occasionally when they helped with retrieval missions, but still, every time I saw them, they sent chills down my spine. They were all skinny, so pale they were almost gray, and had dark circles under their eyes as if they were perpetually ill. It was probably just because they worked so hard, like I did. *I wonder if I look that bad,* I thought, glancing down at my tan, scarred hands, realizing that I hadn't looked in a mirror in a while. My gaze shifted to the soldier's dark suit, and I noticed that the edges of his black coat seemed to fade and rematerialize as he moved. *I must really need a break; that's the second time my vision has been fuzzy in the past couple of days.* I shook my head and followed as a servant led us down a long, carpeted hallway to General Delaney's study, where the general usually discussed business with me. We entered the bookshelf-lined room and came to stand before him.

General Delaney sat at his immaculately carved mahogany desk doing paperwork. Every time I saw him, I was struck by how hard it was to guess his age. Nadia thought he was attractive. His fair skin was mostly smooth, with only the occasional line to break up his otherwise perfect complexion. His eyes were blue against his brown hair and sharp, pale features. Despite his unblemished appearance, a deep hardness in his eyes and faint lines at their corners made me think he had seen more than just a few wars in his time. But for some reason, there was something more today. For the first time in my life, I was suddenly struck with discomfort in his presence. His blue eyes and soothing voice were just a little...much. I had never felt this way before, and it dawned on me again that something had changed in me recently. The draw to the Woods had grown. I was suddenly less interested in beating things out of people. I had taken on Otto as a travel companion, although unwillingly. I was potentially hallucinating stalkers. *What is wrong with me?* I thought as I was suddenly gripped by mild panic. I pushed it down. But something about this place was making me uncomfortable. It had never bothered me before, so it shouldn't bother me now. But I couldn't let it go. *What am I doing here?* I thought. Ruth's words from the morning we left her tree home rang in my head. *"You, my boy, need to learn how to ask the right questions."* I squeezed my eyes shut for a second. *I must just feel guilty for bringing Ruth here,* I thought.

"Benjamin! So good to see you, my boy. I see you brought me what I asked for." General Delaney's words ripped me from my thoughts, and I forced myself to relax. Hearing his joyful voice seemed to calm me down. But not by much. I nodded respectfully but remained silent.

"Thank you for completing your assignment in such a timely manner," said General Delaney with pleasure. "We will sit down and discuss your payment later. But, for now, I would love to get to know this lovely woman. What is your name?" he asked gently, turning to Ruth.

"Ruth," she replied. "And you must be General Delaney," she said with a polite smile.

"That I am. It is nice to meet you." There was a tinge of tension in his tone that I had never heard before.

"Where is the book?" he asked, turning back to me with an inquisitive expression. I retrieved the book from my pocket, where I had placed it after dismounting Jeb, and handed it to General Delaney. As I released the book, I glanced at Ruth. She raised an eyebrow; her look was watchful, as if she was grading me on my performance.

"Ah, thank you!" said General Delaney as he grasped the book. "Now, what can you tell me about this story?" he asked Ruth. "Do you know it well?"

"I do," she replied simply. General Delaney bristled, and I could see him working to conceal something like anger. Why did that simple answer cause such a reaction? Ruth's words echoed in my head yet again. *"Now that is a good question."* What question had it been that I had accidentally spoken? I couldn't remember for a moment; then it suddenly came to me. *Why?*

"If you don't mind me asking, sir, why do you want that book so badly? It's just an old book," I said with a shrug.

I wasn't sure why I asked. He had already told me he was going to use it for funding. But I was suddenly both curious to hear the answer he would come up with and aware that General Delaney would not be pleased with my questioning his motives. Both Ruth and General Delaney looked at me with surprise. Ruth's shock faded into a grin, and that childlike joy returned to her eyes as she turned her gaze on General Delaney. To my surprise, fear flickered across his face at the sight of her smile. That smile, as if she knew something that we didn't.

He regained his composure quickly and smiled at me. But his eyes were dangerous. "Yes, just a book. I happen to like old books. But you should know that this book is more valuable than it appears. It will be sold to a wealthy collector to gain funds for a new phase of remodeling for the Town." His eyes warned me to back off. *It was just a job, and the job is now over,* I told myself. I nodded.

"If you will excuse me," said General Delaney, "I would like to get to know...what did you say your name was again?" he said as he looked to Ruth with testing eyes.

"Ruth," she replied with a polite smile.

General Delaney's eyebrows furrowed, and I saw him fight to conceal his frustration again. "Ah yes, Ruth." His smile hid his disdain. Something about her and the way she smiled bothered him. "Leave us," he said to me. "We will discuss your payment later," he repeated reassuringly.

I dipped my head respectfully and glanced at Ruth. She smiled and gave a slight nod as if to say it was alright. I turned and left, guilt washing over me as I strode toward the door. *What would happen to her if she didn't want to give up the book and the thieves from the cave found out she owned it?* I shook my head as I retraced our path through the long hall back to the front door. *It was just a job, and the job is now over,* I repeated to myself for what felt like the millionth time. *Worrying about her well-being is not my job.*

Forcing the worry from my mind, I descended the large marble staircase and went to find Jeb where I had left him. Seeing him pulled me out of my depressed mood, and I finally felt myself grow calm.

Jeb was curiously investigating one of the carriages near General Delaney's courtyard fountain. As I called him over, one of General Delaney's soldiers frowned at me. "Why don't you restrain that animal as it should be?" he snapped in annoyance.

I laughed. Realizing that I had finished this oddly frustrating mission suddenly left me with a tinge of elation. "Jeb, restrain yourself," I said playfully.

In response, Jeb grabbed his reins off the ground with his dexterous lips and walked to a nearby hitching post. Dropping them over the post, he turned and looked at me, just as I had taught him to do. I laughed at the man's look of pure annoyance as I walked over and gave Jeb a scratch in his favorite spot, watching as the man walked off, casting glares over his shoulder.

I gently flipped the reins over Jeb's head and swung into his saddle. Leaving the reins untouched around his neck, I said, "The Kuzmich Inn." His ears pricked back to catch the words before he promptly began picking his way toward the Kuzmich Inn at a gentle, swaying walk. I enjoyed the ride. Jeb knew how to get to the inn, and though I paid attention to him, it was in the way you might silently pay attention to a friend with whom you were out on a stroll.

As I descended the Crescent Hill, thoughts of the night Jeb had been born came back to me, and I smiled. Mary had joyfully proclaimed how cute he was on the way back from the grassy hills where he was born. We had slept under the stars that night to give him and his mother a rest. It wasn't a long walk to Mary's family home, but it was a beautiful one. Jeb bounded behind his mother during the trip. To our surprise, he was just as curious of us as he was of the world around him. Jeb kept us entertained the whole trip home, nuzzling us any chance he got, sniffing our boots as we rode by, peering into small caves, and chasing after butterflies.

I recalled Mary's words. "He is so curious! I hope that curiosity never leaves him. I shall never make him jaded and robotic like all those other horses, following rules simply because they are told to do so. Never given a chance to ask why."

At the time, I had laughed. "You have been spending too much time with Ivan. That horse would run you over in a heartbeat if you let him," I said jokingly.

"No, he wouldn't!" she exclaimed in playful joy. "I would still teach him how to behave and how to care—how to be gentle. But never do I wish that his curiosity would vanish. For if I could not give him the freedom to say no, how would I know he truly wanted to say yes?" She smiled with glee at her words of wisdom, then laughed at Jeb's wobbly legs as he attempted to run for the first time. He crashed, then stood up and tried again. Her words had stuck with me for some reason. Though she was now gone, and over time other conversations had faded, that one stuck with me. Forever clear, as if it were happening now.

I smiled to myself. Then it came, guilt washing over me. *What would Mary think of me now?* This week was the first time in years that I had allowed myself to think of her enough to summon memories. And now, as guilt came rushing back, I remembered why I had held the memories at bay for so long. The guilt reminded me once again of Ruth. *What will happen to her?* In frustration, I pushed the memory of my beloved Mary and the thoughts of Ruth away, and with them left the feeling of guilt.

Jeb and I walked on through town, watching the people close up shops and listening to the sounds of friends bidding each other goodbye until tomorrow. The sun would go down in an hour or so, and people were finishing up their day's work, gathering the products they sold in the streets and calling their children back to them before heading in for dinner.

Tuning out the laid-back commotion around me, I listened to Jeb's hooves in the muddy street and remembered the war. I took in a deep breath, thinking of the long nights spent riding through rain and sleet. Part of me missed it. Not the war itself—something else. *The simplicity?* I wondered. Knowing what you were supposed to do and how to do it was comforting. Knowing that you had only two options: lay down and die or fight and survive.

As the Kuzmich Inn came into view, I steered Jeb toward the stables. I guided him into a stall, removed his tack, and tossed some hay in the feeder before exiting and closing the stall door behind me. I tossed the stable boy some coins, and he thanked me as I approached the inn's front door—that old, worn, green front door that was somehow so comforting.

Opening the door, I was greeted with a wave of comfortable heat as I stepped in out of the chilly morning air. There were fewer people than usual today. I approached the nearly empty bar and asked Missy where Ivan and Nadia were.

"Upstairs," she responded with dampened excitement. "They've been pouring over a note left for you. As soon as the woman dropped it off, they took it up and read it. They have been wondering over it all evening."

"What woman?" I asked.

"She's about your age, and beautiful," she said with a smile. "Had a book with her. She said you told her to leave a note with Ivan or Nadia if she needed to contact you. I knew you were the one she was talking about because she described your twin pistols. Apparently, you forgot to introduce yourself," she chastised with a grin.

"When did she drop off the note?" I asked, ignoring her teasing. *Is there more than one copy of the book?* I wondered in confusion.

"Just an hour ago. Said something happened, and she thought you could help. The note's a bit odd, though," added Missy with a shrug.

"How so?" I prompted.

"Haven't read it, but it must be because Ivan and Nadia are quite taken with it."

"Thanks, Missy. I'll go up and check it out," I said as I pushed off the bar.

Missy nodded as I headed for the stairs at the back of the room that led to the second and third levels. Most rooms were open for guests, but one was a permanent living space designed to hold a small family. It belonged to Ivan and Nadia, given to them by their parents along with the rest of the inn and bar. I climbed to the second level and found their door at the end of the hall near a set of stairs leading out to the back stables. I knocked on the door, and it flew open to reveal Ivan and his big grin.

"Oh no, I know that face," I moaned as he ushered me into the room.

"I'm glad you are finally here. We have a note for you from a young woman. Beautiful, I might add," he said as he wiggled his brows.

I rolled my eyes. "So I heard. Where's the note then?" I said, holding out my hand.

Nadia handed it to me with a smile. "She was quite interested in you. Kept asking about where you were and what you did for a living. The note's a bit cryptic, but it sounds interesting. Maybe adventure awaits you?" said Nadia with a hopeful smirk.

I opened the note. "I'm glad my notes are kept so private from prying eyes," I said sardonically as I glared at the twins. I looked down at the note.

*"You seek something I have. Meet me at the Woods tomorrow at midnight."*

"I don't see how that's so interesting," I said, downplaying my interest.

"She has something you want!" exclaimed Ivan. "Maybe the book? Isn't that what you were looking for the other night? And if it's the book, then we could use it to get the Beast in the Woods before you hand it over to General Delaney! I'm telling you, this is adventure calling with treasure at its end!" His eyes were wide, and he grabbed my shoulders with an intense grip. "Nadia and I will join you!" he exclaimed, shaking me slightly.

"Ivan..." I groaned. "It could be about the book, but I doubt the woman I met during that ordeal would contact me."

"Why?" asked Nadia, narrowing her eyes.

My gaze shifted to the rafters and back down to meet her eyes. "I may have been in a hurry and practically broken down her front door...without knocking."

Nadia's eyes bugged out, and to my surprise, she burst out laughing. "You like this woman!" she exclaimed.

Ivan's smile melted into a frown of concentration. "How does that add up?" he asked.

"You know Benny; he barges into people's houses all the time for work. But he feels bad about this one! He definitely likes this woman," Nadia declared as her grin widened.

"I do not! Can we stay on topic here?" I snapped.

"No trouble, Benny," said Nadia, still grinning. "If it is her and she does have the book, then we can write down all we need to know before you turn it in, and we can all go hunt the Beast and get the reward! If it is anything like the last time you went after that beast, we will probably end up on a few wild goose chases before we get any good intel, which means we will probably be gone for a while. Missy can run the inn while we are gone. You can't go by yourself. You will need us to help you—you know, with the next war due any time. And you know other people will want the reward if they find out someone is going after it again, so they will probably come after you." She shrugged as if her next point was obvious. "You will need backup just in case." Before I could get in a word, she added, "C'mon, Benny! Adventure awaits! Don't you miss that? The excitement of battles and outwitting those against you?"

"And this adventure could end in a massive reward!" chimed in Ivan with wide, expectant eyes.

"We don't even know if there is an adventure to be had!" I replied. "She just said she has something I want."

"Yes, and other than the book, what could you possibly want from her, unless you are not telling me about another inn you visit for fun?" asked Nadia.

"Yeah! I can't think of anything else she might have that you want. Considering your past, you're not interested in a family, so—" Ivan stopped abruptly when I glared at him.

"Ivan!" snapped Nadia as her hand lashed out and smacked him on the arm.

"Sorry, I didn't mean it like that," he said as he rubbed his arm.

I let out a hard breath and rubbed my forehead. "No harm done, Ivan. You're right. I did go looking for the book and ran into her, and I did tell her to contact me if she found it. But I already found the book and delivered it. There is nothing she could have that I want."

"Unless there is more than one copy in town," Ivan said with a grin.

"And why would I care if there is more than one copy?" I asked.

"Because I did some research on your book, and it could tell us how the Beast came to be, and if we know that, then we might be able to figure out how to kill it, and that would lead to treasure!" pleaded Ivan.

Nadia playfully rolled her eyes. "There are only two theories on that beast in the Woods." She began listing them off on her fingers. "One, the Beast can grant any wish, save that pertaining to life. Or two, if you kill the Beast, you can make life using its soul. We know the first theory is bogus, but Mom and Dad used to tell us bedtime stories of the Woods and how people believed that the Great Beasts wish to use the Beast's soul to make an unkillable leader and that the Delaney family would give a treasure to whoever killed the Beast, thus ending their attacks and the wars. If we succeed, we could split the treasure! You could go wherever you want, and Ivan and I could clean up this place!"

I glanced around at the two beds, the well-worn kitchen, and the old rafters above us. "Yeah, it does need a good cleaning," I joked.

Nadia frowned, glaring at me like a mother exasperated with her son for making a bad joke. "Very funny."

"And what would you two adventurers do if this turned out to be a trap?" I asked. "As Nadia pointed out, there are plenty of people out there who want that reward. If they found out that we are meeting with someone who might have a book that could tell how to catch the Beast, they might think it would be smart to get rid of the competition, who by the way is us. We could have half the world on our tails," I said, thinking once again of the people at the cave.

"That's exactly why you need us at this first meeting as well!" said Ivan.

"We can watch your back," added Nadia, throwing an arm over Ivan's shoulders.

I knew they could. We had shared a childhood and fought together in battle. And a bond born in battle is not one easily broken. *Why not at least check it out?* I thought.

"Fine...but the meeting is not until tomorrow night. I'll meet you here a couple of hours before so we can scope the place out. I suppose we should be prepared to be gone for a while. If this woman has a copy of the book, we wouldn't need to wait for more information from Valdra. We might as well leave to search for the Beast right away, because the longer we wait, the greater the chance someone will find out what we are doing. So, make sure you pack everything you'll need." My words were drowned in their excited chattering, so I left them to their planning and went downstairs to get a drink.

"Off to find treasure?" asked Missy with a smile as I approached the bar.

"It seems that way," I said with a huff as I slid onto a stool. I should have expected this from the twins. After the most recent war had ended, they had nothing left but their parents' inn. They had saved up some money from their time as beast fighters in General Delaney's army, so they retired along with me and spent the next five years rebuilding the inn, turning it into a popular stop in the Town. But Nadia had always been one to seek out adventure. She loved running the inn here, but I had seen evidence lately that she was getting restless, maybe even regretting leaving her life as a beast fighter. Ivan, on the other hand, was just interested in gold. He always had been. He didn't often spend money, but something about the ability to buy whatever he wanted attracted him. A little adventure to get it was nothing; he would gladly fight any battle if it meant finding treasure. If the war had not turned him into a soldier, I was certain he would have become a treasure hunter.

"Will you watch the inn?" I asked Missy as she began filling a mug of ale for me.

"They already asked me. I'd be happy to." She smiled. "They pulled this place back up from nothing after the war, after their parents passed." She shook her head regretfully. "I remember when we were little, their parents used to say this place was like a beacon. A place where others could come to feel safe. Nadia and Ivan have done everything to protect it and keep it running. They deserve an adventure." She grinned as she placed the mug of ale before me.

I nodded. "Thanks."

As I sat at the bar and drank my ale, I thought of what the woman could possibly want. Even if she had another copy of the book, I didn't need it for General Delaney anymore. Ivan and Nadia would want to go after the Beast, as they had discussed. But I didn't want or need the reward. General Delaney always saw to it that I had what I needed. He paid me well. All I wanted to do was go home, take some time off, and maybe teach Jeb a new trick. Yet, I had just agreed to go on this crazy hunting trip with Ivan and Nadia. *Maybe an adventure would do me good.*

"How will you get to the Beast?" asked Missy.

It was well known that anyone who entered the Woods would die. Apparently, a long time ago, people had tried, and they had just dropped dead. No one knew why, so people just stopped trying. Because of this invisible death trap, getting the Beast meant that one had to lure it out of the Woods, but no one had ever been successful.

"I will cross that bridge when and if I come to it, Missy," I said with a tired smile.

She laughed. "You know there are versions of the story that say the Beast is there to lure people to their deaths. Isn't it ironic that now you must lure it to its own death?"

I gave her the best laugh I could muster, but her words stung. In the years after the first few wars, many had sought the Beast in hopes that General Delaney would give them a vast reward. I myself had sought it once or twice but had never even laid eyes on it. Yet for some reason, it had found me. I hadn't been looking for it that day when I saw it in the Woods. *Or maybe I had,* I wondered. Now it visited me in my dreams, and I thought of it almost daily, whether just in a passing thought or getting lost in the pull of its piercing green eyes. I did not want to admit it, but the idea of luring that creature to its death sat heavy in the pit of my stomach. There was something about the mysterious Beast of the Woods that was growing on me, despite the feelings of guilt and fear that often accompanied my thoughts of those eyes.

I abruptly felt like I needed some fresh air. I thanked Missy for the drink and left the bar. I wasn't sure where I was going, but I needed to think. So I tacked up Jeb and rode through town, doing my best to steer away from the Woods.

Eventually, however, I found myself at the edge of the Forest, only a few feet from the Woods themselves, on the main road that arched around the southern half of the Woods. The Town sat behind me, just on the other side of the road. The Forest spread out before me to the north. The Forest's boundary ran both east and west, all the way to the far-off port towns on the Eastern and Western Seas, its surprisingly straight edge only adjusting its trajectory to bend gracefully around the northern half of the Woods. The Woods extended half-way into the Forest, the trees at its edge distinctly different from those of the Forest, causing it to stand out amidst the surrounding plant life. The drooping, vine-covered oaks of the Woods were interspersed with trees that resembled pines with twisted needles and thick bushes, which looked nothing like the typical pine trees and blackberry bushes of the Forest.

Doing my best to ignore the nearby patch of foliage that was the Woods, I focused on the Forest before me. I hadn't been to the other side of the Forest since the most recent war. Though the war had ended only five and a half years ago, it seemed so long ago that I couldn't even remember what it was like on the other side of the Woods. Only that bloody battlefield.

Suddenly, I felt that feeling again. Someone was watching me. I casually glanced around but didn't see anything. I turned back to face the Forest just as Jeb flinched beneath me. There, standing in the shadows, leaning against a tree, was Valdra.

"You have got to stop doing that!" I snapped. General Delaney's personal messengers were not the only ones who found pleasure in scaring me half to death.

He smiled. "Just trying to have a little fun," he joked. "The general has orders for you," he explained as he approached me, his black horse emerging from the shadows behind him.

"Now, hold on," I said, holding a hand up and shaking my head in frustration. "I haven't even been paid for my last job yet. And General Delaney said I could take time off after I completed that mission," I grumbled.

"You will after you do this one last thing," said Valdra in a pleasant tone.

“I am not killing anyone for him.” I glared at Valdra, thinking of the woman I was to meet with tomorrow night.

“I think you just might change your mind when you hear his orders,” he said with a smile. “Delaney wants you to go after the Beast in the Woods again.”

“What?” I couldn’t believe the timing. *First Ivan and Nadia, and now General Delaney, again!* “I have tried going after that thing in the past, and it has never worked!” I snapped. “Why would this time be any different?”

“Because you have this now.” Valdra held up a piece of paper, passing it up to me. “That is the address of a man who can tell you how to kill the Beast. You and anyone who helps you will be handsomely rewarded, of course,” he said with a smile.

“Of course.” I glared. I couldn’t believe this. *The twins will be thrilled.* Then I thought of something. “And what if I refuse?”

Valdra’s smile slipped, and his eyes became dangerous. “It is not our job to question the instructions he gives us. Just do it. It’s just a job,” he said, leaving no room to argue. “When you are finished, come to the mansion, and your payment will be taken care of.” He mounted his horse and turned it toward town. But then he paused, and his shoulders slouched before he turned to look at me, his tone calm. “Relax, Ben. When you get back, we will go out for a drink and have a good time until the next war breaks out,” he said with a playful grin. Urging his horse forward, he rode back toward town, disappearing into the shadows of the homes that lined the street.

*What is wrong with me?* I wondered as I watched him leave. *That’s the second time this week I have challenged General Delaney.* I let out a hard breath. I really did need a break.

It was late now, and I needed to get back home. As Jeb and I traveled back toward town, I still had the feeling that I was being watched, so I stuck to the larger main road, hoping whoever it was wouldn't pounce. I had no fight in me tonight. But just in case, I circled around and took a serpentine route back home.

When we arrived at the house, I let Jeb take a drink as I stripped him of his tack and tended to him and the only other horse in the stalls, my father's black gelding. The stable hands left my father's horse for me to tend to, as they knew I enjoyed it. The horse was retired and spent most of its days in the back pasture of my land with the mares General Delaney had given me as gifts for my heroics in battle.

As Jeb and my father's horse ate dinner in their stalls, I stood and watched the other horses grazing in the rolling, faintly moonlit fields. After a moment, I took the paper Valdra had handed me out of my pocket and read it again. There was no name, just a location for somewhere on the backside of town. Hopefully, the man would be there when I arrived, I would be able to get paid, and this would all be over sooner rather than later. Suddenly, Jeb grunted and kicked the wall to his stall. Startled, I dropped the note and spun around to face him. I left the note where it fell and entered Jeb's stall to check on him. I let out a sigh. He was fine. A cat that had taken up residence in the barn during the last war had gone after a mouse and must have startled him. I patted Jeb on the shoulder as I watched the cat devour its prey.

Suddenly, the hair on my neck bristled. I spun around but didn't see anyone. I felt it again; someone was watching me. I exited the stall and looked around calmly, trying not to give away that I was checking my environment for anyone who could be watching. Still no sign of anyone but the horses. I took a deep breath and picked up the note, shoving it into my pocket as I glanced at Jeb. He didn't seem worried, so I forced myself to calm down. *It is probably nothing.*

I brushed Jeb and my father's horse down and released them into the pasture with the others. Then I climbed to the loft and settled into my bed. Tomorrow, I would check out the address Valdra had given me first thing. But tonight, I needed to rest. *What would I do if I found the Beast?* I wondered. The answer did not come to me, so I closed my eyes and let myself drifted off to sleep with thoughts of mysterious thieves and dangerous adventures roaming through my mind.

# Chapter 5

THE HOUSE AT THE address that Valdra had given me was located on the very edge of town, near where it sloped up into the rolling green foothills of the Southern Mountains. After a restless sleep, I arrived in the early morning, about a half hour after sunrise. As I approached the worn wood house, I heard a commotion inside. I quietly dismounted Jeb and told him to wait for me as I drew one of my flintlock pistols and slowly approached the door.

Stopping short of the door frame, I leaned against the wall and listened. Someone was inside rummaging around, and it didn't sound like they were a welcome guest. The person who lived there was most likely unaware that I was on my way, so it was possible that they had company or were working on a cleaning project. But based on the grumbles of frustration coming from inside, it sounded more like the person was searching for something.

Since it was early morning and people were beginning to start their day, I decided I did not want to deal with whoever was in there on the street where everyone could see. So, leaving Jeb waiting for me in the front, I snuck around back and approached the back door with my weapon drawn and cocked. When I reached the door, I silently wrapped my hand around the handle, turned it, and quietly pushed the door open. As I stepped into the main room, I discovered the culprit.

Standing in the kitchen, bent to one side with her head inside the bottom cupboard, was the woman that Valdra had wanted to kill. Dressed this time in functional trousers and a long fleece-lined jacket, she looked as beautiful as I remembered her, even from this angle, and I was surprised by the relief that washed over me at seeing that she was still alive.

"I assume you knocked when you arrived," I said with a grin. The woman startled so severely that she bumped her head on the cupboard, then stood up, holding the back of her head with one hand and frowning.

"Yes, as a matter of fact, I did knock. Unlike you!" she snapped. "He wasn't here," she said, gesturing to the empty home around her, "and the door swung open when I touched it. So, I figured I might as well take a look," she said defensively.

"For what exactly?" I asked as I holstered my weapon.

Her brow creased above her beautiful brown eyes as she frowned and regarded me with an inquisitive look. Suddenly, her expression softened, and she looked tired. "The book you were after," she said disappointedly as her hand dropped from her head.

"So, you lied," I exclaimed accusingly.

"I beg your pardon?" she said with a look of shock.

"In your note. You lied about having something I wanted."

She took a deep breath. "I was planning on getting it before the meeting."

"Right." I drew the word out sarcastically. "So, you have nothing I want," I stated flatly.

She paused with her mouth open, then snapped it shut. "Okay, I don't have anything you want. I came here hoping I would beat you to the book," she stated.

"And why do you want the book?" I asked curiously.

"I need your help..." She trailed off with a guilty expression.

"Is that what you were going to use the book for?" I asked with raised eyebrows. "To bribe me into helping you?"

"Fine." She let out a small, nervous chuckle. "Evidently, I am not very good at this...Yes, I was hoping that if I had the book, I could exchange it for your help with something."

"And what, exactly, would you need my help with?" I asked. "We only just met."

She let out a hard sigh and pinched the bridge of her nose. "It's a long story."

"Were you planning on telling it to me at our meeting?" I asked sardonically.

"Yes!" She paused with her mouth half open and then closed it with a frown when she realized I was teasing.

"So, tell me now," I said. Then I had a realization. "Wait, how did you even know about this place?"

She blushed. "Um...I may have followed you last night...and saw the note you had."

I put my hands on my hips. "May have?"

"Look, I knew you were looking for the book, and I didn't know how else to find you, so I left you the note to get your attention and was in town following up on a lead on the book when I saw you leave the inn last night and I..." She shrugged. "I started following you..." She suddenly glared at me. "Okay, it sounds worse when you say it out loud," she said as she crossed her arms defiantly.

"Yes. Yes, it does." I glared back at her.

She looked away and raised her eyebrows. "Well, I wasn't *planning* on following you..." she said, as if that would help.

*So she was the reason I felt like I was being followed last night. That doesn't explain the other times, though.* I let my mind wander back to everything that had happened since I had first started feeling like I was being followed. One of General Delaney's soldiers had shown up the night before I met this woman, then I had felt like someone was following me yesterday, and then Valdra had shown up to give me the note. I struggled to hide my frustration. I needed to pay more attention. I couldn't keep track of all these people showing up in the past week and a half of my life.

"So, it was you last night at my place?" I asked, trying to put the pieces together.

She looked at me with guilt in her eyes. "I—"

"Never mind." *It doesn't matter,* I thought. *I need to get this done, and I can't keep getting distracted,* I told myself. I spun toward the front door. "I am not some help for hire service," I lied, "and the person who lives here clearly knew I was coming and fled. So, I guess our business here is done."

But for some reason, I didn't want it to be. For some reason, I had enjoyed the two times I had met this woman in a way I had not felt for a long time. I was not going to tell her that, though, so I walked outside and mounted Jeb, who was waiting for me right where I left him. To my delight, which I was careful to hide, the woman followed me outside.

"At least tell me your name," she said as I cued Jeb forward and we started to walk away.

I found myself wanting to know her name as well, simultaneously realizing how rude I was being and how odd it was that I cared. I pulled Jeb to a stop and looked at her. I didn't know why I was acting like this. *It has been an odd couple of weeks.*

"I'm sorry," I said as I rubbed a hand over my face in frustration. "I am tired and have a long day ahead of me, and I don't mean to be cross," I explained, offering a tired smile. "My name is Benjamin Arlin. Most people just call me Ben. And you are...? I am afraid we both forgot to ask last time we met."

"Yes," she said with a grin. "Something about breaking down someone's door doesn't leave much room for introductions." Her brown eyes sparkled with a teasing twinkle.

I smiled. "Sorry about that, truly I am."

She nodded and reached her hand out to me. "Solace. Solace Devo." As we shook hands, I noticed that, despite her fine features and slender build, she had a strong grip, and the muscles in her bare forearm rippled as she gripped my hand in hers.

I nodded and let out a breath. "Well, Solace, if you need a ride..."

"No, thank you. Where I am going is not far from here, and I have some shopping to do," she said with a polite smile.

I nodded. I tipped an imaginary hat and turned Jeb away from her.

"I still need your help, though," she said hurriedly.

I kept riding and said over my shoulder, "Told you already, I don't do that kind of thing."

She ignored my dismissal. "There is a story that is a family heirloom, and I need to protect it." She took a deep breath. "It has been handed down from generation to generation in my family, told by mouth and memorized so it could be passed on with or without pages that could be lost. At one point in time, there were many of us. But now..." She paused. "But now I am the last one."

"I told you, I am not some help for hire service," I said with a tinge of frustration as I kept moving.

Solace switched tactics. "I think I know where the man who lived here went."

I stopped Jeb. Despite the fact that this woman irritated me, she also intrigued me. I wanted a reason to stay, and it seemed this was it. Plus, returning to Valdra and General Delaney empty-handed wasn't a great option. This alternative sounded much better.

"Why me?" I said as I turned Jeb slightly so I could face her.

"I need you to help me find the man who lived here. He not only has your book, but he also knows how to catch the Beast of the Woods." She took a step closer. "It is said that if one can catch the Beast of the Woods, it will grant any wish one desires, save that pertaining to life itself," she said. She looked at me for a moment, and when I didn't respond, her expression changed. "I know who you are."

"What?" I asked in confusion.

"There were stories of a soldier during the wars with a horse as black as night. He used to rescue those taken by the Great Beasts. Then, when the most recent war ended, he vanished. Many say he was killed in battle. But others say that he still lives. I saw that black horse last night...in your pastures," she said, pointing at me.

I let out a sigh. I knew the stories of the so-called Night Rider. My father used to tell them to me as a child. He even claimed he met him once. But I didn't need another old folktale on my hands. I could find someone else to help me find the man who lived here. I didn't have time for this. "That horse was my father's and was nothing more than a simple battle horse given to him by a friend. Trust me. I fought in the war with my father. I would have known if he was some dark crusader. I am afraid you will need to find help elsewhere." I lifted the reins gently, and Jeb turned and moved forward at a walk.

"I need your help!" called Solace. "Please!"

I kept riding. I was back to being annoyed with her.

"We are all going to die if you don't help me!" she snapped. "You think the war is over, but it's not. You think the good side won, but it didn't. I know the real story of what the Great Beasts are, and it is my duty to protect that story, or this world will forever be lost to those dark beasts that wage war on us so often," she yelled. When I didn't stop, she strode after me. "The Woods have the answer!" she continued. "The Beast within them can grant that the story be protected for all time, and that story contains information that can stave off further war. We are one decision away from death!" she said desperately.

I had met people like her before. People who believed an old story about a king who, in anger over the murder of his son, created the Great Beasts that began waging war on his enemies. Many of them believed that the secret to getting rid of the Great Beasts once and for all was contained within the story they had memorized. I wasn't quite sure how that part of the story worked. But it was just a story. It could not stave off the evils and monsters of this world. Solace sounded just as crazy as all the others I had met. And if she was telling the truth, and she was of the family who spoke the story, then she was what people referred to as a Chosen. According to the story, their family had been chosen for some important purpose. What it was, I did not know, nor did I want to. But Solace was not just any Chosen, she was apparently the last one. *Great,* I thought. *That's all I need—a crazy lady who thinks she has all the answers.* I glanced at her. *Crazy, but smart...and beautiful.* I blinked and looked away.

Suddenly, Ruth's words came to my mind, and I quoted them in frustration. "Death out here or death in the Woods, what is the difference?" I said over my shoulder.

"The difference is why!" Solace yelled to my back.

I stiffened as Ruth's words came back to me again. *"Now that is a good question,"* she had said.

"What did you say?" I asked as I spun Jeb around again.

"The difference is why," Solace repeated more calmly, having finally gotten my attention.

I glared at her, but my frustration was melting into curiosity. *What is it with that question lately?*

"We can stay out here and live or enter those woods and risk possible death. The choice seems easy until you learn why the risk is worth it. It is my generational duty to protect this story, and according to the story I memorized, the Beast in those woods will grant me my wish forever if I can just capture it," she said as she grabbed Jeb's reins to keep me from moving. "I can die in this world, or I can die in that world. The difference is why. I will die in this world because people are not meant to live forever. But if I choose to die there by entering that world to protect this story, I die for a reason, for something that will last far beyond me. And that is the death of a life not wasted."

She looked at me, waiting for a reply. When I did not offer one, she leaned closer and said, "Fine, you are more concerned about living? You are alive, and you have been given a chance to make one decision," she exclaimed, holding up her index finger. "Don't waste what time you have been given. Make the right decision. Choose something bigger than yourself!" she commanded. "Help me. If I die here or there, it does not matter. Only that this story is protected forever. I have no one to pass it to; I am alone. Please help me protect it! You are the only person I know of who can do something like this," she pleaded. "Then you can go back to whatever life you have chosen to waste!" she snapped as she finally released Jeb's reins.

Her words brought a memory to my mind, one that I had tried to forget. A battlefield covered in blood. Bodies of men and women whom my father and I had led into battle against a beast that no one truly understood. The Great Volcano gurgled as it consumed the flesh of the Great Beast we had just lured to its hot cliffs. But in my arms lay my dying father. His words sounded in my ears like a distant echo. *"The war was won long ago, but we fought this battle alone and lost. Yet time has not run out. Do not waste what you have by dwelling on what you have lost. Choose your friends wisely. Don't trust what this world tells you. Do not fight your battles alone."* He had said those words to me before, but I had forgotten what they meant. The war had changed me, and my father's final words had been his last attempt to remind me of the things he had taught me as a boy. But it seemed so long ago. I could not remember the meaning of those words.

"Please. I cannot do this alone," pleaded Solace, almost echoing my father's words. "I have money; I can pay you handsomely."

I looked toward the Woods and the Forest beyond, toward the Great Volcano that rose in the distance, framed by the Northern Mountains. My father's words echoed in my mind again. *"Do not waste what you have by dwelling on what you have lost."* I had not thought of those words since that day. I had pushed them out of my mind. I had lost everything to that war. Mary. My father. Even part of myself. I had thought that working for General Delaney would be a good enough distraction. And it had been. But in forcing myself to forget in an attempt to stave off grief, I had wasted what I'd had. And worse, I had taken others down with me. I had tricked myself into thinking that I was not dwelling on what I had lost. But I was.

*No!* I thought to myself. *I have a job to do. I have been tasked with killing the Beast of the Woods, and that is what I will do.* Suddenly, my mind filled with those beautiful green eyes calling to me. Guilt twisted my stomach, but I pushed it down. *Not now,* I thought. *It's just a job, and Solace's story is just a story. I have been tasked with killing that beast, and that is what I will do,* I repeated to myself.

But Solace wanted to catch it. Working with her would not be easy, because once we got to the Beast, our agendas would be in conflict. I looked at her. She was strong and beautiful, like a flower blooming in the frozen mountains. I did not want to be the one to stomp out her beauty. But I had no other leads. I needed to find the man who knew how to kill the Beast of the Woods. I needed to kill it. That was my job. That was my purpose. I would take the risk, no matter the cost.

"Fine!" I snapped in frustration. "I need to think. We will meet at the Woods as we originally planned. It will be safer to discuss this outside of town where others can't easily eavesdrop."

She nodded. "Will you be prepared to leave right away tomorrow night? The longer we wait, the more we risk someone hearing of our plans and following us."

I nodded. "I will be ready." I paused. "Be careful returning to your home. Someone could already have heard and be waiting there to find out what you know." *Or one of Valdra's soldiers could be waiting to dispose of you,* I didn't add, remembering Valdra's words.

She smiled. "Don't worry. I can take care of myself."

As I turned Jeb toward home, thoughts swirled in my head of what I had just done, what I would do in the days to come, and what I would have to do in the end. *Why does someone always have to die?* I thought to myself. Ruth's words immediately came to mind. *"Now that is a good question."*

Once home, I pondered what this new information meant. After some deliberation, I finally settled on the conclusion that I would just have to trust Solace and then leave her to her fate once she served her purpose. Valdra already wanted her dead, and he wouldn't likely change his mind just because she helped me find the Beast. *Unless there is a way to convince Valdra that she is not a threat. Maybe she could come work for the general?* I brushed a hand through my hair and sighed. I could deal with that problem later. I had not slept well last night and needed rest if I was going to be meeting Solace at midnight. But my dreams were filled with disturbing visions of Ruth and Solace dying. Green eyes jumped out at me, and guilt and fear pounded in my chest when I finally snapped awake. In an attempt to calm myself, I spent the rest of the day making provisions for my land and the animals and people who lived and worked there. Depending on where the man we were looking for was located, I could be gone for a while, which I had not done since the war. But, by the end of the day, it was all settled, and Jeb and I headed to the inn.

When we arrived at the Kuzmich Inn, Nadia and Ivan came downstairs, ready to go, just as I ordered a drink. Ivan had on what was probably one of only two pairs of pants he owned, his only pair of boots, and a well-worn blouse under a leather vest. For weapons, he had his well-used but well-cared-for pistol strapped to his hip, his favorite sword on his other hip, a sheathed knife the size of my forearm at his back between his shoulders, and, of course, his fists. Subtlety was not his forte, and I was glad when he threw on a long jacket, making the weapons less visible.

Nadia, on the other hand, was quite the opposite. Her weapons were completely concealed, as always. She wore a practical cream blouse over functional pants and boots, and she had put her striking red hair up in a classy but sensible bun with loose red curls hanging out in various but organized directions. Though at first glance her clothes were simple and straightforward, her beauty and feminine style were charming and provided a stark contrast to Ivan. I was reminded of the time I had asked her why she always looked nice, even on the battlefield, and she had explained with a grin, *"Just because one can battle a beast barehanded doesn't mean one should abandon her appearance."* She was sweet and joyful, but anyone who had gone to war with her knew that she was quite capable of taking care of herself.

As Nadia threw on her favorite ankle-length green woolen jacket, I reviewed my mental checklist of my own clothes and weapons. Though the twins were somehow always on either side of the battle wardrobe spectrum, I usually fell somewhere in the middle.

I wore practical but clean clothes under my black duster, which covered my twin flintlock pistols given to me by my father, one on each hip. Their silver inlayed ivory handles, carved in the shape of some mythical creature, were always easily accessible beneath my coattails. I also carried a concealed knife in my boot and one in Jeb's saddle.

I turned to the twins as they were buttoning up their jackets. "We still have a couple hours before we have to meet her," I said.

Ivan rubbed his big hands together. "Yes, but one should always scope out a meeting place beforehand. Have you lost your touch?" he said with a grin. Without waiting for a response, he exclaimed, "Let's ride!" and trounced off to the door with a grinning Nadia in tow. I gulped down the last of my ale and gave Missy a tip and a nod. She smiled and waved as we vanished into the night.

Jeb nickered a greeting as we approached, and the twins tacked up their horses before we headed to the Woods. We rode in silence, taking random routes through town to throw off anyone who might be following us. As we exited the Town, it dawned on me that I didn't know exactly where to meet Solace. *Oh well,* I thought. *The Woods are only a half mile or so wide; it won't be that complicated.*

As soon as we reached the road that separated the Town from the Woods, we fanned out without a word, falling effortlessly into a habit of our days fighting wars. We worked together well, as if we were of one mind. Once we had scouted out the entire circle of woods to ensure no one had followed us or was planning on interrupting our meeting, we met back where we had started. It seemed that General Delaney and Valdra had done a good job keeping a lid on the plan to go after the Beast. I just hoped Solace had the same discretion, or else we would have the whole country following us, trying to fight us for access to the Beast. *Not a great way to hunt an ancient creature.*

Certain that no one had followed us, we guided the horses off the road just to the east of the Woods and dismounted inside the edge of the Forest. The moon was bright, so we could keep an eye out for anyone coming along the road, but we would be invisible in the shadow of the trees. We still had over an hour to wait until midnight, though, so we got comfortable.

I tried not to look toward the Woods, but I felt that draw to them, to the Beast within. The beast that Ivan and Nadia were so keen on catching so they could get that treasure in exchange for its lifeless body. The one I had been tasked with killing for General Delaney to supposedly stave off another quickly approaching war with the Great Beasts of the Southern Mountains. The same beast Solace wanted alive to grant her wish that her family heirloom be preserved forever so darkness could one day be vanquished.

"There is something I need to tell you about the woman we are meeting here tonight," I said, turning to the twins. I could just make out their features in the dappled moonlight.

Ivan and Nadia glanced at each other and back at me with questioning looks.

"I met her this morning. Accidentally. She wants me to help her find the Beast of the Woods."

"Ha!" Ivan expressed with glee. "I told you!"

"Shut up, Ivan," snapped Nadia. "What else did she want? And what are we doing here if you already met with her?"

"I didn't want to talk to her in town where people could overhear, so we agreed to still meet out here. And there's something else. Last night, after I got her note, Valdra came with a message from General Delaney. Once again, I have been tasked with killing the Beast. I assume to stave off another war."

"Well, that's convenient," she said suspiciously.

"It gets better. He told me to go visit an address near the back edge of town and get information on how to kill the Beast from the man who lives there. I went to the house this morning, but the man was gone and Solace was there."

"Solace. She's the woman we are meeting? The one you met a few days ago at her house? The one who left the note?" asked Nadia.

I smiled at Nadia's summary. "Yes. But she does not have the book," I stated.

"Then, like Nadia said, what are we doing at this meeting?" asked Ivan with a shrug.

I took a deep breath. "She says that she has a story that has been told in her family for hundreds of years and passed down from generation to generation. Apparently, her family was tasked with protecting it, but she is the last of her people and has no one to pass it on to. So, she wants to find the Beast so she can ask it to grant a wish that the story be preserved forever. She wants me to help her."

"And..." prompted Nadia.

"And she claims to know where the man I am looking for went. He supposedly knows how to lure the Beast out of the Woods. I needed to clear my head and think about it. Having her on this mission complicates things. So I told her we would meet here to finish discussing what she knows."

Nadia nodded. "So you both have to lure the Beast out to get what you want," she stated knowingly.

Ivan frowned. "But if she wants to get the Beast to grant her a wish, surely it has to be alive, Ben," he said sardonically.

"I know." I frowned. "But I don't have any more leads, Ivan. The man wasn't there. Solace wants me to help her lure the Beast out, we both need this mystery man to tell us how to do that, and she thinks she knows where to find him. So, I agreed to help her. She also mentioned payment, though we didn't exactly agree on an amount..." I trailed off. Usually, that would have been the first thing I did, but for some reason, this woman had my mind all twisted around.

"How do you know she wasn't just lying to you?" asked Nadia.

"Yeah! And why did she go to you? Didn't you break down her front door?" asked Ivan.

"She thinks I am the Night Rider," I stated flatly.

Nadia and Ivan stared at me. "Why?" prompted Nadia.

"She claims my father's horse was the Night Rider's horse. She followed me home and saw it in my pastures."

"That's not at all creepy," stated Ivan.

"She's desperate, Ivan," I sympathized. For some reason, I wasn't angry with her.

"So, she doesn't know your intentions then?" asked Nadia.

"I don't think so..." I trailed off, thinking back to when Valdra had given me the mission. "I don't know. She must have been watching when Valdra gave me my orders, but she hasn't mentioned if she heard the part about me killing the Beast. She seemed to think I was only interested in the book." I paused in thought. "Anyways, I could use her help finding this man and luring the Beast out." I looked at the twins. "If we succeed, I have a feeling it will require more than one person to take it down."

"I'm in!" said Ivan.

"Of course you are." Nadia rolled her eyes.

Ivan grinned at his sister's comment, then the smile suddenly vanished and he leaned forward. "But we need to settle on a payment from this Solace woman. If we don't manage to kill the Beast, we can at least get something out of the trip."

Nadia waved Ivan to silence as she sat thinking for a moment, then said, "Okay, I'm in. But if I say we pull out, we pull out. As much as I want that wealth, I also like living."

"Deal," I agreed.

# Chapter 6

AROUND MIDNIGHT, A FIGURE on horseback appeared on the road out of town and approached, stopping only a few paces from our hiding place at the point where the edge of the Forest met the Woods. It was Solace.

"Ben?" she whispered into the night air.

I waited a few seconds to respond, my eyes scanning the edge of town to make sure she hadn't been followed while Nadia and Ivan checked the Forest behind us out of habit. I glanced at Nadia, then Ivan, and when they both signaled the coast was clear, I stepped out onto the dirt road.

When Solace saw me, she opened her mouth to say something, but I held up a hand to silence her and motioned her into the safety of the Forest. She dismounted and followed me off the moonlit road into the shadow of the trees, her horse in tow. Once we had retreated deep enough into the trees that we would be invisible to anyone on the road but still close enough that Nadia could keep an eye on the Town's edge, I signaled that it was safe to speak.

"Who are they?" snapped Solace.

"Solace, this is Nadia and Ivan Kuzmich," I said, gesturing to them with one hand. "They are close friends of mine and will be traveling with us."

"Ben, if someone finds out that we are looking for the Beast and know someone who might be able to help us catch it, we will have the whole country on our tail! They'd better—"

I cut her off. "I trust them with my life," I said, staring at her sternly.

Solace took in a breath as she looked me in the eye, her hands on her hips. Then, after a moment, she gave a brief nod and turned to the twins. "I apologize if I came off as rude. I just need this to work."

Ivan nodded. "Ben says you'll pay. You got enough for the three of us, or are we going to have to split a day's wages?" he said with a joking smile.

Solace nodded. "I have plenty."

"How?" I asked. "No offense, but you don't exactly live in a mansion."

"As I told you earlier, I come from a family who has passed the story down from generation to generation by word of mouth," she recounted.

"You're from the Chosen family," stated Nadia as she watched Solace.

Solace nodded. "My family has always been wealthy. But unlike some in my family history, I felt that riches were not something to be flaunted. I chose to put my money to good use in other areas."

"Like financing hunting parties?" I asked sarcastically.

Solace frowned. "Look, can we just get on with this? We have a long journey ahead of us. The point is, I can and will pay you handsomely."

"Yeah, where are we going exactly?" asked Ivan.

Solace gave me a look that said I would not like her answer. "The man you and I were looking for is a doctor. He once helped heal people who had been injured during the wars with the Great Beasts of the Southern Mountains. He is known for using special healing herbs only located near the base of the Great Volcano. Every spring, he goes there to an island in the river to gather what he will need to make his medicines for the year."

Ivan's smile melted. Nadia went still. I stared at Solace. "You want us to go back to the volcano? You have got to be kidding me! Do you know how many times we almost died trying to lure a beast out there to end the last war? Not to mention what happened once we got there. And this time, we would have to travel all the way there and back before we could even accomplish our ultimate goal of catching the Beast!"

Solace's gaze dropped to the earth at her feet. "I know what you did to end the last war. I can imagine what you lost there, but—"

"No!" I snapped. "You have no idea what we did to end the war. You have no idea what we lost to it!" I yelled as anger flared in my chest.

Solace sighed and held her hands out, palms down, in an attempt to calm me. "So that's it. You will not help me?" She gazed at me with sadness in her eyes. I looked away.

"How do we even know that this doctor can help us?" asked Nadia calmly.

"I have heard stories," Solace mumbled, as if speaking at a lower volume would make us more receptive to the news.

"Stories!" said Ivan disbelievingly. "You mean to tell us that we are staking our lives on stories?"

"Yes," Solace answered plainly. When no one replied, she added, "You don't understand what this means to me, what this means to everyone. I grew up listening to this story. It's a story about the beginning of life as we know it, and it needs to be preserved. History needs to be learned from, or wars, like the ones that you have fought in, will forever control this land and all who live in it!"

"It's just a story, Solace. It cannot stave off war or the evils of this world," I said bitterly.

"But it's not just a story. You can't understand until you know it," Solace retorted. "Please, don't stop now. I know this doesn't make any sense to you. But it is my legacy. And it can be yours too! If you would just help me."

*I could back out now,* I thought to myself, *but I have my orders, and I have a responsibility to follow through on them.* I wasn't about to tell Solace my intentions, though. I looked to Nadia and Ivan. They glanced at each other, then at me. Years of friendship and battle together had given us the ability to communicate without words. Their set jaws and frowns of determination were a clear sign that they were in, and they would not tell Solace of our true mission unless I told them otherwise.

"Okay. We will go," I said, turning to Solace. "But the Forest between here and the Great Volcano contains many dangers, and it can take over a week to get there, and that's if nothing goes wrong. We need a plan," I stated. "We will camp here tonight and put together a travel plan. Then we will set out tomorrow at sunrise. Are we all in agreement?" I asked.

Solace and the twins nodded. The realization of what I was about to do suddenly came rushing over me. I had spent every day since the war ended trying not to think about that day at the volcano, and now I was about to face it head-on. And for what reason? Simply because General Delaney told me to? *I must be losing my mind.* But I knew I would not stop until I had that beast. That was my job.

We decided to camp deeper in the Forest so our campfire wouldn't be visible from the road. As we set up camp, Nadia approached me. "Do you think we can trust her?"

I let my gaze fall on Solace as she and Ivan struck up a conversation. "Well, I know she won't rat us out to any passersby. She needs the Beast just as much as I do."

"You know you don't have to do this," Nadia said as she rested her hand on my arm. "Unlike her, I do know what you lost there. I know what all of us lost. Ivan and I will back you up, whatever you choose. If you want to pull out—"

"I can't," I interrupted her. "The general won't allow it. I have already defied him twice this week, and I think I have run out of rope. If I refused to do this..." I trailed off, and Nadia's expression told me she understood. All three of us knew what it was like to have a commander tell you to do something you did not fully understand. After a while, you stopped asking and just shoved the discomfort down and did the job because it was your duty, and there was always the possibility that you would end up worse off if you crossed the wrong person. "Plus, I thought you and Ivan wanted the reward," I said with a grin.

Nadia laughed. "I think we are all just insane." Her smile softened, and sadness entered her eyes. "Or we are just longing for something bigger than us again."

She was right. I felt it too. I could return to General Delaney's mansion and refuse to hunt the Beast. He would most likely take away my big house and toss me out on the streets with no rank or status, or worse. But losing my wealth and status was not what I feared. I feared what my life would become if I didn't work for the general. I feared what it was already becoming. Pointless. I longed for purpose. For a mission. As much as those days and nights fighting that beast haunted me in my dreams, I missed the simplicity of a cause worth fighting for.

After we finished setting up camp and snagging some dinner, we each began mulling over the beginnings of a plan while Ivan and I took turns cooking the meat. Suddenly, the sound of pebbles slipping down a nearby slope snapped us all from our respective imaginings and conversations. Weapons were drawn as Ivan, Nadia, Solace, and I immediately jumped to the ready. We faced the sound, prepared to fight. But I couldn't believe what I saw. Out of the bushes stumbled Otto, rumpled clothes and all. *You have got to be kidding me,* I thought with a groan.

"Otto, what is with you and scaring the life out of me?" I snapped as I once again holstered my weapon instead of shooting him.

"You know this man?" asked Ivan in surprise.

"I do. Though I'm beginning to think I should have left him to a certain pack of dogs," I said as I glared at Otto.

Otto's jaw dropped open, and he stared at me in shock. "You wouldn't dare!" he said, his voice cracking.

"Who is he?" asked Solace.

"He is an idiot who keeps falling from the trees and landing in my lap," I said as I sat down again. "Where did you come from this time?"

"I came from town where you left me for dead!" snapped Otto. "I spent all that first day looking for a place to stay, and then some hooligan stole my coin sack! So, I camped out here and got distracted examining the trees at the edge of the Woods. I made sure not to touch them because I wasn't sure how far one could go before dying. But they are so different," he said with admiration. "I saw some people enter the Forest and wanted to ask for directions to a satisfactory inn for the night, and it turned out to be you. And I will have you know that I am far from an idiot! I know more about this forest than the lot of you combined!" he said hotly.

"And yet the Forest seems to be the one that has won the fight," Nadia said with a grin as she crossed her arms and scanned him from head to toe.

"Well, I...I simply mean I have studied it," retorted Otto as he pulled his dust-covered coat closed over his rumpled clothes. "One can learn a lot about something without ever setting foot in it. For example, your compatriot seems to have built his bed too close to a blue fire ant hill," he stated, gesturing to Ivan. "He'd be wise to move it over a few feet, or he might very well be blue in the face by morning," added Otto with a lifted chin.

Ivan glanced at his bed; then, having verified that Otto was, in fact, correct, his eyelids dropped to half-mast in deep annoyance.

Nadia burst out laughing. "I like this one, Ben! We should bring him along! Do you remember the time we camped near the Field, and Ivan sat on a horned bee's nest? Maybe Ivan shouldn't travel without him!"

Ivan's frown deepened as Nadia continued laughing.

I couldn't help but smile. Though Nadia was half joking, it might not be such a bad idea. Otto was a student of nature, and he might be able to help with certain sections of the Forest that we would be crossing.

"Nadia, you might be on to something," I said as I wagged my finger at her in thought. "Remember that section of the Forest we would have died in if it were not for that farmer who stumbled upon us on his travels?"

"Yeah, he pointed out all the poisonous plants we almost ate," she said, contemplating my implication.

"Otto," I said, "how much do you really know of the Forest?"

"I have studied every known plant, animal, liquid, and gas in this forest from the Woods to the Great Volcano," he stated with pride.

"Key word being *known*," said Solace warningly.

She made a good point. "Solace is right, but it's better than nothing," I said. "As much as you drive me crazy, Otto, we might need you along for this trip to the volcano."

Otto looked like he was going to agree but then appeared to realize we were volunteering him to come on our journey. "Now wait a minute, why would I go with you?" demanded Otto.

I raised my eyebrows. "You almost agreed to come along with us without considering that?"

"I was already planning on spending most of my time in the Forest," he huffed.

"Then its settled," I said, leaving no room for argument and hoping Otto didn't just walk away.

Otto raised his chin a fraction of an inch. "I will go because I desire to study the Forest in full, not because you have told me to do so," he stated defiantly.

I rolled my eyes. "Do you have a horse yet?" I asked.

"Of course not, thank you. I will walk," he said, absently brushing some dirt from the front of his jacket.

"No, you won't," said Ivan with a shake of his head. "I did that once. When we led that Great Beast through the Forest, we came across a swamp. We were unaware that monsters lived in the swamp, so when I waded in first, my horse got eaten. I had to run through that monster-infested marsh on foot and almost got eaten by some half-blind creatures that were four horse lengths long and would snap at anything that touched the waters. Nadia and Ben made it safely across as their horses could jump from one bank to the next. I ended up having to scramble over frozen tree roots without falling into the water." He frowned. "And yes, it's as hard as it sounds."

Solace spoke up with a concerned look on her face, "It sounds like Ivan makes a great travel partner."

Nadia and I laughed. "You have no idea!" Nadia said and laughed again.

Now it was Solace's turn to frown in annoyance.

Before we settled in for the night, Ivan caught an extra rabbit and roasted it over our small fire so we would have enough food for Otto. Otto and Nadia got to chatting about plants and gases, which was quite entertaining as Otto apparently had never had a woman pay any attention to him before, and he kept stumbling over his words. He eventually relaxed as he realized that Nadia was genuinely interested in his expertise in natural philosophy.

Solace sat near the fire, looking up through the trees at the stars as I began to dig into dinner. When I noticed that Solace was too entranced by the stars to realize food was available, I grabbed two servings worth before Ivan could eat it all and took them to where she was sitting against a log.

As I handed the food to her, she smiled and thanked me but only took one bite before getting distracted by the stars again. I followed her gaze. The dark blue sky was clear, and stars were everywhere, framed by the trees surrounding us.

"They are beautiful, aren't they?" said Solace quietly.

"Yes, they are."

"When I was a child, I used to think that the stars were eternal beings," explained Solace, "set in the sky to watch over us." She smiled at the thought.

"Why did you feel you needed someone to watch over you?" The questions seemed to roll off my tongue without my permission and I immediately regretted it. I didn't usually ask personal questions. "I'm sorry—"

"It's fine," she said with a soft smile. "Let's just say that my family wasn't exactly...stable."

"What do you believe about the stars now?" I asked, curious but not wanting to press the issue I could see still festered within her.

She smiled. "My jaded, mature mind now only believes they are simply celestial bodies that burn so brightly that we can see them from anywhere."

Not wanting the conversation to end, I grasped for something to say. "Yes, but those celestial bodies are a reliable source of protection. They help us find our way in the dark." My gaze dropped from the sky to her face. There was subtle yellow in her brown eyes, which seemed to glimmer like sunflowers in the starlight.

She turned to me with a calm, joyful smile. "Like a compass," she stated. "I have used them to find my way many times, but never have I thought of their direction as a form of protection." Her tone held no criticism, only wonder, like a child who had just learned something new. "Tell me," she said curiously as she leaned back against the log and got comfortable, "have you led many to safety with the stars as your guide? I bet you have wonderful stories of adventure by their light."

I watched her as she settled back and waited for my reply. "Not to toot my own horn, but yes," I said with a grin. "And I have story upon story of my glorious leadership through treacherous lands led only by those shining compasses in the sky," I said playfully.

She laughed. "So it is true?" She grinned. "Even a great leader would be lost and roaming on a cloudy day."

I laughed. "Now, I wouldn't go that far."

As we finished our dinner, we continued chatting and watching the stars. After everyone had eaten, we gathered around the fire to put together a plan. Though we had all been thinking it through for a while, I wanted to run over what the Forest contained so that we would be on the same page.

As everyone took a seat, I grabbed a stick and began drawing a map in the dirt. "These are the Woods," I started, drawing a circle. "We will travel north along the river here that flows between the Woods to the Great Volcano. We will have to pass through three points that will be the most challenging," I said as I held up three fingers. "The first is the Field. It was winter when Ivan, Nadia, and I passed through, so the ground should be softer this time of year and easier to cross. The second is the Valley. Even during winter, this place is damp and foggy, but as long as we don't fall to our deaths in the monster-infested swamp at the Valley's bottom, then we will be fine. The third place is the hardest. This is the river, which is frozen over during the winter, but this time of year, it will be raging and strong..." I trailed off as I noticed Otto was fidgeting. "What's wrong, Otto?" I said impatiently.

He pursed his lips in consideration. "As I understand it, you and the Kuzmich twins were there in the dead of winter, leading a Great Beast to its death in the volcano," he said matter-of-factly.

"Yes, what is the problem?" I prompted.

"Well," continued Otto, "the Forest is an enchanted place. See, it was once part of the Woods, but its power and majesty faded over time. My father was actually studying why the Forest has faded. It once—"

"Otto!" I snapped. "Stay focused."

"Right, so it is springtime. There are different animals, different beasts, different gases, plants, and, well...it is different."

I sighed. Nadia and Ivan groaned, and Solace looked confused.

"So what?" said Solace. "Spring is gorgeous!"

We all looked to Otto. He froze. "I...I..."

"Quit sputtering and focus, Otto," snapped Nadia in an even tone.

Otto frowned, and then, after a moment of gathering his thoughts, he said, "Okay. Benjamin is correct about the three different sections and that they will look different due to the changing seasons. But there are other problems. The first is that the Field is known for...how do I put this...enchanting people. Some come out of there just fine, but others go missing and never return. The second problem is in the Valley. The swamp at its base has been said to produce a mist or fog of some sort during the spring. I have no idea what this mist does because no one who has come in contact with it has ever survived and recorded what happened...at least not to my knowledge," he said with a thoughtful expression. "I am not really sure if it would be a danger. For all we know, it was exaggerated in the few accounts that do exist." Shaking his head, he continued, "The third section of the Forest is, as Benjamin stated, dominated by a huge rushing river that eventually meets up with the Great Volcano. However, when the river is not frozen solid, it is rumored to somehow be boiling hot, and if one falls in, they could be boiled alive," he said flatly. He seemed to be considering something else, then said, "And if my memory serves me right, it all changes on the way back. Just a few days can make a difference in the types of dangers one might face." He thought about it for a moment. "Yes, I do recall reading stories of people who were attacked by beasts and monsters on their way back during the spring. Something about being eaten alive or dying of acute panic," he stated unemotionally.

We sat there staring at Otto. He had to be kidding. "This is a joke, right?" Solace voiced my thoughts.

"Do none of you listen?" said Otto in an offended tone. "I never joke about nature," he stated hotly.

Solace leaned forward. "Well, you'd better come up with a way to get through all those dangers then, Otto, because you are coming with us."

Otto's impassive expression melted into shock and realization. "B-but I..."

"You didn't think of this earlier?" Solace asked with raised eyebrows.

"You didn't give me much time to think," he snapped. "And I was a tad distracted by you all almost killing me! For the second time this week, I might add!"

Ivan suddenly laughed and wrapped a burly arm around Otto. "You really are an absent-minded fellow, aren't you, Otto?" Ivan laughed as Nadia broke into a grin.

"Yeah, he kind of grows on you, though, doesn't he?" said Nadia to Ivan.

Ivan chuckled. "That he does, my sister, that he does."

# Chapter 7

THAT NIGHT I DREAMT of the Beast. Those eyes, green and intense, watched me, piercing through me like a knife. I longed for them more and more. Suddenly, I snapped awake and looked around me. I was just in camp. I settled back down and stared at the stars through the trees above. The urge to go to the Woods had grown. I didn't know why, but I wanted to see the Beast again, especially now that we were leaving and would be gone for a while.

I sat up slowly and checked to make sure everyone was still asleep. Ivan was sprawled out and snoring loudly. Nadia was curled up neatly on her side. Solace was lying behind me about four feet away, and Otto was curled up in the fetal position, gripping his blanket as if his life depended on it. They were all asleep. I grabbed my pistol belt and headed toward the Woods.

The Woods were only a few hundred yards south of us, between our camp and the Town. As I approached the distinct foliage at the edge of the Woods, I felt that draw to them again, to the Beast within. But when I got to the Woods' edge, there was no beast.

After searching for what felt like forever, I turned my back on the Woods to leave, but as I was turning, movement caught my eye and I looked back to see what was there, drawing a pistol in a smooth habitual motion. I froze when I saw it. There, in the branches of a tree on the outer edge of the Woods, it sat, barely visible. Its green eyes stared down at me from its shadowy perch. Its long tail swayed gently behind it. The Beast of the Woods sat so close to the edge of the Woods, its black fur shimmering in the moonlight, that I felt I could reach out and touch it. I felt myself being pulled to the Beast, but the looming death that I knew would come to any who passed into the Woods made the decision to remain outside easy. Yet somehow, it still hurt not to go.

As it watched me, the Beast's pink tongue washed over its whiskers, which caught the moonlight as they moved. Its black, rounded ears were pricked forward, totally focused on me, and its piercing green eyes held me in a trance I found I did not want to break. Still, I shifted away, and something in the Beast's eyes changed. It had seen, in my subtle movement, that I had chosen this world. Without a sound, the Beast vanished into the shadows.

Suddenly, my chest ached, and I felt guilt and panic rise within me. *Why are these feelings suddenly cropping up so often?* I wondered. *I have never had this problem before.* Still mulling over that thought, I turned to head back to camp.

As I approached the camp, I saw Solace sitting up, leaning against a tree. She watched me as I walked toward her and took a seat next to her. We were far enough from the others that we could talk in lowered voices without waking them, and it looked like she wanted to do so.

"What's up?" I asked, hoping she wouldn't ask where I had been.

Solace looked in the direction I had come from and remained silent for a moment before she turned to me and asked, "Why did you agree to help me? You seem to have plenty of money and a job. It can't just be for the payment."

I thought about my answer carefully. *How much should I tell her?* "I met an elderly woman recently who told me that this doctor has the book I have been looking for," I lied. I would have to talk to Ivan and Nadia later to make sure we kept our stories straight around Solace.

Solace nodded slowly, a skeptical frown creasing her fine features. "Based on Otto's descriptions of the Forest, this may be more dangerous than I thought. Maybe we should wait until the doctor returns." She studied me with inquisitive eyes.

I took a deep breath. I wasn't about to tell her my real reason for being here, so I gave her a half-truth. "The man I work for, General Delaney, wants the book sooner rather than later. Plus, from what we know of all the danger, the doctor could die in the Forest and never make it home." It was true that the general wanted this done now. He would have paid me for the previous job if that were not the case. But the doctor surely knew the risks of his travels and had resources. It was a flimsy lie.

"Ah," responded Solace as she held my gaze.

I knew she didn't quite believe me.

"You don't like your job, do you," said Solace, more as an observation than a question.

I raised my eyebrows in surprise, then laughed. "I have just been working nonstop since the war ended, and I probably need a break," I said with a smile, attempting to cover up my discomfort at knowing she could read me so well.

"So, you live for your work," she said with a grin.

I laughed. "I just like to have something to do."

"You don't have a family to take care of?" she asked.

I examined the dirt on my boots. "I did once."

"What happened?" She caught herself. "I mean, you don't have to answer that," she said, a little flustered.

"It's okay." I didn't know why it was okay. But I felt comfortable talking to her. "Most of my family were killed by a Great Beast during this last war. Only my father, one of my brothers, and I survived." I paused. "Then they were both killed in a battle to defeat that beast." I recalled the day my father lay dying in my arms. A blood-soaked battlefield filled with the bodies of men and woman we were charged with bringing home safely.

"That's why you joined the fight?" Solace prompted, interrupting my thoughts. "To defeat the beasts that killed your family?"

I shook my head. "I had fought in smaller battles during the previous war. I joined then because I was needed. I wasn't a beast fighter back then—I was just a young foot soldier. I was usually assigned to defend large towns that were not often attacked or sent on missions to gather supplies. But the last war...Only days after it began, most of my family was killed. So, I joined the official ranks of the soldiers sent to kill beasts. I didn't know what else to do. My father had fought in many wars as a beast fighter, and he tried to warn me of what it would do to me, but I didn't care at the time."

She nodded.

It was still early enough to go back to sleep, and we both needed rest for the journey, but a question had been burning in my mind since she first tried to convince me to go on this crazy death trip.

"Back when you said the difference between dying here and dying there was 'why,' what exactly did you mean? I mean, I heard your explanation, but few people think of asking why when presented with death," I asked, eager for her response. I wanted to know what was with this question "Why?" and, funny enough, *why* everyone was so enamored with it.

Solace smiled. "You have been wondering that all this time, yet you still agreed to come?" she asked.

I smiled, unsure how to answer.

"Okay," she said. Her expression twisted in thought as she considered the best way to explain it. "I was once told that life is a series of questions and answers and that, when faced with a crossroads, one must ask the question that *needs* an answer, rather than asking the question that gets the answer you seek." She gazed at me with her sparkling brown eyes. "The question 'Why?' was the question that seemed to need an answer. Why was I willing to die there?" She paused, then said with a grin, "Plus, it seemed to get your attention."

I laughed, but her explanation reminded me of Ruth's words yet again. *"You, my boy, need to learn how to ask the right questions."*

The next morning, we all cleaned up camp and tacked up the horses. Before we had gone to sleep, we had all agreed that there was no way around the three main sections of the Forest. According to Otto, they stretched out in multiple directions, and it would take us twice as long to go around them. So, we decided on a straight shot through the middle, following the river that would lead us from the Woods to the Great Volcano. Once we got to the volcano, the river would end up being part of the problem. But we would cross that bridge when we came to it. *If we make it that far.*

Ivan and Nadia tacked up their gray dappled horses while Solace went into the Town to purchase a horse for Otto. I took the opportunity to mention to Ivan and Nadia what I had told Solace the night before, so we could keep our stories straight. When Solace returned with a mule, Nadia and Ivan couldn't stop laughing at Otto's disgust.

"Otto, this is Betsy. She will be your ride," Solace explained. Otto cringed but reluctantly took the reins from Solace.

"They didn't have any horses?" I asked, holding back a smile.

"They did, but none that Otto could handle. Betsy is the calmest ride I could find," explained Solace as she stifled a smile as well.

"What is your problem with horses and their like anyways?" asked Ivan, turning to Otto.

"They are filthy creatures that would throw you in a ditch the moment they had a chance. Moreover, I dislike the idea of sitting upon a carriage with its own wits," replied Otto, holding Betsy's reins as if they were snakes.

"You do realize that carriages are pulled by horses, right?" Nadia teased.

"Of course," Otto said. "But I don't have to interact with them. That's what the driver is for."

"Well, you'll have to get used to interacting because it's going to be a long journey," said Ivan. "Try feeding Betsy by hand before we leave. It'll help her get to know you."

Otto reluctantly grabbed a handful of grass and held it out to Betsy. She grabbed the grass in her lips and, in doing so, left a streak of slobber on Otto's hand. He froze with his hand outstretched, and a look of pure disgusted shock fell over his face. Betsy nuzzled his hand, then went on to investigate his hair, turning his already unkempt hairdo into a wild mess. Otto remained frozen and stared straight ahead like a rabbit hoping it would vanish if it sat still enough.

Ivan chuckled and walked up behind him, placing a gentle hand on each of his shoulders. "Relax," said Ivan. "She is just investigating. Think of it like...a handshake," he suggested. Otto frowned. But before he could protest, Ivan interrupted. "Trust me. Just introduce yourself."

Otto's gaze slowly shifted up to Betsy. "It's..." His voice cracked. He cleared his throat and tried again. "It's nice to meet you, Betsy. I am Otto Bilden."

Ivan leaned in. "Good. Now, when she is done shaking your hand, offer her more grass." Otto waited for Betsy to finish investigating him and then offered her more grass. She took it happily and bobbed her head a bit as she ate. Otto flinched.

"Relax," said Ivan. "She won't eat you. She is just enjoying herself."

Otto rolled his eyes. "How do you know she won't eat me? What if I get on her and she decides she hates me?"

Ivan laughed. "She likes you, Otto. You might be a lost man-child, but you're not that bad really."

Otto's expression softened. "You think so...?" He flinched. "Lost man-child!" he snapped as Ivan chuckled. Regaining control of himself, Otto took a deep breath and cleared his throat. "Right, well, I know how to ride, thank you. I can take it from here."

Ivan nodded. "Didn't doubt you for a second," he said with a wink.

Once Otto was stiffly settled into his saddle, we set off north, following the river toward our first obstacle, the Field. As we rode,

I glanced back toward the Woods. Something caught my attention, and for a moment I thought I saw them again. Those eyes. I shook my head and turned back to the task at hand.

The forest floor stretched out before us, crowded with trees of all kinds. Now that it was springtime, they were blooming and gaining new leaves. The old leaves from the fall and winter had been trampled into the ground. Small animals of various kinds moved about in the underbrush as we rode by. Deer appeared in the distance, chewing as they watched us pass through their home. Even a fox appeared to investigate the commotion, though it was careful to keep its distance.

It took us the better part of the day to reach the Field. And each time we passed a break in the trees, Otto would ask if that was the field we sought. But when we finally arrived at the edge of the Field we were seeking, he simply stared in awe.

It looked completely different from when I had seen it last, for it had been covered in ice then. I sucked in a sharp breath as an image of bloodied bodies draped over saddles flashed before my mind. Drops of blood leaving a trail on the frozen landscape of the Field. I shook the image from my head. That was just a memory. It was spring now, and green grass spread in all directions out from the trees and bushes where we stood. The Field rolled and dipped in gentle hills that blocked our view of the other side. If I had not traveled across it once before, I would not have guessed an abrupt line of trees marked the opposite boundary. A similar boundary sat a few feet in front of us, its trees providing cover as we observed the open space before us. There was nothing but grass and the small river flowing down the Field's center. No flowers, no trees, no animals. Just an open field.

"Can you tell why they call it the Field?" snorted Ivan to Solace.

We all gave Ivan a united stern look, under which his joking expression melted.

Solace returned her gaze to the obstacle before us, then encouraged her horse to approach the distinct line where the trees of the Forest gave way to the open field. But suddenly her horse spooked. It reared up and came down in a prancing trot that took it nowhere, and Solace struggled for a few moments before she got it to calm down.

"What was that?" asked Nadia as her eyes habitually scouted out the tree line and the bare landscape before us for any danger.

Ivan and I looked at each other. Then, wordlessly, I cued Jeb to move forward. He didn't budge. When I cued him again, he stomped a front foot and tossed his head. Ivan and I looked at each other again, and then he repeated the same thing with his horse. Same response.

"What is happening?" Otto asked Nadia.

"Ivan and Ben have trained their horses to tell them when something is wrong. They will move if asked a third time. But now we know for sure; the horses don't want to cross the Field."

"Is that a bad thing?" asked Otto.

"Horses are smart, and they can sense things we can't. If they don't want to go, they have a good reason," replied Nadia, eliciting a loud gulp from Otto as he eyed the horses, then the empty field.

I glanced at everyone, getting nods of commitment from everyone but Otto, who simply stared at me blankly, apparently unsure why I was looking at everyone. I ignored him and looked forward to the Field ahead of me. Jeb would go if I asked him to again, but he was telling me his opinion, and more often than not, he was right. But this time, I didn't have a choice. I cued him to move forward, and he did with a slight nervous prance in his step.

The others followed close behind, and we picked our way through the Field, following the small river that ran through it. The twins' horses and Jeb remained calm but tense, and we made sure to pay attention to their responses to the environment. Betsy seemed more or less unbothered, but Solace occasionally had to reassure her horse to calm it down from a tense prancing trot. As we rode, there was an eerie silence, broken only by the rustle of grass and the quiet bubbling of the river. There was no birdsong or chirping of insects, and no one wanted to speak, as if our silence was the only thing keeping us safe from whatever was making the horses nervous.

Only stopping occasionally for water at the river, we rode for hours as the sun beat down on us. There didn't seem to be any prey in the whole field. Even the river had no fish, so we ate rationed bread and cheese.

As the sun dipped lower in the sky, we simply stopped where we were and made camp, as there were no trees for cover. Though we had seen no signs of life other than ourselves and the grass, we set up camp in a circle around our small fire so we could see in all directions, just in case.

Once camp was set, we quietly watched as the sun got lower and lower on the horizon. As darkness fell, something caught my eye in the distance. Some kind of creature, approaching slowly. I pulled a pistol from its place in my belt, and Ivan drew his sword.

I dared to speak. "Who's there?" I whispered. But I got no response.

Ivan stepped forward. "What do you want?" he called out.

Still nothing. But now, the creature was nearer. It seemed to glow in the dark like a lantern, and as the sky turned even darker, I noticed there were no stars here, only the moon. But even its light was strangely faint, despite the cloudless sky.

As the setting sun disappeared completely below the horizon, the Field was plunged into near-total darkness, and everyone froze, staring at the only bright source of light—the approaching creature. The creature stopped and seemed to turn to face where it had come from. Then, suddenly, the Field behind it came to life with glowing lights. There were more of them!

When they were close enough to see in detail, I was stunned. They were the most beautiful creatures I had ever seen. Golden, shimmering robes wrapped and flowed around their miniature frames as they danced in the moonlight. They seemed to float above the grass, though they had no wings. Despite the moon's dim light, somehow its reflection on their robes made them shine like golden stars. Their faces had no clear features and their bodies were only about a foot in height, yet they moved with the grace of a dancer, filling the Field around us like giant fireflies.

"What are they?" whispered Solace as she stared at them in astonishment.

"I don't know...Otto?" I asked without taking my eyes off the creatures.

"I have no idea; I just know this place is enchanted or cursed or something to that effect. I would advise that we be cautious. They might be...dangerous," he said, careful to keep an eye on our visitors.

"I doubt it," said Ivan. "They are beautiful. I've never seen anything like them!"

Putting away our weapons, we watched the creatures in awe as they floated through the air. Time seemed to pass without us as we watched them all throughout the night, unable to take our eyes off their shimmering golden bodies. Even Otto was eventually caught up in their beauty.

Before we knew it, it was morning, and as the sun rose, the creatures vanished along with the darkness of night. We broke camp quickly, and unlike the day before, we spoke as we traveled, marveling at the creatures we had seen in the night. Ivan wondered aloud if they were actually made of gold. Nadia wondered if they were real or just a figment of our imaginations. Solace said she had felt like she could just reach out and touch one, and Otto scribbled in a notebook like a madman.

I smiled as I remembered the creatures. We had all had rough lives—well, all except Otto—and it was nice to see something that took us away from all that; something so beautiful it had made us each forget the pain in our hearts from the lives we had lived and the hardships we had each suffered. But as we traveled on through the dull landscape and the noonday sun beat down, the topic and mood changed. No one could wait until darkness to see the stunning dance again, and we began to voice our theories about why the creatures only came out at night.

"You probably can't see them in daylight," Nadia said simply.

"Or they are nocturnal," suggested Otto before making another note in his book.

"I feel like I might die of boredom if I don't see something other than this field," Solace complained with arms held wide to gesture to the empty landscape around us.

"I was thinking the same thing," I said. "I thought yesterday went by slowly, but today just won't end. And it is so hot out here!" I began rummaging around in my saddlebags for my water costrel.

As soon as we saw signs of sunset, we set up camp and anxiously waited for the creatures. As the setting sun once again plunged the Field into near-total darkness, the creatures appeared, but I was surprised to see how they had changed. They were even more beautiful than before! Their golden bodies still shimmered, but this time there were hints of rainbow colors glinting off their flowing robes. Their show began again, and none of us could stand to take our eyes off the magnificent sight.

# Chapter 8

ONCE AGAIN, THE CREATURES entertained us all night. We were all tired as we packed up and began to travel the next day. Little to no sleep had left us exhausted, and we barely had the strength to climb aboard our horses. As we rode through the Field, our exhaustion only worsened.

"We need to make camp early tonight and get some sleep instead of watching the light show," I said to everyone.

They each nodded in agreement. And a couple of hours before sunset, we set up camp and slept. We were so tired we didn't even take off the horses' or Betsy's tack. We just left them saddled, reins thrown over their necks. We didn't even have the energy to set up our beds. We simply lay down and slept where we fell.

In the midst of a dream, I heard a voice, almost like a song, that woke me but stopped the moment I opened my eyes. The creatures were back; they had woken everyone before beginning to dance in their increasingly beautiful robes. *Why did they wake us?* I wondered. But the question vanished from my mind as they performed their show. Their golden robes shimmered with rainbow colors and reflected bits of dust in the air, creating a light display more beautiful than I could have possibly imagined.

"They woke us to show us their new dance," said Solace in wonder.

We were all mesmerized, our eyes locked on their performance, and I felt my surroundings fade away as I became entranced by their beauty. In awe, I reached out toward the one closest to me, and my finger touched the hem of its robes. Suddenly, like a bolt of lightning, those green eyes jumped to my mind's eye. I was so startled that I felt as though I had been snapped out of sleep. I felt tired, my body heavy with exhaustion as I was once again aware that I had gotten very little sleep over the last two days. I had no idea how much time had passed since we had been woken for the light show, but it was still dark.

I looked around and noticed that Jeb was acting odd. He was prancing in place and stretching his neck out toward me, as if he wanted to come to me but something scary was in his way. Then my gaze fell on the others around me. Dark circles surrounded their eyes, and their skin was pale, but their lips curled into smiles as they gazed at the creatures around us. I suddenly realized what was happening as Otto's words echoed in my mind. *"The Forest is enchanted or cursed or something to that effect."* They were entranced, and I knew I had to snap them out of it.

I stood up and ran to Ivan. Grabbing his arm, I yelled, "Ivan, snap out of it. It's a trick!"

But Ivan suddenly turned on me. "No," he yelled, "they are mine!" The circles under his eyes seemed to darken as he spoke, and when I looked into his eyes, they were filled with a fire I had never seen in him before. "Do not take them from me!" he yelled.

Ivan reached for his sword and slashed out at me; I barely dodged his blade as it sliced through the air an inch from face. I scrambled backward, suddenly aware that the creatures were facing me. I could see now that darkness twisted at the hems of their golden robes.

Turning back to Ivan, I stepped forward and grabbed his shoulders. "Ivan, snap out of it," I yelled. But he pushed me away and lashed out with his blade, coming after me like a possessed bear defending its kill. The others were still enchanted with the creatures. The creatures turned back to face those still entranced as if they were pleased that Ivan had not responded to me and no longer considered me a threat. I had to think of something fast before Ivan killed me.

Ivan charged me again, and the piercing green eyes of the Beast of the Woods came to my mind. *They startled me from the trance,* I thought. *That's what I need to do. I need to startle them!* As I scrambled to avoid Ivan's relentless violent charge, my mind raced, searching for a way to startle them all at once. *My pistols!*

Ivan's sword slashed through the air, barely missing my ear as I dodged the blade and reached for my flintlock. I aimed the loaded revolving triple-barreled pistol at the night sky and pulled the trigger. The piercing sound of the gunshot rang in my ears, breaking the silence around us. Everyone flinched, broken free of their trances, instinctively ducking at the sound of a gunshot. The creatures' heads snapped around in perfect unison to look at me, and their golden coverings vanished, revealing the creatures below. Their appearance was similar under their golden facade, but they were now dark. They still had no eyes, though they seemed to look right at me. They had mouths filled with tiny sharp teeth, which gleamed in the moonlight.

In my peripheral vision, I could see Ivan shaking his head, dazed, slowly coming to a realization of what he had almost done. Then, I heard Otto scream. He had seen the creatures' true form as well.

"It's a trick!" I yelled. "We need to get out of here!"

Everyone began scrambling for their horses and the creatures burst into motion. Teeth bared, they sped through the air toward us with surprising swiftness. Solace struggled to calm her horse enough to get astride, and even Betsy was antsy as Otto tried with all he had to get aboard her.

The creatures let out piercing shrieks as they raced toward us. Ivan grabbed Otto by the back of the shirt and practically dropped him on top of Betsy as Nadia and I joined him in a dash to our horses. We each called them by name, and they came running up next to us as we swung into the saddles without breaking stride.

We sprinted along the river, using it as a guide to keep us near the center of the Field. *Thank goodness for the moon,* I thought. Without it, we would have been lost in total darkness, for as dull as it was in the sky, the moon's reflection on the river was somehow bright and shimmering like a light leading us to safety. I suddenly hoped we were headed in the right direction as I realized again that the stars were non-existent here. *Even a great leader is lost without his bright compass,* I thought.

Exhaustion made it hard for us to hold on as the horses sprinted across the land, dodging holes in the ground and jumping over hollows rather than running up and down the dips in the rolling landscape. Nadia's horse stumbled and caught itself as she struggled to stay on, her body weary from little food and sleep.

The creatures pursued us in swarms, seemingly growing in number. They flickered in and out of the darkness with only their high-pitched screams and teeth shining in the moonlight telling us where they were. One more day with no sleep, and we would have been easy prey for them.

Suddenly, I heard Nadia yell from ahead of me, "There! The edge of the Field! Maybe they won't follow us!"

I looked ahead and saw the hazy moonlight dancing off a line of trees in the distance. We raced through the Field with the edge in sight, but as we reached it, the creatures only hesitated for a moment before plunging in after us. We darted through trees as the sun began to rise to our right. *Thank goodness, we are going north!* Animals of the Forest darted in every direction and birds flew out of our way as we crashed through the underbrush. One by one, the creatures of the Field began to give up the chase as the sun slowly rose, and finally, with one last bone-chilling shriek, the remaining few fell back and vanished as the sun broke the horizon line and light poured through the trees around us.

We pushed our horses just a bit farther, then skidded to a halt in a small clearing among the undergrowth. All of us checked our flanks, double- and triple-checking to make sure the evil creatures were truly gone. *No wonder that field was empty,* I thought. *They must have eaten every living thing.* I shuddered at the thought.

Exhausted, we slipped from our saddles and fell to the ground. "Is everyone alright?" I called out.

Each person called back with affirmation that they were unharmed. I looked back in the direction we had come. Though we had gone in knowing the Field might be enchanted, we had barely escaped with our lives. *From now on,* I promised myself, *I will be careful not to let what I see and covet determine my actions.*

"We need to sleep, but not here. Not this close to the Field," I said, still trying to catch my breath.

We picked ourselves up off the ground and led the horses on foot through the Forest with the river as our guide. Once we reached better cover near a huge tree, we stripped the horses and Betsy of their tack and slid to the ground. Within minutes we were all asleep.

When we awoke, it was around noon. We gathered our things and checked to see what had been left behind in our frantic escape.

"All of the food is gone, Ben," said Solace. "Those golden ghosts must have stolen it on the first night."

I realized she was right. I couldn't recall eating anything since our first night in the Field. We must have been so enchanted by the creatures that the thought didn't even enter our minds.

Solace looked at me with sudden realization. "It's a good thing we forgot to untack the horses last night, or we would never have made it out of there with our tack and blankets."

"I know," I said solemnly. "We need to give the horses a break today. We will travel as far as we can on foot for now and make camp early." Though much less so since our recent rest, everyone was still too tired to agree out loud, so each simply fell into step behind me as I led the way.

For the next few hours, everyone remained silent. Even Otto's detailed explanation of every plant and animal he saw was absent. We listened to the sound of our footfalls and nervously paid more attention to the Forest around us. Though we were out of the Field, we were all still on edge.

"Why am I doing this, Jeb?" I asked, keeping my voice low so the others couldn't hear as Jeb plodded along next to me. His ear swiveled to the side to catch my words. "I keep telling myself I am doing it because it is my job, but..." Suddenly, Jeb tensed next to me, and his ears swiveled forward, then back and forth one at a time, alerting me to his uncertainty.

I stopped and my fist snapped up as a signal to the others to do the same. I watched the bushes around me and knew from years of battle with the twins that Nadia and Ivan were watching the trees and bushes behind us. After a moment passed, I heard Jeb release a heavy sigh, and his tongue flicked out to lick his lips.

I lowered my fist and stroked Jeb on the shoulder. "I agree," I said calmly as I took one more glance at my surroundings. "This place stresses me out too, buddy," I added as I kept a comforting hand on Jeb's neck as we continued on.

We rode until we reached a large, moss-covered boulder near a slight bend in the river. I recognized the boulder from our last trip through the Forest, when we had camped in its shadow. About an hour's ride from here, the land began to slope up and the river disappeared underground at the base of a hill. On the other side of the hill lay the Valley.

"Let's camp here," I said. "We'll reach the Valley in the morning."

If Ivan and Nadia recognized this spot, they didn't say, but they seemed familiar with the area, stopping their horses right where we had stopped during our winter trip. While I started a fire, they went off to see if they could find us some dinner. But they returned with only a small number of berries we all consumed within minutes. Despite our fears that we might have to make a mad dash through the Forest again tonight, we took the tack off the horses to let them relax. It was more important to make sure they were rested and strong, as they would need to carry us during the remainder of this journey. We ensured all our belongings were easily accessible and set up a watch rotation. I took first watch while everyone else settled in for bed, except Otto. He was sitting on a log near the fire, scribbling in his book while the others went to sleep around him.

"You need to sleep, Otto," I said as I approached and sat in front him, my back against a stump. "We all need to be ready to leave first thing tomorrow."

"I don't need sleep, I need to record everything I see, or else we might never get out of here alive," he said without looking up.

I sighed. "It's not your fault, Otto. You were right. The Field is enchanted. You warned us from the start, and we just..." I trailed off. "It's not your fault. We should have seen it coming."

"I am the one on this mission that is supposed to keep us all from dying!" he snapped irritably, his eyes still locked on his writing.

"No, Otto, that is my job. And, in your defense, I kind of forced you to come."

Otto leaned forward over his notebook and began scribbling more intensely. I got the impression that he was hiding something.

"I did force you to come, right?" I asked. He didn't respond, but the corner of his eye twitched in a flash of tension. "Otto?" I said sternly as I leaned toward him. "I can't be galivanting through this forest with a bunch of people who are hiding things from me. This forest is dangerous enough as it is."

Otto sighed and straightened. His haughty, rich boy expression faded. "I might have let you force me..." he said, finally looking at me.

"Why?" I asked.

He fidgeted with the corner of his notebook for a moment before explaining. "I come from a rich family," he began.

"I would have never guessed," I said flatly as I leaned back against the stump.

He frowned, then moved on. "I had a grand mansion that I lived in with my father and mother and their servants. They were great people. Kind to everyone..." He trailed off and was silent for a moment before continuing. "I lied. It was my mother who studied natural philosophy, not my father," he admitted. He moved on. "She was poor, but my father fell in love with her and they married. She loved everyone and everything and constantly wanted to learn. She was always trying to get me to try new things and connect to the people around me. She used to tell me that our wealth was not something to hoard but a blessing to be shared. But I..." He hesitated for a moment. "Let's just say I didn't appreciate what I had." He looked down at his hands. "Just before the most recent war started, my mother left on an expedition to study the Woods. But then the Great Beasts came and destroyed everything. Though my father and I survived with most of our fortune intact, my mother was never heard from again." He paused. "Some say she never made it to the Woods and was most likely killed in the first attack..." He gazed into the large fire we had started in hopes that it would keep the golden ghosts away. So far, so good.

"But you don't believe that, do you?" I asked.

Otto looked at me. For the first time, he looked...normal. Relatable. "I studied the Woods and the Forest during the war and every day since. I thought maybe she might have taken refuge here. But then I heard your story about taking that beast here and, well..." He shrugged. "Either way, I had to look for myself."

When I didn't respond, Otto looked at me with inquisitive eyes. "You lost someone to the war?" he asked.

I clenched my jaw. Since the war ended, I had tried not to think about what I had lost. I couldn't even remember the last time I spoke about my family until Solace asked a few nights ago. But being in this forest brought back memories. Memories of leading the Great Beast to its death, and memories of returning through the Forest after watching my father die in my arms. His blood had stained my clothes and I had stood in the freezing river desperately trying to wash it out. But it wouldn't completely fade, and I had been forced to wear it home. That trip back to the Town had been the worst of my life. We had draped the bodies of the slain over the few surviving horses and towed them behind us. Coming back after previous battles, I had felt triumphant. But that time was different. I had no one to return to. The last of my family had died on that battlefield, leaving me with nothing but pain. A pain I had buried deep for years. But I realized that when I told Solace about my family, talking about them hadn't made the pain any worse. Still, at Otto's question, I felt myself want to push the pain away again. Part of me still didn't want to face it. But I was here now, in this forest. *So why not start talking about them again?*

"I lost everyone," I said simply.

"Oh," said Otto. "I...I'm sorry."

I nodded. "Thanks," I said quietly. For some odd reason, it felt good to get it off my chest, and to Otto, of all people. I chuckled.

Otto raised his eyebrows. "I was just trying to be nice," he said, his high-and-mighty tone returning. Its sudden presence turned my chuckle into an outright laugh, and he frowned.

"I'm not laughing at what you said," I managed. "I just didn't think you, of all people, would care enough to ask."

Otto considered my response and then shrugged. "A few days ago, you would not have been wrong."

I laughed again at his honesty and Otto finally allowed a small smile to form on his lips. Then I thought of something.

"Why did you lie about your mother being the natural philosopher?" I asked.

He looked at the ground. "Where I come from, it is not...acceptable...generally speaking, for a woman to work in that field. I just didn't know how people would react here."

"But your father is a rich man, and he married her," I stated.

Otto smiled. "Yes, he did, and the townsfolk hated him for it at first. But he laughed at them and said that a smart and wise woman is more valuable than any riches he could acquire." He shrugged. "The people eventually came around. I just didn't know how the rest of the world would respond, so I lied."

I nodded. "Well, I would advise you to take a lesson from your father and never let the world stop you from doing what's right. Your mother sounds like a wonderful woman," I said as my gaze fell to Solace, asleep near the fire.

A small sound came from the bushes across camp, and Otto flinched. "Don't worry," I said. "It's just Jeb." I had a habit of keeping track of where Jeb was because he could clue me in to any nearby dangers.

"Why do you let that thing wander around as if it owns the place?" Otto said incredulously.

"What part of his behavior tells you he thinks he owns the place?" I asked with a grin.

Otto's brow furrowed. "I just mean to say that an animal like that should be tied so it doesn't wander off."

"He won't," I said with confidence.

"How do you know that?" asked Otto.

"I know because I trust him, and he trusts me." Otto looked confused, so I continued, "You know, when Nadia and Ivan and I met, we were only, say, fifteen. Ivan was training a gorgeous horse." I smiled at the memory. "For being as big and loud as he is, Ivan has a surprisingly gentle side. I remember I approached him as he was working with the horse in a pasture, and it clearly did not want to do what he was asking. I remember laughing when I saw Ivan ride the horse toward a gate out of the pasture. The horse stopped and threw its head up in protest. I expected Ivan to keep telling the stubborn horse to go through the gate. But to my surprise, he didn't."

Otto frowned. "What did he do?"

I thought back to that day. I could see it as clearly as if it were yesterday. "He gently told the horse to keep going, using a word rather than his legs. When the horse took one unsteady step forward and stopped, instead of pushing harder on its sides to tell it again to go forward, he simply said 'Okay' and then backed the horse up one step. The horse sighed and licked its lips, and Ivan scratched its mane. They stood there like that for what seemed like forever. Then, the horse backed up another step, and Ivan nodded, giving it a good scratch on the neck again before dismounting." I shook my head as I recalled my surprise at the sight. "They went back into the pasture, and the horse worked smoothly for a few minutes before Ivan tried the gate again. To my surprise, though still hesitant, the horse walked through the gate when asked to do so that time. Then, as soon as the horse was through, Ivan began scratching its rump until the horse's nose stretched out and its lip curled in pleasure." I chuckled at the memory.

"Why did he let the horse push him around like that?" asked Otto in confusion.

"I wondered the same thing," I said with a smile, "so I asked him. When he exited the pasture, I remember I ambushed him and told him he was doing it wrong. That the horse was being stubborn, and he couldn't let it win. I remember he looked at me and asked, 'Why?' I was so taken aback by the question that I couldn't answer for a moment. When I finally gathered my thoughts, I explained that the horse would learn that it could win all the time, and once it figured out that Ivan wouldn't force it to obey, it would never want to work for him." I frowned at my own lack of understanding at the time.

Otto nodded. "That is what my father's horse trainer told me. Never let them push you around. You're the one in charge and they will feel much better when they know that." His expression twisted in disgust. "It didn't help. I still fell off, and I still don't like them."

I chuckled and continued with the story. "I had been told the same, but Ivan's father had taught him differently. I remember Ivan laughed and said that my statement didn't seem to make much sense. I was so confused. I had never heard of anyone thinking they could let their horse tell them what to do. So I asked him what he meant; I thought my statement made perfect sense. Ivan looked at me and asked, 'So you are saying that a horse only works because we force it to?'" I mimicked the confused tone Ivan had used at the time. "I wasn't sure where Ivan was going with that question, so I just told him yes, that was what I was saying."

"What did Ivan say?" asked Otto, now invested in understanding.

"Ivan just nodded, then asked me another question," I continued.

"What question?" asked Otto.

"He asked me, if I was right, then why did the horse go through the gate the second time?" I thought back to what had happened and told Otto, "I explained that because Ivan worked the horse in the ring and showed it he was in charge, the horse understood and followed orders the next time. Ivan just nodded again and asked, 'Isn't that horse strong enough to just dump me if he didn't want to work?' I paused, then attempted to explain that the horse was big and strong enough to do that, but it might not know that. Ivan just laughed and said he had never met a horse that didn't know it could throw its rider if it wanted to."

Otto frowned. "Exactly why I dislike riding them," he said as he let his gaze fall on Betsy and the dappled grays who stood nearby, grazing.

I chuckled, then continued the story. "I thought back to all the horses I had ridden, then argued to Ivan that he was right, the horse did know it could throw him, but still, he shouldn't let the horse win. At that point, Ivan smiled and told me I might need to rethink my logic. He said that it sounded to him like I thought his horse knew that it could throw him off whenever it wanted but chose instead to just suffer as Ivan forced it to do everything it hated. Ivan pointed out that he didn't think that made sense."

"What did you say?" asked Otto.

"I nodded and asked, if I was wrong, then why do horses let anyone ride them?"

Otto considered that for a moment. "That is a good question," he said.

I nodded. "That is exactly what Ivan said! Then he went on to tell me the answer. He said horses do as we tell them to because we put them in a round pen they can't escape from. Then we do what we want. Sometimes we break them, or other times we lie to them and tell them we are becoming their friend, but then we push them around and ignore their feelings. We make them long for a connection by leaving them in the pen all alone and turning our back on them after telling them we want to be their friend. Yet, the only thing they truly learn from any of that is that they have no choice but to give in due to exhaustion, confusion, or fear of being alone. In short, we do nothing but exploit their fear and innate need for connection."

Otto nodded thoughtfully. "Well, he isn't wrong..."

"That is just the conclusion I came to as well. But Ivan had piqued my curiosity, so I asked him what he was doing instead. And he replied, 'I was giving him freedom to choose.'"

Otto looked surprised. "Well, that's just absurd! If horses had a choice, they would run right over us!"

"That's exactly what I said!" My voice raised slightly in agreement. "But Ivan had an interesting response. He asked me a question. He asked if I thought our horses hated us so much that if we let them decide, they would just run to the mountains and never return. He explained that if that was how a horse felt about him, he was definitely doing something wrong. Then he added an interesting point. He explained that if an animal is willing to work when it is given no other choice, how much more willing would it be if it made the choice itself to stay and work? What if it trusted us instead of working just to avoid us? Then Ivan reminded me of how the horse went through the gate the second time. He explained that the horse went through because it knew Ivan would not force it into something it was not ready to do. It trusted Ivan because they had worked on building trust. Ivan pointed out that yes, maybe the horse would have gone through that gate the first time if he had forced it to. But if the horse only did it because it had no other way to avoid the discomfort of the mental and physical pressure that Ivan would have to apply to force it through, how would Ivan know if the horse truly understood what he did?"

Otto frowned. "What did he mean by that?"

I considered the question for a moment, coming up with a better way to explain Ivan's point. "Basically, Ivan meant, how would he know that the horse truly knew what he was asking if the horse was so focused on avoiding fear, rather than listening to Ivan's words? Ivan pointed out that he didn't want a horse that would only do as it was told because it had no other option. Rather, he wanted a horse that would listen for his words and pick them out in the midst of all else. He wanted a reliable horse that would respond and obey because it had a relationship with him and trusted him; because it chose his words over every other option."

Otto looked to Jeb. “So that is what you do with Jeb. That’s why he chooses to stay?”

I nodded. “Jeb and I have known each other since the day he was born. My wife raised him until he was three years old and then gave him to me as a present. Ivan had taught her how to work with him the way he worked with his horses. He taught her how to build trust with him and teach him what her words meant. When she gave him to me, I did the same. Ivan helped me, and by the time the first war we were old enough to fight in began, Ivan, Nadia, and I were the only new recruits with non-military horses willing to enter war zones.” I considered the reason why, as I had never explained this to someone before. The answer I came up with brought a smile to my face. as it was a concept that Ivan had taught me. “They were willing not because they were tougher or smarter than other people’s horses, but because they trusted us, and we trusted them. Because we had taken the time to teach them what our words meant, and we had learned their unspoken cues,” I told Otto.

Otto looked at Jeb. “How do you get him to come back?” he asked.

I followed Otto’s gaze to where Jeb was grazing. “I taught him his name. He knows it, and he knows my voice. He will come when I call.”

“What if he is too far away to hear you?” asked Otto.

I smiled. “He won’t wonder that far off. Our bond isn’t something that just happened one day. He doesn’t have to work to make me care for him; he chooses to *because* I take care of him, because I give him the freedom to choose. And every day, we do something that will strengthen our bond. Because of that, we are always close enough, always there when the other calls. Always at the forefront of each other's minds."

"Like family," said Otto, finally smiling at Jeb.

Mary, my father, my siblings, and my mother...their faces flipped through my mind like the pages of a book. I had buried their memories for so long. It had been too hard to think of them. I had slept in the barn and spoken to no one of how they had died or what their deaths had done to me. But now, looking at Jeb, I suddenly realized I had told two different people about them within just a few days. For the first time in a long time, the bond I had with them, though no longer flesh and blood, but spirit and mind, seemed to tug at the edges of my heart once again. But this time, the grief was no longer unbearable.

"Yes..." I said quietly. "Like family."

# Chapter 9

Once Otto finally settled in to sleep, I sat in silence until it was time to wake Solace for the second watch. Ivan took the third, then Nadia. There were no disturbances during the night, but this forest apparently had some secrets to hide, so we were all a bit on edge. At sunrise, Nadia woke us all to get ready to leave.

As we were tacking up the horses, Nadia approached me. “We need to find food,” she said. “I don’t know how much longer we can last without it if we want to have the energy to ride or walk.” She laughed ruefully. “I even tried some of the grass the horses were eating. I would not recommend it, though.” She paused, looking to Otto, who was attempting to give Betsy a handful of grass without getting slobber on his hand. “Otto has started gathering random plants that he says are safe to eat, but at some point, he might be wrong...” She trailed off.

“I know. Just keep your eyes peeled,” I instructed. “We don’t know exactly what to expect in the Valley, but it probably won’t be good. We need to find food before we get there.”

She nodded. “That’s what I was thinking. I’ll send Ivan ahead to scout out the Valley while we look for food.”

As Nadia gave Ivan instructions, Solace, Otto, and I mounted up and headed out. The twins soon caught up, and Ivan rode on ahead astride his gray dappled gelding.

Gradually, as we traveled, we began to see more and more berries scattered among the leaves of bushes almost as tall as the horses' backs. Otto examined them closely, trying to determine if they were safe, but Nadia grew impatient and tried a few, claiming that tasting just one of each kind wouldn't kill her, even if they were poisonous. Some of the berries were plump and brightly colored, but Nadia claimed they were bitter and not nearly as good as the beautiful dark blue, purple, and red ones, which were much sweeter. She didn't seem to have any adverse reactions to the berries, and Otto soon concluded that they didn't appear to be any of the dangerous ones he knew about. So, we decided to risk it. We all gorged on the sweet berries as we rode through the Forest, dodging puffs of yellow pollen that erupted from the plants as we picked each berry. *If we aren't careful, we might all end up with sneezing fits and stuffy noses,* I thought to myself as I swatted at the annoying pollen and grabbed another handful of berries to shove into my mouth.

Solace was in the lead, and she stopped when she reached the place where the river disappeared underground.

"What now?" she called back.

"We just keep going straight up the hill," I said. "The river flows beneath this hill and under the Valley, and then it reemerges on the other side."

Otto paused from collecting berries to scribble in his notebook, red juice from his fingers staining the pages.

As we continued, Nadia made sure to gather extra berries for Ivan, and we eventually met up with him at the top of the hill, on the southern rim of the Valley. The Valley stretched out below us to the east and west in a green marshy mess, its northern bank concealed by distance and fog. It was filled with massive mossy trees, their exposed roots big enough for horses to walk on. Green plants floated on the surface of the water, half concealed by a hazy greenish fog, and patches of land appeared through the fog like stepping stones across the marshy landscape. Those patches of land would be our best route. *I hope it will be easier to cross than last time.*

Ivan looked at me. “Do you think that swamp monster that attacked me is still down there?”

I shrugged. “I sure hope not.”

His gaze shifted back to the swamp below. “We’ll need to stay on our horses and jump from land patch to land patch just in case.”

Otto peered over the edge of the Valley. “There is a chance adult monsters are not around during the spring...” he said hopefully. “The water here might be too shallow for breeding pairs to maintain the population, if they are in fact the size you described. Either that or they are dead, eaten by their young,” he added flatly.

We all looked at Otto. “Are you joking?” asked Solace. “Please tell me you’re joking.”

Otto shivered. “I am afraid not.”

Solace’s face fell to her hands, and after a moment of wallowing in silent horror at the idea, she turned her horse and went back for more berries.

“I’m still hungry, too,” said Ivan after eating all the food we had brought him.

I considered scolding him for a moment, but then I heard my own stomach growl. I spotted an apple tree behind Ivan and said, "Well, let's gather a little more before we go down. Solace, hurry up and bring any extra berries you find for the trip."

We each grabbed as many apples as we could reach and stored them in our saddlebags. Munching on the crisp, sweet fruit, we made our way toward the trail that led down into the Valley. But as we moved toward the slope, I suddenly felt a draw to look toward the Woods. Those green eyes were calling to me, and I turned to look behind me in the direction we had come from. Still astride her horse, Solace was facing me, picking a few more berries. But that was not what grabbed my attention. Behind Solace was a growing yellow cloud.

My mind immediately replayed all of Otto's warnings about the dangers of the Valley, and a jolt of panic rushed through me. "Otto?" I yelled, and I heard Otto and the twins come to a halt as they turned toward me.

Otto gasped from behind me. My gaze shifted to Solace as her fingers wrapped around a delicious-looking red berry. She pulled it off its stem and then froze. We all stared at the place where the berry had been attached to the stem as a tiny puff of a yellow substance spurted from it. I had assumed the yellow puffs were just pollen. I hadn't paid them much attention, as my hungry stomach had been too distracting. The berries had tasted so good, and I hadn't thought of the yellow substance as being dangerous. But now that I looked closely, I saw that it moved like ink in water. It wasn't pollen.

"Not good," said Otto.

Solace was the first to move. Dropping the berry, she clucked her horse into a run and darted past me, down the slope to the Valley below. "Don't just stand there!" she yelled.

Otto was next to me, staring in shock. "It's coming from way back there," he said, pointing.

I followed his finger, which pointed deep into the trees in the direction we had come from. The yellow substance was pouring out from between the trees and bushes we had been traveling through all day. *It must have been building since we first found the berries,* I thought in dismay as I slapped Betsy on the haunches to get Otto moving. The plants must have gradually released more and more of the substance after we had picked them, for now the Forest behind us was so clouded with it that we had nowhere to run but down. We pointed the horses toward the slope and picked our way down the hill as fast as we could without falling. *Not again,* I thought. *Not another near-death experience.* But now wasn't the time. We had to get through this valley without dying.

We rushed down to the Valley's floor but slowed at the sight of the swamp water. Ivan took the lead as I waited to ensure everyone made it safely down the slope. We began hopping from one section of exposed land to the next. But as I looked behind me at the side of the Valley we had just descended, my stomach turned. The yellow cloud had come down the slope and was now mixing with the green fog that hung over the swamp, creating a brown cloud that loomed ever closer.

"Faster!" I yelled, and everyone scattered, taking whatever route they could find rather than riding single file. But the cloud moved too fast. It overtook me first, then everyone ahead of me vanished into its thick darkness. I froze, expecting to start hacking and choking, but nothing happened. *Did we just panic over nothing?*

"Can anyone hear me?" I yelled. The cloud was thick, but if we stayed close enough, we would probably be able to see each other. We had to keep close.

"I can hear you!" I heard Otto respond.

Gradually, everyone called out their locations.

"Is everyone okay?" I asked.

I heard Solace respond, "So far, so good."

"Does an injured pride count?" called Ivan.

"Don't move unless you can see where you are going. How are the horses?" I asked.

Everyone but Solace called out that they were calm enough. Solace's gelding was prancing again, but she said she could handle him.

"Can anyone see the edge of land around you?" I asked.

"No, but I can see something moving in the water," I heard Ivan say. "We all know what that means."

I looked down and stared into the cloud, which obscured the surface of the water. After a moment, a patch of the brown cloud to my left moved as if something were slithering just beneath it. This creature was definitely the same type as the one we had encountered during the winter. But it was smaller. We had a problem. I saw another out of the corner of my eye, and Otto's words about the monsters being eaten by their young rang in my head. *Great,* I thought. *That's just what we need...hungry baby swamp monsters.*

"Go slow, and do not touch the water," I called out.

"Copy that. No need to tell me twice," called Ivan from the front of the group.

We picked our way through the swamp, each taking care not to disturb the water. We could no longer see the sky; the sun was barely visible through the brown cloud surrounding us.

"We need to stay close to each other and keep the sun in the right position," I called out. I looked up at the sun's hazy orange outline. It looked to be just past noon.

We spent the next half hour calling out back and forth and hopping from island to island until we were all within eyesight of each other. Once the sun had moved enough for us to tell which direction it was going, we continued on our way. So far, no one was dying from breathing in the cloud, and no one had been eaten. *Not bad for being exhausted, hungry, and trapped in an evil swamp,* I thought.

When it came time to camp for the night, we huddled around the base of a tree on one of the bigger patches of land. This time, we hitched all the horses and Betsy to the tree, not letting them wander off.

We ate some of our apples, saving a few for breakfast. Then, tired and still hungry, we each drifted off to sleep.

It wasn't until the next morning that we discovered anything was wrong. It started with me. I woke up coughing as the first hazy rays of sunlight cut through the dark brown cloud, and by noon on our second day traveling through the Valley, everyone was sick. We had to slow down because Ivan and Otto were throwing up, and we all had severe stomach cramps.

"Otto, what is this?" I asked. "Is it the cloud?"

Otto wiped his sleeve over his mouth to clear away the remnants of his recent expulsion and replied, "I can't be sure. Stuff in the air goes to the lungs, not the stomach. But you have a cough, so

I wouldn't stay in this fog any longer than we need to. It may be contributing to our illness. But I'd say the fruit is the main culprit. Those berries may have tasted sweet, but it seems they have become bitter in our stomachs. I have been scouring through one of my mother's old journals here and I just found a single drawing that may give us a clue. I don't know how I missed it before. If this drawing is accurate, it indicates the other berries would have been fine. I am afraid the sweet berries were deceptively good..." He trailed off with a thoughtful expression. "It must be the type of fiber," he mumbled to himself. "Maybe it takes longer to break down...or maybe the different chemicals in the berries mixed together and turned to poison in our guts..."

I groaned. *Great, we are going to die in a swamp, and Otto is analyzing chemical structures. How could this have happened? Why am I doing this?* I thought. *I could be home sleeping and working with Jeb if I had just refused to take this job.* But I had no answers to my questions. I could tell myself I was doing it because it was my job and General Delaney would not be pleased with me if I refused, or because I owed General Delaney my life and wealth after I had lost everything, but both of those reasons fell flat. I had known this was a bad idea from the start, but I had gone through with it anyway. With that admission still in my mind, I threw up.

We traveled much slower that day and stayed close enough that we could see each other. Otto began whining, questioning why we were even trying. "We are just going to die here," he moaned.

Nadia glared at him. "I am not dying in this filthy swamp!" she snapped.

"It's okay, we will figure this out," claimed Solace. "What did you all do the last time you were here?"

"It was different then." I concentrated on not passing out as Jeb jumped from one patch of earth to the next. "We didn't eat poisonous berries. And, when Ivan stepped in the water and drew the monster's attention, it wasn't us that scared it off."

"Really?" she said. "What did?"

"The Great Beast," said Ivan.

"The beast you were luring to the volcano to die ended up saving your life?" Solace asked with a slightly hysterical laugh. "How poetic."

Betsy suddenly stopped. I looked at Otto in time to see him grab his saddle with one hand and lean back. For a second, I thought he was going to pass out, as we were all queasy and nauseated from the mysterious illness. But then his hand slowly reached into his saddlebag, and he pulled out a notebook. He gripped the saddle to steady himself as he opened the book and searched for something. Ivan was nearest to him and moved closer as we all stared expectantly at Otto, waiting for an explanation.

"Otto?" I prompted. "Otto, what's wrong?"

His eyes darted over the pages of his book. "The beast you had with you killed the monster," he stated, more to himself than to me.

"Yeah, so what?" retorted Nadia.

Otto's head snapped up so fast he almost fell backward off Betsy. Ivan reached out to steady him. "Easy there, buddy," said Ivan.

Otto shook his head and blinked. He somehow looked like he was going to either vomit or start dancing with joy. "One monster killed the other!" he said enthusiastically.

"What are you talking about?" said Solace. "I think he is losing it, guys."

"No, no, no, I have it!" he said. "Plants! The plants from outside of the Valley are likely what is killing us. Maybe there is a plant inside the Valley that can cure us! I have been taking note of them, and I thought I saw one similar to something I read about in a study on the Valley. I drew it last night while I was trying not to throw up in my bed." He flipped through the pages and suddenly exclaimed, "Here! Swamp blood ivy! It is known to cure all kinds of illnesses, but it is rarely used because of how dangerous it is to get it!"

"Well, we are already here, so it can't be that dangerous," said Solace with a tired shrug.

"Oh, it is!" said Otto, still excited about his discovery. "Many think that it is called swamp blood ivy because the leaves are red and it grows in swamps. But it is actually called swamp blood ivy because it grows under the water only in this swamp, and you could die if you reach in to grab it!" His hair stuck out in all directions, and he looked sick and tired. With his elated facial expression prompted by this discovery, Otto really did look a bit like a madman. "This is great!" he exclaimed. "We won't die here!" With that, he suddenly doubled over and vomited next to Betsy's hooves.

"Wait, you mean to tell me that the only thing in this valley that will save us only grows in the water that, if we disturb it even the slightest, will result in us all being eaten alive by a swarming nest of swamp monsters?" clarified Nadia.

Silence fell over the group, only broken by the sound of Otto's hurling. Suddenly, he snapped up so fast that Ivan had to catch him again to keep him from falling. He wiped his mouth with his sleeve and exclaimed, "Exactly!"

*Great. He really is losing his mind,* I thought. "Okay, we can figure this out," I said.

Ivan and Nadia immediately started bouncing ideas back and forth while I thought through our situation in silence. The monsters would attack at any disturbance of the water, and there was no way around that.

"First, we need to find the plants," I interrupted everyone. "Otto, what do they look like?"

"They look like any ordinary ivy leaf, but red. Sometimes they kind of glow...or at least that is what I have heard," he said, beginning to sound groggy.

"Okay," I said with a nod. *Things are making less and less sense the farther we travel into this forest,* I thought with a frown.

We all got off our horses and leaned over the edge of the water from the safety of the little island we were on. Each of us brushed the brown fog from the top of the water, careful not to disturb the surface. With the fog out of the way, between patches of floating vegetation, we could see the plants, their blood-red hue barely visible in the relatively clear waters. But as we looked closer, we saw that the plants were swaying as monsters slithered between their leaves. *There could be hundreds of those monsters scattered throughout this valley,* I realized with a lurch in my stomach. And according to Otto, they were young and hungry for meat.

"We need to keep moving. We can plan on the way. Then, by the time we decide how to get the leaves, we will at least be closer to the other side of the Valley," I said as I climbed back onto Jeb's saddle. Everyone agreed, and we moved out.

As we traveled, each of us came up with different ideas on how we could get the plants without being eaten by monsters. Ivan wanted to grab the plants and run. Nadia wondered if there was a way to slip something into the water slowly enough that the monsters wouldn't react. Solace kept saying that there must be a way to lull the monsters to sleep, and Otto wondered if there was a way to poison them with plants. I suggested there might be a way to trick the monsters into attacking the wrong spot. Eventually, I began to form a plan.

"Otto, you and Solace might be on to something with the poison or sleep thing. Is there a plant in this swamp that we could use to poison the monsters?" I asked.

Otto looked around and pointed to a small plant that looked like a blade of grass but purple with a white stripe down its center. "That won't kill them, but it might dull their senses if we can crush it so the toxic juices are released and we can get it into their mouths," he stated.

"Perfect. Crush as much as you can to give to the monsters," I said as the plan came together in my mind. "I think we can do this if we pool our ideas. Once the plant is ready, Otto will fling it onto the surface of the water, and the monsters will instinctively bite it. Hopefully, this will slow them down enough that Ivan and I can draw them away without getting eaten. If our distraction is successful, Nadia and Solace should be able to reach into the marsh and get some leaves."

Everyone looked around and nodded. "Sounds good to me," said Nadia.

"Beats just laying down and dying," said Solace.

"We are all in agreement then," I stated. "Let's get going before we all get too sick to make this work." My head was spinning and my lungs burned, but I was not going to give up just yet. It would take more than a few berries to stop me.

While Otto, Nadia, and Solace worked on getting the plants ready, Ivan and I found a good place where we could fight with the monsters. The patch of land we were on formed a long U-shape with only five yards of water between the two banks, and Ivan and I settled on a spot on the south bank, opposite the others. The area was spotted with plants and massive trees that grew out of the swamp, which we could use as cover. While these monsters were not nearly as big as the one we had fought the last time we were here, there could be a lot of them, so we would need some advantage.

As Ivan and I got set up on our side of the bank, Solace and Nadia left Otto to finish preparing the crushed plants and scoped out the best spot to reach the ivy leaves. By the time we were ready, Otto had a pile of the crushed leaves spread out on a two-foot piece of tree bark and was poised to fling it into the water.

"Ready?" I asked. When everyone nodded, I called out a three count, ending with, "Now!"

With one sweeping motion of his makeshift shovel, Otto flung the crushed plant out over the water, attempting to spread it as wide as he could. The second it hit the surface, the water exploded with activity. Long black, green, and brown slimy-looking monsters about five feet long attacked the surface. Their eyes were glazed over white, clearly blind, and their needle-like teeth gnashed violently at whatever had disturbed their waters.

As soon as we saw that the monsters had eaten the crushed plants, Ivan and I jumped into action. I slapped the water with a chunk of tree bark, and Ivan did the same with his sword, drawing the monsters' attention to us. The monsters swarmed toward our bank and Ivan slashed one in half as it launched itself from the water in his direction. Otto had warned me that firing my flintlock pistol in this mysterious fog might set off an explosion, so I used my dagger instead. With only the short blade available, I had to get my feet wet to stab a monster before it could land a bite on Ivan. But as soon as I slayed that monster, more splashed to the surface, seemingly from everywhere, so I retreated onto land just as one leapt clean out of the water, missing my neck by only a couple of inches as I slashed it in half before it hit the water again. As soon as I was back on land, Ivan attacked the nearest monster, and we continued our fight. The plants seemed to be working, but only enough that we barely had an edge on the monsters' speed.

Amid the chaos that Ivan and I were making, I glanced toward Solace to see her holding onto Nadia, who was reaching into the water. She had already pulled some leaves to shore, but Otto had said we would need about three handfuls.

Suddenly, a monster leapt at Nadia, and Solace pulled her back from the water's edge just in time for Solace to plunge a knife into the monster's head. In my moment of distraction, I heard Ivan growl in pain. I refocused on the task at hand and plunged back into the fight to slice at a monster that had its jaws around Ivan's ankle. The monster's body fell into the water again, but its severed head kept its jaws locked on Ivan. I heard a scream from across the water and looked up in time to see Nadia attack a monster that had Solace by the shoulder. She stabbed it twice before it died and then pried its locked jaws from Solace's bloody shoulder.

Otto waved that he had the plants he needed, and Ivan and I pulled back. We ran for our horses, and they carried us from tree to tree, trying to keep as far from the water as possible as we evaded monsters on our way around the U-shaped bend of land to the opposite bank. When we reached the others, they were on their horses and ready to run. We fled north toward the edge of the swamp with monsters swarming in the water below, gnashing at our horses' ankles as we jumped over the snaking sections of water. More large trees appeared out of the brown cloud, their massive roots big enough for the horses to run along, and we took to them. Thankfully, the horses kept their footing as we dodged vines and plants hanging in our path, and we made it to the edge of the Valley with no further injuries.

As the Valley's edge sloped back up, we found our horses scrambling to keep their footing to reach the top. Holding on to my saddle with a white-knuckle grip, I barely managed to stay on. I was so weak I felt as though I would collapse. I could tell that Ivan and Solace were suffering from their bites and the effects of the plant poison as they swayed unsteadily in their saddles. Solace's shoulder was a bloody mess, and Ivan would most likely not be able to walk for a while. Nadia and Otto looked as bad as I felt. We were all barely keeping it together. But we couldn't stop. Not until we were free of this wretched valley.

Once at the top of the hill, the land sloped down before us and spread out in rolling hills covered in trees and bushes, the river flowing through like liquid crystal. Animals were everywhere—grazing deer, birds flitting about in the air and the trees, and rabbits in the underbrush. Everyone let out a sigh. *We made it. Six days in, and we are still alive...at least for now.*

Once we were clear of the Valley, we stopped under the shade of a tree and Otto immediately began preparing a medicine from the ivy leaves that I hoped would cure our illness as Otto thought it would. As Nadia began caring for Ivan's ankle, Otto smashed the leaves into a paste and mixed it with another plant he had picked in the swamp. I dismounted Jeb and tended to Solace's shoulder.

Solace winced as I peeled some of her shirt sleeve from the wound, checking to see how deep the wound went. "Sorry," I said. I grabbed a water costrel. "This is going to hurt."

Solace nodded silently and gritted her teeth while I washed the wound and bandaged it. She took a deep breath as I finished. "Do you think Otto's paste will work?" she asked.

I glanced at Otto, who was too focused to hear the question, and I could feel Nadia and Ivan watching me. I was pretty sure we were all thinking the same thing. If it didn't work, we would die, right here under this tree. It seemed our lives were in the hands of Otto Bilden.

I offered a tense smile. "Otto's smart. He knows what he is doing."

Once Otto's paste was complete, we each took our share. We sat under the tree in exhausted silence for a very tense few minutes. To our deep relief, the paste took effect fairly quickly. As our pain and weakness faded, our spirits lifted, and only a short half hour later, we were all feeling much better.

I clapped Otto on the back. "You did it, Otto."

Otto looked at me. His expression held no hint of his usual haughtiness. “I just used what was given me,” he said.

I smiled and patted him more gently on the shoulder. “Thank you.”

He nodded.

Once we were all feeling strong enough to get back on our horses, we continued on to find a place to camp near the river. We needed to refill our water costrels, and then we needed food and sleep if we were going to survive the rest of this trip. It didn’t take us long to reach the place where the river reappeared from underground, and we soon found a good spot to camp. Ivan, Solace, and Otto filled the water costrels and began building a fire while Nadia and I went off in search of food. We found plenty of animals around, and it didn’t take too long before we had game roasting on the fire. Finally, something was working in our favor.

With food in our bellies, we settled in to get some rest. Just to be safe, we took watch shifts throughout the night. Nadia took the first watch, and I took the last.

As morning light began to pour through the trees, Nadia came up beside me. We stood a little way from our camp, at the top of an embankment. Below and to the east lay a hill, its relatively bare top exposed to the sun’s first rays, turning it golden with dew shimmering in the light. We watched the sunrise in silence. Yellow light, sliced into beams by the tall trees that towered over us, reached through the Forest, bathing the cool, damp morning in rays of welcome warmth. But whatever enjoyment I got from watching the light spread through the land was quickly bogged down with brooding questions. *Why are we doing this?* I thought in discouragement.

I sighed, and Nadia looked at me with a questioning expression. "What?" she asked.

I sucked in a deep breath. "Why are we doing this?" I repeated out loud. "I have been thinking about it all night and..." I trailed off. I had known Nadia for a long time. I could trust her. "I realized the other night that I don't have an answer," I explained. "I could say that we came here because it is my job and you and Ivan wanted an adventure. But the more I tell myself that, the less it sounds true," I finished.

Nadia considered my words for a moment. "What exactly are we doing?" she asked with a smile.

I rolled the question over in my mind. "We are trying to find a man who will tell us how to kill the Beast of the Woods because...I guess because General Delaney thinks that is the only way to stave off more war with the Great Beasts of the Southern Mountains," I stated.

She pondered that for a moment. "Are we?"

"What do you mean?" I asked with a thoughtful frown.

"I'll be honest with you, Ben. I have been thinking the same thing. Ivan and I, I guess we just wanted a break, you know? Something to do outside the inn...Something that will last. Since the war ended, we have fixed up the bar and rooms, but..." she hesitated, "we are done with that now, and we all know the next group of beasts will attack sometime soon, and it will all start over. I just keep wondering what we will leave behind. Ivan seems content to just search for treasure his whole life, but I need something else..."

"So, what are you doing here exactly?" I asked.

She gazed out over the Forest. "At first, I just wanted adventure. But honestly, I feel like I'm searching for something...Something that will last beyond me, beyond an inn." She paused and looked at me. "I guess I'm searching for purpose. I think we all are," she finished.

As Nadia returned to camp, I couldn't help but wonder again, *Why am I here?* If Nadia was right and we came here looking for purpose, why here? Why now? My mind wandered to the Beast of the Woods. Its green eyes shone bright in my mind's eye, drawing me in. Things had been simple before I had seen the Beast of the Woods.

I sucked in a sharp breath and turned to go back to camp. We were still probably two or three days out from the Great Volcano. We needed to get going.

# Chapter 10

As we headed out, I noted that this section of the Forest felt more normal—almost peaceful. Quiet and still, the terrain seemed free of dangerous, unfamiliar creatures and full of familiar ones. Rabbits, birds, deer, foxes, mice, and more seemed content to go about their business as we traveled by, only occasionally looking up to check on us. However, we all paid more attention to the fruit we ate. If Otto was right, our desire for the sweet berries when we were so hungry had likely led us to eat dangerous fruit. *We need to be more careful and not be so focused on our physical desires that we fall for that trick again.* As the day passed, we slowly relaxed. In fact, I felt a little spring of hope as it appeared that we were near the place we had encountered a farmer while on our way to lure the Great Beast to its death in the Great Volcano. The farmer had helped us avoid eating poisonous plants that winter. Until that meeting, I'd had no idea that people lived in this forest. It seemed a dangerous place to make a home. Hopefully, people did still live here. *We might need some help.*

The biggest problems we were facing now were the injuries to Solace and Ivan. They did their best to keep the wounds clean, and Otto used plants from around the Forest to make pastes he said would reduce the pain and hopefully stave off infection. We all knew we would not be able to go much further if they didn't have time to heal, but both insisted we keep moving during the daylight, so we did.

Sometime during our second day of traveling through this section of the Forest, Nadia pulled up next to me with concern in her eyes. "Solace isn't doing great, Ben."

I glanced back at Solace. Ivan was bigger and had sustained worse injuries in battle, so he looked fine, just in a bit of pain. But Solace did look worse. She was slightly slouched, and her lips had definitely lost some color since the last time I had looked at her.

"Have you talked to Otto about her condition?" I asked.

"I did, but he claimed he is no doctor, and he isn't great at telling what an actual infection looks like," she said, keeping her voice low.

I nodded. "Well, last time we were here, we met that farmer. Maybe we should take a detour and see if we can find someone."

Nadia glanced over her shoulder at Solace. "I think that would be a wise move."

Nadia passed on the information to the others while I went ahead to see if I could find any evidence of people. I followed the river north, then paused when a stream split off to the east. The farmer had been on the eastern side of the river, and though it wasn't much to go on, I was prepared to take my chances. If anyone lived out here, they would have to be near a water source. We hadn't encountered any towns along the river the last time we came through here, but maybe, with any luck, this stream would lead me to civilization. I traveled along the stream until sunset, when I finally saw signs that someone else was in the Forest with us.

"I found boot prints to the northeast, maybe a hunter," I told the others when I returned. "Nadia and I will go ahead tomorrow morning and check it out. We will have a better chance of staying safe and getting out fast if we run into a bad situation."

Everyone agreed, and Nadia and I spent part of the night putting together a plan for our trip.

At some point during our planning, the conversation turned away from the mission, and I caught Nadia giving me her mothering look.

"What?" I asked.

"I was right. You like her, don't you?" she said with a smile.

I felt myself blush and opened my mouth to dispute, but Nadia interrupted me.

"Ahhhh, don't you deny it or change the subject. I haven't seen you like this since you met Mary."

I laughed, then let my smile fade.

Nadia must have read my expression. "You shouldn't feel guilty, Ben. Mary would want you to be happy," she said with a soft smile.

"Everyone says that," I pointed out.

"No, I said that. Until this trip, I don't think you have talked to anyone but Jeb about your wife since the day she died. I heard you talking to Solace and Otto, and they didn't say anything about Mary wanting you to be happy, so not one person but me has told you that," she corrected as she crossed her arms. "You are still not letting yourself get over this."

I frowned and looked at her. "I can't—" I began, but Nadia interrupted me.

"You can't what, fall in love? Be happy? As much as you don't want to hear it, Ben, Mary is gone, and there is nothing any of us can do about it. I know how hard it is, trust me. Don't forget what

Ivan and I lost in that war too. And Mary was our friend too. More than a friend. She was family."

My growing irritation suddenly faded, and I let my face fall to my hands. Nadia was right. She did understand, and she wouldn't be saying this if she hadn't already had to face it herself.

"What gave it away?" I finally asked as I looked up again.

"You have been checking on her from a distance like a worried mother hen since she got injured," said Nadia as she sat down and watched me.

I inadvertently looked back toward Solace, then caught myself with an embarrassed chuckle. "Yeah, I guess I have been a bit worried. But not just about her health."

"Then what else are you worried about?"

"I'm lying to her, Nadia," I said tensely. "And I'm not just lying; I am planning on killing the one thing she thinks can keep her family heritage alive. That's a pretty big thing to expect someone to forgive you for just because you fell in love with them." I paused when I realized I had just admitted out loud that I was in love with Solace. "I didn't mean—I—" I sputtered. "I just meant theoretically. Of course I'm not in love with her." I cleared my throat. *And that's not to mention what the general might want me to do to her once we get to that point. Especially if she opposes killing the beast,* I thought.

Nadia laughed. "Well then, Ben, I guess you should keep asking yourself what you are doing here until you figure it out because I personally have a feeling that she now plays a part in the answer." Nadia stood and offered an encouraging smile, then went to check on Solace.

As I watched Nadia walk away, I mulled over her comment and the questions that had been plaguing me. *Why am I here? Why am I doing what I am doing?* I still had no answers, apart from the obvious goal of finding the Beast. Then Nadia's earlier question popped into my head. *"What exactly are we doing?"* I felt like I should know the answer to that too. But for some reason, I still didn't fully understand what I was doing or why I was really here. I felt like I was just moving along, stuck in some time trap that played the same cycle of war over and over again, and I had been lulled into hopelessly going along with it. But on that night when I saw the Beast of the Woods, everything had changed.

The next morning, Nadia and I left camp at daybreak while the others finished waking up and eating breakfast, and we headed to where I had seen the boot tracks. It had not rained and was not windy, so they were still undisturbed. I picked up the trail, and we followed it until we came to a large clearing bordered by trees. Within the clearing was, to our surprise, a village. It appeared peaceful. There were people tending to livestock and children playing about. It appeared, at least on the surface, worth looking into. Nadia and I decided to investigate, though we made sure to keep an eye out for trouble.

The village seemed to consist of a handful of houses loosely arranged around a central gathering area and separated by sprawling fields of green and golden crops. Patches of trees stood here and there, offering shade to the houses and their livestock fenced in nearby. There were cows, goats, and sheep in the small pastures, and chickens roamed among the properties, mingling together so I couldn't tell which chickens belonged to which homes. Upon seeing us, the children scampered off and hid, some probably going to tell their parents of the strangers who had entered their secluded town. As we approached a middle-aged woman tending her garden, I asked if she could point me in the direction of whoever ran the place. She nervously pointed to a house that was slightly bigger than the rest, though not by much, before retreating into her home.

Nadia and I approached the house as a man stepped out of the front door. "Can I help you?" he asked politely, wiping his hands on a towel before slinging it over his shoulder.

Tall, with lean, strong arms and a wide stance, he looked able to handle himself, but his hands were free of any obvious weapons. Unless he was skilled enough to use the towel or his bare hands to kill us, I didn't see any threat, though I remained cautious. His near imperceptible frown suggested that he was not used to seeing travelers in his village, and his wet, reddish-brown hair and freshly cleaned freckled face and hands said he had just come in from working outside and washed up. It seemed an odd time to wash up, as it was a little late for breakfast in a town full of farmers. So maybe someone had warned him we were coming, and he came home to ensure his family was safe from the incoming strangers. If that was the case, the people of this town were very quick to prepare for disaster, and if this man was their leader, he was one to keep an eye on if things went south.

"I hope so," I replied. "My friends and I were traveling through the area, and two of us sustained injuries that need to be treated and given time to heal. They are waiting back at our camp. Do you have a doctor here who could help?"

The man was immediately in action. “Of course, let me come and help you bring them back here. I am Ed Willards,” he said as he shook my hand. “Welcome to the Village. We will take your friends to the Carters’ place. They are our doctors.” He turned and called inside to his family, telling them he would be back soon. “I’ll just get my horse; do they need a cart?” he asked.

“No, they can ride, but the sooner we can get them back, the better. They are not feeling well and are anxious to get settled somewhere they can recover,” I explained.

“I understand. Are they close?” he asked.

“They are about two miles south of here, but there are few paths, and it may take us a while to get there and back since they can’t travel very quickly. Hopefully we can make it back here before noon,” I said.

“Don’t worry, I know some shortcuts. I’ll help you get them back here as soon as possible.”

“That would be great. Thank you,” I said appreciatively.

Once Ed’s horse was tacked up, we headed back to camp. When we arrived, Nadia brought Ed to where Solace was still sitting near the doused-out fire.

“This is Solace. Ivan is over there. Solace is in worse shape than Ivan,” Nadia explained as she gestured to the injured.

“She is tough, though,” said Ivan, giving Solace an encouraging smile and nod.

“Thanks, Ivan,” she said in a weary voice as Ed examined her wound.

“These look like swamp monster bites, which are easily infected .,” he said in a concerned tone. “That might be what you’re dealing with," he told Solace before turning to me. "We should get back as soon as possible."

With a nod to Ed, I helped Solace onto her horse, and we headed off to the Village again.

Ed led us through a shortcut that took us along a deer path through thick bushes, creating nearly a straight shot to the Village from our camp. On the way, Nadia approached me, watching the surroundings as though checking for a trap.

"Ben, do you think these villagers are trustworthy?" she asked.

I shook my head. "We don't have to trust them. We just need their help. Either way, we don't have much of a choice."

Nadia winced. "True."

When we arrived back at the Village, we got a slightly less nervous greeting as people came out to stare at us instead of hiding.

"Sorry about the staring," said Ed. "We don't often see people come through here."

"Where did you all come from? I have been through here once before during the winter and never saw signs of a full village," I said.

He nodded. "We rarely leave the Village during the winter, so we often go unnoticed. We are from the cities along the sea and more distant lands. After one of the first wars, our ancestors came here looking for a place to avoid the Great Beasts of the Southern Mountains as they began to show up in the island countries. We haven't seen any of the Great Beasts come through here since the last one that died in the volcano, but people here are still very cautious. Beasts don't often have much reason to come this far into the Forest, though, and the people of the Town by the Woods usually put up a good fight."

"Well, it looks like a nice place," I said with a polite smile. "I don't know what we would have done if you weren't willing to help."

"It's no trouble," said Ed graciously. He was silent for a moment before he said, "If you don't mind my asking, what are you and your friends doing so far out in the Forest? Those wounds are from the swamp monsters, which are south of here. So you must have come from the Town to end up traveling through that area."

I considered how much I would tell these villagers. They seemed nice, but after everything we had been through, it seemed wise to tell them as little as possible. But I also needed them to help us. *Maybe it would be wise to tell them the truth.* After a moment's thought, I decided on sharing part of the truth. "We are from the Town on the south side of the Forest. We came here looking for someone—a doctor who travels this way during the spring to gather medicinal plants. Have you seen him come through here?"

"I am afraid not. But we are a bit off the main path to the volcano. I assume that is where he is going, as most of the medicinal plants prefer its hot environment," explained Ed.

I nodded. "That is what we figured, too. We would have kept following the river straight to the volcano if Solace and Ivan weren't injured. Hopefully they recover quickly so we can catch up to the doctor before he moves on."

Ed nodded. "Is he a friend of yours?" he asked.

This one would be a bit trickier to get around. I thought quickly. "More like an acquaintance. I was told he could help a friend of mine with a rare disease," I lied. "I couldn't wait for him to get back, so I decided to come looking for him."

Ed smiled. "You must care a lot about this person to risk traveling through the Forest, especially in springtime."

"Yeah." I nodded, unsure what else to say.

Ed showed us to the Carters' house, where we were greeted by a husband and wife, Malcolm and Elena. Brief introductions were made before they immediately began tending to Solace and Ivan.

"It looks like whoever was taking care of them knew what plants to use. Though infection is starting to set in, it would have spread much faster if it were not for that treatment," said Elena admiringly.

"That would be Otto," I said as I gestured out the window to where Otto was dodging Betsy's affectionate nuzzling.

Elena followed my gesture and smiled. "Not the traveling type, I presume?"

I laughed. "Something like that."

As Elena and I chuckled at Otto, Malcolm approached from where he had been tending to Ivan. "As Elena said, there is an infection attempting to set in, and it seems to be impacting Solace more than Ivan. We will need to keep a close eye on her. We can arrange a place for you to sleep and keep your horses until these two are healed enough to continue your journey."

"Thank you, I would appreciate that," I replied.

Malcolm nodded and turned to his wife. "I will be back shortly," he said and kissed her cheek.

I followed Malcolm outside and toward another house. "We don't get a lot of guests here, so we don't have a lot of accommodations, but we will see if the Alves family has room for you," he explained.

He approached the front door just as a woman came out onto the porch. She was short, with her grayish-brown hair up in a bun. Dressed in a gray dress with an apron over the front, she looked like the mother of the town. "Who are your new friends, Malcolm?" asked the woman warmly as Nadia and Otto joined us.

"This is Benjamin Arlin and his friends Nadia and Otto. Benjamin, this is Mrs. Alves," he said. Then he turned back to Mrs. Alves. "They were traveling when two of their comrades were injured, and they stopped here to get medical help. Do you have room for them for a few days while the others recover?" asked Malcolm.

"Of course!" said Mrs. Alves gladly. "I am so sorry to hear about your friends. Come in, and I will make you some food."

"Thank you," I said as I glanced at Nadia with a cautioning look. We could not get soft just because everyone seemed nice. Nadia casually scanned the area around us and then followed me inside with Otto.

The inside of the house was clean and well decorated, with colorful blankets draped over a rocking chair and bench, and a kitchen table that had been carved so the legs looked like they were wrapped in vines. There were multiple rooms down two short hallways that led off from the main kitchen and fireplace area. It looked cozy and refreshing after spending days in the Forest.

"You can use these two rooms at the end of the hall," Mrs. Alves said as she ushered us to our rooms. "I'll put some blankets in here for tonight. You can wash up in back with the rain barrel, and your horses can go in the barn," she explained. "Make yourselves at home. I'll let you know when food is ready," she said as she disappeared back down the hall and into the kitchen.

Nadia leaned toward me. "She seems nice."

I nodded. "Yeah, but don't let your guard down. With our luck, they might try to eat us in our sleep," I said.

Otto stared at me in shock. I chuckled. "I was joking, Otto. Relax." Then I turned to Nadia and whispered, "Keep your eyes peeled." She nodded.

Nadia took the room on the left, and Otto and I took the other room. Since Otto was so desperate for the bed, I let him have it, but Mrs. Alves came in with more blankets for me to sleep on.

Once we were settled, we left our things inside, nothing valuable in them except blankets, and went out to tend to the horses and Betsy. We took their tack off and cleaned it for the first time since we had left the Town. Then we each sponged down our horses and ensured they had food and water before cleaning ourselves up.

Instead of using water from the rain barrel to clean up, I went to the nearby stream, which I had followed to the boot prints the day before. This far from the river, it had dwindled to a small, lazy creek. I removed my leather duster, shirt, and boots and rolled my pants up to my knees before wading in just far enough to keep my pants dry. I scooped up water in my cupped hands and poured it over my head, running my fingers through my thick, now shaggy hair as the water washed over my face. It was still early, but the sun was heating up the air, and the cool water felt good.

As I turned to exit the stream, I noticed a young girl, no older than five, standing on the bank, half hidden behind a tree. She was a little thing, with black hair, a pale complexion, and dark, sweet eyes.

"Hello," she said shyly. "I'm Yuuki! Who are you?"

I humored her, hoping she would go away if I answered her question. "I'm Ben."

She smiled with excitement. "Are you staying at Mrs. Alves's house?" she asked happily as she inched a little farther from behind the tree.

Sighing heavily, I stepped out of the water and began to dry off. "It seems that way," I said dryly.

"Why?" she asked curiously.

I studied her. *There is that question again,* I thought to myself. "Some friends of mine were injured, and Mr. and Mrs. Carter are tending to them until they heal," I told her. "Don't you have somewhere to play other than here?" I asked, allowing annoyance to creep into my voice.

She pulled slightly back behind the tree again at my tone. But after a moment, she prompted, "Are you staying for a while?"

"It seems that way," I repeated as I pulled my boots back on.

Yuuki approached, running from her tree to the tree my belongings were propped against. She looked curious but still unsure about the stranger freshening up in her stream. When she caught a glimpse of my belongings, she reached out to touch my pistols, which were safely wrapped in my pistol belt.

My hand snapped out to grab my weapons and she flinched, taking a fearful step backward. "Those are not for children," I growled. She hid behind the tree again but peered out to watch me put my pistol belt back on. "Don't you have somewhere you should be?" I tried again.

She shook her head. "Not really. I don't have chores until tonight." She went back to examining my belongings. "Why do you have so many weapons and things?" she asked in a small but curious voice.

"For protection," I said flatly as I placed each weapon where it belonged.

With my things back in place, I made my way back toward Mrs. Alves's house. Yuuki followed at what she apparently determined was a safe distance, managing to always keep some kind of tree or shrub between us.

"Protection from what?" she asked, gaining a little more confidence.

I suddenly realized that the villagers were probably quite protected here. This part of the Forest was only accessible by either going through the Forest's treacherous sections or coming in from the sea as these people had done. Yuuki most likely had no idea what monsters lay in the trees and bushes beyond her village.

"From bad things," I said, avoiding any details to make sure I didn't give her nightmares.

"You mean evil?" she asked.

I paused and looked back at her, half hidden behind a bush. *Okay, so she knows more than I thought.* "Yeah, you could put it that way."

"Oh." She thought for a moment. "What do you do if your weapons don't work?" she asked as we came to the house.

Mrs. Alves was outside doing laundry, and, thankfully, she interrupted. "Now Yuuki, leave the nice man alone. He has had a long journey and needs some rest. Why don't you join the other children and go play with the new piglets?" she suggested.

Yuuki smiled. "Okay!" she said and ran off toward the barn where Nadia was tending to some scratches on her horse's withers.

Mrs. Alves smiled, the sun-kissed skin at the corners of her eyes wrinkling. "She is a curious little thing. Sweet-hearted and smart too." She chuckled to herself.

I nodded. "So I noticed."

"Food is ready in the kitchen, by the way," said Mrs. Alves. "I didn't want to interrupt your bathing; it is probably the most relaxing thing one can do after a long journey," she said as she pinned a wet shirt to the clothesline. "But you may help yourself to what's in there. Your friends already ate, and the children will eat later," she explained.

I thanked her and headed inside to grab some food. Before I passed through the door, I glanced around. A light breeze blew through the tall crops and trees. Families were working and laughing together in their fields. Otto had gone to the Carters' to learn more about the Forest and the plants it contained, Nadia was in the barn now playing with Yuuki and the piglets, and Solace and Ivan seemed to be in good hands. This village appeared to be a safe place to stay for now. *I guess we don't have much of a choice,* I thought. We just needed to make sure that Solace and Ivan were okay. I couldn't make it through this without them, and I definitely couldn't make it back home without them. So, for now, we would stay. Hopefully, they would heal fast, and we would be out of here in a day or two. Holding on to that hope, I turned and entered the house.

# Chapter 11

As the afternoon went by, we were all finally able to relax. Otto spent most of his time absorbed in learning from the Carters about the Forest and all the plants and animals it contained. Nadia took to the farm, helping out with chores and getting to know the neighbors. I dabbled in chores and took some time to clean weapons and make sure Jeb was healthy for the journey that we would hopefully be able to resume sooner rather than later.

When dinner rolled around, we all went inside and joined Mrs. Alves at the table with her two children. As we sat down, Yuuki appeared and came to join us.

I must have looked surprised because Mrs. Alves smiled and said, "You met Yuuki at the stream this morning, right?"

"Yes, I did," I said with a smile. "I didn't know she was your daughter."

"I'm not. I just live here," Yuuki said simply as she began picking at the food Mrs. Alves had put on her plate.

"Ah, that explains it then," I said with a smile.

Mrs. Alves smiled, then said, "So tell me, Ben, where are you and your friends from?"

"We are from the other side of the Woods," I said.

Mrs. Alves nodded. "What are you doing way out here in the middle of spring?" she asked curiously.

Nadia took this answer. "We are looking for someone—a doctor who gathers medicinal plants at the volcano every spring."

Mrs. Alves frowned thoughtfully. "Do you not have a town doctor?" she asked.

"We do," replied Nadia politely, "but this doctor is the only one we know of who can solve our particular problem."

Mrs. Alves nodded. "The plants that grow around the volcano this time of year are quite potent and cannot be found anywhere else in the known world. But most doctors are unwilling to risk their lives to make the trip."

"Well, hopefully, we don't miss him," I said.

The conversation steered toward the Village, and we discussed what livestock they had and how they were connected with the seaports and shipping companies that shipped products such as handmade carpets around the world. After we finished dinner, Otto disappeared to prepare his bed, and Nadia and I helped Mrs. Alves clean up the kitchen.

"How did you meet Yuuki?" asked Nadia as she took some dirty dishes to a washtub.

"We think her parents were killed in a storm on the Eastern Sea," Mrs. Alves said. "Ed found her alone at the port when he was in town one day and just couldn't leave her there all by herself. She was only four at the time. So, he brought her back with him, and I took her in," Mrs. Alves said with a sweet smile. "She is a lovely little girl. Kindhearted and smart. She is a little shy when it comes to strangers but always willing to lend a helping hand, and she is wise beyond her years."

"And curious," I added.

Mrs. Alves chuckled. "Very curious. She once got lost in the Forest following a horned bee to its nest, and we had to go looking for her." She smiled at the memory. "Like I said, she is shy toward people, but she is also not easily scared by the world around her. When we found her, she was still so enamored by the hive she had found that she didn't even notice that we were worried until I started lecturing her."

"She sounds like an adventurous little girl," said Nadia with a grin.

"Oh yes! She is always asking to join people on outings and trips to the seaports. She loves to explore, and though she has only lived here for a short time, she probably knows things about this place that none of us do," she said with a smile. "It has cost me my nerves more than once."

The three of us laughed, and Otto emerged from our room to join the conversation. Mrs. Alves began telling us more about the Village and its history. As Ed had told us, these people came to the Village from the seaports and the islands beyond. Mrs. Alves told us of adventures she'd had as a young woman on the seas with her father, who had been the closest thing to a pirate one could be without losing his moral compass. Her father had settled here when she was a young girl after her mother died. Ed and his family apparently came from the Western Sea after a storm ruined their business, and they didn't have enough money to rebuild. The Carters had come out when the Village requested medical help for an illness that passed through, and they loved the people so much they ended up staying. The other four families were descendants of the first three families who had settled here long ago. According to

Mrs. Alves, those original families had come because their homes in other lands had been destroyed by war with the Great Beasts. They had apparently all met on a ship that wrecked on the western coast of the Forest. When they found this place, they decided to stay. Over time, some of their descendants moved back to the islands or headed south to the Town. But a few remained, living here in peace, protected by the dangerous forest that surrounded them.

As we were all getting ready to head to our rooms, there was a loud knock at the door. Mrs. Alves answered it to find Malcolm standing on the porch.

"Sorry to bother you this late, but there is something I need to discuss with our guests," he said.

Nadia, Otto, and I glanced at each other with worried looks as we joined Malcolm outside on the porch.

"Is it something about the injuries?" asked Nadia with worry in her voice.

Malcolm nodded. "It's about Solace. Ivan is healing quite well, but she is faring poorly."

"What do you mean?" I asked, taking a step forward.

"She should be getting better, but I think she is getting worse."

"Is it the infection?" asked Otto clinically.

"Partially. I think fighting off the infection in her condition put her at a disadvantage," explained Malcolm.

"What do you mean by 'her condition?'" asked Nadia, frowning.

Malcolm looked surprised. "You don't know?"

We looked at each other, then back to Malcolm, shaking our heads.

Malcolm took a deep breath. “Well, if she didn’t tell you, then I’m not sure I—”

I cut him off. “We need to know. This is a dangerous journey we are on, and not knowing will only make it more so.”

Malcolm nodded and glanced back toward his house, where Solace and Ivan were recovering. He took a deep breath and met my gaze. “She is dying.” Behind me, Otto gasped as the words sank in.

“Why?” I asked, forcing my expression to remain calm as my gut twisted with a surprising amount of panic.

“I don’t know. This disease is rare. That is why I thought you knew. I thought she was the reason you were looking for this doctor that Ed mentioned,” he said, sounding confused.

My mind scrambled for an explanation to give him, but I was careful to keep my face impassive. “No. Not her,” I said simply. I ran a hand over my face. “I only met her shortly before this trip began. She was the one who told me where the doctor was…” I trailed off.

“That must be why she knows about the doctor in the first place,” Nadia whispered.

I glanced at Nadia and Otto and then turned back to Malcolm. “How much time does she have?” I asked, clearing my throat as my voice broke slightly.

Malcolm shrugged. “I don’t know. The bite infection made it worse. Her energy is down, she has mentioned aches and pains getting worse. She might improve in the next couple of days, but even if she does, she will likely still be weaker than before. I’m not sure traveling is a good idea.”

I suddenly felt guilty for having gotten annoyed at her crazy crusade. She wasn't going on this trip just because she would one day die with no one left to preserve her family's story. She was going because that one day was closer than she had probably expected.

"Is she awake?" I asked.

Malcolm shook his head. "No, but I can let you know when she wakes."

"Please do. I will let her decide if she stays or goes," I said.

Malcolm frowned. "I'm not sure that is a wise idea," he said.

"And why is that?" I asked, slightly irritated.

"I know her type. She will want to go," he said simply.

I let out a hard breath. "Thank you for your concern, but the decision is hers," I said.

Malcolm nodded. "If she wakes in the night, would you like me to come inform you?"

"Yes. I will be sleeping in the back room near the back door. You can come through there so you won't wake anyone else. I'll let Mrs. Alves know that you might stop by."

Malcolm nodded and turned to leave, heading back to his house.

Nadia stepped up beside me as I watched Malcolm disappear into the night. "So that is why she was so desperate."

"It seems that way," I said, lost in thought.

"Do you think she even wants to save her family's story? If the stories about the Beast are true—" Nadia started.

"They aren't," I interrupted. "They are just stories," I said sternly, then turned and disappeared into the house, leaving Nadia and Otto on the porch.

I entered my room and began to get ready for sleep. My stomach was filled with butterflies and my mind was pulled in two directions, caught between my feelings for Solace and my need to finish this assignment. I took a long, deep breath in an attempt to calm myself. As I took off my shirt, I heard a noise behind me and glanced back, expecting to see Otto. But standing in my doorway was Yuuki.

"Isn't it past your bedtime?" I asked crossly.

Yuuki nodded but didn't leave. I took another deep breath and sank down onto my makeshift bed on the floor. "What do you want?" I prompted, suddenly too tired to be irritated.

Yuuki entered the room and sat down next to me. "Why are you sad?" she asked.

I looked at her. "I'm not sad, just tired."

Yuuki frowned at me in deep thought as she examined my face. "You're sad," she said plainly. "Why don't you know it?"

I opened my mouth but couldn't think of anything to say. After a moment, I settled on repeating myself. "I'm not sad, and you need to go to bed," I said as I stood up and shooed her out the door.

As she left the room, she turned and looked at me. "Do you not want to?" she asked inquisitively.

"Do I not want to what?" I said with a heavy sigh.

"Know that you are sad?" she said.

I frowned. I was not in the mood for this kind of conversation. I looked her in the eyes to tell her to leave but stopped, noticing for the first time that her eyes were hazel. They reminded me of the Beast of the Woods, although they weren't quite as green. I shook my head to erase the image. "I'm not sad," I repeated and shut the door.

I wandered back over to my bed and lay down. But I could not fall asleep. Otto ambled in at some point, but I barely noticed. *Why didn't Solace tell me?* I thought. *She could have gotten us all killed!* But then I realized something. I had taken her story at face value instead of investigating to see if there was a different reason she wanted to find the Beast. I had been so focused on my own agenda that I hadn't really looked into her motivations and why she knew about the doctor. Also, I would have come even if I knew she was dying because I had my own mission to complete. So, I really couldn't be angry at her. She had what I needed, and there was no way around that. *So, if I am not mad at her, then what is wrong with me? While I might have trouble with nightmares, I don't usually have trouble falling asleep,* I thought. *Maybe Yuuki was on to something. Maybe I am sad.* I rolled over onto my side. Maybe I was sad because, as Nadia had said, perhaps Solace played a much deeper part in why I had agreed to come on this journey than I was willing to admit. As that thought drifted through my mind, I closed my eyes for what felt like the thousandth time, and for some reason, this time, it worked.

Drawn to the Woods in my dream, I stood at the edge of its branches. They seemed to reach toward me like they wished me to come to them. The Beast of the Woods appeared, but this time not on the edge. This time it was deeper in the trees, its green eyes drawing me in. I took a hesitant step toward the Beast, toward the boundary that kept us apart. I felt sadness sitting heavy on my shoulders, adding to the growing burden of my life. It weighed me down, keeping me from crossing the boundary to enter the Woods. I felt like I might die under its weight. I cried out for help, but the Beast simply watched me. *No,* I thought. *It is not just watching me. It is staring.* Its eyes began to burn something deep inside me. It hurt, but there was something on the other side of that pain that I wanted. I did not know what it was or why I wanted it. But it was there. Then the sadness took over again, pulling me away from the Beast and the Woods it dwelled in, pulling me away from its gleaming eyes and back into the darkness around me.

I awoke to the sound of children playing. Daylight streamed in through the small window, casting a short shadow that told me it was midmorning. The remnants of the dream still hung in my mind as I sat up and let out a heavy sigh. I glanced around the room. Otto was already gone. I must have been tired after not being able to get to sleep for so long last night. *Tired enough that Malcolm couldn't wake me to let me know when Solace woke up? Or maybe she's still asleep. Unless...*But no, Malcolm would definitely have woken me if she worsened during the night. Either way, I needed to go check on Solace and Ivan. I put my boots on over my pant legs and grabbed my shirt before exiting my room and heading out the back door of the house to find some water to wash up for the day. When I stepped out the door, I almost tripped over Yuuki, who was sitting on the steps watching the other children play. She looked up at me and smiled.

"What are you doing in the walkway?" I grumbled.

"Sitting," she stated with a frown, as if confused by my question.

I ignored her and went to the rain barrel. I opened a spout at its base, letting some water flow into a trough. As I turned toward the trough, Yuuki was there next to me. She smiled.

"What do you want?" I asked irritably.

"Can I come meet your friends?" she asked as she clasped her hands behind her back.

"What friends?"

"The ones at the Carters' house," she said.

"I don't know if the Carters want you running around in their house when they have patients trying to rest," I commented.

"Oh." She pondered that statement for a moment. "I'll go ask!" she said happily.

I opened my mouth to stop her, but she was already gone. I sighed. Hopefully she would get distracted between here and the Carters' house. I turned back to the trough and washed up for the morning. The cool water snapped me out of my grogginess, and when I was finished, I pulled on my shirt and went back inside to get breakfast before heading over to see Ivan and Solace.

When I arrived at the Carters' front door, I was greeted by Elena, who welcomed me into the main room. Several people sat around a dark purple braided carpet in the middle of the wooden floor, surrounded by a couple beds and a table that contained medical supplies. Yuuki, who had apparently convinced the Carters to let her meet their patients, glanced up at me and smiled. I ignored her. She was sitting next to Ivan, joined by a few other village residents who were all listening to him tell a story about the time he had fought a giant horned bee, a larger, solitary version of a horned bee. Solace watched from her bed, and Malcolm stood nearby, listening and laughing at Ivan's exaggerated storytelling. Ivan always had a way of telling stories that seemed to hit all the emotions and draw in a crowd. As I watched, Solace smiled at me from across the room. She looked tired but a little stronger.

Malcolm approached when he noticed me by the door.

"Sorry, I was going to come get you when Solace woke up, but she wouldn't let me. Said you needed your rest," Malcolm said.

I nodded. She was probably right. "How is everyone?" I asked.

Malcolm smiled. "Well, Ivan is much better. While his wounds are still healing, the medicine we have here works better than most. He can walk and will be back in the saddle, I'm sure, sooner than my wife recommends."

"And Solace?" I asked, watching Malcolm's reaction.

He took a deep breath before proceeding. "She is stronger and will recover from this wound. But it took a toll on her."

"Do you think she can travel?" I asked as my gaze wandered to Solace. Her eyes were locked on Ivan as he demonstrated how he had managed to dodge the massive bee. Her mouth, slightly open in anticipation of Ivan's next words, curved into a grin as the story took a comical turn.

"I can give her treatment to help her maintain strength enough to travel, but she needs to take it slow, and she really shouldn't be traveling," explained Malcolm.

"Can I talk to her?" I asked, blinking and returning my gaze to Malcolm. "Alone."

He nodded and turned to clear the room. I moved to stand near the end of Solace's bed and waited until the two of us were alone.

"I'm not staying here," she said simply after everyone had left.

I looked at her with a flat expression, not wanting to give away my deep worry. "Why?"

"Because I need to get to the Beast. The only way I can protect this—"

"I mean, why didn't you tell me?" I interrupted.

She sighed. "Why would I? I barely knew you. I still don't. I've only known you for like a week...maybe a little more, but that's beside the point," she protested.

I crossed my arms and allowed a frown to crease my forehead. "You put us all in danger, Solace!"

"How?" she snapped back.

I leaned toward her. "That day in the swamp, I saw you holding Nadia so she wouldn't fall in the water. What if something happened and you let her fall? She would have died long before anyone could help her."

Solace sucked in a sharp breath to spit out a retort, but none came. Instead, she closed her eyes and leaned back into her pillows as she covered her face with both hands. When her hands fell from her face, she was holding back tears. "I'm sorry, alright? I...I just..." She looked into my eyes, forcing the tears away. "You don't know what it is like. I am the last person in my family, and I must protect this story. My parents died at the hands of these beasts just like yours did, and at their death, I took on the responsibility of protecting this story."

I hadn't taken the time to think about how she had come to be the only one left in her line. I could see now that we shared a similar pain, and it cut deep. My mother and Mary had both been killed by beasts that attacked our village. My tone softened a bit. "If you believe all this stuff about the Beast, then why don't you kill it and save your life?" I asked.

"Because this story is more important than my life!" she pleaded, leaning forward as she spoke.

"Why? Why is this so important to you?" I demanded.

Solace hesitated and I saw a look in her eyes that was becoming far too common in my life: guilt. Her shoulders slouched and she nodded. "Okay, you told me your family story, so I guess it is only fair I tell you mine." She took in a deep breath and let it out slowly as if buying time. Then she began. "I grew up in a small village of Chosen ones. My village had its own small band of self-trained warriors who fought beasts simply for survival so we could continue our mission. During the second year of the most recent war, I joined the warriors. I joined later than most but was allowed to train with the others anyway. I was, and still am, inexperienced, but there was one beast that was terrorizing our small village, and I wanted it to end. So, I went after that beast on my own." She shook her head at the foolish decision.

"When I found it, I quickly discovered I wasn't strong enough to fight and kill it alone. Having found out where I had gone, my mother and father appeared at the last minute with the other warriors and scared off the beast, but...they both perished in the battle." Solace held back tears for a moment before forcing her expression to go flat. "I was taken back to our village to heal, but I never fully recovered. I got sick. The two sides of my family both blamed me for my parents' death. They were right, it was my fault. But still they tried to help me. Half the family believed the story held a way to save my life, and the other half believed they couldn't use it without destroying the very thing they were meant to protect. So, they fought." She paused.

"It just got worse until no one was speaking with each other anymore. I couldn't forgive myself and they couldn't forgive me, or each other. Eventually, they sent me away to a doctor they thought could help. I think they just couldn't bear to look at me anymore. When I returned...they were all dead, decimated by beasts."

Solace sighed. "I am the only one left." She looked at me. "And this story holds something more important to me than my own survival. My family fought over their loss and never forgave each other, or me, and we will never have the chance to do so now. This story..." Solace shook her head. "You wouldn't understand unless you knew the story, unless you knew how important it is," she said hopelessly as she sank back into her pillows again.

I let out a breath. I had been selfish to focus only on my own pain. When my mother and Mary had been killed, I blamed myself. I still did. I should have been there to save them, but I was gone, needlessly celebrating a victory over a different beast. I sat down on the end of her bed and looked at her sideways. "Then tell it to me."

Her eyes snapped up to meet mine. "Tell you the story?" she asked, surprised.

"Yes, tell me the story. Help me understand why you value it more than your own life," I said softly as I finally let my worry show on my face.

Solace stared at me for a moment. Whether it was my desire to hear the story or the worry I finally allowed myself to feel and express that surprised her, I didn't know. After a moment, she let out a sigh. "Okay." She sat up in her bed and took a drink of water. I scooted back and leaned against the wall and listened as Solace told me the story she was tasked with protecting.

"A long time ago, before life as we know it today, there lived a mighty ruler known to all his people as the King. The King was beautiful and wise and dwelled in a realm known as the Kingdom, a wonderous place that flowed with a mighty force known as Original Power. The King used his knowledge and wisdom to manage the forces of Original Power and rule the Kingdom with his closest friend and confidant by his side. This confidant was known to the people as the Advisor, for he was their advisor, instructing them in the ways of the King.

"The King diligently taught the Advisor about ruling the Kingdom and helped him understand the Original Power that flowed through its boundaries. But as the Advisor's knowledge grew, so did his pride, and he became convinced that he, not the King, should be the one to rule the Kingdom and wield Original Power. The Advisor coveted the Original Power and tried to take it for himself in hopes that it would give him strength enough to overtake the King and rule the Kingdom for himself. But in his selfish attempt to control Original Power, the Advisor poisoned what little power he managed to take, turning it into a dark and rebellious force that became known as Corrupted Power.

"With this Corrupted Power, the Advisor began to infect some of the people and beasts of the Kingdom, growing the strength of Corrupted Power. All who were infected fell under the control of the Advisor, who rallied these subjects into an army of darkness. With this new, corrupt army, the Advisor attacked the dwelling of the King and attempted to kill him to take full control of the Kingdom. However, the King survived the attack because the Advisor's knowledge and Corrupted Power were no match for Original Power and the wisdom of the King.

"Angered that his trusted friend would turn on him and introduce such evil into the Kingdom, the King banished the Advisor to the Land Beyond, removing his connection to the Kingdom and turning him into a hideous mutation of what he once had been, forever to be known as the Creature. Bitter and selfish, the Creature's very being became like darkness and shadow, and, as his corrupted nature demanded, he vowed to have the Kingdom for himself.

"After a time, the King had a son whom the people called the Prince. The King, together with his son, used Original Power to build another kingdom, the Forest Kingdom. The King and his son filled the Forest Kingdom with creatures and beauty more wonderful than anything we know today. The Forest Kingdom was a special kingdom, for it is said that within this second kingdom, the King placed a light of Original Power itself to sustain the land and all that lived there.

"When the Forest Kingdom was completed, the King and his son placed within its boundaries a prosperous people. The King and the Prince so dearly cared for this second kingdom that they often traveled between the Kingdom and the Forest Kingdom, walking among the people, not only as rulers but as friends of the people. So, the people of the Forest Kingdom were happy. They were grateful for the Original Power that fed their land, and they loved the King and the Prince who wielded Original Power, for the King and the Prince ruled in love and peace, with Original Power at their side. The people even had an affectionate name for the King, the Prince, and Original Power; they called them their Lion! You see, the King and the Prince were one with the Original Power, and together they all led the people with might, as a lion leads its pride.

"One day, the Prince met a poor, beautiful woman from the Forest Kingdom and fell completely in love with her. The Prince loved this woman so much that he went to the King and asked if he would bless them in marriage. The King granted his son's wish, for he saw that the Prince's love for her was strong. So, the Prince and the woman were engaged to be married.

"As an engagement gift, the King decided he would give the Forest Kingdom to the Prince and his bride-to-be for their new home. However, the King knew that the Creature with Corrupted Power was plotting against him, for the King had been watching the Creature and knew he had his eye on this new kingdom. The King also knew that to take the Forest Kingdom, the Creature would try to corrupt the people who lived there, engraving his will on their very beings, filling them with fear and forcing them to bend to his will of darkness. The King knew that if this were to happen, the people would be in misery, separated from their Lion and, thus, the Original Power that protected them from evil. They would be lost to darkness and live out their lives in anger, pain, and suffering. So, before he gave the Forest Kingdom to his son, the King warned the people of this darkness that was born of Corrupted Power. He told the people that the Forest Kingdom was theirs to care for and live in, but if they ever left the Forest Kingdom to dwell in the Land Beyond, they would be consumed by darkness.

"One day, before the Prince and his bride were married, the Creature of Corrupted Power decided he would try to take control of the Forest Kingdom. So, he spun a beautiful lie and gave it to the Prince's bride-to-be as an engagement gift. The Creature told the woman that the Forest Kingdom had been made for the people but that the Land Beyond was hers to take, and the King was just testing her strength as a ruler and leader. He showed the woman the beauty of the Land Beyond and told her that the King simply wanted her and the people to be strong. He told her that if she led the people and they passed the test by taking the land as their own, they would not fall prey to darkness and evil, but the King would give her the Land Beyond so she could rule there.

"With the Creature whispering in her ear, the woman looked and saw the land's beauty and potential for towns and crops, and she was filled with a desire to be the leader of her own kingdom. So, she went to the Prince and told him she wanted the Land Beyond. But the Prince warned her that the Land Beyond was dangerous, shrouded in evil and Corrupted Power. Angry, the woman returned to the Creature and told him what had happened.

"'It is a trick,' the Creature told the woman. 'He does not love you, for it was simply your beauty that caught his eye in the first place. The Prince only wants the Forest Kingdom from his father as a wedding gift. Once you are married, he will have what he wants, and then you and all the people will become his servants.'

"The Creature's whispers filled the woman with shadows of anger, convincing her to believe his lie rather than trust her prince. So, the woman turned to the people and told them of the wonders of the Land Beyond, and they quickly forgot about their Lion and all they had been given. But as they took to the Land Beyond, the people were gripped with a dark force they had never known. The

Creature seized them with his Corrupted Power, and dread fell over them as darkness and fear infected them like a disease.

"In desperation, the people turned back in search of their Lion. They tried to escape the Land Beyond, but the Creature's darkness was now their own, infecting their very blood. The darkness within them tainted everything they touched, even the Forest Kingdom. The darkness that now owned them spread among the people and the earth of the Forest Kingdom, clashing with the Original Power that sustained the land and those who lived there. The darkness of Corrupted Power that now controlled them and the light of Original Power that had sustained them could not exist in peace. The people were trapped in pain and suffering, caught between two powers they could not control in a conflict that threatened to destroy them. They had chosen the Land Beyond, and it had cost them dearly.

"The King saw what the people had done, and he came to them, asking them why they had chosen the Land Beyond. He had made them a great people and placed them in the Forest Kingdom. He had told them of this dark place called the Land Beyond and warned them not to enter there. The King's questions ignited the Corrupted Power within the people, turning it to pain, anger, and selfishness, and they began to quarrel. Some pointed to those next to them, saying, 'They did it first!' Others explained, 'The Creature lied to us!' But worst of all, the Prince's bride stood before the people, and in anger she shouted at the King, 'You trapped us in the Forest Kingdom and plotted to keep us as slaves! The Creature you cast out told me the truth! I led the people here, I have conquered the Forest Kingdom, and with the Creature, I will rule these people and conquer the Kingdom as well!'

"The King was heartbroken by the woman's betrayal and that the people had chosen to leave him and were now unable to separate themselves from the grip of darkness. For what the people did not understand was that the darkness in their souls could not survive in the light of Original Power that flowed freely through the Kingdom. The King knew that if they tried to conquer the Kingdom, they would encounter Original Power at its full capacity—an encounter they would not survive. So, the King left them to the Land Beyond and the Forest Kingdom they had tainted with darkness. He corralled much of the Original Power into the Kingdom, leaving only enough to sustain the people and the land without harming them further, and he placed a powerful boundary that prevented Original Power from colliding with the Corrupted Power of the people and their land.

"So, the people roamed their dark, corrupted land filled with hardships and pain, and the woman rallied them to follow the Creature of Corrupted Power. In pain and darkness, they toiled daily as the power that had sustained them was no longer present with enough strength to stave off disease and suffering.

"But many of the people longed to be with the King and the Prince as they once had, for within their blood was a remnant of Original Power that drew them to their Lion and the Kingdom in which their Lion dwelled.

"Despite the people's disobedience, the King and the Prince wanted to help ease their pain until they could save the people from the darkness they had ignorantly chosen. For the King knew something the people did not. Original Power was written on their hearts because they were born in a land it flowed through. But over time, fewer and fewer people would be born with remnants of Original Power within their blood, and one day, Original Power would mark a final soul. On the day that last soul died, and only that day, the King would banish darkness forever. For the King knew that those loyal to him wished to live, but they would not survive what it would take to eradicate darkness and Corrupted Power.

"To help the people and allow those loyal to him to live, the King planted a small wood in the Forest Kingdom and placed a special beast within it. The King then picked the person he knew was most faithful to him, the one with the most Original Power flowing through his blood. The King told this chosen person, 'The mark I am giving you will grant you passage into the Woods until the invisible boundary that protects you from Original Power is lifted. Until that time, you may enter the Woods, where my beast will dwell. My beast has been given the ability to grant wishes from you and your descendants. From that beast, you may request a wish for protection from the corrupted beasts and the schemes of the Creature. However, each person in your line may only request one wish. So, each must use it wisely and selflessly.'

"So the people sought out this chosen follower of the King and that follower's descendants, calling them the Chosen, to help them seek protection from the darkness and evil that plagued them. But as time passed, the descendants of the Chosen suffered from Corrupted Power and began wishing selfishly, so the King removed their mark of passage, no longer allowing them into the Woods. He told them that they must wait for the beast to come to them, and the beast began leaving the Woods to visit the Chosen when the King told it to. But the Creature continued to spin lies, both small and large. As a result, the people forgot the beast's real name, simply calling it "the Beast." They started to believe that the soul of the Beast could grant life if the Beast were killed, and they began to hunt the Beast. So the Beast retreated to the Woods, vowing to never leave. It is believed that the Chosen still possess the ability to ask for a wish. But due to their selfishness, they are separated from the Beast by a deadly invisible boundary at the edge of the Woods, so no wishes can be granted."

# Chapter 12

I TOOK A DEEP breath and stared at the wall across from me. I could feel Solace staring at me, waiting for my response, but I didn't know what to say. I had heard bits and pieces of the story before, but never the whole thing. It was an interesting story, but I had no reason to believe it was true. Solace clearly believed it, but how could I? It seemed preposterous to believe that the Beast of the Woods could grant a wish or that it could save anyone from the Great Beasts that had attacked our town for as long as I could remember.

"Ben?" Solace said, pulling me from my thoughts.

"I understand the element of forgiveness in this story gives you hope. But how does this story help save people from certain doom?" I asked as I turned to look at her.

"What do you mean? Were you not listening? The Beast was put there so we could ask it for help if the darkness ever got too strong for us to handle! It can grant us what we need to overcome the Great Beasts of the Southern Mountains!"

"So far, we have survived without its help," I said simply.

"Yeah, we have, but what about the people we lost? The people who die in droves every time one of those Great Beasts of the

Southern Mountains rears its ugly head—what about them?" she pleaded.

I nodded. "But according to your story, you and your family were the only people who could get into the Woods without dying, and now you can't even do that because the Beast must come to you. So, even if it were true, the story and the Beast of the Woods are useless," I said. "And if it is the Beast that is so important, then why do you need to protect the story?"

Solace crossed her legs and sat up straight. She paused, swaying slightly as if dizzy, but then shook her head and leaned forward. "You don't believe me now? Imagine how much harder it would be for you, or anyone, to believe me if there were no story that had lasted for thousands of years, being passed down from generation to generation. If I just sat here and told you that the Beast of the Woods could save us all, you wouldn't even still be here." She explained, "It might be the information that people hear, but it is the story that people listen to."

I thought about that for a moment. She wasn't wrong. But I still had no reason to believe her story.

Before I could say anything, Solace threw her hands up in the air. "You still don't believe me!" She took in a deep breath and looked down at her hands for a moment before turning her gaze back to me. "Ben, whether you believe me or not does not make this story false."

I nodded. "And you believing it is real doesn't make it true," I said simply.

Solace stared at me in frustration, then crossed her arms and leaned back against her pillows again, suddenly looking tired.

"Solace..." I wasn't sure what I was going to say exactly, but I couldn't let her believe in a false hope. "I am sorry that you don't have anyone to pass this on to. I am. But you need to let it go and take care of yourself," I said, letting my concern show in my eyes.

She glared at me. "And why would you care if I am taking care of myself?"

I leaned forward and placed my elbows on my knees. I frowned, looking at the floor at my feet as if it held some answer I was searching for. "I just mean"—I hesitated—"you could stay here. We know where the doctor should be. I could take the others and go find him and bring him back here—"

"No," she interrupted me, "I am not wasting what little time I have left sitting in some bed waiting for a doctor. I have a job to do, Ben. There is no one else to do this job. Just me! And I don't care if you think I am crazy. I don't care if you think I am doing the wrong thing. I believe this story. Not because I have been told to believe it by my relatives—some of them gave up on it a long time ago. I believe it because it is true."

I looked at her. "And what if you are wrong? What if it is false, and you *are* wasting what little time you have left?" I pleaded.

To my surprise, Solace's frustration vanished. "I could be wrong. My grandfather once told me that the story has been passed down for so long that some parts of it have been twisted, and people have picked their favorite parts and let some of the most important parts be lost because people would rather they not be true. So, I am probably wrong in some way, shape, or form. But that is not the point."

"Then what is the point?" I asked, genuinely trying to understand.

"The point is this: I believe that the story is true. I believe that the King is real, and I believe that he put my family in charge of protecting this story and communicating with the Beast of the Woods to protect this world. I am dying. I can't pass the message on to someone in my line. But if I ask the King's beast to protect the story, I know it will, and then someone down the line who will live longer than me can figure out how to get back into the Woods and fix what we broke."

"How do you know that?" I asked.

"Because I have faith that the King will honor what he told us, and he will keep us safe through what the Beast was put there to do," she explained, her tone calm and her expression relaxing to match it.

I looked at her. She sounded crazy. The King from her story was certainly long dead. But for some reason, I didn't much care. Maybe it was because I had been having dreams and visions of the Beast since I had seen it myself. Maybe it was because, over the past three weeks, I had developed some kind of bond with it, even though I wasn't even sure it was anything more than a wild animal. I was confused, and for some reason, Solace's story made me feel as if something important was within my reach. *But what?* I still wasn't sure. The fog of grief and uncertainty I had been living in for so long was too thick for me to cut through, and I was too tired to try.

"So, you are risking your life to protect a story that may or may not be true, or possibly passed down incorrectly, because you have faith that an ancient king, who is probably dead, will keep his word," I said in summary.

"Yes," she replied simply.

“And even if he were still alive, why would he keep his word to a people who turned their backs on him?” I asked.

“Because he built his kingdom on love. Because he cared enough to find a solution even after the people had turned their backs on him. Why would he do that if he only meant to break his word?” she asked as she leaned forward slightly, allowing her passion to show in her eyes.

I looked into Solace’s eyes. Beautiful and brown, with traces of gold at their center, they reminded me of sunflowers. Though her body was tired, there was conviction and joy in those eyes—a kind of joy I didn’t understand. One that was not dependent on the world around her but sprang from the purpose that flowed within her. The Beast’s eyes came to me in that moment, but I blinked and turned away.

“Okay,” I said as I looked aimlessly at the wall. “I won’t stop you from coming, but at least promise me you will let the doctor try and help you when we find him.”

Solace considered that idea, then said, “Deal.”

I nodded, satisfied for now, and looked over to the window near the door. Ivan was outside playing with Yuuki, teaching her how to sword fight. I turned back to Solace and noticed she was smiling at me.

“What?” I asked.

“Yuuki is growing on you, isn’t she?” said Solace with a tired grin.

I frowned. “I wouldn’t say that.”

“Oh, but she is,” said Solace as she closed her eyes and leaned back into her pillows again.

I stood and pulled the blanket up higher on her. "Get some sleep. If you are coming with us, you will need to be strong enough to ride."

Solace nodded and rolled onto her side as I turned and headed for the door. "It's not just a story, Ben," I heard her say quietly. "You will see one day."

I didn't know what to say, so I simply closed the door behind me as I stepped out onto the porch. I stood there for a moment, thinking about everything she had just told me. I suddenly wanted to know more about this story. Even if it wasn't true, it was true to Solace, and, for some reason, that made it important to me.

The sound of laughter came to me from around the corner of the house, and I walked over to see Ivan and Yuuki sitting in the grass, watching Ivan's horse. The dappled gelding was standing in front of them, outside the pasture fence, untacked and unbridled, and Ivan was teaching Yuuki how to hold her hand out flat to feed the horse some grass. Yuuki giggled when the gelding curiously nuzzled her dress. As I got closer, I could hear Ivan explaining things to Yuuki.

"See, when you meet a horse, it isn't polite to just go up and pet it without permission," he was saying. "You want to let the horse come to you first."

"But what if it doesn't want to?" asked Yuuki.

Ivan laughed. "Then we should respect that decision. But there are some things you can do to help."

"Like what?" asked a curious Yuuki.

"Well, you can hang out with the horse like we are right now," said Ivan. "When I first got Buddy, I would spend hours in the fields just hanging out with him. He eventually came to enjoy my company and was interested enough to come say hello."

Yuuki giggled as Buddy nuzzled Ivan's shaved head and then his big bushy mustache.

Malcolm came up next to me as I watched Ivan and Yuuki feed the horse. "I'm surprised Yuuki warmed up to Ivan so fast. She is usually pretty cautious around strangers," said Malcolm.

"Really? I got the impression that she likes to ask a lot of questions." I said with a smile.

Malcolm laughed. "She is very curious, but she can get caught between the two—her curiosity and her shyness. She is often torn between her desire to explore nature's treasures and hiding from strangers."

I thought back to the previous morning at the stream with Yuuki and nodded. "Well, Ivan has a way with people. I don't know a single person who doesn't enjoy his company. Even people who don't like him enjoy being around him," I joked with a chuckle.

Malcolm laughed along with me. "I can see that. He has kept our home full of good stories and laughter since he arrived. We have enjoyed his company immensely."

Malcolm's expression turned serious for a moment, and he said, "I just wanted to let you know that although Solace shouldn't be riding on this journey, we have come up with a treatment that should keep her strong enough to do so. Still, I recommend as much rest as possible both now and during the journey," he said.

I nodded. "I plan on making sure she is well cared for, but I will not force her to do what we want. She can make her own decisions. She is a capable person and is quite determined to see this through to the end," I said solemnly.

Malcolm nodded and said that he would start making up some medication to take with us on the journey. His hope was that she would be strong enough to travel in a day or two. I thanked him and then headed toward the barn, where I figured Nadia would likely be tending to her horse as she did every morning.

When I reached the pasture behind Mrs. Alves's house, I met Mrs. Alves on her way to the house with a fresh pail of milk. She smiled as I approached. "You looking for Nadia?" she asked. "She's by the barn, cleaning tack. She put on quite a show this morning, practicing some moves with her knives—while on horseback!" Mrs. Alves shook her head in awe.

I smiled. "I am sure she did." Nadia and Ivan were talented riders, but Nadia was so good she had even been offered a job as a circus performer once. She had turned it down because she didn't like how they treated the animals.

I approached the barn and found Nadia sitting just outside on a bench, bent over her work. I grabbed a cloth and sat next to her. I had helped her clean tack on many occasions, and I knew how she liked it done.

"Solace is coming with us," I said after a moment of cleaning in silence.

Nadia's cleaning paused, and she looked up at me. "Is she better?" she asked, sounding surprised.

"Only a little, but she is improving, and she is determined to come with us," I responded.

"Will she be strong enough to ride?" asked Nadia.

"Malcolm says that they will make some medication that will help her keep her strength, but she will need as much rest as she can get. I respect her decision, but one thing I will not do is let her stay up on watch. And since Otto is not up for the task, or more accurately, none of us are willing to put our lives in his hands, we will have to split that task among the three of us."

Nadia resumed her cleaning. "She could compromise our safety. We already have one person with us who can't fight, and now we are adding another who can't even help with watch. Plus, I know how you feel about her, so your attention will be divided."

"My attention will be fine," I said irritably.

Nadia looked at me with concern in her eyes. "Yeah, so you say..." Her voice faded as she looked back at her tack and finished polishing a metal buckle.

"Ivan is doing well, though," I added.

"That's not a surprise. I have a feeling he could have fallen all the way into the water and still somehow come out alive," she said with a grin.

We finished our work and began gathering up the tack to put it away. As Nadia stood, she smiled. "It looks like someone is quite curious about you."

I turned my head in the direction Nadia was looking and noticed Yuuki watching from Mrs. Alves's back porch. When she saw me look, she shyly pulled back through the door into the house. "I can't figure her out," I said, turning back to Nadia.

"What do you mean?" asked Nadia as I gathered the rest of her tack and we headed into the barn.

"Sometimes she follows me or shows up right behind me when I least expect it, and then other times she hides behind trees and watches me like I am some kind of wild man," I said with a confused shrug.

Nadia laughed. "She is just curious but probably not used to people like you. Notice the lack of soldiers in this village. Sometimes you can be a bit...edgy," she said with a smile. "She probably just wisely keeps her distance in those moments."

"Hmm." I glanced back at the house, but Yuuki was gone.

Nadia and I finished putting the tack away and went to find Otto. We needed to put a plan in place for our travels, especially since Solace and Ivan were still healing. My hope was that we could leave in two days and that the doctor would still be at the volcano or that we would meet him on his way back. When I had checked with Solace, she had explained that, to the best of her knowledge, he most likely left the Town the day before we did. So, we should catch him just in time, which was good because there was no guarantee that he would travel the same route back or even that he traveled this route at all. It was faster but more dangerous than a less direct route.

Once we found Otto, we gathered in the Carters' house with Ivan and Solace, and, as Malcolm finished dressing her wound, we began piecing together our next steps.

"When can we leave?" I asked, turning to Malcolm.

"While I still advise that Solace stay here, she is improving today, so you should be able to leave the day after tomorrow, as long as she takes the medicine we made for her and keeps her wound wrapped and dry," he responded.

"Can she go any sooner?" I asked.

Malcolm considered my question. "I wouldn't advise much sooner than that. Possibly tomorrow evening, if you wanted to travel at night, but no earlier than that. She needs to rest."

I nodded. "Okay, thank you, Malcolm. I really appreciate your help." We shook hands, and Malcolm left us so we could discuss our plans.

I turned to the others. "Okay, this doctor we are after will probably be about three or four days ahead of us by the time we leave here unless he took a longer, safer route, in which case we will beat him there."

"To my knowledge, he usually takes the shorter route. He goes fast," said Solace.

I nodded. "Okay, then we will have to travel fast to make sure we get there before he leaves." I turned to Solace. "Do you know how long he usually spends gathering plants for his medicines?"

Solace shook her head. "I am afraid that, at this point, we will just have to hope he is still there when we arrive or that we meet him on his way back."

I nodded as Solace voiced my own hope, but it was Ivan who responded.

"Hope it is!" he said with excitement.

Everyone smiled and mumbled their agreement. I turned and pulled out a map of the Forest and the surrounding areas that Mrs. Alves had provided us. This map had been developed by people in the Village who had explored the Forest not too long ago. They had made the map to help them keep track of what locations were safe during each season. The map showed the river we had been following as it snaked its way through the middle of the Forest, starting at the Woods and ending at the Great Volcano. The section of the river between the Village and the Great Volcano was labeled as unpredictable during the spring months. But it was still the fastest way to the volcano.

"Okay, we are going to keep to the path we were planning on taking, which will lead us through this part of the Forest along the river," I said as I gestured to the map. "The river starts getting warm about here, and its temperature will supposedly reach the boiling point by the time we reach the barren land near the Great Volcano," I explained. I glanced at Otto. "Otto, you have been studying the Forest with Mrs. Carter and the rest of the villagers. What exactly is between that volcano and us?" I asked.

Otto considered the question for a moment before responding. "During the spring, that section of the Forest is unpredictable. A few villagers have told me that the Great Volcano and the boiling water are really the only problems, but a couple of people said they have seen things there—things they can't explain." Otto rubbed his chin in thought. "Actually, they don't even know how the river works. By all intents and purposes, it should not be boiling. The whole thing is a mystery. In short, they ultimately advised that we simply avoid the volcano and the waters near its base, especially during the spring."

"What was it like during the winter?" asked Solace.

"Frozen," said Nadia flatly.

I nodded. "Well, it's spring now, so we won't need to worry about ice. What we need to do is stick close to the river like we have been doing. It will get wider and meet up with the lava rock around the base of the volcano." I recalled our trip up there to lure the Great Beast to its death. Even in the winter, that place had been hot and miserable once we got close to the volcano.

Otto chimed in. "I heard that the river mysteriously mixes with uncooled lava, making the water even more dangerous."

I raised an eyebrow at that seemingly impossible detail. I hadn't noticed anything like that when I was up there in the winter. But I had seen plenty of the impossible on this trip, so it shouldn't surprise me that there might be more. "Well, since we aren't planning on being that close to the volcano, hopefully, we won't have to deal with that part. What we will have to deal with is here." I pointed to a place on the map about two-thirds of the way between the Village and the point where the river supposedly mixed with the lava. "This is the widest part of the river, and it has a small island in the middle. Solace, you mentioned that's where the doctor probably is," I said, turning to her.

She nodded. "That's what I've been told."

"That's what the villagers have said too," added Otto. He pointed to the tiny dot of an island on the map. "That island is bigger than it looks on the map. According to several villagers, that is where all the best medicinal plants grow, so that is most likely where we will find the doctor."

"Did they tell you how to get to the island?" asked Nadia.

Otto shook his head. "They said people have done it, but the river behaves differently each year, and sometimes there are strange natural—and unnatural—occurrences. It is a bit of a guessing game."

"What kind of strange occurrences?" asked Ivan with a raised eyebrow.

"One person said there are sometimes mirages, even when it's cold. Other people said there is red rain. The river is quite fascinating. As you mentioned, it has been recorded that in winter it is frozen, even in the hot area near the volcano, and in spring there is the issue of the water boiling. That should be impossible, especially since people have said that, despite the water's heat, the area is not nearly as humid as one might assume. Most of it sounded a bit too far-fetched, though maybe not, considering we are in the Forest..." He trailed off and was silent for a moment. But before I could interrupt, he added, "There was one strange occurrence that sounded interesting. There was mention that sometimes you could find a few floating volcanic rocks that might be stable enough and large enough to be used as rafts." Otto crossed his arms and rubbed his chin as his gaze grew distant. "I am quite interested in how they develop and why they break away from the other lava rock," he pondered. "A couple villagers mentioned that they can hold weight. One said she saw a wild horse cross the river on one, which makes no sense, for many reasons. Why would a horse cross the river? How does such a porous rock hold weight and not get hot? Why w—"

"Otto, please focus," I interrupted, my shoulders sagging slightly.

Otto blinked and looked at me. "Sorry." He cleared his throat. "Anyway, if the rumors are true, they could be a useful tool if they have developed this early in the spring. Ed mentioned they often don't show up until summer."

"Okay," I said. "Well, we will have to cross that bridge when we come to it." I glanced at the map. "We will maintain our trail up the river until we reach the island. Otto, is there anyone who knows more about what we will run into?"

Otto shook his head. "These people mostly come from the seaports; not many of them have traveled toward the volcano. They mostly avoid that area, as they get their medicine from the seaports each spring. It is safer that way."

"Then why do people go to the volcano at all?" asked Ivan.

"Because the medicinal plants that grow there are highly sought after. They sell in the ports for more money and are much more potent and effective than other medications. But it's a dangerous trip, so people often use what they have instead. It usually works the same way. It just takes longer for the body to respond," replied Otto.

"Okay, let's stay on topic here," I said. "Since we are not sure what exactly to expect, we will need to stay close and stay sharp. No one has mentioned those golden ghosts living on this side of the Village, but I think we should be prepared anyways. Ed says he thinks the weather should stay clear, so we will camp during the day and travel at night. I would rather be awake if anything attacks us. Hopefully, the stars and moon will provide enough light for our travels, and if things don't work out, we will reassess as needed. We should try to bring enough food from this village to last us until we can come back through here on our return trip." Everyone nodded in agreement. "Ivan, Solace, you both need to be careful. You're both still healing, and we can't afford any more delays." They both nodded in response.

Elena happened to enter the room then, just as our meeting was coming to a close. "Malcolm said you're planning for your trip," she said "You can take our pack mule for your supplies. That way, your horses will not be exhausted."

"I wouldn't want to take your livestock; you have already done—"

"It's nothing," she interrupted me. "We can get another one at the seaport this spring if something happens and you can't bring it back," she said with a smile.

"Thank you," I replied.

I turned back to the others. "Does anyone have any questions?" They all shook their heads. "Okay, Ivan, you gather the medication for you and Solace and then get some rest. Nadia and I will make sure we have all our tack and weapons ready for whatever lies ahead. Otto, talk to the villagers and make sure you get as much information as possible on anything that can help us make it through this section and the trip back. Solace, you need to rest if you want to go with us. So, sleep as much as you can. Everyone needs to sleep tomorrow," I said to the group. "Then we will spend the afternoon making sure we have rations for the trip, and we will set out at sunset."

# Chapter 13

THE NEXT DAY, WE all slept in as late as we could, none of us coming out of our rooms until after noon. Once we were all rested enough for night travel and Ivan and Solace were prepared, we gathered food with the help of Mrs. Alves, the Carters, and a couple of other families in the Village. Gathering food for the trip didn't take long, so we spent the rest of the afternoon individually preparing for the mission. We had all made friends here, and I was caught off guard by the melancholy mood as we said our goodbyes. But when the time came, we packed up and were on our way.

We traveled along the river all night. The stars were out, so we found our way relatively easily, and we were surprised by the ease of our travels. We made good time, and by the next morning, the river's waters were already warmer. Around noon, we found a good place in the shade of some trees and set up camp. Nadia left to get food, while Otto stayed back to care for Ivan and Solace. I went to the river to fill our water costrels.

As I crouched on the riverbank, Solace came up beside me to wash her face in the calm, warm water, and I watched her out of the corner of my eye. She looked tired, but if there was anything she had proven by this point, it was that she was a fighter, in more than one way. Not only did she not let her illness stop her, but she didn't let the views of others stop her either. She believed in the story more than anyone else I had met, yet she didn't seem bothered by the idea that I might think she was crazy. She fought for what she believed in but did so gracefully. Though she could get under my skin and certainly wasn't perfect, she seemed to live life with a focus I had only seen in soldiers on the battlefield. She had no clear enemy to fight. *Yet she is still fighting.* That thought brought a question to mind.

"Can I ask you something personal?" I asked her.

She looked at me, thinking for a moment. "Sure, why not?" she said as she sat down on the riverbank next to me.

"We have tried in the past to find where the Great Beasts come from. They live in the Southern Mountains, but no one has ever succeeded in finding them until they emerge and start a war. The rest of us have given in to the fact that we cannot find them until the next war starts. So why are you fighting when there is no enemy to fight?" I asked.

"Just because you can't see the enemy doesn't mean it isn't there," she said. "Just because something is beyond our view or understanding doesn't mean it's not a part of reality in life as we know it."

"So, you think you can figure this out when no one else can?" I asked with a grin.

She smiled. "No, but I think that I can choose to keep fighting. I think that I can choose to never give up even when everyone else does." Solace smiled to herself. "My mother used to tell me, 'If everyone else forgets, you be the first to remember.' Of course, she was referring to being polite, but I think it applies here as well."

I chuckled. "So you will fight until your last breath to do your part in a war that we cannot always see and do not always understand," I said, more to myself than to her.

Solace leaned toward me. "Why not?" she asked with a smile.

"Don't you get tired of people..." I paused, trying to think of a more tactful way to ask the question, but Solace beat me to it.

"Thinking I'm crazy?" she said with a sparkle in her eye.

I laughed nervously. "Yeah, I guess that is what I was thinking," I admitted. "But I was going to say it made you look...different." I shrugged. "Most people strive to fit in. Don't you get tired of people thinking you are crazy? These days that can be dangerous."

Solace laughed and asked, "What sane person ever changed the world?"

I chuckled softly and nodded. Though I knew she was exaggerating, as not all influential people are crazy, she made a good point. When I thought about it, it was the people who stood up and stood out who eventually changed things. The people who were strong enough to stand up under pressure and not care that the world might cast them out—people like Solace.

"The key, my friend, is to still care about the people who think you are crazy without letting them stop you from accomplishing your mission." Solace's words pulled me back to the conversation.

"Why would you care about the people who think you are crazy?" I asked. "Why should you give people like that any thought at all? The world doesn't care about you," I said, letting my mood darken.

Solace nodded. "I care because people are worth it, Ben. People are always worth it." She looked at me. "I don't have to spend time with people who think I am crazy or let them walk all over me, but I do care about them."

"Why?" I asked, genuinely curious.

Solace considered that for a moment, then responded, "Because of the story."

"The one you are trying to protect?" I clarified.

She nodded. "That story is about a king who loved his people, not because of their behavior, but despite it. He cared enough to provide for the people who had betrayed him and to give them instructions for how to get help, even if that help would only last for a moment. We often get help only to take it for granted or waste it. Yet he still offered it."

"But if he loved his people so much, then why didn't he just fix everything?" I asked.

Solace smiled. "I don't know," she said, "but I am quite enjoying figuring that out."

I looked into her eyes. She did enjoy it. She enjoyed the process, the relationship with the story that seemed to have some of the answers. "What if you are wrong?" I asked.

Solace's eyes drew me in as she answered. "What do I have to lose?" she asked.

As I gazed into her eyes, I suddenly realized why I was developing feelings for her. Her soul was what I saw each time I gazed into her eyes. Her soul was beautiful, so full of life. So full of hope. But I could see something else in her eyes now. Something that was distracting her and possibly even worrying her. I could see a flicker of uncertainty.

"You feel like you are missing something from the story, don't you?" I asked.

Solace nodded. "You ask a good question. Why didn't the King just fix everything? I have asked myself that same question. My ancestors have told this story generation after generation, but every time I tell it, I feel like something is missing. I must protect this story, not just to save the information about the Beast, but for whoever might one day fix what is broken. I must keep it safe until the rest of the story can be written," she explained.

I finally let myself accept what I had not been able to acknowledge for weeks. No, for years. I felt like my story was unfinished, like I had lost my purpose and was going nowhere. Like I was standing at the edge of a cliff with nothing in front of me but emptiness. I felt hopelessly lost in a world that was going swiftly nowhere but to pain and destruction. That was the real reason I was on this journey. I could have disobeyed General Delaney. I could have gone back and told him the doctor was gone. But Solace had shown me that day at the doctor's house, in a matter of minutes, what it meant to fight for what you believe in. And now she had shown me what it meant to fight no matter what, a lesson I had thought I had learned on the battlefield. But I was now realizing that I had only learned part of what it meant to fight. What Solace understood that I did not was what it meant to fight for what you believe, whether you are struggling or safe, hurting or comfortable, in motion or stagnant. What it meant to care about something more than yourself. I had once had that, but it had been taken away. I had spent so much time allowing what had been taken from me to drain my energy that I hadn't even thought to look at what I still had. Until I met Solace.

"What?" she asked softly.

She watched me, her eyes gentle, and her tone held such warmth that I began to wonder...Was she beginning to feel the same way about me as I did about her? *No. I can't do this right now. Stay focused on the mission.* "Nothing," I said.

I looked away and continued filling the water costrels. But just then, the Beast's eyes came to me in my mind's eye, and I realized something. I had looked away from Solace just now like I had looked away from the Beast in the Woods that night before we left on this journey. *Why do I keep doing that?* I suddenly felt like everything I needed was right here, or there in the Woods, or somewhere near me. But I just couldn't get to it. I remembered trying to get to the Beast in my dream, but something had held me back until I plunged into darkness.

I shook the image from my head and glanced at Solace.

"Do you think I am crazy?" she asked.

I smiled. "Definitely," I said with a playful grin. We both laughed.

I finished filling the water costrels as Solace stood and returned to camp. I couldn't help but wonder what would happen once we found the doctor. He knew how to get the Beast to come out of the Woods and would hopefully tell us without much prodding, but then what? We would have to travel all the way back through the same sections of the Forest. I was glad the villagers had enjoyed our company enough to invite us to stay on our way back. I was not looking forward to the journey home.

As I stood to return to camp, I spotted something small moving through the bushes near the edge of camp. Ivan saw me looking and made a questioning gesture. I motioned him to follow me, and, with weapons ready, we flanked the bush where the motion had stopped. As we readied ourselves for a surprise attack, there was a small sound, like a whimper. Ivan and I exchanged confused glances, and Ivan stepped around the edge of the large bush, peering inside.

"Hello there," he said in a soothing voice as a smile spread under his mustache.

Confused, I stepped back to give him room as he came out. To my surprise, sitting in Ivan's arms was Yuuki.

"What are you doing here?" asked Ivan gently.

Yuuki remained silent. Ivan sat down on the ground, placing Yuuki next to him as everyone gathered around.

"Give her some room, people," said Ivan as he spread his burly arms wide. "Now, why don't you tell us how you got here?" he said, turning back to Yuuki.

Yuuki's bottom lip stuck out, but then she said in a quiet voice, "I wanted to help you, so...um...I followed you."

"Yuuki!" I snapped, but Ivan interrupted me with a glare before turning back to Yuuki.

"Well, now, that is sweet, but it's dangerous out here. You could have been hurt," he said.

Yuuki shook her head. "I have lived alone before," she said in a small voice.

"Well, living on the docks in the seaport is much different from living out here," said Ivan.

"I travel here all the time when no one is looking," she said. "I like it out here."

Otto piped up, "Ed did tell me that he used to take her with him on trips to the seaport but stopped because she kept running off to explore the Forest."

Yuuki nodded and repeated, "I like it out here."

*This part of the Forest doesn't seem too bad,* I thought. Cloudy weather was the worst we had run into at this point. Yuuki exploring out here without getting eaten by something wasn't all that farfetched.

"What are we going to do with her?" asked Nadia. "We can't take her with us. Mrs. Alves will be looking for her."

Yuuki shook her head again. "I left a note," she explained, as if that solved everything.

"You left a note," I repeated. Children really did think life was simple. Her child scribble was probably illegible.

Yuuki nodded. "I told them I am with you and that I will be safe."

I frowned. We couldn't go back; we were already rushing in hopes that the doctor hadn't turned back and headed home already.

"What now?" asked Ivan with a shrug.

"She can travel with me," said Solace. Everyone looked at her in surprise.

"Solace, they will be worried about her," I responded.

"She left a note, and you know as well as I do that we can't go back now. We will lose a whole day, and that might be all it takes to make this whole near-death experience a waste," she said.

Solace was right, but the people in the Village would be missing Yuuki, and they had no way of knowing if she was actually with us. Plus, it looked like a storm was rolling in from the south.

Everyone was looking to me for an answer. Finally, Ivan said, "I vote she stays." Solace agreed, then Nadia and I looked at each other.

I looked at Otto. "What do you think?"

Otto seemed surprised by the question, as it was likely the first time I had asked his opinion about something other than natural philosophy. "Um, I don't think it wise, but she can't be sent back due to lost time, and she can't be left alone, as that is not what one does with a child of her age. So, I am afraid we have no other option."

*One of us could go back with her.* But I shot the idea down as soon as I remembered that Ivan was still not completely healed. Though he could fight, having at least two people fully prepared to fight was safer. That left Nadia and me. If I left, it might put the others in more danger than they could handle right now.

"Fine," I said, "she stays. But Solace and Ivan, she is your responsibility," I said as I pointed to them.

They both nodded in agreement, and Ivan began showing Yuuki around camp.

Nadia came up next to me. "This could slow us down more."

"It better not," I responded sternly as I looked at Ivan and Yuuki. "Ivan and Solace will have to make sure of it."

We all slept as much as we could that day. Sleeping during the day was hard when there were no caves around. But there were trees, so we were able to set up a makeshift tent and sleep with our blankets pulled up over our eyes. We were all tired from traveling all night, so it worked out well enough in the end.

As the sun began to set, we packed up and headed out. But we moved slower this time, as the clouds were rolling in and it was becoming harder to see as the stars and moon faded from view.

"It looks like it might rain," said Ivan as he examined the sky.

Otto nodded. "Most likely," he stated. "Then again, I have been told that the clouds are relatively perpetual the closer you get to the Great Volcano. There is a possibility that rain won't come until later. But heavy rains should be expected."

"Great," said Ivan. "That's just great."

We continued on through trees and bushes, and sure enough, the closer we got to our destination, the thicker the clouds got and the darker it became, making it nearly impossible to travel at night. As a result, we eventually had to change tactics. We traveled until it was too dark to see our way, then we slept until morning with a night watch rotation between Nadia, me, and, because we were running low on people who were up for the task, Otto. Thankfully, we made it through the night alive and woke in the late morning the next day.

We traveled all day through misty rain that only got worse the farther we went. Ivan was feeling well enough to take care of himself, but Solace and Yuuki would be at risk if they got too cold. *Hopefully, it will warm up as the river gets warmer,* I thought to myself.

We stopped later in the day and found a place to build a fire. Nadia set up a covering made of branches and made sure there were small openings to let the smoke out. We all gathered close to warm up before setting out again to travel until nightfall.

By Otto's calculations, we would arrive at the island by late morning the next day, and we were in for a full-on rainstorm. But, on the bright side, Yuuki was an avid traveler for someone her size and age, and Solace seemed to be holding up well.

The next day, we packed up and ate as we traveled. The river we were following had grown much wider and looked like it had reached a boiling point. The green trees and bushes of the Forest began to thin and become more sparse as we neared the volcano. The ground became rockier, and we had to keep an eye out for geysers, which became more frequent as we traveled. The first time we came across one, I narrowly missed getting hit by the boiling hot water and steam that spewed from the ground.

In the late morning, just as Otto had predicted, the island came into view. Lava rock covered one side of the island, forming what could be described as a rugged but apparently solid shoreline. Beyond the island, in the near distance, towered the massive volcano known as the Great Volcano. Much of the island was covered in trees thick with vegetation, including what looked like vines and various smaller plants intertwined with their branches. The island was bigger than I remembered it being. It looked like it would take a couple hours to walk its length. The water around the island appeared to be just barely boiling and contained chunks of the floating lava rock Otto had previously mentioned. As Otto had suspected, there were few of these rocks, and none appeared big enough for even two people to stand on. To make matters worse, the geysers were everywhere, spewing steam and boiling water, and the rain was starting to come down harder, making much of the terrain slippery.

“Let’s camp here and figure out a way to cross,” I called to everyone.

We found a place to set up a shelter under some nearby trees, and while Solace and Yuuki rested, Otto, Ivan, Nadia, and I got to planning.

"We could wait for the doctor to come to us," suggested Nadia.

I had thought of that, but it would be risky. "I don't think we can do that. I don't know for sure if he will come this way or if he is even here. We need to find a way to cross so we can search the island," I responded.

We decided to let Otto stay with Solace and Yuuki, and the rest of us split up, looking for any way we could cross the river to the island. Nadia went north, toward the volcano, Ivan wandered around close to camp to see what he could find, and I headed south down the riverbank.

As I walked along the edge of the river, I suddenly had that feeling again—the feeling that someone was following me. I hadn't felt it since we left the Town. The hair on the back of my neck stood on end as I let my gaze wander across the terrain around me. Nothing. *There is no one out here,* I told myself. *Just the people you came with and the doctor.* I walked a little farther but paused when I thought I saw something in the corner of my eye. I glanced around, wondering if Yuuki had snuck out of camp to follow me. But still, I saw nothing.

I continued to travel along the bank, testing out a few floating lava rocks to see how much weight they could hold. Otto was right, they were mysteriously buoyant and could hold weight, so it was possible that we could each go across separately, on individual rocks. But they were not large and would be difficult to balance on. Suddenly, movement caught my eye again, and I turned to my right to see a man standing in the distance, on the barren riverbank.

I glanced around, wondering where he had come from, but when I looked back, he was gone. *Was that who has been following me?* I wondered. *If it was, why did he decide now was a good time to let me see him?* I asked myself, confused.

I grabbed a pistol and scanned the area around me. When I didn't see anything, I turned to head back to camp to warn the others that someone might be following us. But I was stopped short by the sight of the man I had just seen on the bank. He was standing several yards away, smiling. He wore a long brown duster and a wide-brimmed hat. He had no weapons that I could see, and his hands were at his sides so I could see they were empty. I relaxed slightly but made sure to keep my distance and watch my surroundings in case he wasn't alone.

"Hello, my friend! What are you doing so far out here?" the man asked politely. "This is a dangerous part of the Forest," he added, gesturing to the landscape around us.

"Who are you?" I demanded as I placed my pistol back in its holster.

The man put his hands up as if fending off an attack. "No need to be hostile. I don't bite," he said with a disarming grin. "I just wanted to tell you to be careful out here."

"And why would you want to tell me that?" I asked, my hand still near my pistol.

The man chuckled. "Just doing my good deed for the day. I have been traveling these parts for years, keeping an eye on what goes on out here so I can report to a village nearby," he explained as he took a couple of steps forward.

"The Village?" I asked, casually backing away. "They didn't tell me they had someone out here," I said, my eyes narrowing.

"Oh, they don't know I am out here this year. I come in from the port every few years or so and make observations. I stop by the Village before returning to the port to let the merchants know what they can expect to come from this area of the Forest, product wise, that is."

I nodded. I didn't know much about this area of the Forest, but his story seemed plausible. Even so, I kept my hand near my gun. Based on how our journey had been going, this could be a trap, or worse.

The man turned to leave, but then he stopped and turned back to face me. As he moved, the edge of his coat appeared to smear as my vision seemed to blur again, just like it had at General Delany's mansion and the cave. I blinked, trying to clear my vision, then stared at his jacket, but it looked normal. *I must be more tired than I thought,* I told myself.

"You need to take charge of your companions," the man said in an obvious warning. "This part of the Forest can play tricks on your mind. You are the only person in your group who can lead them through this safely."

"How do you know about my companions?" I asked with a suspicious frown.

The man smiled. "No one comes out here alone."

*The doctor does,* I thought as I clenched my jaw. "Why are you telling me these things?" I asked, paying close attention to his movements in case he reached for a weapon.

"Because I have met people like you before. A great leader, but one who values the opinions of his followers. In battle, that is helpful. But here, it can be dangerous. This place can play tricks on you, and if you do not take charge and rule over them, they will take over, and you will all end up in danger," he answered.

"Thanks for the advice," I said, watching him carefully.

"No problem," he said as he turned and disappeared into the trees a few yards back from the riverbank.

As I turned to go back to camp, I kept scanning the area around me. Patches of hardy grass grew here and there, but no one was in sight. The man had surprised me, and I didn't like it. I should be more observant. If I wasn't, I would fail. The thought of failing with so many people relying on me brought back a flood of war memories. Memories of the journey back down the volcano after we had killed the Great Beast, when that second smaller beast had shown up, catching me and my companions off guard. Beasts of any size were rare in the Forest. But still, I should have paid closer attention. If I had, perhaps my father and brother would still be alive. Or perhaps if I had been in charge of that mission, I could have ensured we all returned home safely. I pushed the painful memories aside as the man's words echoed in my head, describing me as a great leader. It was true. I was a good leader. Many people had told me so during the war, and I had led many people in and out of battle. I just hadn't taken the time to think much of it before.

For some reason, the trip back to camp seemed to take forever. I thought of Ivan taking the lead to say he voted for Yuuki to stay. I thought of Nadia at the start of this journey, telling me she would pull out if she didn't like how the trip was going. I thought of how Solace irritated me sometimes and how Otto thought he was above everyone else. Maybe this man was right. Maybe my followers were taking too much control. If we were going to get through this, I had to take the reins.

When I finally arrived at camp, everyone was arguing. Ivan and Nadia were fighting about who was better at making decisions, and Solace was angry that everyone was telling her she had to rest when she should be leading the way because she knew more about this doctor in the first place. Otto was complaining that he knew more about the types of plants the doctor would be looking for, so everyone should follow him. With the words of the man at the river echoing in my head, I strode into the center of camp.

"Everyone, shut up!" I snapped. They all looked at me with angry expressions. "I don't know what is going on, but you have all got to get it through your heads that this is a dangerous place. We cannot afford to get distracted. I have been running this mission, and that is how it will work until it's over."

To my surprise, Nadia stepped forward. "Ben, you have been compromised. You care too much about Solace's well-being. No offense, Solace," she added before turning back to me. "And you cannot lead us if you are too focused on her."

"Oh, and I guess you are the one who should take over," I snapped in frustration. A slight panic arose in the pit of my stomach. Solace did not need to know how I felt about her. I stole a brief glance at Solace and saw a hint of surprise in her eyes at Nadia's comment. But I could not tell if it was a good surprise or bad.

"Yes, I—" started Nadia.

Ivan interrupted her. "Don't get all high and mighty now, sister! You know your strength is in the shadows, not the lead."

Nadia's eyes turned hard as she glared at her brother. "You know *you* can't do it. You're still lame!" she snapped. "And I am perfectly capable of leading. I have done it many times!"

Solace frowned. "Just because someone is injured doesn't mean they can't take charge," she said, anger boiling below the surface like a geyser ready to blow.

Otto raised an eyebrow. "I assume you are referring to yourself? You can barely ride, let alone lead," he said irritably, lifting his chin.

"Look, would everyone just stop arguing?" I snapped, my voice raised. "We need to figure out how to get across this river, or this whole trip will be a waste."

Everyone scowled as they muttered some form of agreement. We each presented our ideas for how to cross the river, but a heated argument developed once again. It was only broken up when we all finally couldn't handle each other any longer and parted ways to various spots around camp. After a few minutes of ruminating on everyone's disrespect, I took advantage of a momentary break in the rain to go stand by the river and think. I had no idea why everyone was being so stubborn. I had led this group through this whole trip. Now we were on the last leg of the journey, and they all decided to turn on me.

As I stood watching the steam rise from the boiling river, Yuuki appeared next to me. We stood in silence for a moment, but then I realized I had no idea where Yuuki had been during the argument.

"Where have you been?" I asked in a stern voice that even surprised me.

Apparently used to my edginess, as Nadia had called it, Yuuki clasped her hands behind her back and twirled her skirt back and forth as she gazed at the river. "Looking for a way to cross the river like everyone else," she said.

I shook my head. "It's dangerous here, Yuuki. You need to stay in the camp."

"But I found one," she said, looking up at me.

"I'm sure you did, but you can't just wander off," I said irritably.

"But I didn't," she said, her bottom lip jutting out.

"Don't whine at me, Yuuki. You were the one who came on this trip without permission!" I snapped. "Go back to camp and stay with Ivan or Solace," I said, pointing toward camp.

Yuuki reluctantly did as I told her, and I let out a sigh. *At least Yuuki knows how to take orders.* As I gazed out over the river, I noticed that there were more lava rocks coming downstream. We were each going to have to get across individually on those rocks. There was no other way.

I turned and went back to camp, where I found everyone arguing again. "Be quiet and listen," I said. "We are crossing on the rocks. They are not big enough for more than one person at this point in the year, so we will each pick one and ride it across."

"That is insane!" exclaimed Solace. "You know I am too weak to do that," she admitted.

"So, you were complaining about us thinking you were too weak to travel, and now you are complaining that I want you to put in some effort!" I snapped. "Make up your mind!"

More arguing ensued, and I shook my head in frustration. We had spent the better part of the afternoon going around in circles like this, and I was suddenly tired. I pinched the bridge of my nose as a headache began to burn in my temples and between my eyes.

As I stood like that, listening to the arguing around me, I felt a slight tug on my coat and looked down to see Yuuki.

"What do you want, Yuuki?" I said with a sigh.

"I know how to cross," she said quietly.

I frowned. "Yuuki, let us figure this out, okay?"

Yuuki looked at the others. "Mrs. Alves says we shouldn't argue," she said with a frown.

I was not in the mood for this. "Well, sometimes people argue, Yuuki. It's not a good thing, but it happens." I looked down into her hazel eyes and noticed for the first time that they were filled with little bright green flecks. In my mind's eye, they faded into the image of the Beast of the Woods, staring back at me with those intense, almost glowing green eyes. My dream of the Beast flashed back to me. I had been pulled back into darkness. *But why?* I wondered. The answer suddenly sprang to my mind. *Me.*

# Chapter 14

IN MY DREAM, I had been consumed by darkness, separated from the Beast because of guilt, pain, and sadness from the things I had done. In my state of hopelessness after losing my family, I had taken jobs as a killer for hire, and the things I had done weighed me down with regret. In the dream, and in life, my choices were like a weight on my shoulders, pulling me into darkness that I didn't have the strength to battle. Looking down at Yuuki, I suddenly felt like a fog was lifted. I shook my head and thought through what had happened throughout the day. *Why are we all suddenly at each other's throats?* I asked myself. I let out a sigh. *We must all be tired.* I turned to go for a walk to clear my head, but about three minutes in, I realized that Yuuki was following me.

"Yuuki, I told you to stay in the camp," I said with an irritable sigh.

I grabbed Yuuki's hand and we headed back to camp. When we arrived, everyone was still in a sour mood, and Otto and Nadia were refusing to talk to each other. Thankfully, the rain had let up and the sun was attempting to break through the clouds, but it didn't do anything to improve our moods. Yuuki's words echoed in my mind. *"Mrs. Alves says we shouldn't argue."* I remembered the words of the man on the riverbank. *"I have met people like you before. A great leader, but one who values the opinion of his followers. In battle, that is helpful. But here, it can be dangerous. This place can play tricks on you, and if you do not take charge and rule over them, they will take over, and you will all end up in danger."* I looked at Yuuki, and her hazel eyes once again brought back the image of the Beast in the Woods. I glanced up at the people around me and realized that I had taken the advice of a stranger. And to make matters worse, one I was suspicious of. *Why?* I thought. *What is wrong with me?*

Yuuki tugged on my coat. "I can help," she said confidently.

Still questioning my leadership abilities, I decided to humor her. "How can you help?" I asked.

"I know how to cross," she said, pointing at the river.

"And how would you know that?" I asked as I squatted down in front of her.

"I thought of it when the man came to tell me I was smart," she said as she twirled her skirt back and forth again.

I frowned. "What man?" I asked, tension building in my chest.

"A man. He came and told me I was smart and should do it on my own. But Mrs. Alves always tells me to get help from adults," she said frankly. "He tried to tell me not to, but Mrs. Alves told me not to do what strangers tell me, so I tried to tell the others. But they wouldn't listen," she explained with a frown. "So, I came to tell you because you are not a stranger," she added proudly.

The simplicity through which she saw the world brought a faint smile to my lips. "You did a good job, Yuuki. What did the man look like?" I asked as my expression turned serious again.

She shrugged. "Um...just like a man. He had a long brown coat and a hat."

*The man by the river.* His warning came back to mind. "*This place can play tricks on you, and if you do not take charge and rule over them, they will take over, and you will all end up in danger.*" Suddenly, I had a thought. *What if the man's message was true, but he worded it in a way that would get me to focus on ruling the others rather than the true danger?* I thought. *What if it isn't the people I need to rule over, but the tricks?* I stood and went to the center of the camp.

"Did anyone else see a man around here earlier?" I asked, interrupting their brooding.

Ivan was the first to respond. "Yes, actually, there was a man who showed up and chatted with me for a bit. I almost killed him because he startled me so bad, but he seemed harmless after I calmed down."

Nadia nodded in agreement. "I saw a guy as well. We talked, but he didn't stick around for long."

Solace and Otto nodded as well, each explaining they had spoken with a man. For the first time in a while, we all agreed on something.

"What did he tell you?" I asked.

Everyone thought for a moment, then Solace responded first. "He just pointed out that I knew more about this doctor than the rest of you and that I should take the reins from here on out," she said.

Nadia frowned. "He told me almost the same thing, just a slightly different version." She considered that for a moment. "I don't know why I didn't realize this before, but it's odd that he even knew why we were here," she said, confused.

Slowly, we all came to the realization that we had each been deceived into arguing with one another. The man, whoever he was, had tried to convince each of us that we were better equipped to lead the way, and we fell for it. *Well, except for Yuuki.* I glanced at her, then at the others.

"We have been tricked," I said simply. "Again."

Otto piped up. "That makes sense. It would follow with our track record so far," he said clinically.

Everyone glared at him. "You're not helping, Otto," said Solace.

"I merely meant that it is entirely plausible that we all got drawn in by something that isn't what it seems, as that has happened a lot on this trip," he elaborated.

"Well, why didn't you just say that then?" said a still irritated Ivan.

"Okay, everyone calm down," I instructed as diplomatically as I could, motioning with my palms down. "We need to keep an eye out for anything suspicious and keep working on figuring out how to cross the river. We need to cross before dark. I don't want to waste any more time arguing, and I would like to be able to head back by tomorrow at the latest."

Everyone grumbled an agreement, and I felt Yuuki pull on my coat again. I looked down at her. "What?" I asked.

"I have an idea," she said again, this time pleading.

I opened my mouth to tell her to stay out of the way and let us think, but then I thought of the Beast in the Woods. What had kept me from the Beast were the choices I had made and the weight I carried because of those choices. Maybe I needed to change something. *What is the harm in letting Yuuki voice her idea?* I thought. So instead of telling her to be quiet, I shoved my pride down and took a lesson from Ivan.

I squatted down and looked at her. "What is your idea?" I asked with a smile.

Yuuki clasped her hands together. "Back in the Village, my friends and I would play a game where we had to sit in the river, each on our own log, and hold hands to make a raft out of them because we didn't have any string to tie them together. Then we had to work together to keep the logs from floating apart as we let the river take us to the other side," she said. "Maybe we could each stand on a rock and hold hands and get to the island that way."

I stared at her. Why was it that there were five adults with many more years of life experience, and it was the child who came up with the most helpful solution to our problem?

Nadia spoke up. "That's actually not a bad idea, Ben. Then no one rock would have too much weight on it, and we would be able to use each other for balance as we float across."

I nodded. "You're right." I looked at Yuuki. "Okay, Yuuki, we will give it a go," I said as she smiled bashfully.

For the next half hour or so, we managed to stay on task long enough to gather some satisfactory rocks along the riverbank north of our camp and plan out how and where we were going to restrain the horses and Betsy. Though our realization that someone or something was trying to deceive us had helped us argue a little less, we still bickered and almost slipped into the boiling water a couple times because of it. By the time we had gathered rocks that were big enough to hold each person, we had realized we would have to let go of our pride and work together to get this done, or some of us could die.

Since we didn't know exactly what to expect on the island, I figured we would need everyone's skills, and we couldn't leave Yuuki here alone, so we decided we would all have to cross. There was also the fact that sinister things were happening here. That mysterious man had gotten to us all, and I didn't want to leave anyone behind with a threat we didn't understand. With all of us going, we would have to pack light and make sure the horses were secured until we could get back. Hopefully, we would only be gone for one night.

"This is how we are going to do this," I said as I gathered everyone around. "We will get on the rocks one at a time, holding hands to keep us together. Ivan, you are the strongest, so you will have to stand on land and hold us near the bank long enough for everyone to get on their rocks. Can you do that with your bad leg?" I asked.

"Sure thing," he said playfully as he made a fist and flexed his muscle. For the first time all afternoon, we all cracked a smile.

"Okay, I will get on first, then Otto. Up next will be Solace and Yuuki, then Nadia, and Ivan last," I said. "As we get on, we will pull together to keep the rocks close to each other. Otto, is there anything we need to know about these rocks or the water?"

Otto considered my question. "These rocks are very unusual. I have tested them a few times and they do seem to hold out the heat, at least for a little while. However, we need to be very careful to avoid being splashed with the water. We also need to be careful about navigating the river flow, as the currents seem to fluctuate in intensity for no clear reason. I think it would work best if weight were distributed as evenly as possible on each rock. The best way to do this would be to have everyone sit or kneel instead of standing. However, based on the way these rocks feel, we would need to move quickly and probably couldn't sit for much longer than a few minutes before the heat would pass through our clothes and possibly burn us," he explained. "Once we are all on, we will need to shift the weight toward the island. That means the most weight needs to be on the side we are moving toward, so we will have to be strategic in how we form up once we are on the rocks. Also, breathing could get harder in all this steam, and as you have probably all noticed, we are sweating, which will make it harder to hold on to things." His voice lowered. "So, just stay calm and don't panic," he said, as if to himself more than anyone else.

"Okay, we will all sit down on the rocks. Solace, can you take Yuuki with you and have her sit on your lap?" I asked.

"Yes. It might take me a bit longer to get into position, but we can do it," she said, giving Yuuki a wink.

"Just remember, once we are all on the rocks, we will have to steer this thing," I said. "Since Ivan weighs the most, we will need to somehow turn the raft so that he is closest to the island. His weight will pull us in that direction, but we may have to lean with him to make sure we get all the way across."

Otto piped up again. "Once Ivan gets on his rock, as long as we all stay as close together as possible, his weight will shift the raft away from the bank and toward the island."

"Okay, we will have to help each other onto our rocks, then hold on to one another so we can pull together. We should also make sure that Ivan and I are next to each other to keep most of the weight on our side to use as leverage. Do you think that will help, Otto?" I asked.

"It should. We could also hold onto each other's clothes so we could keep a better grip and let go with one hand if needed. That would also allow us to pull together and organize ourselves in pairs so we do not have to try and hold together a flexible circle. Ivan's initial weight shift when he gets on his rock should push us in the right direction, especially if we lean with him. But remember, each of us must be careful not to lean too far, or we might fall off the rocks." Otto paused and considered something. "Also, once we let go of the riverbank, the river's current might spin us out of control, which means we will need to give it a bit of a push in the right direction so we will at least have momentum toward the island even if we do lose control."

I nodded and looked to Ivan. "Can you push off with something after you get on your rock?" I asked.

"It's possible. I could use a long branch to push off and help guide us," he said.

Otto nodded. "That should work. Just make sure the branch does not spend too much time in the boiling water, or it may wilt," he added.

Ivan nodded in affirmation, then turned to me and added, "Once we get out there, we need to have a way to make sure we don't float down the river past the island."

We all turned to look at the island, then back to where we had gathered our rocks. We had stashed our rocks north of our camp, where the river had carved a small inlet into the lava rock and earth that made up the beach. We had gathered the rocks there so they wouldn't float away, but we would have to pull them out one by one to get on them. If we got on them while they were trapped, it would be too hard to get into position to catch the current. From where the rocks were concealed, the island sat about fifty yards south and about twenty yards out across the water. This was going to be a challenge.

Solace suddenly pointed. "What about that tree on the edge of the island? The one with the bushes under it and big vines hanging from its branches. It has a low-hanging branch that has not yet grown into the water. Could we grab that branch or the vines?"

I nodded. "Good idea. But there is no place to get on land right there, as the foliage is too thick, so we will have to hold on and work our way to the beach over there." I pointed to the island's northwestern side, where the trees opened up to a small beach, which was really just an outcropping of lava rock that was even with the water level.

I looked at Nadia. "Since you are the most agile, you should be on Ivan's left so you and Ivan can grab the first branch on that tree."

Nadia agreed, but her brow furrowed as she asked, "How are we getting back when this is all over?"

The question had crossed my mind a few times. "I haven't figured that out yet. If we could find a way to keep the rocks from floating away, that might help. But other than that, we will just have to hope that however the doctor plans to get back will work for all of us." There was a moment of silence as I hoped that was the case and we wouldn't be stranded there until winter. I could only imagine the others were thinking the same thing.

Another possibility came to me. "Ivan, you have your big knife with you, right?"

Ivan nodded. "Never leave home without it!"

"Could you use it to carve a small boat from a tree?" I asked.

Ivan raised his eyebrows. "I could. It would take a while, but it is possible."

"You mean like that door you carved for the inn after that beast destroyed it?" asked Nadia with a smirk.

Ivan rolled his eyes, "It worked," he claimed. "And this is a boat we are talking about. It doesn't have to look pretty—it just has to be functional. I can do functional."

"True," said Nadia with a shrug.

With a nod, I looked to Otto. "Could a wooden boat make it across the river?"

Otto winced. "It depends on the wood used and how thick it is. Maybe once...maybe."

I nodded. "Then, worst case, one of us makes it back and can figure out a way to get some more lava rocks to those still on the island, or we can try grabbing ahold of some lava rocks as they float by, though it doesn't look like any get close enough to the island for that. For now, we will just have to hope the doctor has what we need."

With that hope in mind, we began putting our plan in motion. It was probably nearing three in the afternoon now, and, if all went well, we should be able to make it to the island just before dark, camp there, and then find the doctor in the morning. Ivan went off to find a big enough stick to steer us, and Otto studied the river currents hoping to find an accurate path to our landing point. Solace explained to Yuuki how she would sit in her lap so Solace could keep her safe from the water, while Nadia and I stood on the bank rehearsing what we were all about to do.

"Remember, Solace will be holding on to you. If you lose your grip, she might die," I told Nadia.

She frowned. "If it's only Solace you care about, then why don't you sit there?" she snapped.

I took in a breath. "Nadia, I didn't mean it like that."

She sighed. "I know. I don't know what has gotten into me. I am sorry."

"I know, so am I," I said as I looked across the water to the island. "This place has taken its toll on all of us, and I think we were unprepared after we got used to the comfort of the Village. Plus, I don't know what was going on with that man we all saw..." I trailed off.

Nadia took in a deep breath. "Do you think it was a hallucination?"

"I don't think so, because we all saw the same thing," I said.

She nodded. "Well, whatever or whoever it was, I can't help but think what might have happened if we had tried to cross while we were still arguing."

"We wouldn't be crossing at all. We would still be arguing and not even aware of Yuuki's idea," I said with a smile.

Nadia looked at me. "Yeah, what prompted you to listen to her?"

My cheeks puffed out as I took in a breath, then let out a sigh. "Honestly, I think I'm crazy."

"Why?" she asked.

I looked at her and then past her to everyone preparing for the trip that could kill us all. "The Beast of the Woods. I have seen it face-to-face." I looked at Nadia for her reaction.

"What? When?" she asked, her eyebrows springing up in surprise.

"About a week before this all started. I was riding out by the Woods when it came to me, right to the edge. It just sat there and looked at me with these piercing, almost glowing, green eyes. But someone came around the corner, and it vanished." I sat down on a rock. "I thought I was losing my mind, but I have felt...I don't know...drawn to it, to the Woods, ever since. Anyway, Yuuki's hazel eyes reminded me of the Beast's eyes, and it kind of snapped me out of my own head. I just thought, what's the harm in listening to her idea?" I said with a shrug.

Nadia slowly sat down next to me. "Is that why you took this mission in the first place? Because you knew you might have a chance to kill the Beast now that you know it's real?"

I ran my hands over my face. "Honestly, I don't know why I took this mission. For a while, I told myself it was just a job. Then I told myself I needed it. I needed a break from the Town. I needed to get away. Even the reason you just mentioned probably crossed my mind." I paused and looked out over the river. "Maybe I really took this mission because it gave me an excuse to get closer to the Beast."

"What do you mean?" asked Nadia.

"I can't explain it, but it's like...it's like I need it. The Beast. It's like when I see it, I am close to finding something...Something I can't explain, but something I need. Something I have been longing to have for a long time," I attempted to explain.

"Peace," said Nadia as her gaze seemed to become unfocused.

I looked at her. "What?"

She smiled and turned toward me. "You have probably been longing for peace. To be free of the darkness that surrounds us. War, death, pain, loneliness, lack of purpose...the hopelessness of a world stuck in a cycle of war." She looked down at her hands. "I know it because Ivan and I have had this same conversation. Not the part about the Beast, but about that thing we long for that we don't have and can't seem to reach."

I leaned forward and propped an elbow on each knee, letting my face fall to my hands. She wasn't wrong. Though I had pushed it out of my mind for so long, I was longing for peace, which was something this world did not offer. For some reason, that thought reminded me of the old lady with the book, Ruth, and her words suddenly jumped to my mind. *"Maybe it is what that world has that this world lacks,"* she had said. My dream of being consumed by darkness flooded my memory. That must be it. I had wanted something from the Beast. That world—the Woods—had something this world lacked. Perhaps it was peace, or maybe it was something else; I had no idea. But I was suddenly gripped with a desire to find out. Worry twisted my stomach as I remembered my mission to kill the Beast. I didn't want to kill it. I wanted to learn from it. I wanted whatever it was that I was so desperately missing.

"Don't forget about the legends," Nadia said, interrupting my thoughts.

"What legends?" I asked, lifting my head.

"You know, the ones that say the Beast of the Woods will lure you to your death, like a siren," she said plainly.

I thought back to when I had stood on the edge of the Woods that night when we had decided to start this trip. I had felt drawn to the Beast, but the ever-looming threat of death from entering the Woods had stopped me. The Beast hadn't seemed angry at my choice, but almost sad, like it wanted to connect with me just as much as I wanted to connect with it.

"I don't know. It seemed different from what I have heard about sirens. It wasn't pretty or singing. It wasn't the way it looked or the way I felt physically or even the way it made me feel about myself that drew me in. It was...I don't know...it was like it had something...some part of me." I shook my head. "I know that sounds crazy."

Nadia pursed her lips. "Maybe not."

"What?" I asked, surprised.

Nadia shrugged. "After what I have seen in this forest, I don't know that I would be surprised."

I considered that for a moment. She had a point.

"I should tell Ivan that you saw the Beast," Nadia pointed out. "If something happens and the Beast turns out to be targeting you specifically, the more backup you have, the better."

I nodded. "Go ahead."

"Have you told Solace yet?" she asked.

I looked toward our camp, where the others were securing supplies and animals. "No," I said simply.

Nadia reached forward and grabbed my chin, pulling my gaze to hers. "You need to tell her the truth, Ben." She released my chin. "You told Malcolm that this trip was dangerous enough without people keeping secrets. I suggest you take your own advice," she said, holding my gaze until I nodded.

"I will," I agreed.

Nadia stood. "Good, then let's get going. It will get dark soon, and we need to make it across before then."

We returned to camp to ensure everything was set on this end and ready for our return. Otto claimed there were not many carnivorous animals roaming around, so the horses and food should be safe. But just in case, we put the food in one of the few nearby trees, and Ivan and I built a makeshift fence out of rope with bells attached every few feet. The twins' horses and Jeb had been taught to stay within the rope. Hopefully, Solace's horse and Betsy would not break through. We set up the fence in an area with a little bit of grass, though this close to the volcano, the ground was mostly dark lava rock with little ground cover. The grass wouldn't last long, but we didn't have much choice. If all went well, we would hopefully be back in the morning.

# Chapter 15

As we were finishing up with the horses, the sky decided it would be a great time to water the earth again, and it started to rain heavily. It was the last thing we wanted, especially since we were already sweating from the heat of the river. The rain would make it even more difficult to hold on to each other and stay on our rocks, but we would have to work with it. Once our camp was secured, we gathered where the rocks were stored and began moving them out of the miniature lagoon one by one, each person holding onto their own rock with a branch pressed firmly into the rugged top to keep it from floating away.

"Is everyone ready?" I asked once we were all in position.

Everyone nodded, and with that, I replaced the pressure from my stick with pressure from my foot and shifted my weight onto my rock, with Ivan holding on to one hand to keep me from floating away while Otto got into place. The rain had made the rocks a bit slippery, so I was careful not to move too fast. But once I sat down, time would be against us because of the heat flowing through the rocks from the boiling water. Using my free hand to grab Otto's outstretched hand, I crouched and settled on the rock in a seated position as gently as I could. I felt Otto's grip tighten as the river tried to carry me away from shore, but then it loosened as he quickly repeated the process with his own rock, followed close behind by Solace, who was holding his other hand, and Yuuki. Solace had instructed Yuuki to hold on to her in front so that Solace could use both hands. Nadia held Solace's free hand as Solace gingerly climbed onto her rock, slipping momentarily but managing to get on without any burns. Ivan shifted his weight backward as the current from the river increased its grip on the growing raft of rocks and tried to pull it away from the riverbank. As I looked to Ivan, I could see him struggling to hold his footing as the ever-increasing rain pounded into the bank where he stood.

Once Solace and Yuuki were settled, Nadia took her place on her rock. When we were all in place, Solace and Otto shifted their grip from holding hands to holding on to the clothes of the person in front of them. Otto held on to my clothes, while Solace held on to Nadia's clothes from behind as we pulled together so the rocks were lined up in pairs, with Ivan's alone near the shore. Nadia and I held Ivan's left hand and wrist as, in his right hand, he grasped a long, stiff branch he would use to help guide us. The three of us formed a triangle, with Otto behind me and Solace with Yuuki behind Nadia. Once we were all in place, Ivan scrambled onto his rock, his foot just missing the boiling water as the raft was taken by the current. Nadia and I shifted from holding Ivan's hand and wrist to grasping the back of his leather vest with both hands. The makeshift raft went into a slow spin as Ivan barely managed to push off the riverbank with his branch.

With all of us now on our rocks, we had to fight to keep them together without pulling anyone off their rock. The rain began pouring harder, adding to the chaos of the moment and making it hard to see where we were going. With most of our weight on one side, the raft drifted toward the island, carried along by the current. Though they were on the back of our makeshift raft, Otto and Solace had to hold on just as hard as everyone else so they could lean back to balance the weight and make sure the raft didn't flip over.

The raft was caught in the current and spun more than we had thought it would. As we spun so I faced upriver, boiling water droplets splashed against my rock and hit me. The urge to shift away from the scalding hot water was overwhelming, but I held on and held my ground, as did the others.

The raft continued downriver toward the island, continuing its slow spin until Ivan was in front as we headed toward the brush slightly upriver from the low-hanging branch. We reached the island much faster than expected due to the speed of the river current, which threatened to splash us with boiling water. As we neared to the island, Ivan dropped the branch he was using to help guide us. He reached out to grab the low-hanging branch, but it slipped through his hand. My heart sank at the failed first attempt to attach ourselves to the safety of the island. We were all drenched in warm rain, and so was the branch. With the first branch now out of reach, Ivan's other hand snaked out in desperation to grab anything he could get a hold on. All of us pulled on each other, trying to keep the raft in one piece as Ivan managed to grab some more flimsy-looking tree branches. As the current pulled us downriver, Ivan let out a loud fighting growl as he gripped the branches and attempted to bring us closer to shore. I released my grip on Ivan with my left hand and reached toward the bank to grab a branch as well, anchoring us in the current and pulling us a little closer to the bank. The rain poured down, and we all struggled to hold on to each other. With Ivan and I holding the raft more or less in place, Otto released his grip on me with one hand and grabbed onto some branches as well. But Solace, who was holding on tight to the back of Nadia's clothes with both hands, wasn't anchored to Otto, and the current slowly started to separate our makeshift raft and pull her and Yuuki farther downstream. Ivan, Otto, and I repeatedly shifted from one branch to the next until we ended up in a near straight line with Solace and Yuuki at the end. Nadia released one hand from Ivan's back to lock on to Solace with a forearm grip, but just as she did, Ivan's rock hit the rugged beach, and the jolt caused his wet vest to slip out of Nadia's grasp. Nadia and Solace floated past the main landing point but were able to keep their grip on each other, and Nadia grabbed another bush just a few feet downriver from our intended landing point.

I lost my grip on Ivan as well, but as he rolled onto the beach, he managed to grab my hand before I lost my grip on the branch as well. He immediately bounded to his feet, and with his help, I slowly stood and stepped from my rock to the beach while Ivan hoisted me up by my coat. Otto did his best to hold onto the spindly branch of a bush, but his other hand began to slowly shift down my coat as I made it to land. There was no way to secure the rocks, so they just floated on down the river without us. *I really hope the doctor has a way off this island,* I thought.

Otto tried to stand and follow me, but before I could grab his hand, he lost his footing and fell toward the water. Ivan lurched forward and grabbed him by the back of his shirt before he could hit the water. Instinctively, I grabbed Ivan to keep him steady, but Otto still had a hold on my coat, so I grabbed a nearby tree with my free hand to make sure we didn't all fall in together. Thankfully there was a good handhold, and I managed to hold on long enough for Ivan to lift Otto onto the safety of land.

Nadia and Solace were still downstream, holding tight to a bush, with Yuuki clinging to Solace. As soon as Ivan, Otto, and I were on land, we ran to help them. It took the three of us to make a chain and pull them back toward the beach. Once we were in position, Nadia smoothly crawled off her rock, keeping her weight low to keep her footing on the slippery rock as she and Solace tried to maintain their grips on each other despite their rain wet hands. With everyone but Solace and Yuuki on the land, Ivan was now able to simply reach out and grab Solace.

As Ivan pulled Solace off her rock, the rock spun slightly as it got wedged against the bush, and Yuuki's tired, wet grip finally slipped. Solace was pulled to land, but Yuuki dropped back onto the rock and began floating away from the shore. Without thinking, I immediately dove for her as everyone scrambled to grab my clothes or any part of me that they could and form a chain to keep me from falling into the water. I grabbed Yuuki's dress, and heat surged through my foot as I planted the sole of my boot in the boiling water to keep from going headfirst to my death. As soon as I grabbed Yuuki, I felt myself being pulled from behind, and the two of us were launched backward, where we all landed in a pile on the rugged ground, clear of the water line.

Though we all wanted to lie there and take a breath, the rain was coming down so hard that we felt like we were going to drown, and the river's edge was creeping closer and closer, steadily rising due to the heavy downpour. We picked ourselves up, and Ivan grabbed Yuuki, shielding her from the rain as I wrapped an arm around Solace. We made our way to the relative cover of the tree line, which we immediately found was concealing some small caves. We took shelter in the nearest cave that was up high enough to be safe from flooding. We were all too exhausted and wet to speak, so we just sat there, each soaking in thoughts of how close we had come to being boiled alive.

Thanks to the heat of the boiling river, we did not have to worry about being cold. But nonetheless, we made a fire and tried to dry out our clothes as much as possible as the little daylight that was able to make it through the clouds and rain began to fade. Solace was so exhausted that she fell asleep almost as soon as she stopped moving. Yuuki soon joined her, once Otto had dabbed some salve onto the small burns on her arms and hands where she been splashed with boiling water droplets. Otto then began tending to Nadia's left hand, which had been cut at some point by one of the branches she had grabbed, and I did my best to tend to some burns on my foot. Thankfully, those were the worst of our injuries.

With everyone settled in for the night, I joined Ivan at the mouth of the cave. We sat there in silence, each of us in thought, watching the rain while the others drifted off to sleep. Thin waterfalls dripped off the rock above us, falling across the mouth of the cave and hitting the ground below, where they created small streams that flowed down toward the beach. The sound of the rain hitting the stone and plants around us created a hypnotizing effect that seemed to numb my depressing thoughts.

After a few moments, Ivan glanced back toward Solace. "Nadia told me about the Beast of the Woods," he said calmly.

I nodded.

"Why didn't you tell us sooner?" he asked.

I shrugged. "I didn't think it was important at the time...and I thought you would all think I had lost my mind."

Ivan chuckled. "We all know I'm the one missing some marbles."

I laughed with him. I should have known that Ivan wouldn't be bothered by the news. He might look like a bear and be skilled in battle, but he had a way with people that stemmed from a respect for all living things—something that many believed contradicted his outward image. But it was one of my favorite contradictions.

"I can't believe we didn't die," Ivan said with a hard sigh. "And little Yuuki made it, too. I almost thought we lost her for a minute."

I looked back at Yuuki, who was asleep next to Solace. "Hopefully, this doesn't scar her for life," I said, more to myself.

"Nah," said Ivan, waving a hand through the air. "She is tougher than she looks," he said with a grin.

I smiled. "Yeah, I guess she is...Smart, too," I added. "We wouldn't have gotten out of our own way if it weren't for her."

"Maybe," said Ivan, "but I heard she had help."

I raised my eyebrows. "From who?" I asked, confused.

Ivan smiled. "The Beast," he said as he looked at me.

"What do you mean?" I asked with a thoughtful frown.

He shrugged. "Nadia said you were reminded of the Beast by Yuuki's hazel eyes, and that pulled you out of your own head long enough to realize that you should try something other than your own idea."

I thought about that for a moment. I hadn't realized it until now, but he was right. And this wasn't the only time. Every time we were in trouble, it was the Beast that pointed me in the right direction and helped open my eyes to what was really going on around me.

"I don't know what to do with this, Ivan." I sighed.

"With what?" he asked as he fiddled with a stick.

I shook my head. "Everything. The Beast. Solace. How am I going to handle things when we get back to the Woods?"

Ivan considered the situation. "One step at a time, brother, one step at a time. Things might not look clear now, but one day...one day we will have the whole story," he said as he slapped a burly hand on my back. "Then, when you look back to this point, the point when you didn't know what to do with what you had, you will remember what it feels like, and you will be able to help the next person." Something in his tone told me he was silently seeking answers of his own. For what dilemma, I was not sure. Maybe the allure of treasure had begun to lose its shine.

Ivan patted me on the back once more and stood, moving deeper into the cave to settle down for some rest. Darkness had fallen, and it was time for us to sleep. Thankfully, there was no one on the island but the doctor, and he had no idea we were here, so we could all sleep without setting up a watch. Tomorrow we would find the doctor, then somehow cross the river again, and, finally, head back home. I looked back to the rain falling outside the cave and mulled over Ivan's words. *I hope you are right, Ivan,* I thought to myself. *I hope you are right.*

The edge of the Woods was near, so near that I could reach out and touch it. As I stood there, I called to the Beast. I wanted it to come out. I wanted to see its eyes. The Beast came to me, its green eyes glimmering in the moonlight. I was so happy to see it; it was like a long-lost friend. I suddenly felt myself falling, pulled away from the Beast again. But this time, at the feeling of fear and guilt, I instinctively reached out to the Beast for help, as if it could somehow save me. To my surprise, it reached out to me with a forepaw and grabbed my hand. The moment it touched me, a flash of light burst between us, and I saw something. I didn't know what it was, but I knew I wanted it. It was what that world had that this world lacked. I pulled away from the Beast to reach for it, whatever it was, but the light faded and darkness engulfed me. The Beast's eyes held my gaze, and though it spoke no words, I knew it was calling me to come back.

Suddenly, I was jerked awake. I reached for a pistol but stopped short when I saw Yuuki sitting next to me.

"What's wrong, Yuuki?" I asked, letting out a relieved sigh. It was just a dream. Again.

"Miss Solace won't wake up." Her voice was small in the dark cave.

I was immediately up and moving. Ivan and Nadia must have felt the commotion because I saw them sit up as I ran to Solace.

I grabbed Solace's shoulder and shook it. "Solace!" I said desperately, panic filling my body.

Solace shifted slightly but didn't wake up. I relaxed some, knowing she was alive, but my heart sank when I saw her forehead. She was dripping sweat, not just clammy from the heat of the river like the rest of us.

Nadia appeared next to me as I felt Solace's forehead. "She is burning up," I said.

Nadia grabbed a water costrel and put it to Solace's lips. She drank, but only a small mouthful. "We need to find that doctor," said Nadia. "He might have something to help her."

I glanced around the cave, taking in the condition of each person. We were in a bit of a tight spot. Solace clearly couldn't go anywhere, and I honestly wasn't sure what to do with Yuuki, but I figured she should stay in the cave just to keep her from wandering off and getting lost. Otto was in the best shape out of all of us, but he was the only one who knew how Solace's medication worked. That left Ivan, still healing and sore, Nadia with a cut on one hand, and me with a bad foot. *I wanted us all to stay together, but we will have to make do with what we've got,* I told myself.

"Otto, you will stay here with Solace and Yuuki. I don't think there is anything on this island that will hurt you, but keep your eyes open anyway—that means staying awake." I handed Otto my knife and, ignoring his look of shock at holding the weapon, began making sure my pistols were dry and clean before loading their three revolving barrels with dry powder from my powder horn and lead balls. "Nadia and Ivan will come with me. The more people we have, the faster we will cover ground and find the doctor." I looked to everyone. "Any questions?" They all shook their heads, except Otto.

"I don't understand children," he said, looking a bit frantic.

Ivan smiled. "Not a problem, Otto." Ivan squatted down to speak to Yuuki. "You be good and stay here with Otto, okay? We will be back with help."

Yuuki nodded. "Okay."

Ivan stood up. "She's a good little one, Otto. She will stay here. Just try giving her something to do that will keep her in the cave," he said as he slapped Otto on the back.

Otto stumbled forward under Ivan's strong hand but nodded in affirmation before glancing at Yuuki with a wary expression.

Ivan and Nadia grabbed their weapons, and the three of us headed out, leaving Otto to watch over Solace and Yuuki.

The rain was still falling, but much lighter now. Once we got our bearings, noting we were on the northwestern end of the island, we split off in different directions, Nadia to the east side of the island, Ivan along the west side, and me down the middle. Part of me wondered if we should have just waited on the other side of the river until the doctor came back. I shook my head. I didn't need to think of that. We were here now, and we would have to work with what we had.

Ignoring my sore foot, I trudged across the soggy ground as the rain slowly soaked through my clothes again. There were plants everywhere, but it didn't look like much else lived here. Otto had mentioned at one point that there wouldn't be animals on the island, except maybe birds, as they had no way of crossing the river during the spring, summer, and most of the fall. Then again, someone had apparently seen a horse cross on a rock, though I was inclined to believe that was just a hallucination. In addition to the low chance of an animal being able to cross the river in spring, during the winter everything was covered in a thick layer of ice, making it impossible for anything to live here for long. But plants were everywhere this time of year as the wind, rain, and heat created a small tropical paradise in the middle of this death trap of a river. With the backdrop of the glowing, lava-encrusted volcano in the near distance, this mysterious island actually looked pretty spectacular.

I rounded a large boulder covered in the roots of a big jungle tree and continued through the underbrush. There were no signs of trails or any human activity, so the doctor must not be on this part of the island. I walked for about an hour before I exited the trees on the other side of the island. The beach that stretched out in front of me took my breath away. Cooled lava rock ran along the edge of the water, just like the beach we had landed on, but the river flowed much more gently here. Between me and the water, this beach was covered in all kinds of plants I had never seen before, each a vibrant color so bright I couldn't remember when I had last seen so much color. Delicate plants, sparkling with raindrops, grew in all shapes and sizes, covering the rocks that made up the beach. White, pink, purple, and blue flowers dotted the vines and ground cover. Some were striped, others had the most intricately arranged petals, and some were like glass, transparent and shimmering as the sun briefly peeked through the clouds.

In the middle of the beach was a man. He was sitting near a basket, gathering different parts of the various plants, careful not to disturb the vines they grew on. As I stared at the magnificent scenery before me, Nadia and Ivan came out of the jungle on either side of me and stopped when they saw what I saw. While the jungle behind us was all greens and browns, this place seemed to have every color in existence in the form of a plant.

Once we all recovered from our awe at the striking scenery, we worked our way through the delicate plants toward the man picking them. As we got closer, I saw that he was probably a little shorter than me and a bit broad in the middle, with a long gray beard and hair pulled back in a low ponytail. He was dressed in a dirty blouse and a pair of brown trousers. He had clearly been working all morning, maybe even since before sunrise, as he looked hot and tired. As we approached, he stood up and brushed some dirt off his pants. Understandably, his expression was full of confusion, and he glanced around as if trying to discover where we had come from.

"Good day to you!" he called out after apparently determining that there were no other unexpected visitors about.

During my walk across the island, I had decided to use my relationship with General Delaney to get this man to come with us. While my main intention was to ask him how to lure the Beast out of the Woods, Solace also needed his help. With all his special plants from this island, surely he had something to treat her condition. Plus, if I could convince him that General Delaney wanted him back in town, then he could care for Solace on the trip back. Otto had been doing his best, but he was no doctor. I could ask this man about the Beast later, but for now, I needed him to come help Solace.

Once we were close enough to converse, I introduced myself. "Hello, doctor. My name is Benjamin Arlin."

The doctor reached out to shake my outstretched hand. "I'm Dr. Darcio Batin. I would say it is nice to meet you, but I am not sure why you are here. I have never seen anyone else on this island," he said suspiciously.

I nodded. "I am here to take you back to the Town. General Delaney has requested your presence as soon as possible."

Dr. Batin remained silent for a moment, then said, "I understand...But I must confess that I have work to be done here, and I cannot return to the island this year once I leave. The trip is too dangerous to be made more than once."

I nodded. "I understand your situation, but I am afraid you will need to come with us now. Not only has General Delaney called on you, but one of my companions has fallen ill, and we need your expertise to help her," I said, leaving no room for argument. "She is with the rest of our party on the other end of the island."

The doctor hesitated and glanced around the clearing. "Okay, I can help your friend, but once again, I must stress that I cannot leave this place yet. These plants are very delicate and must be harvested in a specific w—"

"Like I said, I understand your predicament," I interrupted, "but we will have to discuss your departure from this place later. For now, our companion needs your help," I stated a little more forcefully.

Dr. Batin eyed me with narrowed eyes but nodded. "Okay, lead the way," he responded.

*That was easier than I thought it would be,* I thought to myself. I glanced at Ivan and Nadia. Ivan shrugged, and Nadia raised an eyebrow, telling me she was just as surprised as I was at how quickly he agreed to come with us. I nodded to her to confirm I understood her concerns, and the three of us exchanged glances, silently agreeing to keep an eye on Dr. Batin and watch each other's backs.

We trekked back the way I had come, leaving behind the colorful beach and heading back into the green and brown jungle, weaving through the trees and rocks as quickly as we could. As we traveled, I noticed the rain was beginning to fall harder, and the doctor began asking questions. While I was skeptical and remained mostly silent, Ivan was all too happy to tell him the story of how we had made it onto the island.

We arrived back at the cave in a little less than an hour to find Otto still waiting with Solace and Yuuki. The doctor immediately went to Solace's side as it was obvious something was wrong with her. He felt her head and instantly began giving orders. Otto had already raised her feet and covered her with more dry clothes. So, the doctor moved on to the next step. He reached into his bag and pulled out some vials. Each was filled with a different plant. He instructed Otto to take certain plants out and combine them to make a paste while the doctor made a different paste. One paste was placed in Solace's mouth, and the other was rubbed on her neck and under her arms over what the doctor said were areas that contained lymph nodes. *Whatever those are,* I thought.

Once they were finished, the doctor looked up. "She is ill with something I cannot cure, but I can help stave off the symptoms and cure her fever."

"What do you mean you can't cure it?" I snapped. "You are supposed to have the best medicine in the world!" I forced myself to push down the panic rising in my throat as I suddenly realized how desperately I did not want to lose Solace. I knew I had feelings for her, but I had not suspected until now just how strong those feelings had grown.

"I can't work a miracle!" he snapped back. "I just know plants. What she has is terminal." He took in a breath, and in a quieter tone, he added, "I'm sorry."

I stared at Solace. I couldn't deal with this right now. We needed to get moving. "She will have to travel. We must leave as soon as possible to get her back to town," I said sternly. "And get you to General Delaney," I added.

The doctor frowned. "Fine, but she needs to rest. I have a specially made boat that I cross the river with. We can cross two at a time. But we need to let her rest for now."

"Why can't we just go right away?" inquired Nadia. "It's almost noon, so we have time to get back on the road if we can cross now."

The doctor shook his head. "You don't get it. She is dying. If she does not get some rest, then she will not make it back to town at all!" he said, raising his voice slightly to make the point clear.

"Where is your boat?" asked Nadia as she crossed her arms.

"It is on the south end of this beach," he responded.

"I didn't see a boat," said Ivan.

Otto piped up. "It is most likely not on the water as it would eventually melt or wilt, depending on what it is made of."

The doctor nodded. "He is right. I pull it up onto the rocks in the jungle to make sure it cools off when I am not using it."

I glanced at Ivan and Nadia. None of us liked the idea of staying here any longer than we needed to. If we carried Solace, we could move now. While carrying her would slow us down, it would be faster than staying here until her fever broke, and it would do less damage than making her walk. *If she even could at this point.* "Okay, we will carry her to the boat on a bed. That way, we can move, and she can rest."

"I will need to get my things. I cannot leave them here! There are people counting on me to bring back that medicine," demanded the doctor.

"Fine. You and Ivan can go grab your things, and Nadia and I will get the boat ready. Where is it located exactly?" I asked.

The doctor hesitated for a moment, then said, "Go down to the other end of this beach and up the hill a bit. It is stored in a small cave there."

I looked at Nadia and she nodded, ready to go. As we left the cave, Ivan informed me that he and Otto could put together a makeshift cot to carry Solace before he and the doctor set out to retrieve the doctor's supplies. Nadia and I headed down the beach to find the boat, and as we walked, Nadia came up beside me.

"What are we going to do if this guy doesn't know how to get the Beast out of the Woods?" she asked. "We came all this way, and he can't even cure Solace's illness, so what if he is not as smart as she thought?"

I glanced over my shoulder to the mouth of the cave and then back to the beach ahead of me. "I don't know," I said as I forced myself to calm down and focus. "Let's just hope we didn't come all the way out here for nothing," I added in frustration.

# Chapter 16

NADIA AND I FOUND the boat right where the doctor had told us it would be. Stored in a small cave created by a tree growing over a pile of rocks, the boat was definitely unique. It looked like Dr. Batin had found a large lava rock and hollowed it out, reinforcing it with wood on the inside.

We dragged the boat out of the cave through the rain to the center of the beach, directly across from the cave entrance, where we would keep it on land until we were ready to leave. We flipped the boat upside down to keep the rain out of it, then headed back. When Nadia and I got back to the cave, Ivan and the doctor still had not returned with all his equipment, so we began preparing Solace. We wrapped her up in my coat to protect her from any splashes of water, then gently placed her on the cot that Otto and Ivan had made, which consisted of our jackets and some large leaves they had found. While we made sure we could get a good grip on the makeshift cot, we discussed who would go across in the boat first. I initially suggested that Otto go first with the doctor's supplies, but as Nadia and Otto began discussing that plan, I began to wonder if it wouldn't be better to have Solace cross first just to get her settled. Then she would have time to rest and recover while the rest of us crossed. Before I could bring up my idea to the others,

I suddenly wondered if I shouldn't mention my worries about Solace. Nadia had already claimed that I was compromised by my worry for Solace, and I didn't want to give them more evidence that was true, especially since Nadia had announced my feelings for Solace to the whole group. Then I realized there was another problem. Even if I did tell them to send Solace across first with Otto, Otto wasn't strong enough to move Solace out of a boat. Plus, it was still raining, which would make it even harder for him to move her on his own. *Nadia could do it.* I would rather leave Solace's life in Nadia's capable hands than Otto's nervous ones. Then, Otto could go across next with the doctor's supplies, and Ivan could go alone. That would leave the doctor and me to go last. I needed to keep an eye on him, so I was not about to let him cross on his own. *There is also the problem of getting the boat back to the island after each trip. We will need to work out a way to get the boat back and forth across the river since it can only carry up to two people at one time.*

My thoughts were interrupted when Ivan and the doctor returned. Once everyone was ready, we headed out to the boat to discuss plans on how to cross. The rain had turned to a heavy downpour, and the wind had picked up, adding to the already challenging situation. As we trudged across the beach, Ivan voiced the question that I had been pondering.

"How are we going to get the boat back to the island for each trip?" he wondered out loud.

"I have been thinking about that. I think whoever is on the other side with the boat will have to take it back upriver and give it a push. Then we will have to try and catch it," I suggested.

"That doesn't sound like a great idea," said Nadia. "Too many variables."

I nodded. "I had a feeling you would say that." I raised my eyebrows. "Anyone else have a better idea?" I asked, looking around at the group.

"We could just have two people row across and then one person bring the boat back," suggested the doctor.

Nadia shook her head. "The current is too strong after all this rain. One person alone would get washed downriver before they could make it back to the island."

The doctor shrugged. "That's how I do it."

"Well, it might work for you, but you've probably never had to row the boat over in a current like this." She sneered irritably.

The doctor considered that. "True. I usually just wait for it to pass."

"We could try that," said Nadia.

The doctor winced. "It might take a few days. It is hard to tell with these storms. Sometimes they come fast, but others stay for a while." He glanced at the dark sky filled with rain clouds. "This one looks like it will stay for a while."

"Which means the current may only get worse," I said.

"In this current, I don't think even I could keep the boat on track," said Ivan. "We only made it here because we were going with the current and managed to push off hard enough to get across before we passed the island. But it's been raining and storming almost constantly since we got here, so the current is even stronger now."

For a moment, everyone was silent. Then, of course, Otto spoke up. "I have an idea!" he said, raising his hand.

"And that would be?" I asked.

"The doctor has rope, a bow, and some arrows." Otto looked at the doctor's supplies and then looked to the doctor. "Why do you have a bow and arrow? There is nothing to hunt," he said, confused.

The doctor shrugged. "Some of the trees here produce edible fruit, and it's easier to get it down that way."

Otto peered back into the doctor's bag, then shrugged.

"Otto, you were saying..." I said.

"Ah, yes. Anyway, once the first person gets over, they could shoot a rope back here so it spans the river between the opposite shore and this island. We could tie each end to a tree, and that rope could act as a guide. Then all we would have to do is tie a small section of rope to the boat so it is slung over the guide rope, and then the boat won't float downriver out of reach. Then that first person could tie a third length of rope to the boat and shoot the other end over here to someone on the island, and we could just use that rope to pull the boat back to the island each time. A horse could also be used to pull the boat back the other direction, once someone gets over there and sets it all up, that is."

I looked to Ivan and Nadia. "That's not a terrible idea. It needs some improvement, but I think we could do something with it."

Ivan nodded his head. "It could work. If the ropes are long enough."

"Yeah, but there is one problem," said Nadia. "Otto and I had discussed Otto going over first with the doctor's supplies, but Otto can't shoot worth beans."

Otto glared at her, his brow furrowed. "How do you know? You have never seen me try!"

Nadia smiled at him. "No offense, but am I wrong?"

Otto's frown deepened. "No," he said plainly.

Nadia held back a grin and turned to me. "Told you."

"What if we got rid of the bow and arrow and just had one person hold the rope, or even just tie it to the boat as they cross the first time?" suggested Ivan.

I interrupted the conversation before someone else could speak. "That should work, but Otto still doesn't know how to rig the horse up to pull the boat back across."

"Good point," said Ivan with a nod.

Otto remained silent, obviously not wanting to agree or disagree.

"Nadia is lightweight and strong, so she can cross with Solace. Then Otto will go with the doctor's supplies and Yuuki, then Ivan will go alone, and then the doctor and I will bring up the rear," I said, leaving no room for argument and hoping no one questioned me.

Everyone nodded in agreement.

With that, Ivan and I measured out the two ropes the doctor had. They would cut it close, not leaving us much room for tying them to objects or holding on to the ends, but they would do, so we proceeded with the plan. Ivan placed Solace in the boat, and Nadia climbed in after getting one rope tied high in a tree so it wouldn't sag too close to the hot water while she crossed, holding the other end. Ivan and I held onto one end of the second rope while Nadia took the other end with her. We pushed the boat to the water's edge, and Ivan gave it a push so strong that it was halfway across the river within seconds, its movement aided by the wind and current. The boat carried Nadia and Solace downriver a bit farther than we had hoped, but Nadia managed to grab a branch from one of the few trees that lined the shore. Once she had a good grip, she began pulling the boat into a position that would allow her to get out. Still keeping the ropes that stretched across the water as tight as she could, Nadia wedged the boat in between some rocks and climbed out, dragging the boat as far out of the water as she could on her own before tying off the two ropes. Once the ropes were secure, she took a moment to catch her breath, then lifted Solace out of the boat as gently as possible and carried her upriver to our camp.

With Solace safely tucked away, Nadia returned to the boat, untied the ropes, and took them with her as she towed the boat upriver to our camp, slightly upriver from our position on the island. She tied the guide rope to a nearby tree and tied the second rope to the boat, making sure to keep them above the water. Then she retrieved some more rope from our camp, tearing down the horse enclosure to do so. Grabbing a shorter segment of rope, she tied one end to the boat's side, looped the rope over the guide rope, and tied the other end to the other side of the boat. Then Nadia tied a fourth rope to the boat, keeping one end of that rope with her so she could rig it to her horse and pull us back upriver.

Once the boat and ropes were set up, Nadia pushed the boat back out into the water and watched as we pulled it downriver to our position, guided by the rope that spanned the water. Once the boat reached us, Otto and Yuuki hopped in as quickly as they could without getting burned by splashing water, and the doctor and I loaded the doctor's supplies into the boat with them. We all had to move quickly, or, with all the heat rising from the river, the ropes would get too hot to handle.

By the time the boat was all loaded, Nadia had rigged up her horse to pull it back upriver. Ivan waved to her to signal we were ready, and Nadia's horse pulled the boat across the river in no time. With the wind and rain now in full swing, Nadia would not have been able to do it herself. The process was repeated until everyone was back across the river except the doctor and me.

Instead of leaving the guide rope strung out over the water, I cut it loose from the tree on the island and brought it with us. The rope might come in handy, and I didn't want to waste it. As soon as the doctor and I were ready, Nadia's horse pulled the boat upriver one last time. Finally, we were all safe and sound back across the river, with no more injuries to speak of.

Once we were all safely on land, the doctor informed us, "My camp on this side of the river is much farther upstream. I have supplies that I must retrieve, along with my horse."

I glanced at Nadia. "Can you go with him to retrieve his things?" I asked.

She nodded and looked to the doctor. "How far?"

"Not sure exactly. I'd say about an hour's walk," he said.

Nadia looked at me. "We can take a couple horses. We will be back as soon as we can."

The doctor frowned.

"What?" asked Nadia, crossing her arms.

"It's just that I don't usually ride...other people's horses. Mine is very docile, you see." He cleared his throat. "I would rather walk."

Nadia raised her eyebrow. "You want to walk for an hour?"

"Well...I would prefer—" he started.

"Fine." Nadia turned to me with eyes wide in annoyance. "We will walk, apparently."

I chuckled at Nadia's annoyance, allowing myself to feel some joy now that we were all back from the island, safe. For now. "Take your horse. You both can ride back once you retrieve the good doctor's horse."

Nadia nodded and I watched as they headed off toward the distant looming volcano. The volcano framed my view as they disappeared behind a cluster of sparse trees that somehow still grew here, and I thought back to that day. The day my father had died in my arms at the base of that volcano. The day I had lost what little I had left. My gaze shifted to Solace. *Now it is happening all over again,* I thought. *But this time, somehow, it is happening before I even have something to lose.* She was dying, and there was nothing I could do about it. To make matters worse, whether she lived or died mattered more to me than I wanted to admit to myself.

With the Nadia and the doctor gone, I busied myself with checking on the horses and getting our food down from where we had stored it in the trees. Then, in an effort to stave off the nervous feeling in my gut due to the situation with Solace, I began checking and rechecking all our belongings and tending to the horses.

As I saddled Jeb, Ivan came up next to me and put a hand on my shoulder. It pulled me from a daze in which I hadn't even realized I was lost. I glanced up at Ivan with a questioning frown.

"You look like you are trying to outwork your own mind," he said with a knowing look.

"I'm fine," I replied as I turned back to what I was doing.

"That's just it," replied Ivan. "You are far from fine, my friend."

I shook my head. "I'm fine, Ivan. Go find something useful to do," I said irritably, rain trickling down the back of my neck.

Ivan crossed his arms and leaned on a nearby tree. "I can't...You already did it all," he said jokingly as he gestured to the packed-up camp. "Did you realize you set up a shelter from the rain, or were you in a haze when that happened?"

I looked around me. Nadia and the doctor had probably arrived at the doctor's camp by now and would be back in less than an hour since they were probably on their horses now. And Ivan was right. There was nothing left to do. My gaze fell on Solace again, and my stomach twisted in worry. I let out a hard breath and leaned my forehead on Jeb's side. His calm breathing somehow helped me relax.

"You love her, don't you?" said Ivan gently.

I straightened, walked over to a nearby log that was far enough away that the others wouldn't hear us, and sat down. Ivan joined me, and we watched Otto and Yuuki tend to Solace.

I didn't want to talk about this. I was tired. Nadia had already gotten me to admit that I had feelings for Solace and had even brought it up in front of Solace back when we were all fighting after that mysterious man had shown up. I had not told Solace about my feelings, though. I didn't want to let myself admit I loved her. But the more I thought about it, the more I knew I had already done so. I loved her, and there was nothing that could change that.

"I didn't want to," I finally said out loud.

Ivan looked at me, waiting for an explanation.

"I didn't want to start down this path again," I added hopelessly.

Ivan considered my response. "What path would that be?"

I watched Solace. "I do love her. But it's too late now," I said. "She'll be gone soon. I am losing everything all over again."

Ivan looked at her. "I wouldn't give up just yet."

"I'm not giving up..." I said as uncertainty washed over me. I shook my head.

Ivan took a deep breath. "Solace is on this journey because she has something that none of us have ever really had," he said, looking at me. "She has faith, faith like I have never seen...We won many wars with the Great Beasts of the Southern Mountains, but each time, we lost a battle within ourselves. We lost hope. After every war, we grew to see that everything was worthless, hopeless—that it would all end at some point. So, we moved on and just did as we were told or what we thought would make us happy until the next time we would be lost in war." Ivan shifted his gaze to the fire. His expression made me wonder again if the reward for the Beast's life was losing its attraction, outweighed by something maybe even he had not yet fully latched on to. "Nadia and I lost ourselves in work at the inn and our daydreams of adventures and wealth." Ivan looked at the ground. "You lost yourself to loneliness, to fighting a battle alone, to pursuing what you thought was your purpose, doing what someone demanded of you simply because you thought that was the only option."

I frowned to myself. *Leave it to Ivan and Nadia to cut right to the heart of the matter,* I thought. But Ivan's words reminded me of my father's last words. "*The war was won long ago, but we fought this battle alone and lost. Yet time has not run out. Do not waste what you have by dwelling on what you have lost. Choose your friends wisely, and don't trust what this world tells you. Do not fight your battles alone.*"

Ivan sucked in a deep breath. "Solace, though..." He chuckled to himself. "She is something else...or has something else."

"Yeah, faith in a story that probably isn't true," I pointed out.

Ivan frowned. "No..." He looked at me. "She has faith in a king who vowed to protect his people if they would just ask him to."

I looked at him. "You really believe that story?" I asked, my voice raising slightly in disbelief.

"She does," he said simply. "And she believes it enough to come out here on what might be her last trip ever, risking her life and enduring pain because she believes that this story is real and that it contains the secret to surviving these wars."

"That story means nothing," I declared. I was tired. I was tired of the struggle and my constant confusion. Tired of not knowing why I was here or what I was doing.

Ivan shrugged. "It means something to her. So, the question is, what does she mean to you?"

I covered my face with my hands, trying to clear the fog that had plagued my mind since this journey began.

"Why are we here?" Ivan asked, realizing on a different level the importance of that question.

I took in a deep breath and looked up at the sky as if it would help me. "Ivan—"

"Just try to answer the question, Ben," he interrupted. "We have almost died more times on this trip than I care to count, and I have come to realize that we all started this journey completely for our own benefit," he said with raised eyebrows as he acknowledged the selfish motivations for our actions. He leaned over to me and added, "This trip might have started out as a quest for adventure and wealth to remedy our boring, purposeless lives, but now it is different. It means something, and it's high time we all admitted that."

I sat up straighter and stuck my tongue in my cheek, unsure how to answer him. *Maybe he is right.* I had spent so much time trying to figure out the answer to what seemed like a simple question. Why had I come here? Maybe that was the simple answer. I had done it for myself, because I had lost everything and wanted some of it back. Because I wanted something more than just to take orders from a rich man on a big hill.

"What do you want me to say, Ivan?" I asked tiredly. "Do you want me to tell you that in the beginning I didn't know why I was coming out here? That I put you all in danger because I was lost, alone, and wanted something in my life to make a difference instead of waiting around to just repeat the same fight in the same place that will most likely end in the same way?"

Ivan was silent for a moment, then he said, "What changed?"

I looked at Solace. Suddenly, I felt fragile and deeply exhausted, and panic began to fill my bones. "I am losing it, Ivan," I said, trying to hold back the fear rising in me. "I can't do this again," I admitted through gritted teeth.

"After this last war with the Great Beasts, you disappeared, Ben," said Ivan. "Not to make you feel worse, but you lost it a long time ago," he said with no trace of his usual joking attitude. He was serious. "You have got to let someone be a part of your life—be your family. You live in your barn, you talk more to your horse than you do to humans, and you hate your job, although you won't admit that to anyone except, funny enough, your horse!"

"I know how horrible my life is, Ivan, so thank you for the reminder," I snapped back.

Ivan stood and grabbed my arm as I rose to leave. "You have got to admit to yourself that your reasons have changed, Ben." He looked to Solace. "She is your reason now, and if you would just let go of your past losses and move on, you would be able to see that. You don't have to forget the people you have lost, but you need to move forward with your life and stop living in the past."

I shook my head. "I can't. You don't get it. I can't do life like you and Nadia can. I have nothing to go back to. I have nothing but my skills in war, and there is no war until the next horde of beasts shows up! And when those beasts show up, we will fight, and they will die as they always do, and then it will all start over again."

"Life is war!" Ivan snapped. "You are better at this than you think. And if you would just let go and let other people help you, you would not be fighting it alone!" he said sternly. Ivan pointed to Solace. "If you won't fight for yourself anymore, then fight for her."

I looked at Ivan. "And what if I fail?" I said, allowing my fear to crease my brow for a moment.

"Then we will move on to the next thing," he said in a calmer tone as he spotted the change in my expression. Ivan took a step closer and threw a heavy arm around my shoulders. "We got this, brother. Take a lesson from Solace and have a little faith."

"Faith in what?" I asked.

Ivan considered that for a moment. "In the power of a story," he said simply.

I took a deep breath, my cheeks filling with air, and let it out slowly. For the first time since my father had died, I felt like I was going to cry. But as I forced myself to calm down, the feeling subsided, and I turned to Ivan.

"We got this, brother!" he repeated. "Don't give up now. She needs you just as much as you need her."

With that, Ivan returned to camp for food, leaving me sitting on the log next to Jeb. *Have faith in the power of a story.* My mind replayed Ivan's words. As I let that idea distract me from worrying about Solace, I remembered what Solace had told me that day in the Village. *"It might be the information people hear, but it is the story people listen to."* I looked at Solace as I recalled my question to Ivan. *"What if I fail?"* I had asked. *"Then we will move on to the next thing,"* he had responded. *But what is the next thing? What could possibly give me more purpose than Solace?* I shook my head and forced myself to move on, but echoes of my conversation with Ivan kept drifting through my mind.

It was still a while before Nadia and the doctor showed up with all his belongings. But once we were all together again, we packed up and headed out with the boat in the doctor's cart and Solace resting inside the boat.

As we rode, I kept pondering Ivan's words, and, slowly, they convinced me to let go and accept my circumstances. I had come here initially because I was told to and probably because I thought there was some kind of purpose in searching for the Beast of the Woods again. But Ivan was right; this journey meant something more now. Solace had changed everything, and it was high time I admitted that.

Over the next few hours, the sparse terrain transitioned into thick forest once more. By the time we made camp that evening, we were all drained and sore. Crossing the river twice in less than a full day had taken its toll. On the bright side, Solace's fever had broken, and she was now awake but still regaining strength, along with the rest of us. None of us had the strength to hunt, so Otto and the doctor gathered edible plants instead of wild game. Otto worked on turning the plants into a stew, cooking in a pot from the doctor's supplies and stirring with a large wooden spoon. Everyone gathered around the fire, Solace wrapped in an extra blanket and propped against a log. She was still pale, but it was good to see her sitting up and speaking quietly with Yuuki.

As we waited for the stew to cook, I decided it was a good time to tell the doctor the real reason we needed his help, apart from caring for Solace. I sat down next to the doctor and thought through what we knew about him so far. He still seemed reluctant to go back to the Town, but he had come with us without much fuss and appeared to be a nice enough fellow. But I just couldn't be sure how he would take the news that what we really needed from him was to know how to get the Beast out of the Woods, which we could have figured out back at the island if it weren't for Solace's condition. Even though she was getting better, I wanted the doctor to accompany us at least to the Village, where she could get some much-needed rest before we started the journey home.

Uncertain exactly how to proceed, I decided a straightforward question was the best idea. "How do we lure the Beast out of the Woods?" I asked.

The doctor looked at me in surprise. "What?"

"You heard him," said Nadia, joining the conversation. "How do we lure the Beast out of the Woods?"

The doctor opened his mouth, but no words came out. After a moment, with everyone staring at him, he finally found words to explain. "I...There is a gas that can motivate it to come out."

"Like smoking out bees?" asked Otto.

The doctor's eyebrows raised. "Yes, like smoking out bees," he exclaimed. "This gas can dull its senses, and it can be lured out by..." He paused for a moment to gather his thoughts. "Well, by a meal."

"I thought it was some ancient creature that doesn't eat," said Ivan.

The doctor shook his head. "That is just a myth. It eats...people." He paused as if trying to come up with a better explanation but then settled with, "Just like the Great Beasts of the Southern Mountains."

Suddenly, Otto yelped and staggered back from the cooking pot, spoon in hand. Everyone turned to look at him.

"What's wrong, Otto?" I demanded.

"This leaf!" he said in shock. "This leaf is poisonous!" He held the large spoon gingerly out in front of him.

"What leaf?" asked Nadia, hurrying over to look at the contents of the spoon.

"This leaf that the doctor put in the soup! He is trying to kill us!" he yelled, pointing to the doctor.

I stood up. "Now, Otto, calm down. Maybe he just grabbed the wrong plant when you were out gathering food," I suggested.

Otto shook his head. "No, this plant is poisonous, and every doctor I have ever met has told me that, so he would know!" Otto dipped the spoon back into the pot and looked inside as he stirred. "And there is a ton of it in here!"

We all looked to the doctor. For a moment, everyone seemed to freeze. Then, suddenly, the doctor made a run for it. Ivan grabbed at him, but Nadia was closer. She grabbed his wrist and wrenched it behind his back. A knife seemingly appeared out of nowhere in her hand and she rested the blade on his neck. The doctor froze.

"So, it's true!" yelled Nadia in accusation. "You are trying to kill us!"

Solace turned toward the doctor, her face pale. "How could you?" she demanded hoarsely.

I frowned; this didn't make any sense. He had helped Solace at the cave when he could easily have killed her, and we hadn't done anything to threaten him.

"Why are you doing this?" I demanded.

For a moment, he looked small, and I thought he would make up some excuse to explain away his actions. Then, suddenly, his timid demeanor vanished. A horrible smile spread across his lips. "You have no idea, do you?"

"What are you talking about?" I demanded as I drew a pistol, pointing it at his chest.

"You so desperately want to know why you are out here?" he sneered. His eyes suddenly filled with hate and his face twisted in anger. "You are here to die!" he yelled as he grabbed Nadia's arm and yanked it away. She tried to grip him harder, but he managed to twist the knife from her fingers and run for the trees surrounding us. Thankfully, Ivan had moved to protect his sister's flank, and he swung his big fist through the air, landing a punch that knocked the doctor out cold.

# Chapter 17

IVAN SECURED THE UNCONSCIOUS doctor with ropes, and we leaned him against a log in the middle of camp, where we could keep an eye on him until we could figure out what had just happened. Otto dumped out the poisonous stew and began making a new stew that would be safe to eat.

"What just happened?" asked Solace, her eyes wide with shock.

"I have no idea," I responded, genuinely confused.

My mind was reeling, trying to figure out what this meant. Was there something in the air here that had poisoned the doctor's mind? Was that what had made us see the man on the riverbank and begin to argue? Or was there something else going on—something much worse?

"What are we going to do?" asked Nadia.

I frowned. "We are going to figure out why he tried to kill us," I said with determination. "But we can't do it here. If something happens and he escapes, we may never know why he wants us dead. Or worse, he may succeed. Let's just get to the Village, and we will interrogate him there."

"We can't put those people in danger," said Solace, her brow furrowing in concern.

"We won't be. Once there, we will be able to make sure he is secure, and we will not let him out of our sight. Plus, we will have the others in the Village to help us make sure he doesn't succeed at whatever it is he is trying to do," I said.

While Nadia and Ivan did their best to make sure that the doctor was secure for travel and could not escape his restraints if he woke up, Otto searched the doctor's things and concocted a mixture of plants to keep the doctor out of commission until we could get him back to the Village. We were all tired, and I needed time to think before we started interrogating him, or he might be able to work us all back into a frenzy like that man by the river.

The next morning, we traveled through the Forest along the river's edge, and I remained deep in thought about the events of the night before. This section of the Forest was not all that bad, and the weather grew more pleasant as we traveled, so things went smoothly. Thanks to Otto and the medicinal plants the doctor had prepared, Solace's condition had improved by the time we reached the Village late that afternoon. However, she was still weak, and once the villagers had greeted us, she was immediately taken to the Carters' home once again. Next, we took Yuuki back to Mrs. Alves, who was so happy to see Yuuki was okay that she didn't even get mad at her.

"Believe it or not, Mrs. Alves, we couldn't have done it without Yuuki," I told her as I patted Yuuki on the head.

Mrs. Alves gave a tight, worried smile. "I don't even want to hear about it. The worry has already frayed what little nerves I have left."

I chuckled. "Well, you should be proud of her. She is a smart and tough little girl," I said with a smile.

Once Yuuki was back with Mrs. Alves, the rest of us sat down with Ed to discuss what to do about the doctor.

"He might be dangerous," said Ivan, leaning against Ed's kitchen table and biting into an apple.

"What do you mean might be?" responded Nadia. "He tried to poison our food."

"Yeah, but he could have been intoxicated by something in the Forest," said Ivan. "Like whatever it was that might have made us all mad at each other."

Otto nodded. "That is plausible, considering everything that has happened."

I sighed. "I think that was just us being angry and taking the advice of a total stranger because we were tired and prideful."

Otto nodded again. "That is more likely," he stated clinically.

"Well, we won't know until he wakes up," said Ed. "I will make sure he is secure here and let you know when he is awake."

"Are you sure you are okay with him staying here? I didn't want to give him a chance to escape in the Forest, so I thought this would be the best bet. But if you don't think this is safe, I will find a way to do this elsewhere," I said.

"Don't worry about it, Ben. We might live relatively protected lives here in the Village, but that doesn't mean the lot of us haven't had to handle some sticky situations before," he said with a grin. "You will stay in the Village, and I will keep an eye on the doctor. In the meantime, let's make sure you all get food and rest."

I nodded. "Thank you, Ed. I really appreciate it."

With that, we parted ways, leaving the still unconscious doctor with Ed. Ivan, Nadia, and I stopped by the Carters' to get our wounds checked and attended to. Nadia's hand was the worst, but

Otto had done a good job keeping it clean, so the Carters didn't need to do much other than give her some medicine for the pain and change the bandage.

After our visit to the Carters' house, where we left Solace still resting under the watchful eyes of Elena and Malcolm, we returned to Mrs. Alves's house for much needed food. Then Nadia spent the rest of the evening trying to teach Otto how to use a bow and arrow while Ivan and I made sure the horses were in good shape and healthy enough for continued travels. Just after sundown, Malcolm informed us that whatever Otto had used to knock out the doctor would probably last until early morning, so we bedded down for the night.

The next morning, Ed came over to let us know that the doctor's drugs had worn off, and he was now ready for questioning. So, Ivan, Nadia, Otto, and I headed to Ed's, and when we arrived, he led us into a room where he had tied the doctor to a wooden chair. As Ed left, closing the door behind him, I sat on the bed and looked at the doctor, who was now fully awake. There was no fear in his eyes, only hate. Hate I did not understand. *Do I know him?* I thought. *Did I do something to him in my past?*

"Why did you try to kill us?" I asked sternly.

The doctor smiled. "You don't get it. You are so blind to reality. You choose to ignore what is real because you are too weak to deal with it!" He sneered.

I frowned. "You did not answer my question," I said flatly. When the doctor only laughed, I glanced at Nadia, giving a subtle gesture.

She darted forward so fast the doctor had no time to realize what was happening until it was too late. A small knife leapt into Nadia's hand, and she plunged it into the doctor's thigh. She left the knife in the wound, most likely for dramatic effect and to prevent him from bleeding out before we got what we needed. Just before the doctor released a scream, Ivan slapped his big hand over the doctor's mouth and held it there until his screaming subsided into whimpers.

"You stabbed me!" he yelled in shock as Ivan released his mouth. The doctor stared, eyes wide, at the knife sticking out of his leg.

"Yes, she did," I said plainly. "And she will do it again, or worse, if you do not tell me the truth, right now."

Fear crept into the doctor's face as he realized he was facing people who had done this type of thing before. He worked up an ugly laugh as he grimaced in pain. "You were never supposed to make it this far," he said through his laughter. "You were supposed to die in this treacherous place in your attempt to learn how to kill the Beast," he said menacingly.

"What are you talking about?" demanded Nadia. "Did someone tell you to kill us, or are you just insane?"

"Someone did." His evil smile twisted as he continued to laugh.

I signaled to Nadia again. With speed that made her movements look like one graceful motion, she slipped the knife from his leg with one hand and grabbed the wound with the other, squeezing it with a fierce grip as Ivan covered the doctor's mouth again, smothering another scream.

Blood seeped from the knife wound, and I heard a heavy thump behind me. I didn't react, as I knew it was Otto passing out. I had expected it. But if I responded, I knew the doctor would see it as a sign of weakness. So I left Otto to lie where he fell and kept my gaze locked on the doctor.

"Okay!" he yelled as Ivan released him again. Panting from the pain, the doctor opened his mouth to speak. "You..." He took a deep breath as pain contorted his face. "You were asking too many questions. So, I suggested that you be sent out here on a wild goose chase to find a way to kill the Beast. You have no family left so you wouldn't be missed, and if someone did go looking, they would believe you died trying to find me," he said, breathing heavily.

Suddenly, I lurched from my seat and grabbed the armrests on his chair. The doctor recoiled in fear as I put my nose mere inches from his face. "Tell me now who it was that sent you, or I will stab you in places that hurt much more than you ever knew possible!" I growled.

The doctor's eyes darted away, then back to me before he snarled his response through clenched teeth. "Valdra is coming for you. He knows you are here, and he is coming for you. Your precious General Delaney was fed up with you asking questions about why he wanted the book, losing interest in doing what had to be done, and challenging him and his commands." The doctor looked me in the eye as he repeated, "Valdra is coming for you. His soldiers can come and go as they please faster than you or me, fading in and out like darkness itself—demons wielded by the hands of General Delaney. Martecytes."

Suddenly, I remembered the people at the cave that night with Ruth. Their shadowy coats had moved like fog. I had thought it was my mind playing tricks on me, that I was seeing things. Then the image of the man at the river came to mind.

"That man at the river, who was he?" I demanded.

"One of General Delany's precious Martecytes there to make sure you died. How do you think Valdra knows where you are?" he sneered.

I stood and paced the room. "All this because of a book? That doesn't make any sense."

The doctor laughed. "You don't get it! That book, your ill friend—they are more important than you realize. Valdra is coming. He will be here sooner than you would think possible, and he will destroy them both!"

I couldn't believe it. The very people I had worked with for so long, the very people who had fought with me, and taught me, were now trying to kill me over a book. *But why?* I had not acted like the people General Delaney had tasked me to eliminate in the past. They had betrayed him and put the townspeople in danger. I had only asked questions. Something else was going on here, and it had all started with that book. I motioned Nadia to one corner of the room where we could speak in hushed tones.

"We need to get out of here, or we will put this whole village in danger," said Nadia worriedly.

"I know." I crossed my arms. "They will be coming by the shortest route, straight through the Forest—the way we came. If they can move the way he says, they are probably almost here already. But if we can find a faster way around the Forest, we might be able to beat them back to town. We need to get that book and figure out why it is so valuable to General Delaney."

I turned on my heel and walked to the door, stepping over Otto. As I pulled the door open, it got stuck on Otto, and I had to slide him out of the way before I could exit. Once out of the room, I went to find Ed. Hopefully, he would know about a different route around the Forest.

I found Ed on the porch, looking a bit worried. "That sounded intense," he said.

I took a deep breath. "I am sorry, Ed, but I have unknowingly put you all in danger," I responded as Ivan and Nadia stepped onto the porch behind me. "It turns out that someone wants me dead, and his soldiers are on their way here. We need to leave. Is there a route that will take us around the Forest?"

Ed nodded. "I can take you to the Eastern Seaport. There are some ships there that travel through the islands of the Eastern Sea. The trip is dangerous but fast and can get you back to town faster than if you went by land."

"I wish we had known that on the way out here," commented Ivan with a disappointed frown.

Ed shook his head. "These people don't take normal passengers. They would not have let you on board."

"That might work, Ben," said Nadia. "With people like that, we might not be found as easily."

I shook my head. "If Valdra is getting here soon, that means he has some way of knowing where we are that we don't know about. Not to mention the fact that if the doctor is not exaggerating and Valdra can get here faster than we think possible, then he is traveling faster than we did." I sighed. "If he can get here that fast, then he can get back that fast. And as soon as he knows we have left, which might very well be sooner than we think, he will turn around, and he might beat us back."

"It's a close call, but we might be able to get there in time. Where is the book?" asked Nadia.

"The only copy I know of was with General Delaney the last time I saw it," I responded.

"Then we will have to break in and grab it," said Ivan with a shrug before looking at me. "Did you really defy Delaney's orders?"

I shook my head. "No. I asked a few questions and have been less than interested in doing dirty work lately, but that shouldn't have driven him to want me dead." I frowned in confusion. "We need to get that book and figure out why it is so important to him," I repeated.

"First, we have to get there without getting caught by Valdra and his men. Our best bet is the sea," said Nadia.

I nodded in agreement. She was right. If we were to have any chance of getting back, we needed to leave now and get a head start. And the only way we could do that was by boat, or we would come face-to-face with Valdra and his soldiers, and we were in no shape to fight them. I had worked with Valdra for years and knew him well, but if he was after us, we were in grave danger.

"Okay, we will go by sea," I said. "We need to leave as soon as possible—"

Suddenly, a crash behind us interrupted me. I glanced at Ivan and Nadia, and after a moment of confused hesitation, all four of us rushed inside to the room where we had left the doctor. When we arrived, we found Otto standing in the middle of the room with a dazed look on his face, and the chair was tipped over on the floor, the doctor still securely tied to it. Blood pooled on the floor around the doctor's head. He was dead.

"Otto, what happened?" I demanded. But I was pretty sure he didn't know. Based on his expression, he was still not quite himself after passing out and might do it again after seeing the blood on the floor. But it appeared the doctor had tried to escape, falling and hitting his head on the corner of a nearby table in the process.

"I...I don't know. I just..." stammered Otto as he swayed slightly.

I let out a frustrated growl. "Never mind." I had needed the doctor to tell us more about what was going on. But now we had nothing but the knowledge that Valdra was coming, and we needed to leave.

Ignoring Otto, I turned to Ed. "Tell me about these ships."

"The ships are not well known, and they only dock at night," responded Ed.

Nadia's expression twisted in thought. "What exactly do they do?" she asked.

Ed smiled. "They...transport things."

Otto seemed to have recovered enough to throw in his two cents. "Those would be called merchant ships," he said with a confused expression, as if stating the obvious.

Ivan laughed. "He means they smuggle things, Otto. Things that are not legal."

Otto's eyebrows raised in shock. "Oh my." He looked at me. "We are going to entrust our lives to pirates?"

Ed lifted a shoulder. "They are not quite pirates, per se...They keep a low profile and avoid fighting with people to ensure their cargo goes unnoticed...and last time I checked, the cargo might be illegal, but it shouldn't be."

"So, pirates with a moral compass," said Nadia with a smirk. "How do you know these smugglers?" she added.

Ed hesitated as if unsure whether he should answer.

"Mrs. Alves," I said, suddenly remembering a conversation I'd had with her about her father. She'd said he was as close to a pirate as one could get without losing his morals.

Ed smiled and nodded. "She might seem like the mother of the town, but she had quite the adventurous childhood and has many connections in...that world," he said with raised eyebrows.

"How long would it take to get to the Eastern Seaport from here? Could we make it in time?" asked Nadia.

Ed nodded. "The Eastern Seaport is a little over a day's ride from here if you go fast. If you left this afternoon and rode straight through without stopping, you could get there by tomorrow night."

"Will there be a ship in port then?" I asked.

"Not sure. I heard Mrs. Alves talking about a ship last night, though, so maybe. She keeps track of those things," he added.

"Why?" asked Nadia.

Ed shrugged. "Like I said, she has an adventurous past. I don't usually ask questions. We all have things we keep to ourselves on one level or another."

I nodded and stepped forward. "We need to get out of here as soon as possible. I have no idea when Valdra will get here, but when he does, if we are here, I would not put it past him to kill everyone in the Village just to make sure no one knows what we know. But if there is no evidence we were here, he might just pass through."

"I can take care of that," said Ed with a confident nod. "And the doctor's body. Don't worry."

"What do we know?" asked Ivan.

I shook my head. "We don't know much of anything at this point, but he doesn't know that and probably wouldn't care even if he did."

Ed nodded. "Let's head to Mrs. Alves's house and get things sorted."

As we left Ed's house to make arrangements with Mrs. Alves, I sent Otto to update Solace and get anything from the Carters that Solace would need on the trip. "There is a ship in port right now," said Mrs. Alves once we had arrived and told her of our plan. "Captain Bates's ship. It is the only one of its kind that runs through the islands this time of year, and the eastern port is a common stop for them," she said. "They docked for repairs after a run-in with one of the leviathans. I am not sure if they were headed toward the Town, but I will make sure they get you where you need to go."

"How can you do that?" I asked.

Mrs. Alves smiled. "Don't worry. Just be ready to leave within the hour, and I will take you there and make sure you get on that ship."

We immediately began gathering our things and packing up the horses. We collected everything we needed for the trip to the ship and all the medicinal plants we would need for Solace to last us until we arrived back on land. She had improved under the Carters' care and was just strong enough to travel. But she wouldn't last long without their medicines.

As Mrs. Alves had instructed, we were ready within the hour. But once everything was taken care of and we were prepared to head out, a thought came to mind. *If I know Valdra, he will kill anyone who was on this journey with us.* The only way to give the villagers a chance was to leave now and hope that Ed could make it look like we had never been here. Just maybe they would be safe. Then again, maybe not. There was a chance the man at the river might have seen Yuuki.

As we gathered to leave, I approached Mrs. Alves. "I am concerned about Yuuki," I said, not wasting any time.

Mrs. Alves gave me a worried expression. "Why?"

I took a deep breath, trying to think of the right way to handle this. "Valdra is a brutal man. If the doctor was right, that means that Valdra knows exactly who was with us on that island, including Yuuki." I looked Mrs. Alves in the eye. "She may not be safe here...Her presence might even be a threat to everyone in town."

Mrs. Alves's face creased with worry as her gaze moved to where the children were watching the commotion. "She has already asked me multiple times if she could go with you. She has never really fit in anywhere, and the short time she spent with you..." She paused, tears threatening to spill over. Then, her gaze locked on to mine. "She should go with you. She will be safe with you; I know you will keep her safe."

I took a step back. *That wasn't what I had in mind.* "I...I was going to suggest Ed take her to the Western Seaport until this is over," I clarified.

Mrs. Alves shook her head. "I have not seen her warm to anyone as fast as she has to you and your friends. I know it is a lot to ask, but she will be safer with you. We have no idea when this will be over, and she has no one to stay with at the port. It is either here or with you. And if she stays here, we may all die," she said.

Solace had approached halfway through the conversation to find out why Mrs. Alves looked so sad, and now she looked at me.

Placing a gentle hand on my arm, she said, "She has a point, Ben. We can take care of Yuuki until we figure this all out."

I looked from Solace's reassuring gaze to Yuuki, who was watching us from a distance. When she saw that I was looking at her, she took that as a cue to join us. I let out a hard breath as she reached our group.

Mrs. Alves crouched down next to her. "Yuuki, you are not safe here anymore," she said in a gentle tone as she tucked a strand of hair behind Yuuki's ear. "You need to go with Ben and Solace."

Yuuki locked eyes with Mrs. Alves and nodded solemnly. "I know."

Mrs. Alves smiled and hugged her. "I love you, little Yuuki."

Yuuki hugged her back. "I love you too, Mrs. Alves."

Mrs. Alves chuckled and wiped away some tears. "You are a smart little girl," she said as she wrapped her in another hug. "Stay close to Ben and Solace; they will take care of you."

She nodded, and in a sad voice, she said, "I'll miss you."

"I will miss you too," replied Mrs. Alves. "Now go get your things and ride with Solace."

Yuuki hesitated for a moment, then wrapped Mrs. Alves in one more hug before running off to the house to grab her few possessions. When she reappeared, she had a small pack over her shoulders and was carrying a stuffed bunny doll. Yuuki found Solace, who was now astride her horse, and, with the help of Ivan, climbed aboard to sit in front of her.

With everything and everyone secured and accounted for, we waved goodbye to our new friends and followed Mrs. Alves, headed for the safety of the Eastern Sea. As we left, I fell to the back of the group and looked over my shoulder at the Village. I had started this journey not knowing what I was doing or why. Now it felt as if a fog was beginning to clear from my mind. I was here for a reason. I shifted my gaze to the people in front of me. All my plans had changed. I had started the journey lost and hopeless, with no purpose to speak of. But now I had Solace. *Maybe I was meant to be here...for her.* I did not know what the future would hold, but I knew I could not waste what little time I had with her. I would find a way to save her.

# Chapter 18

We traveled through the night and all the next day, arriving at the docks of the Eastern Seaport just before midnight. The docks were empty of people but filled with all kinds of ships and cargo that would offer good cover if a fight ended up going down before we got on the ship. Mrs. Alves told us to wait by the cargo that was to be loaded onto the ships, then disappeared into the dark shipyard. After what seemed like forever, she returned and led us through the stacks of cargo arranged near the docks. As we left the cargo area, we were careful to stay parallel with the docks but away from any prying eyes.

We continued south down the length of the seaport until we passed the last dock and started down a path that led through the base of a rocky outcropping, its walls growing taller as we went. The path eventually curved around a tall rock face that was filled with pockets of small caves and waterfalls, and I felt as though we were in a completely different world from the seaport. Then, just when I was beginning to get suspicious of being led into a trap, we wove through some large boulders and rounded a corner that opened into a massive cave on the water.

As we picked our way down the rocks to the makeshift docking port on the beach, I was stunned to realize that I was not looking at the night sky with a partially visible moon but rather a magnificently camouflaged pirate ship. The ship was a curious one. It seemed to resemble more than one kind of ship, and despite its size, it had oars. But it was beautifully crafted. The ship's hull was painted to blend in with the dark blue, almost black, waters below it, and the three masts held sails that were a beautiful matte blue and gray color that made them almost disappear against the midnight sky. As we came up next to the ship, I noticed that what I had thought was the moon was actually an elegant symbol on the main sail. Three thin silver circles overlapping at various points encased a silvery image of a sitting lion holding a broadsword in one paw. The double-edged sword was held so it covered half the lion's face. As a strong breeze tugged at the sail, I noticed that at certain angles, I could see the likeness of a lamb, safe between the lion's front paws. As moonlight shone through the sail, the image seemed to mysteriously resemble the moon itself.

"Hurry, this way," urged Mrs. Alves, snapping me from my analysis of the ship. "They are to set sail soon."

With haste, Mrs. Alves led us, still on horseback, right onto the ship, its deck busy with the crew preparing to depart. As we dismounted our horses, a tall sailor in a long, dark blue jacket approached us with a welcoming smile, walking with a brisk stride that made me wonder if he had ever been a soldier. Though his jacket appeared more formal than any of the other sailors' clothes, he wore no captain's hat upon his dark brown hair, and his uniform had no insignias or other additions to identify his rank or any military experience. His clipped, clean look and undecorated captain's jacket made it hard to determine where he might be from or what his purposes on the high seas could be, which was probably exactly the image he intended to produce.

Mrs. Alves gestured to the man with one hand and said, "This is Captain Nathanial Bates. He has agreed to take you all, and your possessions, through the islands to the port near your town."

I reached out to shake the captain's outstretched hand and noticed a smaller version of the image on the sail etched into the cuff of his coat. "Benjamin Arlin," I said, introducing myself as my eyes shifted from the symbol to his eyes. "Thank you for accommodating us at the last minute."

He offered a slight bow, and with a grin, he said in a deep, smooth voice, "Last minute is my specialty, Mr. Arlin. Welcome aboard."

As Mrs. Alves said goodbye to us, one of the crew informed Captain Bates, "Christopher says the *Lyonsword* is prepped and ready to sail."

"Thank you," Captain Bates responded. "Set sail as soon as Mrs. Alves is on land, then please show our guests to their quarters." With a curt nod and a clipped but even tone, the man responded with a "Yes, captain" and was off to complete his tasks.

As the man left, Captain Bates turned to me and said with a smile, "There is work to be done, so I must leave you with the crew. But I would be delighted if you could join me in my quarters for a meal once you are settled in."

"We will be there," I responded.

With that, the captain disappeared in the commotion of the crew as we turned to wave goodbye to Mrs. Alves. She waved from the shore as the *Lyonsword* was rowed out to sea, where the winds caught up the sails, pulling us out into the night.

The horses were stowed below deck in an area that looked like it had carried livestock before. It contained sections like stables that were bedded down with hay. Because of limited space on the ship, we were given one corner of the sleeping quarters on the level below the deck, but above the horse stalls, in which we would have to arrange ourselves. The crew's sleeping quarters were well maintained and looked more comfortable for their occupants than I would have expected on a pirate ship. We were given cots and hammocks as beds, and we each claimed our own space, just big enough for us to sleep in, except for Yuuki, whom Solace said could sleep with her. Once we were settled in, we headed to the captain's quarters.

The captain's quarters were nothing like the exterior of the ship. While the ship was built to blend in to its surroundings on the outside, the captain's quarters were built of unpainted mahogany, with blood-red curtains and golden accents. Cushioned seats lined the far wall under windows that looked over the water at the stern of the ship. On the port side was a made bed, and in the middle of the room was a mahogany map table and chairs. Off to the starboard side was a bookcase, a desk, and storage. Though it was a beautiful cabin, it was not so fancy as to make me think the captain was a wealthy man. Instead, it seemed to be built for purpose rather than flair.

As we approached the captain's desk, he was speaking with a crew member who looked a little better dressed than the rest, though his jacket was not as well cared for as the captain's.

"Benjamin, this is Christopher Ores, my first mate," said Captain Bates as they finished their conversation.

We each greeted him with a handshake and then, as Christopher left, I turned to the captain and introduced my companions.

"It is nice to meet you. So sorry we couldn't go through formal introductions sooner, but duty calls," said the captain with a smile. He gestured to some fruit and drinks on his desk. "Please, take some food; you are probably hungry after your travels. The cook will be providing more food later. But for now, eat as much as you like," he said politely.

I nodded. "Thank you, sir."

The captain eyed me for a moment, then said, "You are a military man, are you not?"

I smiled. "I am, sir. What gave it away?" I asked as I grabbed Yuuki's outstretched hand to stop her from pulling a plate of grapes off the desk. I gave her a warning look and she grinned innocently up at me as she took only a handful rather than the whole plate.

He smiled. "I have served in the battles with the Great Beasts as well. It takes one to know one." He gestured to the seats under the windows at the back of the cabin and said, "Please, sit down. I know the space in here is limited, but I would love to get to know my new passengers."

Once we had all gotten some food, we took our seats. The curved couches under the two windows were just big enough to fit three of us on each side, and the captain positioned himself at the edge of his map table, where he could stand facing us.

"So, tell me Benjamin, what made you want to board my ship rather than one that docks during daylight?" he asked politely.

I had been considering how much to tell this captain, but Mrs. Alves had said he could be trusted. "We are in a bit of a bind," I said, deciding to tell him the truth. I hadn't been completely honest with anyone for a while, and it felt odd, almost dangerous.

Captain Bates chuckled. "That I gathered. Mrs. Alves doesn't bring me just anyone. She knows this ship is as much a secret as a ship this size can be, and she would not waste my time with ordinary travelers."

I nodded in understanding. "We traveled to the Great Volcano in search of a doctor who gathered medicinal plants there," I began. "I was recently tasked with figuring out how to lure the Beast out of the Woods. The doctor was supposed to have the solution to that task. However, it turned out that I was deceived. I was sent there by General Delaney, the man I have spent my entire adult life working for. It seems that his use for me has come to an end, and I have been asking too many questions," I explained.

The captain considered my words carefully. "So you are on the run," he said, his expression serious. "What are your plans when you arrive at your destination?"

"General Delaney has a book that he tasked me with retrieving. It was my questioning of why he needed this book so badly that broke the camel's back, so to say." I leaned forward and placed my elbows on my knees. "I need to get it back. I need to know why he is so afraid that I may discover why he needs it," I said plainly.

The captain nodded slowly. "And where is this book now?"

"Last I saw it, it was with General Delaney," I replied, leaning back in my chair again.

The captain looked at me. "You gave him this book?" he questioned.

"Yes, sir," I responded, not quite sure why that was the part of the story he was choosing to verify.

"And where did you find this book in the first place?" he asked.

I glanced at Nadia. Her eyes were narrowed slightly in suspicion. She wasn't impressed with this line of questioning.

"All due respect, Captain, but why do you need to know?" I asked as I slowly sat up straight so I could watch his reaction.

The captain lifted his chin and regarded me with a frown that suggested he was unsure if he should be upset or intrigued. He held my gaze without wavering. "Last minute might be my specialty, Benjamin, but I like to know my cargo and what dangers it may bring," he replied in an even tone that left no room for argument.

I nodded. "Okay, then you should know that I don't entirely know why they want me and my crew dead. I don't know anything about the book except where I got it, and up until this morning, I didn't even know it was valuable enough to kill people over." As soon as the words left my lips, I thought about the man General Delaney had instructed me and Valdra to dispose of. Up until this moment, I had thought that man was a deserter who was trying to steal from General Delaney. But now that I thought back to it, I realized that was probably not the case. He may have wanted to keep the book to learn from it. Had the general actually ordered him killed because he wanted to read the book?

"And where did you get the book?" Captain Bates asked again.

"The mountains," I replied. "There was an old lady who lived near the base of the Southern Mountains. I was tasked with retrieving her and the book and handing them over to General Delaney."

"And you succeeded?" he asked, eyeing me.

I nodded. "Yes, sir."

The captain contemplated what I had just told him, then shifted gears. "Tell me about the people who have come for you. My crew are avid fighters, but I like to know what I might be getting into."

I shook my head. "I doubt they will follow us," I responded.

Captain Bates nodded. "Still..." he said, watching me closely.

Noting the captain's watchful eyes, I explained, "Their leader's name is Valdra." I paused at the sight of the captain's eyebrows raising. "You know him?" I asked.

"Of him. He leads a group of soldiers called Martecytes. Dangerous. They can move like shadows. Some say they are not really human, but ghosts. Others say they are neither. In reality, they are simply infected with a mysterious shadow that makes them...powerful."

*Infected with a shadow? How would that even work?* It didn't make much sense to me, yet I remembered what the doctor had said about them fading in and out like darkness. And there had been those people outside the cave and the man by the river. *Maybe I wasn't just seeing things and the edges of their clothes really did move like fog,* I thought as my stomach twisted. *Or shadow.* All the times General Delaney's soldiers had given me an odd feeling or seemed to appear out of nowhere suddenly made a terrifying amount of sense. "I have met some of them. I worked with them for years. The people of the Town do not dislike them," I said, confused.

The captain nodded. "General Delaney is not who he says he is, Benjamin. You would be wise to watch yourself," he added warningly.

I let out a breath. “I am starting to realize that.” Then a sudden thought crossed my mind. “Do you think they will be able to follow us across the water?”

“If they know you came this way, they might try. I am not sure how they get from one place to the next exactly. But they can move through town as shadows, reaching different locations much faster than any normal man could,” he explained with a look that said he had experienced their cunning in the past.

Ivan frowned. “How does one fight them if they are shadows?”

The captain chuckled. “Though many believe them to be ghosts, they are not. They are beings that can be beaten. You just have to know how,” he replied.

“Do you know how?” asked Nadia.

“Aye, I have fought one a time or two. They are merciless creatures,” he said, his eyes losing focus for a moment.

“How do you beat them?” asked Solace.

The captain looked at me and studied me for a moment before turning to Solace to answer. “There is an ancient power that very few know of these days. The Martecytes fear it. It is the only thing they fear,” he said ominously.

I frowned, but Solace’s pale face lit up. “That sounds promising,” she said, her tired eyes filled with excitement. “Can you teach it to us?” she asked.

The captain turned serious. “Power is not ours, Solace. You would be wise to never forget that,” he warned. Then his expression softened. “You all need rest,” he said as he stood and reached out a hand to end the meeting. “Thank you for being honest with me, Benjamin. I do appreciate it. My crew and I will do what we can to get you to your destination as soon as possible. If there is anything else you need, please don't hesitate to ask," he said with a smile.

"Thank you, Captain," I said as I stood and shook his hand.

The others stood as well, and we all took what food we had left over and headed to our quarters. We had been traveling for more than a full day and night and were ready to turn in. As we crossed the deck, one of the crew members came up to us and introduced himself.

"Welcome aboard the *Lyonsword*! I'm Eric," he said, shaking my hand.

He was about my height, with bright red hair that one could hardly miss, pale, freckled skin, and a thin but fit build. Like all the crew we had seen, his clothes were well-worn but not quite ragged.

"Ben," I replied simply, before gesturing to the rest of my crew. "This is Nadia, Ivan, Solace, Otto, and Yuuki."

Eric smiled. "Quite the group," he said, glancing at Yuuki. "Not what I'd expect f'r those on the run," he said curiously.

I returned his smile. "We weren't on the run until this morning."

"Ah!" replied Eric with an exaggerated nod. "I see now. Well, make yourselves at home. The captain's a good man, and the crew might be rugged, but we don't often bite," he said with a grin.

"Thank you, we appreciate your hospitality," I replied with a smile.

Eric nodded again and scampered up the mast to the nest above, where he could keep an eye on our surroundings. We headed below deck, nodding to the crew who waved as they worked the sails, and found our way to the sleeping quarters, where we each hunkered down for the night. It was only minutes before we were rocked to sleep by the gentle swaying motion of the ship.

Dreams swirled in my mind during a restless sleep. But suddenly, I snapped awake, unsure what had woken me. I grabbed my pistol but stopped short as I noticed Ivan crouched in front of me.

"What are you doing, Ivan? I almost shot you!" I whispered.

He smiled. "Nadia found something that I think you should see," he explained as he stood and headed down to the lowest deck where the horses were stowed.

I glanced back at Solace to make sure we hadn't woken her, then got up and followed Ivan farther into the belly of the *Lyonsword*. As we reached the side opposite where the horses were held, I saw Nadia crouched in the shadows, looking at something.

Nadia stood and stepped into the light of the single lantern that hung from the ceiling. "Before you freak out and yell at me for snooping around this guy's ship, hear me out," she said, holding her hands up, palms out.

I crossed my arms. "This better be good, Nadia, or the captain is going to throw us off the ship, or worse!"

She nodded. "Didn't you think it was a little odd how he reacted to your story about the book?"

I frowned. "Yes, I thought it was odd, but that doesn't give us permission to go snooping around his ship!" I whispered through gritted teeth.

Nadia ignored my anger and continued, "Well, I thought it was odd as well, so when I couldn't sleep, I came down here to clean tack and started thinking. What if he knows more about this book than he is letting on?" she said with raised eyebrows.

I stared at her. I was angry that she was snooping around, but she had a point. *Why would a captain of a pirate ship be so curious about whether I had succeeded in giving the book to General Delaney?*

"Go on," I said slowly.

Nadia smiled. "So, I started looking around the ship and talking to the crew, who seem nice, by the way," she added. "Anyways, I came down here to look around after one of the crew told me they tend to keep valuables down here. I didn't mean to, but the ship rolled, and a barrel fell over, hitting this spot on the floor that sounded hollow. When I checked it out, I found this..." Nadia gestured to the shadow she had been crouched in, and I stepped forward to look.

Nadia had pulled up floorboards, revealing a hidden compartment below them. "What have you done?" I snapped at her. "Nadia, this guy is clearly smuggling things. We already knew that! You are going to get us killed!" I said, struggling to keep my voice quiet.

"Look inside," she said as she crossed her arms.

I hesitated as I attempted to burn holes in Nadia's face with my glare, but Nadia's expression was insistent. If she thought whatever was in there was important for me to see, then it probably was. I glanced around me, checking the dark corners behind barrels and supplies before leaning forward and looking into the hole in the floor. Nadia had dug away some hay, revealing a bag. The bag now lay open, and I looked inside. To my surprise, the bag was filled with books. I crouched down in disbelief. *Could it be?* I wondered. It had no mark in the corner. I opened one of the books and flipped through it, scanning a few pages. *It is!* This story started out differently from Ruth's book, but it was definitely similar. These were not just any books. They had something to do with the one I had taken from Ruth. The one that General Delaney thought was so rare that he had sent me after an old lady to get it. But here, in the belly of the *Lyonsword*, was a whole bag of them!

"Surprised to see so many?"

The voice startled all three of us and we spun around, taking a collective step back and placing our hands on our nearest weapons. Standing in our only escape route, Captain Bates stood watching, leaning against one of the horse stalls with his arms crossed.

The captain raised an eyebrow. "Going to try and kill me on my own ship now, are you?" he said menacingly as he rested his hand on the handle of his own pistol.

"No," I said in as calm a voice as I could muster. "You just startled us is all."

He nodded slowly as his gaze shifted to the opening in his ship's floor. "I should kill you," he said in a cool tone as his dark blue eyes lifted and met my brown ones.

Knowing we had been caught and there was nothing we could do about that, I decided there was no option but to move forward. "Why do you have these books? How did you get your hands on so many?" I asked.

The captain looked at me for a long moment as if he were deciding whether telling me before he killed me would be a waste of breath. Then, to my surprise, the captain straightened, suddenly looking tired. "A friend," he said simply as he turned and headed to the stairs.

Ivan turned to me with a questioning look. "So...he isn't going to kill us?" he asked.

I glanced at Nadia, who looked just as confused as I felt, then I followed the captain. "Stay here. I will fix this," I said sternly when Nadia and Ivan tried to follow.

Nadia opened her mouth with an apologetic expression. "Ben—"

"Stay here!" I snapped as I disappeared up the stairs. As I came out onto the deck in the early morning darkness, the crew seemed completely unaware of what had happened below deck, but a few of them glanced at the captain as he strode across the deck to his quarters. Though they seemed to know something was up by the captain's mood, they only glanced at him with questioning looks as he walked by before returning to their work.

The captain disappeared into his quarters but left his door open so I could follow. Once inside, I closed the door and turned to face him.

"I do not appreciate having guests rummaging through my ship," he said sternly as he poured himself a drink.

"I did not intend to go rummaging through your ship, Captain, but it happened, and now I know. You are smuggling these books. Why?" I demanded.

The captain looked at me with calm eyes. "Why should I tell you?" he asked in an even tone before raising his glass to his lips and taking a swig.

"This is not how I wanted this to go, and I understand if you want to throw us off your ship or even kill us, but you must understand that I will protect my crew. When you started asking all those questions about the book, I got suspicious," I admitted.

The captain raised his chin a half inch. "I know it was not you personally who searched my ship and found the books," he said, eyeing me as he spoke.

"That is beside the point, Captain. Punish me as you see fit, but whatever you choose, I need to know about those books," I demanded.

The captain sat down in his chair and observed me with an analytical frown. After a moment, he said, "Before we continue with this discussion, there is something I need to make very clear. I am not going to throw you off my ship...or kill you...but if anything like this happens again, that will change," he said. "Am I understood?"

"Yes, sir," I stated with respect. Considering what had happened, that was highly gracious of him.

The captain remained silent for a moment, then gestured to the couches under the windows. "Have a seat, Benjamin," he said.

I sat down and waited for him to proceed. He looked at me for a moment before speaking again. "Benjamin, I want to trust you," he said plainly. "I do. I see that your interests may align with mine, and I respect you taking the fall for your crew. Apart from their actions this morning, I like you," he said, the tension finally disappearing from his voice. "I think you are a respectable man." He paused. "Is my judgment of your character misplaced?" he asked as he locked eyes with me.

"No, sir," I answered with confidence.

He nodded. Finally, he let out a sigh and leaned forward. He placed his drink down with thoughtful precision before resting his elbows on his desk and steepling his hands at his chin. "The truth is, I was going to tell you about the books last night. But I wanted to see what you would do."

I winced at the idea that we had not passed the captain's little test.

To my surprise, the captain smiled. "Not once have you tried to deny what happened or put the blame on someone else. Your only concern was for your crew and for gaining understanding about that book. I find that response to be...curious. But sufficient. All is forgiven," he granted.

I raised an eyebrow. That was not what I had expected to hear.

The captain continued, "Benjamin, I have the books because, as you know, I am smuggling them. But do you know why I am smuggling them?" he asked.

I shook my head. "No."

"I am smuggling them because General Delaney wants them gone. He hates them."

I frowned. "But he seemed so interested in the one I retrieved for him."

"You mean the one he made you take from an old lady in the Southern Mountains," he said plainly. It was more of an observation than a question.

I contemplated how that sounded. "I know it was wrong. But it didn't seem like he wanted to get rid of the book." Suddenly, I realized that if General Delaney wanted the books gone, then he likely wanted Ruth gone as well. I let my face fall into my hands. "What have I done?" I groaned. "He probably killed her," I said, more to myself than the captain. I looked at him. "Why did he want that book?" I asked, now knowing that it had cost an innocent old lady her life.

"To keep it from the people. To keep them from knowing the story it contains," Captain Bates explained.

"What story is that?" I asked.

The captain smiled. "A story about a prince."

The captain poured me a drink before continuing. "The book used to be in print, just as common as any other book. However, General Delaney has gradually gotten rid of more and more of them so that the people will not know the truth about the Beast of the Woods."

I stared at the captain. "It talks about the Beast?" I asked in surprise.

He nodded. "It does."

"But the only story I know of that talks about the Beast is only told by the Chosen family. It has never been in print," I said, confused.

The captain nodded. "The story they told was a different version." A slight frown creased his brow as his eyes lost focus for a moment. "This story is a bit different. Their story was about a king. This one is about a prince." He shrugged. "The details have changed over time. The one you took from that old lady was probably the original. The general has been looking for it for a long time."

I shook my head. "Just another story that has been changed by time. Why do people keep putting false hope in these stories?" I asked in frustration.

"The story was originally supposed to be told by the Chosen. But there are no more of them alive, Ben. The last one died in the most recent war with the beasts, and he was not much of a believer in the first place. Their story died with him. This book is all we have left," he explained.

I shook my head. "That is not true."

The captain leaned forward. "What do you mean?"

"Solace," I said simply. "She is the last of that family line."

The captain's eyebrows lifted. "Really...?" he said as he fell into thought. "I have been working on getting these books back in print for decades now, and I have never met an original storyteller from the Chosen family in person..." His voice trailed off as he looked at his door, toward the crew's sleeping quarters.

"I must know what is in that book," I said to the captain.

"Yes, you must," he said. With that, the captain leaned back in his chair and began to tell me the story contained in the book that had set this whole journey in motion.

# Chapter 19

"A LONG TIME AGO, there was a prince and a king who dwelled in a realm called the Kingdom, a place that flowed with Original Power. The Prince, a man who loved to build things, joined his father, the King, and they used this Original Power to create a wonderous new land. They filled it with people and creatures of all kinds, and it grew into a kingdom known as the Forest Kingdom. Together, the King and the Prince ruled these two kingdoms with Original Power by their side.

"Then one day, the Prince fell in love with a poor, beautiful woman. The two were engaged to be married, and the King prepared to give them the Forest Kingdom as a wedding gift. But then the Prince was betrayed by his future bride, and the people followed her to a place called the Land Beyond, a dark and corrupted land ruled by an evil being called the Creature, who wielded a dark power known as Corrupted Power. When they entered that land, the people and the Prince's bride-to-be were corrupted by darkness. They tried to escape it, but in doing so, they corrupted the Forest Kingdom as well.

"As they fell under the control of Corrupted Power, the people's selfishness grew, and they didn't stop with corrupting the Forest Kingdom. The Prince's bride-to-be and the people who followed her vowed to conquer the Kingdom as well and take it as their own. But the King knew that if the people tried to enter the Kingdom to conquer it, the Original Power in the Kingdom would kill them. So, the King placed a powerful boundary between the Forest Kingdom and the Kingdom to protect the people until the time was right for him to vanquish all evil. But, desiring to relieve the people's suffering, the King also placed a beast within the Forest Kingdom, housed in the Woods, and he gave the Beast the power to grant a wish to a chosen few. However, those chosen few began to wish selfishly, so the King banished them from the Woods for their own safety and extended the boundary of Original Power to surround the Woods.

"The Prince was utterly heartbroken by the horrible betrayal of his bride and the people, and by the pain they suffered because of the choice they had made. So, the Prince went to his father, the King, and explained that he still loved the woman and the people, despite what they had done. The King told the Prince they could save his bride-to-be and the people, but doing so would come at a cost. The King told the Prince that to protect the people from darkness, the Prince would have to take on their darkness himself, using his power to overcome what they could not.

"'You are of me, my son, and infused with my Original Power,' he explained. 'You must battle their darkness and win back the affection and allegiance of the people. My power in you will keep you safe from the darkness of their land, but you must enter that land and overcome their darkness. You must take the darkness from the people. Once you have taken hold of their darkness, you must cross the boundary to the Woods that I have set so that the light of the Original Power will burn the darkness away. But there is a price to pay. No darkness can enter the Kingdom. All who enter here with any darkness in them will die by the light of Original Power! When the darkness is fully consumed, and all are safe in the Kingdom, you must go to war with the Creature and vanquish him and his followers to destroy the influence of Corrupted Power forever.'

"Knowing the sacrifice he would have to make, the Prince left the Kingdom and went to the people. Protected from corruption by the Original Power he possessed, the Prince lived as a commoner in the Forest Kingdom, telling those who wished to know of how he would save them. But the Creature continued to feed the shadows of anger within the people, convincing them the Prince was their enemy, and their anger grew until they hated the Prince.

"One day, the people gathered at the Woods, shouting in anger at the Prince, telling him to leave them, warning him they would take his father's kingdom soon. But the Prince allowed their anger to build, for as they condemned him, their darkness was exposed, and he could take their darkness into himself. Their angry shouts, their selfish ways, their rage, and even their lust for blood—he took it all.

"The Creature, realizing what the Prince was doing, flew into a panic. He attacked the people with his Corrupted Power, trying to fill them again with darkness, with shadows of fear and doubt. But the Prince had begun to absorb the darkness, and he just took that darkness, too.

"Now, with a hold on the darkness that was infecting the people, the Prince looked to the Creature from his position at the edge of the Woods. He declared in a loud voice, 'It is over. I have won.'

"Before the Creature could respond, the Prince stepped backward through the invisible boundary into the Woods. A loud clap of thunder sounded as the darkness and light collided. The light of Original Power blazed like fire through the Prince as it burned the darkness he had taken from the people. It blazed so bright and hot that it purged the darkness from him, but the Prince fell to the ground, dead.

"At his death, the Beast of the Woods released an earth-shaking roar, like that of a mighty lion. For the Prince had given his life, and the King had lost his only son.

"As the Beast's roar ended, a silence fell over the two kingdoms, and the people stood staring into the Woods, where the Prince lay dead. Then the Beast of the Woods appeared next to the Prince's body. 'Do you see?' asked the Beast. 'Do you see what your selfishness has cost?' But the people did not answer.

"Seeing that the Prince was dead, the Creature turned to the King and roared, 'I have won! Your son is dead, and the people are lost to my power from now on!'

"As the King approached the body of his lifeless son, tears flowed from his eyes, for he loved his son, who had willingly given his life to win back the people they both so dearly loved and the woman who had led them astray.

"Looking to the Creature, the King spoke. 'Once, I barred the people from the Kingdom so they would not be killed by my power. But I did not leave them alone in this land,' he went on. 'I gave some a special marker that covered their darkness and granted them passage into the Woods, where they could ask the Beast for help living under your corruption. But darkness still ruled over them, and their marker was corrupted, so I banned them from the

Woods for their own safety. But now, my son has done what they could not. He has taken their darkness from them, and they will come to know what he has done for them.'

"'But still, I can whisper in their ears and possess their bodies!' The Creature said mockingly. 'They are trapped forever in this land. Your son may have pulled the darkness from them, but it has forever stained their hearts,' said the Creature with a grin. 'Here they will dwell with me forever. They are hopeless! You cannot have them! They will never be fully free of me, and they will forever be lost to you!'

"The King shook his head. 'Not forever,' declared the King, 'for my son will vanquish you once and for all in one final battle.'

"The Creature forced a hearty laugh, though fear was gnawing away inside him. 'There is no battle to be fought!' he declared. 'I will hold them captive, for their Lion has been broken—your son is dead,' he roared as he strained to build up confidence within himself. 'Your people are left all alone in my world and have no hope, and without hope, they have nothing.'

"The King smiled. 'My work is not yet finished. For it is hope that I shall leave them.' With that, the King reached down and touched his son. The Creature watched in horror as light poured from the King and filled the Prince, for the King loved his son, and in love, Original Power is strongest. The lifeless body of the Prince was filled once again with life, and he rose to his feet with a radiant glow! The Creature cried out in horror as the barrier of protection between the two kingdoms was torn, and a gate was made in the boundary that separated the two kingdoms, a gate guarded by the Prince himself.

"The King spoke to the Creature with the Prince standing by his side. 'The Lion has won. My son now stands between the people and my power. The people have hope. For they can see that, through my son, they may have protection from your darkness and even enter the Kingdom if my son allows it. But one day, when Original Power has marked the last soul, my son will end your rule and the need for this boundary by destroying you and this land.'

"The Prince had fought the darkness of the people and won. But the Prince soon vanished. No one knows where he went or why he left. In his absence, the darkness took over once again. But the story says that one day, the Prince will return and vanquish the Creature and its evil beasts forever. But until that time, the Beast of the Woods will be a light to the gate that will one day provide the people with a way home to the Kingdom."

I took in a breath as the captain finished the story.

"Over time, this story has been forgotten," Captain Bates continued. "With the Prince mysteriously missing, the Creature of Corrupted Power held fast to the people, twisting truth into lies. And so, the gate was lost." Captain Bates shook his head at the thought. "But the Beast of the Woods remains as a beacon to the gate, though no one knows where the gate truly lies. Some believe it is within the Woods, guarded by the Beast. But the deadly boundary has prevented anyone from entering to look for it. Others believe that since the story says the Prince guards the gate, it is located elsewhere. Whatever the truth is, the Creature has seen to it that we do not find out. He draws our attention to other things. Lies too attractive to ignore. The story goes on to explain that, in desperation, the Creature of the Corrupted Power formed another lie—the lie that the Beast of the Woods is what remains of the darkness and Corrupted Power. The rumor is that if one could catch the Beast and deliver it to General Delaney, they would be rewarded with a wish and riches beyond their wildest dreams." The captain leaned back in his chair. "The story explains that the Great Beasts of the Southern Mountains are creatures made by Corrupted Power. Apparently, they attack us to keep people subjected to the Creature and to kill the Beast that will show people to the gate." The captain paused, then added, "Near the end of the story, it says that the Great Beasts of the Southern Mountains were made to resemble the Beast of the Woods, so people would think the Beast of the Woods was evil as well. That is how it got its name." He shook his head. "Its true name has been forgotten. The name 'the Beast' was given to it by the Creature to convince people it was evil like the Great Beasts. But the Beast is not evil—it is a glimmer of truth in this darkened land."

I frowned in confusion. "So one story says there is just the Beast and the Chosen, and the other says the Prince actually helped save the people?" I pondered aloud, more to myself than to the captain. "It is just a different version of the story Solace knows," I said as I met his gaze. "Except that the Prince has apparently abandoned us in this version."

The captain shrugged. "It may be just another version, but it is important that you understand, this story is not just any story. It tells us that there is a way to get rid of the beasts. They rose to power because the darkness we chose came to life and wants to keep us prisoner." He leaned forward. "We must not let it. That is why I smuggle these books. This story needs to be preserved so people know what these beasts are and why they are here. They are agents of evil—an evil we cannot defeat on our own."

I shook my head. "These stories that people keep telling me, they are just stories, but everyone seems to think that some small detail within them will save us all from something that has been plaguing this world since it began," I said in an irritated tone.

The captain smiled. "Maybe they are just stories to you, Ben," he said as he leaned forward, "but stories can change the world."

Suddenly, Christopher burst through the door. "Captain, it's back!" he said urgently.

Captain Bates lurched from his chair and chased after Christopher, out of the cabin. Confused, I followed. "What is back?" I asked. But my answer came as I exited the captain's quarters. The sun was just breaking the horizon to our left, and its orange glow outlined a ship in the distance.

"It's them, Captain," yelled Eric from the nest above us. "I can barely make out their flag, but it's them."

The captain began shouting orders. "To the oars! We need to disappear into the islands before they get too close!"

"Who is it?" I asked.

"The *Punisher*," he said as he ran to the wheel. "It is one of General Delaney's ships. Its main purpose is to capture and kill people like me, people who protect the story. They have been tracking us this entire trip. They would have surely caught us if it weren't for the leviathan attacking us both last time."

Shouts went up around us as orders were yelled from person to person and the crew took up their positions to get the ship moving faster.

Captain Bates spun the wheel, turning the ship toward the first island that had come into view. "Let's hope they are still too damaged to chase us down. If they are, we can lose them in the islands!" he yelled.

"Is there anything I can do to help, Captain?" I asked, turning to face him.

"We can always use more oarsmen in this situation," he said, gesturing to a trapdoor that led below deck.

"I have just the man," I said with a grin. I ran across the deck and descended the stairs to the second level. "Ivan!"

Ivan's head snapped up, woken from a deep sleep. "I'm here!" he yelled, beginning to draw his sword.

"Ivan, we need help in the oars room," I said. "Nadia can help, too!"

As I explained to them about the ship on the horizon, we ran to the oars room, took up places among the crew, and began rowing the boat with the rest of them, adding to the light wind that pushed the ship toward the islands. It felt like forever before we finally heard the call to begin slowing the boat instead. Then the order was given to stop and let the boat drift. Sweating, Ivan, Nadia, and I looked around.

"What's happened?" I asked the man leading the group.

"We have made it to the islands, but we need to hide. The first island might seem obvious, but if they are just passing us to head to the port for repairs, they will go right past us. There is no reason to waste energy," he said.

The ship was steered into a cavern on the first island, which was more of a large rock than an island according to some of the crew, and was tucked out of sight of the other ship. It felt like ages before we got the signal that the *Punisher* had passed us by, headed to the eastern docks we had come from. Everyone heaved a sigh of relief. Some even yipped and hollered in joy. Nadia, Ivan, and I looked around with smiles on our faces. So far, we weren't dead.

The rest of the day, the whole crew was on watch for the leviathan that roamed the waters of the Eastern Sea. A large female was known to come to these islands to give birth this time of year. No one really knew how many there were, but the captain had already encountered a male in the open sea. The last thing we needed right now was a fight with an indestructible angry mother sea monster. We floated from small island to small island, guided by oarsmen and the rudder, waiting until the sun set to set sail in the open ocean again.

The Eastern Sea held a few small collections of islands. We were among the first group of islands on the eastern side of the Southern Continent. According to Eric, it usually took about a day to make it through this first patch of islands, and about two, depending on the weather, to get through the second patch of islands to the seaport closest to the Town, making our trip about three days. Based on the current weather patterns, the captain estimated that we would most likely arrive on schedule.

That night we set sail in high winds, headed through open sea toward the second patch of islands. I spent every waking hour studying the book and going over Solace's story with her, trying to figure out what I was supposed to do next. If the stories were true, they basically explained that the Great Beasts of the Southern Mountains were made by the Creature, which wielded what was called Corrupted Power. The Creature's power had infected various animals that took over the land and would fight to give their master more and more control. One story said that the Beast of the Woods was there to grant a wish to a member of the Chosen family to stop each evil beast as they came. But the other story said that the Beast was there to show people the way to a gate that would lead them to the Kingdom, to safety, though I didn't entirely understand that last part. But there was a deadly boundary around the Woods, and no one could get into them without dying.

Since there was no special power that I knew of, I was confused about what kingdom the stories were talking about until I had another conversation with the captain on our first day among the second group of islands, our second day of sea travel. I was sitting on the deck discussing the stories with Solace, who was gradually getting worse. I had been trying to keep her mind off her situation, and the stories seemed to help. I even humored her when she started rethinking how to get access to the Beast. Even though I was still pretty sure its powers were just a myth, I went along with the conversation. Solace and I both decided it was an easy decision. If we stayed outside the Woods, we would live. If we entered, we would die. But if the Beast exited the Woods, it wouldn't die. So, the choice was easy. Our original plan had to work. We would have to lure it out.

Our conversation moved on to other topics, and Captain Bates approached us while we were in the middle of a discussion about the unseen kingdoms and all the various beasts, good and bad. "You look as though you are trying to solve a riddle, my friend," he said joyfully as he approached. "What troubles you?"

I shook my head. "These stories don't make sense. If they are just stories, then fine. They make sense. But if I am to expect them to be real, where are these kingdoms that they talk about?

Why is everyone putting so much faith in a story about people who are dead now? There is no such thing as darkness turning into creatures and light burning darkness out of people," I said in frustration. I took a deep breath to calm myself and watched as Nadia began teaching Otto how to aim a pistol at a nearby plank of wood.

Captain Bates chuckled. "Oh, but there is, my friend." He leaned against the gunwale and looked at me with a mischievous smile. "This world is in a fog. General Delaney has everyone believing that the world works one way, when in fact, it works quite differently," he said.

"So, you would have me believe in outlandish power?" I asked skeptically.

The captain considered that. "Power, miracles, fantasy, call it what you like," he said simply.

"And you have seen this power?" I asked.

"You have not?" he asked with raised eyebrows. "Did you not cross the Forest in springtime?"

"Everything we saw has an explanation, even the golden ghosts," I explained, sounding less confident than I had hoped.

Otto fired the pistol and then slouched, having missed the mark.

"And what explanation would that be?" prompted the captain, apparently aware of the training session behind him and unconcerned at the sound of the shot.

"They are just creatures. Nature," I said with a shrug.

"And what of Valdra's Martecytes? Are they just natural?" he asked.

I thought back to how they had materialized out of nowhere at the cave. I had thought my eyes were playing tricks on my mind, but then both the doctor and Captain Bates had mentioned their mysterious abilities.

"If this power is real, then why have I not heard of it before?" I asked, trying to convince myself it was all just myth. I watched as Nadia lined up a demonstration shot, aiming at something I couldn't see.

The captain smiled. "Because everyone knows the most convincing lies are based in truth."

"And what lie would I be believing that would make me not notice this power you speak of?" I asked, frustrated that he might think I was not observant enough to notice something so obvious.

"The lie of self-sufficiency," he said with a grin.

Nadia fired, the smile on her face indicating she hit her target spot-on. Otto's jaw dropped.

"What do you mean?" asked Solace, who had been listening closely.

"I mean, my dear friend, that we were not designed to live alone, apart from the King's power. But we took it upon ourselves to believe that we could do everything ourselves and that power was no longer needed. We built machines, we came up with equations, we cured diseases, and we abandoned the one by whom we were made," he explained. "We fell under the control of a twisted power we were not made to survive."

"But all those machines, cures, and equations are good things," said Solace with a frown.

The captain smiled. "And therein lies the truth that makes the lie so convincing."

I thought back to the Forest and all the times we had nearly died. Each time it had been the Beast of the Woods that had pulled my attention in the right direction. Each time I was lost, my connection with that beast was what had led me to safety.

"The Beast of the Woods," I said. "Is it of this Original Power?" I asked.

The captain nodded. "I believe it is. Why do you ask?"

Nadia reloaded the pistol and handed it to Otto.

"I have seen it," I said, not caring, for the first time, if Solace knew.

The captain straightened. "You have seen it?" he said with wonder.

Solace looked at me with a tired but triumphant smile. "I knew it," she said, before letting her eyes close. "That night at the Woods, the night before we left..." she mumbled as she rested her head on my shoulder.

"What was it like?" the captain asked.

"It was..." I chuckled to myself, "...mysterious."

We all laughed. "I believe you, my friend," said the captain. "Do you believe now?" he said inquisitively as Otto lined up a shot.

"In miracles or in stories?" I asked.

"Both," he said with a smile.

I glanced down at Solace. The story had brought us together. Whether the story was true or not, I was not sure, but it had played a part in changing my life when I thought I had nothing left. I let out a silent breath. Solace's decision to rest her head on my shoulder rather than lean back on the bags behind her was not lost on me, but I chose to ignore it in hopes that I had mistaken the gesture. It would be easier to do what I must if she did not return my affections.

"Maybe." I absentmindedly returned my attention to Otto's lesson.

Otto fired, hitting the edge of his target. He smiled at his near hit.

The captain shifted his weight to leave. "Don't take too long, for we must all choose."

As the captain returned to his duties, I turned my attention to Solace. She had fallen asleep. Her pale face still held the remnants of a smile. She believed. *Why can't I?* I thought back to when I had started this journey. I had begun the journey because I felt that it was my job. But Ivan and Nadia were right. Things had changed. I was here for Solace now. I was finally ready to admit that, but still, I felt like the fog in my mind had not yet fully dispersed.

In that moment, a moment that seemed so simple, with me and Solace sitting next to each other on a ship in the Eastern Sea, I let myself feel my love for her. I looked at Solace and knew, as I had the day we left the Village, *I am fighting for her. I am here to help her accomplish her purpose.* I suddenly felt another piece of my mental puzzle click into place. The mission I had set out to complete no longer existed. I was not sure what I believed about the stories, but I knew one thing for sure. I believed in Solace. Despite her condition, she was fighting. *And she will no longer do it alone,* I thought to myself. But even as I had those thoughts, my fear of losing her tugged at my heart. I set my jaw and pushed aside the fear that despite my change in mission, the outcome might be the same—the Beast and Solace both dead.

I leaned back just far enough to wrap a tender, firm arm around Solace. Pushing myself forward and up into a crouch, I scooped Solace up in my arms. She stirred slightly, repositioning her head on my shoulder as I stood. I would be by her side. No matter what happened. I would do whatever it took to save her. And though it would break my heart if she did not make it, I would not give up. I would move on to the next thing. I would finish what she started. As I approached the hatch to the deck below, I saw each person who had come on this journey with us. Ivan was cleaning his weapons. Nadia was now reading over Otto's shoulder as he scribbled in his journal. Yuuki was curled up near some hammocks in a small nook made of barrels and blankets. *No,* I thought to myself, *we will finish what she started.*

I descended the stairs below deck, placed Solace in her bed, and covered her with a blanket. Otto came down and got her to swallow some medication before we left her to sleep. With Solace sleeping, safe and sound, I climbed back up from the lower deck and walked to the gunwale with Otto in tow.

"She is not doing well, Ben," said Otto, sounding concerned.

I looked out over the water as I leaned my forearms on the ship's gunwale. "I know," I said calmly.

"I am sorry I can't help her more," he stated.

"No, Otto, it is not your responsibility to save her from something like this." I sighed. "You have done more than I ever thought you would. Thank you."

He nodded. "You are welcome."

I heard a clang of swords behind us, and we both whirled. I let out a sigh of relief as I saw two of the ship's crew members clash their swords together in a friendly sparring match. I heard Ivan's hearty laugh and watched as he stood and brandished his freshly polished sword at the two men.

"Now that's a good way to get your head chopped off," he bellowed playfully as he stepped toward them.

The sparring crew members, Dan and Casey, had seemed to strike up a friendship with the twins in the short time we had been on board. The two friends turned to Ivan. "You could do better, my bumbling friend?" asked Casey with a teasing grin.

"Aye, I could do better!" Ivan bellowed in return.

"Ha ha ha!" the man laughed and said with a grin, "I challenge you to a duel!"

Ivan held his sword in a steady grip and crouched, ready to spring into action. "I'll have you on your arse in nothin' flat!" he gloated.

With that, they lurched toward each other, and their swords met in the clang of metal on metal. They jumped and slashed, turning the main deck into their playground as they threw insults back and forth, laughing, and occasionally commending each other on their fighting skills and cunning. At one point, they swung a little too close to Otto, who stumbled out of the way with a look of shock on his face. We all roared in laughter as Otto's eyelids drooped in annoyance. He straightened his shirt and went to find a less death-defying location, where he began rummaging through his notes on the Forest.

Nadia soon joined the game as well, shifting the balance to two on two, with Nadia and Ivan against Dan and Casey. Even little Yuuki watched the spectacle, darting between people, trying to keep a good view of the action. It had taken her a bit of time to warm up to the crew, and I was beginning to wonder if that might not be a good thing. She had grown on them, but they had rubbed off on her. She cheered the duelers on and laughed as Ivan scooped her up onto his shoulder in celebration of besting Casey. Soon, the crowd was cheering as Nadia got the upper hand against Dan.

The high spirits remained until we arrived the next night within sight of the hidden port where we would be docking. But the mood darkened a bit as we continued toward land. The wind began to whip about and rain came down hard, forcing the crew to spend the remainder of our trip fighting with the sails. But thankfully, the leviathan was nowhere in sight, and we made it to the secret port in one piece.

As we approached the dock, the crew prepared to tie down the ship to the secluded single dock, which had been built specifically to accommodate a ship this size. The captain expertly maneuvered the vessel into the small space, barking orders to his crew until the ship was secure. As the crew finished tying off the ship, Nadia, Ivan, Otto, Solace, and Yuuki made their way to the main deck with our belongings and horses. The captain spotted me and waved me over. Leaving Jeb with the others, I joined him at the gunwale.

"Where will you go now that you have read the book and know the story?" he asked.

I had been thinking about it all day. "I need to go see the Beast of the Woods. I need to know why I have been so...connected to it," I said. *And to see if it can save Solace.*

"You be careful, Benjamin," he warned. "Those Martecytes are not to be trifled with."

"Yes, sir," I said with a small smile.

The captain must have heard the discouragement in my voice because he said encouragingly, "You are almost there, my friend.

I shook my head. "I am sorry. I don't mean to ruin the mood."

"It's her, isn't it?" he asked, looking toward Solace and the others.

I nodded. "I am not sure how much longer she has."

"She is a fighter. Do not give up on her just yet," he said, patting my shoulder. "Plus, she has you," he said with a smile.

"What if I am killing her?" I asked. "I mean, if she had not come on this journey, maybe she would have a better chance of surviving."

Captain Bates laughed. "A woman like her cannot be killed that easily," he said with a smile. "She is too strong for that."

An idea had been floating around in my mind, and I needed to get some clarity on it before I left this ship. "You speak of this power in the stories. If it still exists, can the Beast show it to me? Can it save a life with the power?" I asked.

The captain's face took on a more serious expression. "Some believe that what the story says about the Beast granting wishes means it can grant a life."

"But one must kill it to do so," I said hopelessly.

The captain nodded. "So they say...Someone always has to die," he said with a distant look on his face.

"Why?" I asked. "I don't get it. Why does someone have to die?"

The captain shrugged. "I don't know." He leaned against the gunwale and looked out over the water, which was now calm. "But I can tell you this. Many people die at the hands of those evil beasts, but it is said that the one good beast, the Beast of the Woods, can stop that. If the Beast does have power we don't understand, there is a chance it could save us all from the Great Beasts of the Southern Mountains. So, if the Beast of the Woods must die to save Solace's life, think about what you would be killing. Think about what you would be taking from the people."

I nodded in understanding. Killing the Beast in exchange for one life might condemn all others to death at the claws of the Great Beasts. I pondered that dilemma as the captain and his crew helped us off-load our horses and supplies. Solace tried to help, but she barely made it off the boat with her horse in tow before Ivan ordered her to sit down before she passed out. She complied and fell asleep while we finished.

Once we had all our belongings back on land, I turned to the captain and offered him an outstretched hand. "Thank you, Captain. It has been a pleasure."

"The pleasure is all mine, Benjamin. You and your crew are welcome aboard any time," he said as he shook my hand firmly. "Before you go into town, there is someone I think might be able to answer your questions about the power we talked about," he said. "I have only met her once, but she seemed to know a lot about this kind of thing."

"Who is she?" I asked.

"I don't remember her name, but she is staying with a friend. She is working out a deal to ship something with us. Look for an inn between here and your town called the Pint Inn. If you travel fast, you should be able to reach it in two days. Tell them Captain Bates sent you and wants to talk to our new client," he explained.

"Thank you, Captain," I said with a smile.

"Until next time," he said, responding with his own smile and offering a respectful bow before returning to his ship and setting sail once more, on a mission to share the book and the story it contained.

# Chapter 20

WE HEADED WEST TOWARD the Town, which was a straight shot inland from where the *Lyonsword* had dropped us off. I had to figure out what was true and what was false about this story and the Beast of the Woods, so we followed the captain's instructions and looked for the Pint Inn.

After riding all night and the next day, Solace was barely able to stay on her horse. I stayed near her, ready to catch her if she passed out. Finally, we came over a small hill as the sun's last rays were vanishing into night and saw what we hoped was our destination. At the base of the hill was a building with glowing lights and some stables, all surrounded by an old wall marred by the attacks of beasts long dead. We headed down the hill, and I instructed everyone to wait at a distance while I went to check it out. The inn was not all that impressive. Its old, unpainted wooden walls and shabby garden gave it the look of a place weary travelers might stop if they had no other options. But that was probably how it had stayed under the radar while still providing a great spot for smugglers to discuss business. Hanging on a lamppost was a sloppily made sign that read "The Pint Inn. Room for a night. Stay longer at your own risk." The words were followed by a carving of a beast, signaling that beasts posed a danger in the area.

I approached the door in the wall and knocked. After a moment, the covering on the door's window opened, and a man with a scruffy red beard looked out at me suspiciously. "Here for booze, a bed, or both?" the man said grumpily.

"Captain Nathanial Bates sent me," I said with confidence.

The man's eyebrows raised, and he leaned as far forward as the bars of the makeshift window would allow to glance around me. "Anyone with you?" he asked in a more polite tone.

"Five more," I stated.

The man nodded. "Bring 'em over," he said, then closed the window shutter and opened the door.

I looked back at the group and waved them over. Once we were all inside the wall, I turned to the man. "We are looking for Captain Bates's new client," I said, watching the man's reaction.

He nodded. "Leave your horses with the stable guard and follow me," he said, waving a hand in the direction he began walking.

I helped Solace from her horse and handed her off to Ivan, signaling to him that I would keep an eye on our flank. I scanned the area as we left the horses and followed the man into the inn. It was busy with all sorts of people. Some played cards at the tables, others drank and laughed at the bar. Still others sat alone in corners keeping to themselves. We followed the red-bearded man as he ascended a flight of stairs to the rooms above. He led us to a room near the back and gestured to the door. "In there. Just knock and tell them what you told me," he said before disappearing down the hall to return to his duties at the door.

I glanced back at the rest of my group to gauge how they felt about the situation. Seeing that they were all waiting for me to decide what would happen, I turned to the door in front of me and knocked.

After a moment, the door was pulled open about three inches, and a man looked out at us. "Who are you?" he asked with a frown.

"That is not important," I stated. "I am a friend of Captain Nathanial Bates, and I need to speak with his new client," I demanded.

"Let him in," a familiar voice said from somewhere in the room.

The man looked back at whoever had spoken, then returned his gaze to me and reluctantly opened the door to let us in. As we entered the room, I stopped abruptly when I saw who it was who had spoken.

That knowing smile creased her lips when she saw me. "Well, hello, my boy!" said Ruth in a joyful voice. "Where have you been off to these past few weeks?" she asked with a gleam in her eye.

I stared at her in shock, as I had been sure General Delaney had her killed. "You...you're alive!" I exclaimed, not sure what else to say.

She smiled. "That does appear to be the case," she said with a slight nod. Ruth looked past me and waved to Otto. "Hello, Otto. How have your travels been?"

He smiled. "Quite adventurous!" he responded, looking proud of himself.

"I am sure they have," said Ruth as her eyes met mine. I had somehow missed that look. The one that made me think she knew something I did not. "And who are your new companions?" she asked, glancing at the others.

I gestured as I introduced them. "This is Nadia, Ivan, Solace, and Yuuki. They—and Otto—have been traveling with me."

Ruth nodded. "It is nice to see you are not alone anymore," she said with a smile.

"Ah, well, Nadia and Ivan are old friends. Solace and Yuuki I only met more recently," I explained.

Ruth nodded again. "I see." She glanced at the man who had let us in. He gave a polite nod and left the room, closing the door behind him.

"Come, sit. You all look tired," said Ruth, returning her attention to us. "Tell me, why did you want to see me?" she asked as she gathered some teacups for us before she shuffled over to a table and sat down.

"I...I didn't know it was you," I said, gathering my thoughts as we all followed her and found places to sit. "Captain Bates simply said he had a new client who might be able to help me learn about the Beast and the stories and the power that they speak of," I explained, finally recovering from seeing Ruth alive.

"Why do you want to know about that?" she asked inquisitively, pouring us all some tea.

I took a deep breath and glanced around at my companions. Solace was already asleep, but the others smiled knowingly. "That is a bit complicated," I said, allowing a lopsided smile to form on my lips.

Ruth raised her eyebrows. "Is it?" she responded. "I have found in my many years that often things are much simpler than we make them," she replied with a twinkle in her eye.

I nodded. "Well, where should I start?" I asked, mostly to myself.

Ruth shrugged. "The beginning is always a good option," she said as she grabbed a teapot and filled her cup.

I chuckled and began the story. "A few weeks ago, I saw the Beast of the Woods." I heard Otto gasp behind me and begin to speak, undoubtedly full of questions. I ignored him. "It came to the edge of the Woods and met with me. I didn't understand why. I still don't. But it did...change me...somehow." I frowned in thought. "Everything I had tried so hard to stave off for so long—my bad memories, my feelings of hopelessness, guilt—it all came rushing back when I saw that beast's green eyes," I recalled. "Then I was tasked with retrieving the book from you. I met Solace during that time," I clarified. "After I dropped you and the book off with General Delaney, I was tasked with killing the Beast of the Woods. I had been given the same task a couple times in the past, but I, and many others, had never even succeeded in finding the Beast, let alone figuring out how to kill it."

Ruth nodded. "As has been the case for a long time."

I agreed, then continued, "When I was tasked with killing the Beast, I was told that there was a doctor who could help, who knew how to lure the Beast out of the Woods. Solace was looking for him as well, because she is the last of the Chosen family line."

Ruth's eyebrows raised in surprise as she looked to Solace, asleep in the corner of the room.

"She needs to lure the Beast out because she wants to ask it to grant a wish. She wants to protect the story that her family has been tasked with telling for hundreds of years." I watched Solace as her chest rose and fell slightly with every exhausted breath. She was continuing to get worse. Her already pale complexion was even more so. She had dark circles under her eyes and had taken to falling asleep any time she stopped moving. "Now we know why she was so insistent," I said, looking at Ruth. "She is ill with something no one can cure," I said sorrowfully.

Ruth looked at Solace for a moment before turning her attention back to me as I continued the story. "We traveled through the Forest, retrieved the doctor, and then promptly learned that it was all a trap. General Delaney apparently did not like me asking questions about the book, and he had tired of my loss of interest in the dirty work he had tasked me to do from time to time. So, he sent me through the Forest, hoping I would die on the way. But when none of us died, the doctor tried to kill us. It turns out he, Dr. Batin, worked for General Delaney."

Ruth nodded. "I know of the doctor."

"You do?" I asked, surprised.

She nodded. "You might be surprised what an old lady in the mountains can know."

I nodded. "I am sure I would be," I said with a smile.

"Continue your story," prompted Ruth with a wave of her hand.

I took a deep breath. "Anyway, I don't really understand why General Delaney wants me dead. I don't get why questions over an old book would send him over the edge. So, I decided to try to find the book."

"Did you?" Ruth asked, her eyes widening just a touch.

I glanced around at the others. "Yes, I found it."

"With Captain Bates." Ruth said the words more as a statement than a question. "Did you read it?" she asked.

"I was told the story, then I read it. But...it doesn't make sense," I said in frustration. "It tells the story of the Beast, just like Solace's story. They are similar in many ways. But they are also different." I filtered through what I could remember of the stories in my mind. "I don't know what to believe. They are just stories, but for some reason, General Delaney thinks they are valuable enough to kill for."

"Just stories, you say." Ruth looked at me with steady eyes. "And yet you are here, asking to know more."

I let my gaze fall to the floor as I considered her words but then noticed Ruth studying me, so I responded with a shrug, unsure how to answer.

"There is another reason you seek this knowledge, isn't there?" she asked.

I should have known Ruth would be able to tell. Looking at Solace to make sure she was still asleep, I wondered if I should tell the truth. Solace couldn't hear me, so why not just say it? "Solace is ill," I said plainly. "I...I thought if the power was real, and the Beast was made by the King, that maybe it could save her life before she..." I paused, not wanting to say it out loud.

"Dies," finished Otto.

I glared at him. Nadia reached forward and placed a hand on his arm as his expression turned confused and surprised at my clear displeasure.

Ruth glanced around the group and then back at me. "Stay the night. Solace is tired and needs rest, as do you all."

"There is an army of Martecytes after us, Ruth. I cannot stay. I cannot put you in danger again," I said insistently.

Ruth looked at me. "You are right. You cannot," she said with that knowing smile and a glint in her eye. "You may stay or leave. The choice is yours," she stated as she reached for the teapot to refresh her cup. But I saw her watch my reaction from the corner of her eye.

I glanced at the others to make sure no one was opposed to staying. Only Nadia gave me a look that might have signaled she wasn't sure. I nodded, acknowledging her uncertainty, but set my jaw in an expression I knew she would understand. I nodded to Ruth. "Okay. We will stay."

Ivan, Otto, and Yuuki followed Ruth behind a large curtain that hung across the other end of the room, creating a small space where we could stow our things and sleep for the night. Nadia hung back and pulled me to the side. "Can we trust her?" she asked.

I nodded. "That is one of very few things I am certain of. She is trustworthy."

Nadia responded with a clipped nod, and we followed the others to our sleeping quarters. It was a bit cramped, but it would do. There was only one small bed, which I assumed Ruth slept in, but when I brought it up, Ruth insisted that we give it to Solace. The rest of us would sleep on the floor.

Once we had deposited our things and each claimed a small section of floor to sleep on, we all filed back into the main area of the small room. Ruth went to the stove in the far corner and began filling bowls with stew and handing them out, and I gently shook Solace awake and handed her a steaming bowl. When we had our food, we all sat and ate until we were full, something we had not done since we left the Village six days before. We struck up some casual conversation while we ate. Ruth told the others of the day she had met Otto, and I finally told them of how Jeb and I had saved Otto from the dogs. Solace caught my eye during the story and smiled. I couldn't tell if she found my story funny or endearing, and I tried not to let myself spend too much time hoping it was the latter. I was distracted from my thoughts when Ruth explained that she had found Captain Bates after leaving General Delaney's.

"I am getting old, and it is now someone else's job to protect this story," she declared. "Captain Bates has been shipping a version of the story, but I am working on getting the true story, the full story, back in print."

"Where did he get his books if not from you?" I asked.

"There was a printer who secretly kept them in circulation. But word is he recently passed away. That is why the captain was open to meeting with me. He has nowhere else to get copies," she explained. "A new network of printers will need to be established, and he seemed a good choice to help with that process."

After dinner, everyone headed to bed except me. Solace had fallen asleep on my shoulder again, so I helped her to bed but then came back out to the main part of the room. I had too much on my mind and no desire to sleep. Solace was sick. We were being chased down by someone I knew was capable of killing us, especially since he had an army of evil Martecytes. Another war was due to begin any time in the next six months. *And I am pretty sure that I am now homeless and jobless,* I thought to myself. I let out a heavy sigh.

Ruth approached the table and sat down. "Are you going to stay up all night?" she asked.

I shook my head. "I'm not tired," I mumbled as I stood to fill my cup again.

"We both know that is not true," she said plainly.

I returned to my chair with a full cup and leaned back, letting my gaze rest on the curtain that concealed Solace and the others from view.

"I don't want to lose her," I said quietly.

"Solace? Why would you lose her?" asked Ruth.

I looked at Ruth, trying to gauge what she meant. "She is dying."

Ruth shrugged. "That may be the case. But you may still find a solution. Plus, that is not the only reason you think you might lose her," she said, her knowing eyes watching me as I shifted uncomfortably under her stare.

"What do you mean?" I asked.

Ruth smiled. "You are looking for a power that you claim you don't believe in so that you can save her. So, you are doing what needs to be done for that part of the problem. What is the other part of the problem? What is the weight you carry heavy on your shoulders?" she asked. "The one that you cannot even try to solve."

I stared at her. "I..." I let out a sigh. I might as well come clean. "I am lying to her," I said in a tired voice. "She wants to protect her family's story, and to do that, the Beast must be alive. I want to save her, but to do that, the Beast must die." I shook my head. "I was planning on killing it from the start anyway," I mumbled. "But I want to be there for her. I feel almost as though, maybe, it is my job to help her complete her mission...but I don't want to lose her, and if she could be healed, the story would be safe until she could find a different solution to preserving it..." I trailed off as my justification of my own plans seemed to fall flat. "But she values her mission more than her own life..."

"You think she wouldn't forgive you?" Ruth asked with a serious expression on her face.

"She doesn't even know how I feel about her," I said dismissively, though I had my suspicions that she did.

Ruth continued to watch me with her wise eyes. "She does," she said simply.

I looked at her in surprise. "How do you know?"

"She chooses to sit close to you. She seeks you out and wishes to be seen by you. She looks at you as if you are the only thing that exists, just as you look at her," she said softly.

I closed my eyes. I had thought I had seen her return my affections a few times, but I had told myself not to accept it. I had told myself that it would be easier to watch her die if she didn't love me.

I shook my head. "She has no idea who I really am...the things I have done...that I have lied to her." I looked at my hands. "Even if she did love me, I don't deserve her love," I said hopelessly. "And not just because of my intentions with the Beast. I have blood on my hands. I have for a long time."

Ruth glanced toward the curtain, her expression tensing with what looked like a hint of regret. But then her expression faded into a soft smile, and she looked at me. "Thankfully for us, true love is not bound by what we deserve."

I stared at the ground. "You think so?" I asked, allowing myself a brief moment of hope. Then I realized what Ruth had said. "Us?" I asked. "You've been in love?"

Ruth chuckled and nodded. "Of course I have."

"What happened?"

She looked across the room, and her eyes lost focus. "The last time I saw him, he gave me a gift and a mission." She smiled. "I have almost completed it and will soon see him again," she said with hope in her eyes. She sat up a bit straighter and changed the subject. "You said you read the book. What information did it contain about the Beast of the Woods?" she asked.

I took a deep breath, trying to get my brain to switch gears. "It told of a people who left their prince for a darkness they did not understand and described how their prince saved them from it. The Beast was created as a source of power. It said that the Beast can grant either a life or a wish for assistance in fighting the darkness."

"Did the story you read tell of a gate?" Ruth tilted her head to one side slightly.

I nodded. "It did mention a gate. It said the Beast would lead you to it. I assume it meant the gate was in the Woods, as that is the only place the Beast has ever drawn anyone." I frowned. "Why are you asking these questions? I thought you read your copy of the book."

Ruth's expression darkened for the first time since I had met her. "The book I had, I wrote. It was different. You must be careful, Ben. General Delaney is not what he seems. He has twisted the story and made it incomplete," she warned. "He has ensured that people do not know the truth about the Woods."

"The Woods?" I asked. "What do you mean?"

She shook her head. "You said it yourself once. When posed with the question of whether to enter the Woods, the threat of imminent death makes that choice easy. But it is not as easy as one might think. The general has used that twisted story to convince people that there is only one choice to be made about the Woods. Stay and live or enter and die. But that choice only seems easy. Only until you read why. Until you read what really happened."

"How did he twist the story? What is missing?" I asked, taking her sudden seriousness as a good sign that I should heed her advice.

"The stories you have heard and read are one and the same, broken in two and twisted into lies," she said with a frown as she wagged her finger at me. "It was not just a king or a prince. It was both. It was not just a people; there was a woman leading them to darkness, corrupted by the Creature of Corrupted Power," she said intensely. "And the Prince did not—" She suddenly froze. Her brow furrowed and her head tilted as if she were listening to something. She stood abruptly. "You must leave," she commanded. "You must go to the Woods and meet with the Beast," she said as she flung back the curtain and began grabbing our things and waking the others.

"What is wrong?" I asked, caught off guard by her sudden urgency.

"They are coming for you," she explained as she handed me some of my things and looked up at me. "The Martecytes. You must get to the Woods before they find you."

I had no idea how she knew they were coming, but I trusted her. I grabbed Solace and helped her stand, and we all headed out the back door to the stables. The sky was just beginning to lighten in the east with the first hint of sunrise. As the others loaded up and swung into their saddles, I turned to Ruth.

"I can't leave you here," I said. "He will kill you!"

She smiled. "Go. I will be fine. My life is not his to take," she replied as she grabbed my arm and looked me in the eye. "Enter the Woods, Ben. Remember the story. Enter the Woods and go to the Beast as you have been longing to do," she commanded.

"But I can't enter the Woods," I protested.

Ruth shook her head. "Go. Enter as I have told you."

The man who had let us into the room earlier came up behind her with something wrapped in a black cloak. I had no idea when she had told him to bring her the object, but Ruth took it from him and looked at it with something I thought was sadness. She stroked it gently and closed her eyes for a moment, taking in a deep breath.

Then she opened her eyes and handed it up to me as I swung into Jeb's saddle. "Take this," she instructed. "I am no longer the one called to wield them in this land. They will protect you and help you. Do not lose them. Always keep them near you," she instructed. "They will offer you guidance."

I pulled back part of the cloak to see what she had given me. It was a sword and a shield. The kind used centuries ago. But the silver metal was gleaming as if they were brand new, and their design was simple but beautiful. All I could see were the sword's hilt and the edge of the shield. The hilt had a subtle pattern of shallow ridges in the metal that wrapped around the grip and crossbar, making a design that resembled a tree. The grip was wrapped in black leather, with a green ribbon tied just below the crossbar, the only spark of color amidst the beautiful silver and black. The shield looked plain, but I could see the edge of a design at its center.

I covered them again and bound them to Jeb's saddle before looking to Ruth. "What about the story? You said it is not complete," I asked in haste.

Ruth shook her head. "You will find what you need in the Woods. Now go!"

I turned Jeb away from the inn but looked back in time to see that Ruth and the man were gone. I looked ahead at Solace, who was riding double with Nadia. Yuuki was riding double with Ivan, and Otto was on Betsy. Holding the reins of Solace's riderless horse, I took up the rear as we headed out of the door in the wall, with Ruth's words still echoing in my head. *"Enter the Woods, Ben. Remember the story. Enter the Woods and go to the Beast as you have been longing to do."*

# Chapter 21

We traveled as fast as we could considering Solace's deteriorating condition and made it back to town by midnight the next night, exhausted from our travels with little sleep on the way. When we entered the Town, we went straight to the Kuzmich Inn to figure out what to do next.

"Welcome home!" said Missy as we entered. The inn's bar was closed this time of night, when there was only one person to tend it, so the bar was empty, and Missy was cleaning dishes.

Without responding to Missy's upbeat greeting, Nadia approached her with instructions. "Missy, we are placing someone in our room. If anyone comes in asking if we were here, tell them you have not seen us since we left town a couple weeks ago."

Missy's brow furrowed. "What's wrong?" she asked. She looked to Solace as Ivan carried her up the stairs. "What happened? Is she okay?"

Nadia shook her head. "The less you know, the better, Missy. Please, just don't tell anyone we are here," she said as Otto, Yuuki, and I followed her and Ivan up to Nadia and Ivan's living quarters on the second floor.

"Okay," said a confused Missy as she watched us disappear up the stairs.

Ivan and Nadia's home was located at the end of the second-floor hall, right next to the back door, and consisted of a large private room that was split into two bedrooms connected to a small lounging area. When Ivan put Solace down, her knees buckled, and he caught her just before she hit the ground. He gently picked her up again and carried her into Nadia's room, placing her on the bed and covering her with a blanket.

Otto immediately began giving her what was left of the medicinal plant paste. "Ben, I don't think this is doing anything at this point. She doesn't have long," he said, sounding worried.

I turned to Nadia and Ivan. "I need to enter the Woods," I said as I unwrapped the sword and shield that Ruth had given me.

"You can't, Ben! What if the story about the Prince is wrong?" challenged Nadia. "You are going to enter those woods just because some old lady told you to? Or is it just because that beast might be able to save Solace? If you go into those woods, you will die, and for nothing!"

"I have to try, Nadia. We don't know if any of those stories are true. But Ruth told me to enter the Woods, and I trust her," I responded.

"What if she is just a crazy old lady, Ben?" asked Ivan, concern etched in his tan face.

"I am going. That is final. I need to see what is in there. I need to try and save Solace," I said with determination. I could find a way to save Solace's story later. If I needed to, I would kill the Beast to save her life. The captain's words rang in my head. *"If the Beast of the Woods must die to save Solace's life, think about what you would be killing. Think about what you would be taking from the people."* I pushed the memory from my mind and headed to the back door.

As I stepped outside, I heard a commotion behind me and turned around to find Ivan and Nadia geared up and prepared to follow me.

"Stay here!" I commanded.

"No!" Ivan retorted defiantly. "We are coming, and you know you can't stop us!" he said, locking eyes with me.

He was right. They would come. I could see in his eyes that there was nothing I could say that would make them stay behind. They would do what it took to protect me. They had always had my back, and they would not stop now. Still, I tried one more time.

"I need you to protect Solace," I said, attempting a more friendly tone.

Nadia frowned. "Otto learned some things on that ship, so he can watch her. Plus, it will be less conspicuous having her in here with him. Valdra has never met him," she explained.

I frowned and looked at Otto, who had been watching our exchange.

"Nadia has taught me a few things since this journey started. I will protect Solace with my life," he said with conviction. I hesitated, worried that Otto wasn't capable. But as I looked at him, I knew he would try; I could see it in his eyes. Maybe Nadia was right. Maybe he was our best bet.

I nodded. "Fine," I said as I pulled my pistols from their holsters and handed them to Otto. With Otto's limited training, he would need something that could be used at a distance and offer multiple shots. "There are three shots in each pistol. They are already loaded." I grasped his shoulders and locked eyes with him. "Protect her," I said. He nodded and gripped the pistols with confidence, though a small flicker of fear in his eyes showed me he was not overconfident. That would do for now.

Nadia, Ivan, and I left out the back door, making sure to be as quiet as possible. We mounted our horses and headed out through town, going as fast as we could without drawing attention to ourselves. At this time of night, people galloping through town on horses would likely bring unwanted attention. Once we made it to the Woods, we headed for the north side, where we could be hidden from view in the Forest's trees.

"Stand watch out here," I told Nadia and Ivan.

I turned to face the Woods, looking up at the thick trees that formed their dark edge as I gathered what little confidence I had. I had no idea what I was doing. I was acting on the hope that an old lady from the mountains knew what she was talking about, despite all the rumors about this place. I was hoping that the story of an ancient king and prince was true—a story I could not yet allow myself to fully believe. I was acting on the small chance that the Beast in the trees before me could save a life. The captain's words came to me again. *"If the Beast of the Woods must die to save Solace's life, think about what you would be killing. Think about what you would be taking from the people."* I shook my head. I could not think of that. I needed Solace. I thought of the night we had spent stargazing in our camp, the night before this journey had started. I had watched her stare at the stars with awe, her eyes like sunflowers in the moonlight. That was the moment I had started loving her, though it had taken me a while to admit it. *Even a great leader is lost without his compass,* I thought.

I checked to make sure the sword was secure at my side and took the shield from its place at my back, hoping it could protect me if I did run into trouble. Then I closed my eyes, knowing Nadia and Ivan would defend me to the death if someone should find us here. They had my back. All I had to do was move forward. So that is what I did. Without letting myself think of anything other than Solace, I stepped forward, crossing the deadly edge of the Woods.

The bushes and trees were so thick I had a fleeting thought that I would not make it through the Woods' edge, not because of its deadly invisible boundary, but because of the dense brush and trees. To my surprise, I came out on the other side of the thick boundary, alive. I had closed my eyes to protect them from the underbrush and branches as I pushed through, and now I willed myself to open them and look back at the wall of foliage behind me. *I'm not dead!* I thought in surprise. *There is no deadly invisible boundary!*

Staring at the thick foliage of the Woods' edge, my heart pounding in my chest, I forced myself to turn back around to look toward the center of the Woods. As I turned my back on the dense trees I had fought through, I could just barely see through the trees ahead of me to the Woods' center, where the foliage was thinner.

With a deep breath, I pushed through the remainder of the trees and approached the center of the Woods. As I drew closer, I saw that the foliage didn't just thin out, but there was a small grass-covered clearing at the center. Within that clearing, perched on a large rock, was the Beast. Its green eyes watched me, framed by shimmering pure black fur. Its elegant body was well muscled, and its long black tail dangled off the rock, the last couple inches calmly flicking back and forth. Its gaze pierced through me, seeing everything. I felt exposed. I could not turn back now, but walking forward, I felt the weight of what I must do to save Solace. I could see more clearly now the power in the Beast's eyes, glowing from within as if its very soul was made of Original Power, and I knew it could save Solace. *It is true,* I thought in wonder. *It is a being of the King in the story, and I must kill it to save the life that is so dear to me.*

The Beast's eyes drew me in. I wanted to know more about it. I felt as though it was a friend. Its eyes held joy; it was happy to see me, for I had finally chosen to enter its world. Those eyes had guided me, even saved me. But the intention in my heart weighed heavy on my shoulders. *I have to kill it,* I told myself as I fought back tears. I had no idea why its life felt so precious to me. But I knew the only way to get a wish of life granted was to take the soul of the Beast.

I approached the Beast as if in a trance. My mind reeled as I forced myself to stay on mission. *I am here to kill it,* I forced myself to remember. *I am here to save Solace.* As I reached the Beast, I grabbed the hilt of the sword Ruth had given me and pulled it from its scabbard. The sword felt heavy in my hands, reflecting the weight of my decision. I fought again to hold back tears, but I was losing that battle, for the Beast meant something to me now. I felt as if part of me would die the moment I took its life.

As I stood there with the sword in my hands and a dark intention in my heart, the Beast just watched me. It stared into my eyes, never breaking its gaze. Though I knew it made no sense, I closed my eyes. I could not bear to look at it as I killed it. I raised the sword, poised to strike down the magnificent being before me.

"Why are you doing this?" The Beast's voice was deep and commanding, and my eyes snapped open in shock at the sound. The guilt of my intentions was overwhelming. But I spoke.

"I...I need to save a life," I responded, unsure what else to say.

The Beast's eyes were intense, but its voice was somehow comforting. "And you must kill me to do that?" it inquired.

"Someone always has to die," I said hopelessly as I felt my body weaken with grief.

The Beast's voice was calm and steady, but its depth cut through me like a knife. "Someone did die," it said.

Panic shot through me. *Solace? I am too late!* I thought as I stumbled forward, letting the sword and shield clatter to the ground. I fell to my knees as the weight of that thought took hold of me. I had failed. "Solace, is she dead?" I forced myself to ask.

"What do you seek?" asked the Beast.

"I seek life," I said in desperation. "I do not want to lose her...I can't."

"You love enough that you would give up part of yourself in killing me," the Beast stated, more an observation than a question. "Who told you I must die to save a life?" it demanded.

"The stories. They tell of a kingdom. The kingdom you came from," I explained. "One of them explained what power you hold."

The Beast's eyes seemed to penetrate deeper within me. "Did you not hear what the woman said? The stories are one. The true story has been broken in two, and the Creature has twisted its truth," it explained, echoing Ruth's words.

Solace was dead, and I had nothing left but the Beast before me. I had nothing left but the story. "What is the truth?" I asked, letting everything that weighed me down float away. Giving in, I let it all go.

With no further words, the Beast reached out to me. Its paw touched my chest, and its tail wrapped around my waist. Suddenly, light surrounded me. The Beast's true name rang out in my mind, though I had no idea how I knew it. Adournath. I did not catch the meaning of the unique name as my attention was captivated by a brief image that flashed before my mind's eye of a large, scaled animal offering me something. But before I could fully grasp what I saw, it vanished, replaced by a vision that played out around me. I looked up in awe as the vision came to life. The story of the King and the Prince played out like a dance. I saw a wonderous kingdom, one of power and light radiating from a stone placed in a fountain at a magnificent castle. Somehow, I knew it was the Kingdom from the story.

The Kingdom spilled out around me in a vision like a waterfall. Then a man I somehow knew to be the Advisor attacked the King. The King banished him from the Kingdom, and the Advisor became a creature of darkness as he had in Solace's story.

Then time seemed to pass, and the King had a son, the Prince, and together they made the second kingdom from the story, the Forest Kingdom. They placed within it a small stone that glowed with Original Power. But the Forest Kingdom had a different name in this vision, one I could not understand, spoken in a different language. But that was not the only difference. As the name vanished from my awareness and the vision continued, I saw that this story was different from the versions I knew from Solace and the captain's book. Some differences were clear, and others were so hazy that I felt I had no time to process or even fully notice them.

The vision continued, showing that the Prince fell in love. The King blessed the engagement and offered the Forest Kingdom to the Prince and his bride-to-be as an engagement gift. Then the Creature appeared and tried to take the Forest Kingdom. He whispered in the ear of the Prince's bride-to-be, who looked strangely familiar. She led the people to the Creature and his dark land of Corrupted Power.

The visions played out as Solace's version of the story had, but with a different ending. The Chosen family did fail, as they had in her story. They chose to use their wishes for evil, and their mark of passage into the Woods was taken from them. The Beast did have power, but only power the King had granted. Its soul could not grant life. But the people hunted it anyway, so the Beast retreated to the Woods upon the King's orders.

But unlike in Solace's version, the story continued.

"What is this?" I breathed as I sank back onto my heels, staring in awe at the vision around me.

"The truth," said the Beast.

At the Beast's words, the image of the scaled animal with its outstretched gift flashed through my mind again. But this time, I could faintly hear its words as its gift seemed to meld with the Beast's tail, creating a belt around my waist. "Have hope, my friend. For the truth is a treasure worth knowing." As the belt was secured, the vision erupted again in vivid detail around me.

The Prince's sacrifice played out next, and I saw that the version Solace told and the version in the book I'd read were two halves of one story, as Ruth and the Beast had said.

In my vision, I could see the Prince standing at the edge of the Woods. With a mighty hold on the darkness, he looked to the Creature. "It is over," he said. "We have won."

Then, the Prince's bride-to-be lashed out in rage at the Prince's words, and I noticed a detail that was missing from the book. The Prince did not step into the Woods as the book had said. Instead, corrupted by the darkness she had chosen, the Prince's bride-to-be pushed the Prince backward through the boundary at the Woods' edge. It was almost as if that one final push solidified the Prince's hold on darkness, and the Prince, allowing it to happen, absorbed the darkness of the people. The moment the Prince's bride-to-be pushed the Prince into the Woods, a loud, crashing thunder sounded as darkness and light collided within him. The Corrupted Power that now filled the Prince collided with the Original Power that flowed through him. The collision erupted with such intensity that the Prince fell to the ground, dead, just as the eruption faded and darkness covered the land.

At the sight of the Prince's death, the Beast of the Woods appeared in the vision, releasing an earth-shaking roar as it had in the book. The King had lost his only son, and the Prince had given his life to save a bride who had betrayed him and a prideful people who followed her.

As the events of the story unfolded before me, I was struck by how familiar this bride-to-be looked. Then, I suddenly realized who she was. She was Ruth, as a young and beautiful woman. *But how could that be? This story took place hundreds of years ago.*

My shock at seeing Ruth faded as a silence fell over the land in the vision. For the story did not end with the Prince's sacrifice.

Now the Beast of the Woods appeared next to the body of the Prince, as it had in the book's version of the story. "Do you see?" said the Beast to Ruth. "Do you see what your selfishness has cost?"

Ruth was gripped with terror, for though darkness covered the land, the Prince had taken it from her heart, and she knew the truth. She had betrayed her Prince for a lie. Now she saw that, despite what she had done, the Prince had given his life to save those who had taken his.

Ruth collapsed to her knees as tears flowed from her eyes. In desperate sorrow, she wailed, "I have destroyed the one who truly loved me, the only one who could have forgiven what I have done."

The Creature watched this all unfold before him, and, seeing that the Prince was dead and darkness covered the land, he turned to the King with a broad grin. "I have won! The people may see the truth now, but your son is dead, and the people are lost to my power!" he roared. "I still hold power in this land, and your son, now dead, will never again be able to rid them of my darkness."

The King stood over his son's body with a tear in his eye, for he loved his son. But his son had been willing to give his life to win back the people they so dearly loved and the woman who had led those people astray.

Turning his gaze on the Creature, the King spoke. "Once, I barred the people from the Kingdom so they would not be killed by my power that flows through its boundaries. But I did not leave them alone in this land. For I gave some a special marker that covered their darkness and granted them passage to the Woods, where they could ask the Beast for help and protection. But darkness still ruled over them, and their marker was corrupted, so I banned them from the Woods for their own safety. But now, my son has done what they could not. He has overcome their darkness."

The Creature laughed. "He has overcome nothing! He is dead, and darkness prevails! What can he do for them now? I will whisper in the people's ears as I have before and enslave their minds!" the Creature said mockingly. "Your son may have pulled the darkness from them this time, but it has forever stained their hearts, and he is not here to save them," the Creature growled. "I will bring them back to me. They are trapped forever in this land, for I have corrupted your precious forest kingdom. Here they will dwell with me forever. They are hopeless! You cannot win!"

The King shook his head. "Not forever, for one day, my son will vanquish you forever in a final battle," he responded with undeniable authority.

The Creature forced himself to laugh, though fear was building inside him. "There is no battle to be fought. Your son is dead. He cannot defend the people any longer! I will hold them captive, for their Lion has been broken, and like a lamb your son died and was consumed," he said, building up his confidence as he grew louder. "Your people are alone in this dark world, and they have no hope," he repeated. "Without hope, they have nothing!"

The King declared, "My work is not yet finished, for it is hope that I shall leave them. I will give them a new marker. One they cannot corrupt."

With that, the King reached down and touched his lifeless son. The Creature watched in horror as light of Original Power poured from the King and filled the Prince, for the King loved his son, and, as the author of Original Power, in love that power was strongest. The Prince's body was filled once again with life, and he rose to his feet with a radiant glow of Original Power, a light amidst a dark world.

The Creature cried out in horror as the barrier of protection between the two kingdoms was torn, and a gate was made between the kingdoms, a gate guarded by the Prince himself. With a dark kingdom flowing with Corrupted Power on one side and a light kingdom flowing with Original Power on the other, the Prince now stood, a guide and a guard, between two powers only he could control, a marker that none could destroy.

The King spoke to the Creature with the Prince standing by his side. "The Lion has won today. For the people now have hope, hope that one day they will pass through this gate my son now guards and enter the land flowing with Original Power. But because of their decision to choose the Land Beyond, both the people and the Forest Kingdom have been infected by Corrupted Power. And all that is ruled by Corrupted Power must be destroyed if the people are to be truly free. But until the time is ripe for destruction, the choice is theirs, as it always has been, for I will not force the people to choose me. So, I will give them what they want. They will have the Forest Kingdom, their darkened land. There the people will dwell between worlds, between the Land Beyond and the Kingdom, for they must choose between the two. When the time is right and the last one has chosen, I will allow my son to vanquish you and this land, and all who have chosen darkness will perish with you. For if I were to destroy all corruption now, all would be lost no matter their choice."

As the vision continued, I saw the people begin to choose. For some, the allure of the Land Beyond was strong, for there they could have their own way no matter the pain it cost others. But for others, the safety and peace of the Kingdom tugged at their hearts. Those who chose the Kingdom searched for the Prince, their only way home. Those who found the Prince were protected on their travels through the Forest Kingdom and seemed to be granted a place in the Kingdom.

But unlike in the book, the Prince did not mysteriously vanish after he rescued the people. Instead, the Creature appeared again.

Seeing that the Prince had provided a way for the people to escape his control, the Creature desperately formed a lie. Like a massive illusion, the Lie began to engulf the Forest Kingdom, changing its appearance until it was as if the Forest Kingdom and the Kingdom had never existed. All that the people had once known of the two kingdoms, including their Lion, began to vanish, leaving the people alone in a shroud of darkness to walk in a world fabricated by the Creature.

"When this lie is at its worst, the people will be alone!" the Creature shouted to the King. "They will not see the true form of the land they live in, the land where your gate dwells! They will not see your gate, and they will not know of the Kingdom; they will not know they have a choice!" he declared in rage. "The people under this lie will be mine!"

But the King and the Prince knew that hope was not that easily destroyed. "Your powers are limited," said the King to the Creature. "For though the people may not always see their Lion, they are not alone. They know of the Woods and my beast that dwells there, and he will show them the truth. They have the story of my son's sacrifice, which gives them hope. By heeding my words and entering through the gate, the unseen will become seen."

As the Forest Kingdom and all that was part of it began to fade away, the Prince walked to the edge of the Woods, for it was the final place to be covered by the Creature's lie. The Prince spoke to the people, saying, "I have loved you always and always will. Listen to the one who guards the story and the disciples she chooses after her. Remember what I have done for you. Tell the story to your children. For if you wish to be free, you must follow truth and hope to the gate I have made for you. Be ready, for, in faith, you must accept the truth and stand with me against the dark forces of this world."

"Tell us, who is the guardian, the one who guards the story?" cried the people in a loud voice.

The Prince turned to Ruth, his betrothed. She still knelt, with tears in her eyes, and bore on her face the shock of seeing her prince alive. Ashamed of what she had done, she looked to the ground. Barely holding back sobs, she said, "I have betrayed you, and I accept my place in this horrible land. I do not deserve to know the truth and see your kingdom again one day."

The Prince knelt before his bride. "I have loved you always; that is why I came to this land to do what had to be done. I did it not only so that you and all the people could be safe but so that one day you could rule by my side." The Prince reached out and, gently lifting her chin, he looked into her eyes. "Do you believe that I still love you?"

With fresh tears welling in her eyes and trembling hands, she replied, "Yes, for only the truest form of love would cause such an act to be done."

"Do you love me?" he asked her gently.

"Yes, and I will love you all of my days!" she responded.

With that, the Prince took the corrupted mark of the Chosen. With Original Power, he melted it like metal, purifying it until it glowed orange. The Prince fashioned the molten metal into what looked like a sword and a shield, though I could not see it completely. When cooled, the pieces shone like no other armor ever made.

The Prince then gave the armor to the bride he so deeply loved. "With this shield, you will have protection from the Creature, and with this sword, you will be armed with my father's words to battle the darkness and evil that still roams this land. For I have a mission for you. You may choose to come with me now or to help the people. But I ask that you choose to help the people, for I love them also, and through their faith, the Lie will be reversed, and one day, what is unseen will be seen. When the unseen becomes seen, we will be wed, and you will rule by my side."

"I will help the people, my prince. For I love you, and I will do as you ask," replied Ruth through her streaming tears.

The Prince continued, "You must lead the people to the truth. For the Creature's power has its limits. He cannot conceal every detail. But do not forget me, for things will not be as they seem. Tell the story of my sacrifice to all the people, for my father has placed in it the power of hope. Help the people, for I love them; through their faith, they will be set free of darkness. One day they will be free of this lie, and if they choose to enter the gate, they will be welcomed into the safety of the Kingdom."

"But when will we see each other again?" pleaded Ruth.

The Prince took Ruth's face in his hands and whispered a promise. "We will see each other again when love unites the Chosen and the Guardians of the story and what is unseen is made seen." Then, in the vision, the Prince leaned closer to Ruth and whispered something to her that I could not hear. At hearing the Prince's words, Ruth shed a tear. Whether it was one of joy or sorrow, I did not know.

Filled with love for Ruth, despite all that she had done, the Prince planted a gentle kiss on her lips. But before their kiss ended, the Prince vanished under the Creature's lie. Where the Prince had stood, the Woods remained, for the Creature could not hide the Beast or the Woods in which it dwelled. Within the branches of the Woods, the King's beast remained as a beacon to the gate that would one day make the unseen seen.

With the Prince gone, Ruth did as he had asked. The vision showed that she did not forget him. She told the story, wrote it in books, and spread it to all the people she could find. But, in desperation to keep the people imprisoned and under his control, the Creature worked tirelessly to busy people with war and to corrupt the story. He first tried to break the story into two parts, and then he twisted the story's two halves until even Ruth did not fully remember all the details.

To keep the people from searching for the story, the Creature sent his corrupted beasts and creatures to attack the people and his unseen armies to whisper in their ears the messages of hopelessness, anger, and fear. He fought for control over them, filling the world they could see with his dark, Corrupted Power and driving them to the Land Beyond. But in the vision, I saw the King. From an unseen kingdom, he watched over his people, and armies of light fought the armies of darkness to protect the Prince's betrothed and the people who believed the story she guarded. It was then that I believed it all. I knew faith would one day make the unseen seen.

# Chapter 22

THE BEAST'S PAW DREW back from my chest, and with a jolt, the vision ended. Silence fell on the Woods.

"Pick up your sword," instructed the Beast, breaking the silence.

Speechless from the vision, I reached out and grabbed the sword. As my grip settled around the sword's hilt, a new sight appeared around me. Not a vision. It was as if the moment the sword settled into my grip, a fog was lifted, and my eyes were opened. The world around me played out in a reality I had never seen before. Two worlds in the same place, connected by the Woods, one dark, one light. White light poured over the land, revealing things I had never known or seen. The Forest had a name, as did all the other places I had known my whole life. I could hear them spoken, although by whom, I did not know. They were spoken in a language I had never heard. The Beast looked to the trees around us, and they seemed to turn transparent at his silent command, revealing the Town and the land around me. The words I heard faded as I focused on my surroundings. Before me was a battle. A legion of the soldiers of light battled with a legion of the soldiers of darkness. I recognized some of the soldiers of darkness. *Martecytes!*

"What are they fighting over?" I asked in breathless disbelief.

"Look closer," instructed the Beast.

As I looked at the soldiers of light, I realized they were not fighting a full-fledged war, but battles, many battles. The people of the Town moved as if there were nothing happening around them. But the soldiers of light engaged in battle before some of them. Creatures of darkness followed closely on the heels of those who had no soldier of light to protect them.

"Who are they?" I asked in astonishment.

"Those of darkness are the Creature's armies. Those of the light are the Lion's Sword," explained the Beast. "The armies of the Prince himself."

I stared in stunned silence at the fighting around me. I could hear it. I could see it. I could feel it moving around me. It was no vision. It was real!

"This world is shrouded in a lie," said the Beast, its voice deeply penetrating yet calm. "The people cannot see. But the soldiers of Original Power fight to defend the people in the name of the Prince who protects them even now from the darkness of Corrupted Power. The war was won when the Prince overcame their darkness, forever opening his gate for those who will seek it out. But the land was covered in the shadows of the Lie by the Creature of Corrupted Power. Now, the armies of light fight for the people, for those who wish to escape this darkness and seek the gate."

My father's last words suddenly became clear. *"The war was won long ago, but we fought this battle alone and lost. Yet time has not run out. Do not waste what you have by dwelling on what you have lost. Choose your friends wisely, and don't trust what this world tells you. Do not fight your battles alone."* I remembered the stories my father once told me. Stories of the Night Rider, a rider on a black horse who wore a symbol of a prince and fought to protect a true story.

Solace's words about my father's horse belonging to the Night Rider jumped to my mind. But then, something caught my eye, pulling me from my thoughts.

I looked to the edge of the Woods, where there stood two soldiers. One dark. One light. One on the outside of the Woods. One on the inside. They both watched me.

"Who are they?" I asked.

The Beast looked at me. "They are the ones who follow you. The ones who fight over you," said the Beast. "The sword you hold was fashioned from the mark of passage. When wielded, it shows you the armies of the Prince and the armies of the Creature of darkness."

*That is what I felt,* I realized. *That is who has been following me.* I turned to the Beast. "Why me? Why am I here?"

"You are here for a purpose, Ben. This world needs the truth. The Creature of Corrupted Power has covered this land in a lie. He has blinded the people and trapped them in a path they believe is right but is swiftly leading to their destruction."

"The Great Beasts of the Southern Mountains," I breathed in realization.

"The Great Beasts of the Southern Mountains were made by the Creature of Corrupted Power," the Beast explained. "He corrupted the King's beasts, who once looked similar to me. He wants people to believe I am evil as well. The Creature now sends his beasts out to keep a hold on people's minds, to keep them trapped in shadows of hopelessness and fear." The Beast's green eyes held my gaze. "You must share the story, Ben, as Ruth once did. You must tell them the truth."

"Why?" I asked. "What good does the story do? They should come here, to you, so you can show them what I just saw!"

The Beast shook his head. "They will not come to me. They have forgotten this land's true form. For that knowledge was lost when they believed the Lie—the Lie of hopelessness spun by the enemy. They need the story, for it is the story they will listen to. It is the truth that will set them free."

"What should I do?" I asked as I stood and sheathed the sword. The armies of light and darkness vanished as I released the sword's hilt, and I looked around in surprise.

"Go, print the story in full," said the Beast, commanding my attention again. "Bring it back to the land and to the people. Give them hope, Ben," commanded the Beast.

"How?" I asked.

"The story will give the people hope for the future and show them the truth, for truth is power, and through it, you will find strength to fight the battles to come."

Still perched atop the rock, the Beast again placed a paw on my chest, and before me, a man dressed in beautiful white and blue robes appeared. On his head was a shimmering pure white crown. *The Prince!* I thought. *He is alive. It is all true!* On his chest, a pendant held his cloak in place. The pendant's silver surface seemed to flicker between multiple images as he moved. Though I barely saw each one as he shifted to step toward me, I noted there were three distinct images. One was familiar, a curious but beautiful design, but I couldn't place it. The other two I had never seen before; one looked to be a crest of some kind, and the other had two identical S-shaped symbols connected near the middle.

I stared at the Prince in awe as he stepped forward and spoke to me. "Do you believe in miracles?" he asked. "Do you believe I and these kingdoms are real? Do you believe the truth?"

"Yes," I responded with confidence, "I believe."

"Then you have become one of us." The Prince reached out and picked up the shield I had let fall to the ground. As he did, I saw that the symbol on the shield matched the familiar image on the Prince's pendant. The Prince then took from my scabbard the sword Ruth had given me, the sword he had made with his own hands and given to his betrothed long ago. It didn't all make sense, but I knew it was true.

"Kneel," instructed the Prince.

I knelt.

"My betrothed has completed the mission that she accepted out of love for me. For she has spread the truth to those who must hear it in this land. Now, I have chosen you to be the last of her disciples. In your land, they are known as the Night Riders, the Guardians of the story. The Chosen and the Guardians are now one; the time has come. With this sword, you will fight alongside the armies of Original Power and lead the people to see the truth." The Prince extended the blade and rested it on my right shoulder before moving it to my left. "You are now a soldier of my army. Tell people of the truth and make the unseen seen," he commanded. The Prince gripped the hilt of the sword, blade down. "Stand," he instructed. He held the sword out to me. "If you believe in me, take this sword and the shield you received with it, and go. Spread the story to the four corners of the earth, for faith will show you the gate that can free this land of the Creature's dark lie. In faith, heed my father's words and make the unseen seen."

"I will do as you command," I said, taking the sword and shield and bowing my head. As I lifted my head, a question began to burn in my mind. "May I ask my prince a question?" I asked respectfully.

"You may," he replied.

"You said that the Chosen and the Guardians are now one and that we will be soldiers of your army. But I thought Solace was the last of the Chosen. Is Solace...alive?" I asked.

"Solace is alive," the Prince responded, "for though she has not seen me here, her faith has led her to me. She will fight in my armies, as will you, and she will become a mighty warrior, for together you will be the last Night Rider."

Relief washed over me. I could barely believe it. But this prince I had so recently thought was only a story stood before me. And I believed he spoke the truth. I bowed. "Thank you, my prince."

With my head bowed, I felt the sensation of the Beast's paw lift from my chest. I lifted my head. I was outside the Woods. Its thick, tree-lined edge was before me, and the Beast watched me from within its branches, those green eyes glowing, intense and wise. Then the Beast turned away and was gone.

"What happened?" said a worried Nadia as I stared at the Woods in front of me. "Was that the Beast? Why didn't you kill it?"

Silence hung in the air around me like fog, only broken by Nadia's voice and the echo of unanswered questions that filled my mind. *How is Ruth still alive if she was the woman in the story? How does the sword allow me to see the armies of light and darkness? Why is it so important that the story be spread to the four corners of the earth? Why was the truth of our reality revealed to me and not Solace, a Chosen?* I took a deep breath and calmed my mind.

"Ben, what did you see in there?" asked a stunned Ivan as he peered into the branches where the Beast had vanished.

My mind settled on one thing. The Prince's command. *"The Chosen and the Guardians are now one; the time has come. With this sword, you will fight alongside the armies of Original Power and lead the people to see the truth. You are now a soldier of my army. Tell people of the truth and make the unseen seen."*

I turned on my heels and walked away from the Woods toward the road. "I saw the truth," I said simply. The twins followed me to the horses and we mounted in silence, though I saw them glance at one another with raised brows. Likely sensing my urgency, they asked no more questions, and we rode back to the Kuzmich Inn as quickly as we could. I needed to see Solace. I needed to see with my own eyes what the Prince had told me—that she was alive.

We rode through town, and images of what I had seen flowed through my mind as I looked at each person we passed. They had no idea what was happening around them. They had awoken this morning just like all the rest and walked through life in a fog, just as I had, believing a lie.

We pulled up to the stables of the Kuzmich Inn and dismounted the horses. I ran up the steps and through the back door, Ivan and Nadia following close behind. I swung to my left, opened the door to Nadia and Ivan's home, and stepped across the threshold with anticipation pounding in my chest.

As we burst through the door, I heard Ivan and Nadia gasp behind me. There, standing in the center of the room, healthy and alive, was Solace! I stopped dead in my tracks and stared at her.

She raised her eyes to meet mine in an affectionate gaze. Those beautiful eyes. I smiled as I noticed that they now held flecks of green within them that hadn't been there before, a reminder of what the Prince had done for her this night, and for all of us so long ago when he sacrificed himself at the edge of the Woods. I held Solace's gaze and walked to her, barely hearing as Otto explained that she had suddenly come to and stood, healthy, as if she had never been sick.

Stopping before Solace, I placed a gentle hand on her cheek. I couldn't speak. I had returned to this town and the Woods with the intention of saving her life. But it turned out that she'd had all she needed. Faith had saved her. Faith in a story I now knew to be true without a shadow of a doubt. But there was one question left to ask. Not one of faith but of love, and in this moment, I knew she would tell me the truth. *Does she love me back?*

"I'm okay, Ben," she whispered with a soft smile. She reached her hands up and placed them on either side of my face.

There was no doubt in her eyes, only love. "I know," I whispered. Her soft smile broadened. My heart skipped a beat, and I knew I had her love just as she had mine. I lifted my other hand and delicately held her face as I gazed into her joyful, wise eyes. I leaned forward. I paused, watching her reaction as I leaned just a little closer. "I want to kiss you," I said, just loud enough for only her to hear.

"I would like that," she said quietly. With that, I planted a passionate kiss on her lips. I knew now that she would not leave me, that death would not take her from me. She was safe, not in my hands, but in the hands of our prince.

Our lips parted, and she looked up into my eyes. Her eyes were filled with understanding that I had once marveled at. But it was no longer a mystery to me. "Do you still think I am crazy?" she asked as a playful grin spread across her lips. "Do you think I am too different?"

I smiled. "Yes," I joked. "Crazy..." I couldn't take my eyes off hers. "Different...but just as different as you should be," I whispered. Then I grinned as something she had once said came to mind. "But what sane person ever changed the world?" I asked, repeating the joke she had made to me after we left the Village the first time.

Solace laughed, and her laughter shone in her beautiful eyes. Then she let out a sigh as we wrapped each other in a hug.

As we embraced, I faintly heard her whisper, "I no longer bear this burden alone."

"Never," I responded so only she could hear.

I finally lifted my gaze to the people standing around us, watching. Everyone stood there with looks of confusion on their faces, waiting for my explanation of what had happened. Well, everyone except Yuuki, who was sitting on the floor clutching her stuffed rabbit toy, staring at Solace and me with a look of pure joy on her face as if she could barely contain herself.

"What did you see?" asked Nadia. "Back in the Woods."

Solace and I parted from our hug, but my arm remained over her strong shoulders. "Captain Bates was right. There is power in this land," I answered. I felt like a new person. The fog was lifted from my mind, and I was filled with clarity. I knew my purpose. I knew what I had to do. "Ruth was right, too; the stories are one. But they have been twisted. There are lies within them, and the two parts are two halves of the same story. That is why she called on those who followed her to help protect the story," I explained.

"Wait, protect the story? You mean like in the stories about the Night Rider?" asked Ivan.

"That's right. Solace and I will take up the Night Rider's name. The Beast was meant to lead people to the gate, and now it will help us show people the truth. We need to print the real story, the true story."

"What is the true story?" asked Ivan.

"Yes, Ben. What did you see?" repeated Nadia urgently.

"The truth is that the story is true, and not only is it true, but the Prince lives. I saw him with my own eyes! He was the one who saved Solace with Original Power, and he told me to spread the story to the four corners of the earth and break the Lie to make his kingdom seen. He explained that Ruth chose me as the last Guardian." I grabbed the hilt of Ruth's sword. "And he told me that this sword would help me on my way," I said as I drew it from its scabbard. For the first time, I noticed the sword had writing on it, though I did not recognize the letters. They were ancient. Beautiful.

Ivan stepped forward and looked at the sword. "Wow," he said in awe. "I have seen a lot of swords in my time, but none with that kind of writing on it. What does it say?" he asked.

"I don't know, but I think I know a couple people who might," I said with a smile.

"Who?" asked Otto.

"Captain Bates and Ruth," I explained.

"What are we going to do?" asked Nadia, finally calming down slightly.

I looked at them each in turn and said, "Solace and I have been tasked with repairing the story and finding the gate. We will get the story back in print, spread it to the four corners of the earth, and break the Lie to make the unseen seen. We will take up the mantle of the Night Rider and do as our prince has commanded us to do."

"Why do we need the story so badly if we could just take people to the gate once we find it?" asked Ivan.

"Because the story can change people," said Yuuki.

We all turned to look at her. "What did you say?" I asked gently.

"Mrs. Alves always says that a good story can help even the meanest person change his ways," she said with raised eyebrows.

I smiled and crouched down in front of her. "You are right, Yuuki," I said as I tussled her hair. "And we are going to help as many as we can."

I stood and looked to Nadia, Ivan, and Otto. "I know I sound crazy, but if you will give it, we could use your help. Valdra and his army will be after us and will stop at nothing to ensure the true story never sees the light of day and that no one can find the gate. I could use your help, and your friendship."

The three glanced at each other and back at me. I had found what I had been missing, and I could see they had as well. We had found family—a purpose more fulfilling than any adventure...a treasure worth more than gold.

"We will follow you to the end of the earth, brother!" said Nadia with a grin.

"We pledge our swords to the Night Rider and the mission the Prince has given you," announced Ivan.

"I pledge myself as well!" declared Otto.

Nadia and Ivan drew their swords, and we touched blades. Solace drew her dagger and placed it on top. Then, Otto drew the pistols I had given him to protect Solace, and he touched them to the pile.

Yuuki tugged my coat, and I looked down. "Can I come too?" she asked hopefully.

We all laughed, and Ivan picked her up and put her on his shoulders.

"Of course, you can come, Yuuki," I said with a grin.

With that, we pledged ourselves to our king and prince. We pledged ourselves to the mission that we had been given. I had once fought for a man who would kill his soldier just for asking a question about a book. But now we would fight for a prince who had given everything to save a people and a bride who had cast him away. *That,* I thought to myself, *is a man worth fighting for.*

"What now?" asked Solace.

"We need to print the true story, distribute it as the Prince commanded, and find the gate to the Kingdom," I explained.

"Isn't the gate in the Woods?" asked Ivan. "It seems like the most logical place, since the Beast is there, and the Beast is supposed to lead people to the gate."

"I am not sure. I saw the Prince in the Woods in a vision, but I didn't see the gate. Anyway, we can't go back there right now. Valdra is coming, and we need to find Captain Bates. He can print and smuggle the books around the world." I looked at the sword in my hand before sheathing it again. "Plus, Ruth will know what this sword says. Hopefully, she is with the captain. So, we will find them first."

Suddenly, a thump sounded from somewhere below us. We all froze. I had heard muffled voices coming from downstairs, but that was not unusual in the inn, so I had ignored it. But that thump meant trouble. I grabbed the door and opened it a crack, trying to hear better. I heard Missy trying to calmly tell someone that the rooms were full but that she could show them around. Someone was here. Someone she thought was dangerous. The thump was a signal that she and Nadia had worked out years ago. Missy would drop an empty ale bottle on the wooden floor and pretend to trip over it, giving her a chance to bang on a particular part of the wall behind the bar that would make a sound we could hear loud and clear in this room only. Her signal to run.

"He's here," said Nadia. "We will go out the back!"

Ivan secured Yuuki in his arms, and we all grabbed what we needed and entered the hall, heading for the door as fast and as quietly as we could. We reached the landing outside and scurried down the steps. We each grabbed our horses and Betsy and quickly threw our tack on them before rushing from the stables.

"Where are we going to go?" asked Solace as we swung onto our mounts and raced from the inn.

I glanced behind us and thought I saw Valdra in the window of Ivan and Nadia's room. He had surely seen us. I turned and focused on where we were headed. "To find the *Lyonsword*," I responded.

We headed out of town toward the Pint Inn. Valdra would likely follow us, but we had no other options. The people at the inn would be able to point us in the right direction in our search for the captain and Ruth.

As we rounded a corner, headed to the path just outside of town, we slid to a halt in the road. Before us stood Valdra, backed by the Martecytes with their dark coats flowing to the ground.

"You have nowhere to run, Benjamin," announced Valdra. "He has won."

We turned to flee in the opposite direction, but we were surrounded.

"Otto, take Yuuki from Ivan and get behind us," I said as Ivan, Solace, Nadia, and I formed a circle around them.

"You have lost, my old comrade," said Valdra with a smile, "and now your time has come."

Valdra and his army leapt at us from all sides. Though they were only humans, infected with a mysterious shadow, they seemed to come as one being, surrounding us in darkness. Besieged by the enemy, I suddenly remembered the sword at my side. I grabbed its hilt and drew the blade from its scabbard. As the blade tip exited the sheath and my grip settled firmly around the hilt, I felt myself connect with the powerful sword, and a loud roar of the Beast rang out in my ears as its eyes filled my mind. My eyes were opened, and I saw the battle around us, light versus dark as it had been in the Woods. But this time, five soldiers of light came to my aid, seeming to appear out of nowhere. Three were astride white horses, and two swooped down from the sky on white flying creatures, which resembled winged lions, but instead of fur, they had feathers and beautiful patterns of scales like a dragon. The soldiers of light stood among us to fight in the name of their prince to protect the people he so dearly loved.

Valdra's Martecytes skidded to a halt as the soldiers came to my aid. But Valdra's eyes locked on to the sword I now held in my right hand. "The Lion's Sword!" Valdra gasped with wide eyes. At first, I could not tell if he was afraid or angry, but finally, his brow furrowed and he growled to his soldiers, "He knows the story!" He held out a hand to one side, signaling them to hold their positions.

I looked to Valdra; we were still outnumbered by at least ten people, so I had to make a show of force. "That is right, Valdra," I replied, raising my chin a half inch. "I know the story, and I believe it. The Prince has sent these soldiers of light to strike you down. They will defend me and my comrades."

With a frown that seemed more irritated than fearful, Valdra pulled his horse back, commanding his soldiers to do the same. "We will come for you, Benjamin!" he yelled. "General Delaney will come for you and destroy the story once and for all!"

Something about Valdra's response to seeing the sword bothered me. He was not backing down out of fear of the soldiers of light, though some of his Martecytes seemed unsettled by them. Instead, it was as if my having the sword and knowing the story had interrupted his plans. What those plans were, I had no idea, but I had no time to debate the situation now; we needed to get out of here before he changed his mind and attacked. Without taking my eyes off Valdra, I spoke one word. "Go!" At my command, the soldiers of light charged Valdra and his soldiers of darkness, pushing them back toward the Crescent Hill and General Delaney's mansion, which dominated its crest.

I turned to my companions to find them all giving me questioning looks. "What just happened, Ben?" asked Nadia.

"This sword was made by the Prince, and it can show the one who wields it the armies of light and dark," I explained.

Solace came up next to me with a grin on her face and a gleam in her eyes. "I can feel them," she whispered in awe. "They are among us, aren't they?"

"They are, and they will protect us," I confirmed with a smile and a nod. I wondered to myself if the sword worked for other people. I would have to test it sometime. For now, though, we needed to get moving.

I looked to the group who had been with me on this journey and would continue to accompany me from this point on. "We must have courage and fight. We have been tasked with a mission and given the tools to accomplish it," I said, holding up the sword. "We must do what our prince has asked of us. We must spread the story and find the gate."

The Arlin Trilogy continues in Book 2

*The Mission*

# About the Author

Ondrea Keigh grew up in the forested Pacific Northwest, in Washington State, before moving to live near the sandy beaches of Florida. She loves to write and will do so at any time and in nearly any place. Her first published story was a short story titled *The Night Rider Adventures: Episode 1 – The Night Rider,* and she has many more stories on their way! Ondrea graduated from Liberty University with a degree in psychology and also holds a certification in dog training. Before becoming an author, she worked as an animal trainer, and when she is not working on a new story, she can still occasionally be found training puppies!

ONDREAKEIGH.COM

Made in United States
Troutdale, OR
11/27/2023

15036825R00235